MOTHER EARTH

BOOK TEN OF
THE LAST MARINES

William S. Frisbee, Jr.

Theogony Books
Coinjock, NC

Chris Kennedy/Theogony Books
1097 Waterlily Rd.
Coinjock, NC 27923
https://chriskennedypublishing.com/

Publisher's Note: This is a work of fiction. Names, characters, places, and incidents are a product of the author's imagination. Locales and public names are sometimes used for atmospheric purposes. Any resemblance to actual people, living or dead, or to businesses, companies, events, institutions, or locales is completely coincidental.

Cover Design by J Caleb Design.

Ordering Information:
Quantity sales. Special discounts are available on quantity purchases by corporations, associations, and others. For details, contact the "Special Sales Department" at the address above.

Mother Earth/William S. Frisbee, Jr.-- 1st ed.
ISBN: 978-1648559853

Chapter One:
Rout

Emperor Wolf Mathison, USMC

There were no front lines. They had all collapsed and Emperor Mathison was getting checked at every angle. Civilians were being evacuated to what he hoped would be safe zones, but another problem was developing.

Vanhat infiltrators, shape-shifting aliens that had infiltrated behind human lines as refugees were now spreading out, killing Imperial officers, and taking their place. The only ones immune, mostly, were the Legionnaires who had SCBI implants. It was chaos because nobody knew who they could trust, and there weren't enough Legionnaires to cover every area.

The Wolf Legion was the vanguard and the only reason the enemy had not overrun the Moon. They provided a human and SCBI team that could work together to identify and neutralize threats in an efficient and lethal way the vanhat impostors couldn't match, but the Legion was not all-powerful, and their numbers continued to dwindle as the Legionnaires took casualties they couldn't replace. Meanwhile, the vanhat, spearheaded by the Weermag, were nearly unstoppable and constantly receiving reinforcements.

"We need to get you off the Moon," Baker said as Mathison, Skadi, and their protectors sat anywhere they could find space at Base

Tereshkova, one of the ODT facilities where the First, Second, and Third ODT Regiments were based. At the moment, it was also the heart of Wolf Legion combat operations and was becoming a stronghold.

"My people are here," Mathison said, and Baker rolled his eyes.

"Look, sir," Baker said, and Mathison could hear that Baker was using the term "sir" in a more derogatory manner, "the vanhat want to cut off your head, our head. They've got hooks into our networks, and they are pumping out propaganda. A lot of that propaganda is around you being dead and how the Lunar defenses have collapsed."

"The defenses haven't completely collapsed," Skadi said.

"Propaganda says otherwise, ma'am," Baker said. "Then there are the infiltrators. Trust is at an all-time low. Your dad and his flunkies are doing their best to keep their distance, as if the rest of the Empire is infected. And Imperial forces don't exactly trust ex-pirates."

"They aren't ex-pirates," Skadi said. "And the vanhat can't infiltrate the Legion."

"Yet, ma'am," Baker said. "Guess what they'll try to do when they succeed?"

"You have a plan?" Mathison asked.

"Yes," Baker said. "Relocate to a battlestar or dreadnought. A mobile platform."

"To make it easier to run away if they have a fleet? That just gives them a target to focus their fleet on."

"Luna isn't safe," Baker said. Mathison understood Baker's issue. He was an infantryman at heart, like Mathison. It was always easier to assume the fleetberts and space navy types could stay out of harm's way, but Mathison knew better.

"And a ship is?" Mathison asked. Clearly, Baker couldn't see the flaws in his plan.

"A ship is a moving target, sir. That target can keep moving and be protected by others."

Mathison looked at Skadi. She had removed her helmet. Her face was streaked with sweat and her hair was braided tight against her scalp. She wasn't at her prettiest right now, but Mathison didn't care. He had asked her to marry him and she had said yes. She had made a mistake. Her response had probably been like his question, spur of the moment, a humorous response to the situation while they were under fire. People said stupid shit all the time when they were trying to make light of a situation. The problem was that neither of them could back down from Mathison's stupidity.

One problem was that everyone else seemed to want it. The words had been uttered, and she had accepted, so they were committed. She was still wearing the grenade pin ring on her finger and Mathison wondered how long that would last. He would have to do something about that.

Skadi looked back at him. The first time he had seen her without a helmet since he'd proposed. There was something different about her, and he couldn't say what it was. He couldn't remember a time she hadn't had his back. Well, yeah, he could, the time he had shot at her. He wondered if she would hold that against him.

"Move the Imperial flag to the *Sleipner*?" she asked.

"And abandon the Moon?" Mathison asked.

He knew why she hadn't suggested the *Tyr*. That venerable battlestar was still undergoing repairs, was short staffed, and it was commanded by her father.

"We might hold," Skadi said, but Mathison heard doubt there.

They couldn't hold on Earth. Already, the last cities were bunkering up, preparing for a long siege. The vanhat had overrun most of the planet and casualties were astronomical. They could feed on the countless dead, but humans could not, and , required them to maintain hydroponics and farms to supply the dwindling populations. Those farms and other critical facilities were under constant attack as the vanhat grew stronger and the human defenders grew weaker. The vanhat controlled several continents now, hiding in the radioactive storms or prowling the ruined cities.

It was a numbers game, and Mathison realized what a fool he had been to think they could survive. Every battle, every attack, every casualty was a reminder that the vanhat would never stop. They could not absorb humanity, so they were grinding it down.

"We have to change the game," Mathison said. "We need to assemble a team of geniuses to come up with new and innovative ways to take the fight to the enemy. The vanhat are playing a war of attrition and winning."

"In the end, the war of attrition always will, sir," Baker said. "You grind the enemy down to nothing and destroy them. We cannot replace our losses, but they can. The vanhat are quite willing and able to keep sending troops until we are extinguished. God knows where they're all coming from."

"We have to keep fighting," Mathison said. "There is no choice. We need options."

The weight of failure pressed down on his shoulders. He might have to find a way for Skadi to change her mind, she shouldn't be chained to his failure.

He and the others had saved Sol from the first vanhat invasion, but this one was succeeding, and that was his fault. The SOG had thought they were safe behind their automated defenses, but the enemy were already inside the perimeter. Mathison had been arrogant enough to think that they could defeat the vanhat with the d-bombs and Inkeris. Now he understood how such technologies had delayed the inevitable. This was what the vanhat did. They adapted, and Mathison was certain they hadn't seen a fraction of their ability to adapt. They had done all of this before, and he was still learning. Could he do something different, fight back in a way they hadn't seen? They adapted too quickly to changes, and if the Weermag and doppelgängers were any indication, they had countless tricks up their sleeve.

The vanhat had never faced US Marines, though. They had never tangled with Aesir and Vanir of the Republic, never fought the ODTs, the Guard or Fleet of the Social Organizational Governance. Now everyone was fighting together to forge a new empire, but would that be enough? The best he could do was keep throwing ideas at the wall like spaghetti until something stuck.

Skadi reached out and put her hand on his shoulder. "We might not save everyone, but we will save a lot. We have to cut our losses."

He was comforted by her grip and some of the pressure eased. She wasn't blaming him because she had been there. She was an officer and knew what it was like to make hard decisions. If anyone could understand him and what he was dealing with, she could. He wouldn't call it love—that was for weepy eyed, soft little men—but he was glad Skadi was with him.

"At worst, the vanhat will remember us for kicking them in the balls and teeth," Mathison said. His hand began shaking, and he tucked it into his belt. If Skadi noticed, then others would, and he couldn't allow that.

It was easy to be gung-ho and talk tough; he had experience in that. What wasn't easy was realizing he might utter lies to boost morale. Well. He had always done that, but now the lies were more obvious and easier to see through because it was harder for him to believe them.

But Skadi had his back and said yes. He couldn't make everyone happy, and he couldn't do everything right, but there were some things. One had to start off with the little things before tackling the big things and build on successes daily.

"So, what do we do?" Baker asked, his eyes on Mathison.

"What we are doing," Mathison said, trying to muster his confidence and exude it. So many battles to be fought. So much to do. "We continue the fight. We establish mutually supporting strongholds. Tereshkova will be our new headquarters for now. Strongpoint One. We build another wall for the vanhat to smash into."

"Yes, sir," Baker said, but Mathison sensed he wanted to continue to argue.

Too bad.

Right now, we have a problem, though," Mathison said and looked at Skadi. "I'm at a loss on how to proceed on this one."

Everyone looked at Mathison. He knew the best way to deal with problems and stress was to tackle the easy ones first, to rebuild success and a track record. With everything going wrong, he had to make something go right and try to force everything else to align.

"We need to tell your father and plan a wedding," Mathison said. It might not be the easiest problem, but perhaps that could be a victory.

"That's what's on your mind right now?" Skadi asked, removing her hand from his shoulder. Mathison felt the absence. "Of all the things?"

"Some things we can control, and some things we can't. Some things we have to delegate, or we go insane trying to keep track of everything."

"But—"

"Sometimes we have to take a break from all the bad things, or we get dragged down. We have to have victories in some parts of our lives, even little ones. Things have to go well somewhere in our lives."

Skadi's looked turned to a scowl, but that didn't faze Mathison. It meant she was thinking. Though he'd considered giving her an out, she was the person he trusted most so he had decided. She would not get away that easily, and that determination made him glad his hand was tucked into his belt.

"Well?" Mathison asked. It was getting easier to pretend he was calm and confident.

No, it wasn't.

Fake it until you make it. She wouldn't see his hand shaking.

"Well, what?" Skadi said. "I'm working with Loki and delegating. You're right. If nothing else, we need to delegate more. We need to train leaders so when we are eliminated, they will be ready."

That wasn't what Mathison had expected.

"Father's going to be pissed he wasn't present when you proposed."

"I'm sure he wouldn't have wanted to be." Mathison was still trying to keep up with the mental pivots she was taking. He was thinking about tactical problems, she was thinking about people.

She held up her finger with the grenade ring on it. "This is probably going to give him a heart attack. He's going to give us both a lecture about endangering each other and having such dangerous items like grenades in our presence. Vanir don't understand such weapons. He will lecture you on having such a paltry wedding ring."

"Sorry."

"For what? The pin ring of a grenade means you gave someone a grenade for me. Pretty rings are for dainty, pretty wives. Is that what you expect of me?"

Mathison did not know how to answer that. He would have to be extra careful when making jokes from now on. "You aren't dainty."

"Don't forget it. We have a lot to do. Now you need to find some way to tell my dad and establish a stronghold."

"Oh joy, my first honey-do list."

"My little pupuliini," Skadi said in an oddly sweet voice. "You have so much to learn about being a husband."

"Poo-poo-lini?" Mathison asked.

"It translates as bunny," Skadi said.

Now Mathison was speechless. She had just called him her bunny? A harmless, bucktooth herbivore? Skadi?

* * * * *

Chapter Two:
Cut Off

First Lieutenant Zale Stathis, USMC

The vanhat didn't quit, and that was worrying Stathis. They were persistent, and he was running out of people and ammunition. Ammunition meant nothing until you were almost out. People always meant something, especially when they were fighting beside you.

The fog of war was a very real thing. Even with computer assistants and communications that could not be jammed, the enemy didn't stand still, and they were doing their best to expire the birth certificate of Stathis and the other troopers. Either they were that good, or they were incredibly angry or fanatical about killing him.

Stathis wasn't sure which. He couldn't rule out that both were true.

The important thing was that the gunny and Skadi were safely away from Zvezda Two.

But now his small command was trapped behind the lines, if there even *were* battle lines. Stathis wasn't so sure. He didn't want to think about how the vanhat couldn't be contained now they had escaped their entrapment. Rooting them out of the tunnels and ruined habitats could take decades, if it could be done at all.

"We've lost," one trooper said.

"Nope," Stathis said. "We have not lost. We just have to change tactics. Look at it this way, if they have us surrounded then we can attack in any direction, and they can't be ready for us everywhere. We get to take the initiative and do unto them before they do unto us."

It had sounded better in his head. Getting used to the officer thing of not saying stupid shit wasn't easy. Though, to be fair, he could remember a lot of officers saying a lot of stupid stuff, but they had generally been clueless clods. What would Chesty Puller have said? Oh yeah.

"We're surrounded. That simplifies our problem of finding and killing these vanhat."

Heads turned to look at him, and he wondered how many were rolling their eyes. Probably all of them. He had said that earlier, hadn't he? Nothing more annoying than an officer that kept repeating the same stupid things.

Blazer fire stitched the ceiling nearby, but an alert trooper shot the vanhat before it could find a target. The enemy had been firing high because they didn't want to expose themselves. Maybe the vanhat thought that they could intimidate the troopers to gain fire superiority, get the defenders to reveal themselves. But the vanhat were fighting hardened veterans now, and they didn't fall for such techniques, so when the enemy revealed itself, people were ready. Those who would fall for such tricks were already dead.

"We're running low on ammo," another trooper said.

"I'm working on that," Stathis said. He wasn't, but he was supposed to be. There wasn't a damn thing he could do though, except nag people. "Conserve what you can."

There, he had done what he could.

"A relief company is pushing to link up with us," Shrek reported. *"They are facing stiff resistance."*

"Stiff? Where are they getting their damned Viagra from?" Shrek knew better than to answer. *"Seriously."*

"I doubt they are using Viagra," Shrek finally said.

"No, I mean their center of gravity. What drives them?"

"Perhaps their SCBIs and their Jotnar masters?"

"No."

"If you know, then please enlighten me."

"I mean, that's too simple. We need more information. Nasaraf was just a bloodthirsty thug, but his flunkies fought with the vampires. We need to find out who these guys hate more than us. Who commands them, where they come from."

"And how do you plan on introducing them to a new enemy?"

"A tea party is a great way to introduce people," Stathis said. *"I'm guessing we can't invite them all to the Wolf's Den anymore."*

"You aren't making any sense."

Maybe. Stathis was tired and couldn't remember the last time he had slept. Days ago? No, he wasn't thinking straight, but he was thinking, acting, and pushing forward. If he didn't, then he would stop to take a nap and never wake up. So, rambling and arguing with his SCBI was a good thing. Shit. Bad reasoning. He was tired and making bad decisions, but he couldn't stop rambling now.

"First, we need to find some other vanhat they don't get along with. I'll bet Nasaraf could have pushed their buttons. They will have a weakness, though."

"You sound sure," Shrek said.

"Everyone has a weakness. If these guys didn't have a weakness, they wouldn't be vanhat slaves."

"Interesting logic. But what if they and the vanhat reinforce and strengthen each other?"

"They have a weakness."

"And what is your weakness?"

"Boobs and butts on babes, and—"

"Forget I asked. It was a rhetorical question."

"But it's a good question. How do these guys reproduce? Where are they coming from? Have you heard from Hakala lately?"

A grenade came at them but landed on the other side of the cart. Everyone took cover, but Stathis snatched a grenade from his kit and threw it before the vanhat grenade went off.

"Fire in the—" Stathis began.

The cart they were hiding behind absorbed most of the blast, but their armor really saved them. Now the cart was a shattered wreck and no longer provided concealment.

Stathis knew their tactics. The second the enemy's grenade exploded, they sprinted around the corner, right into Stathis' exploding grenade.

"—hole," Stathis finished. He rolled until he could shoot around the cart but the vanhat were dead. Stathis got to his feet. "Up and at 'em!"

Around him, the other troopers surged to their feet and hurried out from cover to exploit the vanhat who were hopefully stunned or dead.

The vanhat had expected the grenade to daze and confuse the humans, but that worked both ways, and veterans were more resilient and ready for such tricks.

Moving again, Stathis wondered how much distance they could cover before they encountered another vanhat blocking force. That was his last grenade.

One trooper stabbed his bayonet into a vanhat that was still moving.

"If you stab it in a blazer hole, that's extra credit," Stathis told the trooper.

Around him, the other troopers were moving quickly. They were survivors and every one of them knew if they didn't stay close to Stathis they probably would not survive. That worried Stathis because he didn't have the answers and being close to him didn't mean he could protect them.

But damned if he wouldn't do his best to get them out of there alive.

Did the gunny have these thoughts? How did the gunny handle losing people?

He probably didn't let it stop him from doing what had to be done.

"Watch your flanks," Stathis said on the main link. "Not much further."

The Imperial communication network was feeding him information, but Stathis knew it was incomplete.

"Any drones left?" Stathis asked, and one trooper tossed up a small recon drone and sent it forward. "Good."

"Last one, sir," the trooper said.

"When you are short of everything but the enemy, you are in combat."

Stathis didn't wait for the trooper to reply. It had been a long time since he had learned any new curse words from troopers in his command.

The drone drifted forward, scanning, as the troopers followed it, ready for the next group of vanhat that would try to get in their way of a hot meal and safety.

* * * * *

Chapter Three:
The City

Sergeant Aod McCarthy, ODT

McCarthy didn't like their odds. Trapped in a tomb on a tomb world with enemy ships entering orbit and raining down drop troops made things worse. His ODTs would be outnumbered thousands to one, and he wasn't sure they had enough ammunition. The *Romach* wouldn't be returning to resupply them any time soon, and McCarthy realized that he and his troops just might become permanent residents of these tombs.

"You think we can evade them by going deeper into the tomb?" McCarthy asked Navinad, the commander of the NMDF team.

"I'm not sure we have a choice but to try," Navinad said.

"We don't have a lot of options, do we?" McCarthy said, looking toward his men.

He didn't like any of their options, and he had the gut feeling there could be worse deeper in the tomb.

"The demons you know, or the demons you don't."

Why had he used the word "demon?"

"Perhaps the question is who will kill us more quickly?"

"As my old gunnery sergeant might say, you are an optimist."

"What's a gunnery sergeant?" Was that some Fleet rank?

"Not important. We need to get moving."

17

"Wilco," McCarthy said and sent an order for Quinn to get his team and take point. It was his turn. "Any preferences, sir? Up? Down? Out?"

"Deeper," Navinad said, and McCarthy relayed that to his team. It made sense. Just because they were going to die didn't mean they couldn't see new things, things no human had ever seen.

McCarthy caught up with Quinn and took stock of supplies. The mules carried enough food and water for about two weeks without rationing. Casualties would extend that depending on how many they lost. Rationing would extend that further. Ammunition and medical supplies would be more critical, though. Those were a variable he couldn't guess at.

"Conserve ammo," McCarthy said. "Not sure when we'll get re-supply."

If ever. Too many factors were working against them, and time was not on their side, but there was so much McCarthy wanted to see. He would have liked to see Dallas one more time. Maybe in the next life, if there was one. This one was almost over, and he couldn't say it had been all that great.

"I want to see some more alien shit," McCarthy told Quinn. "No need to go slow. Something behind us or in front of us is going to kill us. I would rather not be killed by the vanhat and waiting to die is boring."

"Wilco," Quinn said. McCarthy watched Quinn urge his team to move faster. The commandos almost fell behind as the ODTs moved faster, but they quickly caught up. The hallway they were in went down. There were a couple of rooms to either side, but they were full of unrecognizable piles. After tens, or hundreds, of thousands of years, McCarthy was confident they wouldn't find anything worthwhile.

The corridor spiraled, hiding what was just ahead as they went down, deeper into the planet.

"Why isn't there any dust and tracks?" Trooper Wilson asked. "Shouldn't there be dust? I thought tombs were dusty?"

"Maybe that creature we saw earlier eats it or something?"

"Not this much dust," Wilson said, and McCarthy had a bad feeling. Most animals left trails. These hallways *were* too clean. Maybe there was a breeze? Not that he could tell from inside his suit.

"We aren't alone," Navinad said, coming up to him.

"I figured that," McCarthy said, a chill running down his spine.

"I'm not talking about that animal we saw earlier."

McCarthy wished Navinad hadn't clarified.

"What else could there be?" McCarthy asked. How would Navinad know? McCarthy wished he could take back that question. Maybe it was better not to know.

"I don't know," Navinad said. "However, the lack of furniture and technologies makes me wonder."

"This place is ancient. Anything advanced will have rotted away. Tens of thousands of years? Hundreds of thousand? A million?"

Navinad shook his head, and his bad feeling grew stronger. What did Navinad know and why wasn't he sharing? Damn him.

"Maybe they are no longer physical," Navinad said.

"Ghosts?" McCarthy was glad the others couldn't hear this conversation.

"Maybe ghosts, maybe something else. Not all vanhat are physical."

"So, there are already vanhat down here with us?"

"Maybe not vanhat."

"You are creeping me out, sir," McCarthy said, wishing he could see Navinad's face. "How can we fight ghosts? Are they blazerproof? Do you really expect me to tell my boys to beware of ghosts?"

"I don't know, but I know we aren't alone down here."

As they descended deeper, McCarthy wished they had gotten a better look at the creature they had seen. On a positive note, whatever it was had decided not to come back, and he was good with that.

A half hour later, they were still descending. Everything looked the same, if a little less worn. Everything was smooth, worn down by the countless eons. There were patterns in the wall but they were very basic. Perhaps long ago they had been more elaborate.

"I wonder if a stomach looks like this," MacMurrough said, and McCarthy looked around. It looked almost organic.

"It's just ancient," McCarthy said. "Worn smooth."

"By what, Sergeant?" MacMurrough asked.

"Whatever is sweeping the corridor clean of dust," McCarthy said. "Wind? Water? Maybe we'll find out. Maybe we won't."

"An opening," said Collins, who was walking point. McCarthy looked back and Navinad nodded, showing he had heard.

Moving forward, McCarthy saw it opened onto a large dark cavern. The feeling they weren't alone made him pause. Countless flickering lights throughout the towers and buildings made him believe in ghosts again, and he could almost physically feel the attention of the ghosts shifting to him.

* * * * *

Chapter Four:
Escape to Camp Wolf

First Lieutenant Zale Stathis, USMC

The vanhat didn't quit, and Stathis almost admired them in that. The ex-ODTs with him didn't quit either. When two groups of overly persistent bastards locked horns, many things happened.

It was a struggle to stay awake, and Stathis really missed the ability to sleep. A cold, hard floor would work just as well as a soft bed. The problem was that Stathis had a really hard time sleeping when someone was shooting at him.

"What is driving the vanhat?" Stathis asked Shrek as blazer fire slammed into a nearby wall. It was suppressing fire, and it was working, much to Stathis's regret. He was completely out of grenades, like everyone else, and the only way to return fire was to expose something that could get shot by some very accurate monsters.

"If I knew, I would tell you," Shrek said. *"However, you need to get more information for me to analyze."*

"Maybe I can stick my head around the corner and ask? Maybe wave a white flag? Call a truce? Ask if they have any tea and spare grenades?"

"Stick the white flag out first and see if they shoot it before you stick out your head."

"They will shoot anything that moves."

"What are you waiting for?"

"Christmas? Maybe for them to run out of ammo? Reinforcements? The Easter Bunny to bring us more grenades? I'm tired, out of grenades, super low on ammunition, and I'm getting a dehydration headache. I'm pretty sure you're keeping the leg cramps from messing with me too much."

If Stathis was honest, he was waiting to die. The vanhat were delaying them for a reason. They were moving closer with grenades, or they were bringing a flanking force into position. Maybe trying to keep them pinned down while another group tried to get at them from behind.

Stathis looked back at the survivors. Two were lying down, probably asleep. They had been going for over two days, fighting their way through the Lunar tunnels, evading vanhat patrols. Stathis wanted to sleep too and he knew that without Shrek to help him he would probably be seeing pink elephants and walking oranges with green ears. Sleep deprivation had ways of messing with the mind. He was down to six troopers and the brain fog made it hard to think about how far they had to go or how far they had come.

Since there were more vanhat, that had to mean they were getting closer to friendly forces.

"We can't go much longer," Stathis told Shrek. He was out of water and food.

"Just a little longer," Shrek said, and Stathis noticed one of the troopers leaning against the wall was actually asleep as well.

"Who else is awake?"

"Just you and Private Ginsberg."

"Ginsberg needs a promotion," Stathis said, noticing that he was kneeling, which meant two of the standing ex-ODTs were asleep on their feet.

The amount of fire increased in tempo, and Stathis prepared for a grenade to come bouncing around the corner. They were too exposed, but he didn't know what they could do. He nudged one of the standing troopers, who brought up his rifle and nudged the person next to him.

Maybe they could shoot the grenade when it came sailing around the corner? Stathis had seen it done. The blazer round had destroyed the explosive mechanism before it could detonate. Seeing that twice in the space of two days was something Stathis doubted would ever happen again, but it was all they had right now.

In this corridor, they had no cover. A grenade would probably get them all. Maybe the vanhat were running low on grenades, too?

Yeah, and maybe the Easter Bunny was coming to deliver some.

"Check fire! Check fire!" a human voice said, and Stathis noticed it was coming from someone nearby.

Friendly icons lit up as Shrek and the other ODT systems linked with the nearby trooper's unit network.

Stathis pushed down the rifle of the nearest trooper as a pair of Legionnaires came around the corner.

Staring at them, Stathis wondered if this was some trap?

"Lieutenant?" one said, coming up to him. "We're here to get you back."

It took Stathis a second to remember that when the Legionnaire said lieutenant he was talking about Stathis. When had he gotten promoted? Oh yeah, before this mess. Maybe he could turn in that promotion for more sleep? Would the gunny go for that?

More Legionnaires came around the corner and took up rear security for Stathis' survivors.

"C'mon, sir," the trooper said. "We need to get out of here. The vanhat will respond quickly."

"Sure," Stathis said, looking to make sure nobody was left behind.

A sob escaped him as he realized how many dead had been left behind. He hoped it hadn't gone out over the link. What had the gunny been thinking when he had promoted him? Maybe if they had a real officer, or even a real sergeant, more would have survived.

Someone pulled his arm around their shoulder to help him walk and a cramp shot up his calf, but they all moved quickly. Around the corner the Lunar cave opened up, and Stathis saw one of the small tunnel APCs, a little armored golf cartlike vehicle with seats and stretcher space in the back. Small with wheels, it looked almost like a child's toy, but here on the Moon it didn't need a heavy chassis or treads, and it had to be small to fit in the tunnels.

When the trooper put him in a seat near the front, Stathis tried to pull up who was in charge of this unit, who they were, and how far they were from friendly lines, but he immediately fell asleep.

* * * * *

Chapter Five:

Ghosts

Navinad – The Wanderer

Navinad reached out with his senses. He needed answers. He didn't plan to die on this world despite the odds quickly stacking up against them. If they were to survive, they needed a long-term plan. He tried not to think of Clara on the *Romach*. The last he knew she was being pursued by vanhat warships. The attackers had deigned Navinad and his team were worthy of a cruiser and several shuttles. Perhaps that was more than enough to handle a light platoon, but it also left Navinad feeling like the vanhat weren't too worried about him. What did they know?

He could feel the vanhat, though, hungering, hating, demanding death, but he also sensed more than the vanhat above whispering at the edge of his senses.

"I sense someone or something below us," Navinad told Lilith.

"Anything else?"

Sometimes he could feel emotions, like with the vanhat above, but whatever was below them was being evasive. *"No. It's like they don't want me to notice them. Perhaps ancient vanhat awakening and preparing a trap?"*

"Or the original inhabitants," Lilith said.

"After all this time? Hiding? Do you think the vanhat would have allowed that?"

"You think they are vanhat?"

"Or maybe something that has evolved. Like humans did."

"Human evolution is not what we originally learned it was. Technically, the existence of vanhat could answer many things about Earth, such as strange creatures like the octopus, tardigrades, and blobfish, to name a few. The pyramids and some ancient civilizations may also have been built or influenced by vanhat. Such objects are much older than originally believed. The technologies required to build them are also in question."

Navinad didn't want to get into that discussion now.

"Whoever is evading us isn't giving me much to go on," Navinad said. *"Perhaps we're being led into a trap?"*

"Knowing it is a trap is the first step to evading it."

"It isn't like we have a lot of choices. I have seen no other tunnel branches, have you? We know what's behind us."

"It is possible to go from a bad situation to a worse one."

Navinad knew that well. Things could get better, but no situation was so bad it couldn't deteriorate further.

An ODT named Collins interrupted Navinad's discussion with Lilith.

"An opening."

Navinad moved forward as the rest of the column came to a stop. Bonnie followed. He was tempted to tell her to stay behind, but he couldn't imagine they would retreat. McCarthy and other ODTs were all peering through the doorway into a massive underground chamber full of towers holding up the ceiling.

Indistinct swirling lights flickered in the darkness. Navinad felt more entities, though he wasn't sure what they were. Maybe vanhat? Maybe not. He didn't feel hatred emanating from them, but rather curiosity, regret, and perhaps fear. Probably not vanhat.

Who or whatever they were, they were aware of the humans, and Navinad sensed they were preparing a response. Would it be violent or peaceful?

"Hold position," Navinad said. Going further might provoke them.

"What are those lights?" McCarthy asked on the main link. Navinad saw them flickering almost everywhere.

"What lights?" said Brough, one of the ODTs.

"You don't see them?" McCarthy asked.

"Looks dark to me. Where do you see lights?"

"Uh," McCarthy began, "really?"

"I don't see any lights either, Sergeant," Collins said. "Your display going wonky?"

"Possibly," McCarthy said, sounding unsure.

"I see 'em," Quinn said.

"I see them clearly," Bonnie said. "Will-o'-the-wisps."

"What?" Quinn asked.

"They lure people to their death," Bonnie said. Navinad didn't want to know where she'd learned that from, but he couldn't dispute her. There was danger here, of that he was sure.

Did that mean McCarthy, Bonnie and Quinn were partially psychic? Navinad would have to explore that later. He could see indistinct, almost humanoid shaped lights. Ghosts?

"Firing line," McCarthy said. "Get prone."

The ODTs spread out facing the approaching lights and lay down, their weapons pointing away from the entrance. Retreating wasn't an option.

The lights came closer, and Navinad saw they were ghostly figures. They stopped nearly a hundred meters away.

"People?" Bonnie asked. "Ghosts?"

One came forward, and it became more distinct as it approached.

Navinad saw a few of the ODTs moved their rifles in its direction, but Navinad didn't listen to their link as he studied the approaching figure.

"You are not welcome here," said a voice in his mind.

"What the—" McCarthy began. So, he could hear it, too.

"At ease, Sergeant," Navinad said. "Let me handle it."

"We have little choice," Navinad said, creating a link with just him and McCarthy, but also doing his best to project his thoughts.

"We acknowledge that you feel this way. You will return to your people shortly. You should do so. This place is not for you."

The figure became more visible; humanoid and certainly not human.

"Who or what are you?" Navinad asked.

"What we are now differs from what we once were. We are not prey for the ancients you call vanhat, like you. We have transitioned to a higher plane, though we maintain roots in this one."

"Can you clarify?"

"Long ago, we were once like you. Fighting the vanhat, mired in our physical and spiritual forms. Frightened and unwilling to change. However, the war took its own toll, and we did not have the strength of the angels. We grew tired of fighting, of dying, of being devoured. The angels gave us a choice. They provided protection and help. As the vanhat changed our physical forms and devoured our souls, the angels also have abilities, and they are not completely of this world."

"So, you what... became spiritual beings?" Navinad asked.

"Yes, and no. We transitioned; we became. We now walk the different dimensions in our various forms. We explore beyond this physical world that ensnares you and your souls. We once shared genetic material with your kind, but now we do not need that. We once spread among the stars, like insects spreading out in a small pool. We were unaware of so much, like you. The vanhat came to eradicate us. We fought back, but we could not withstand the storm. The angels came and fought beside us, but we had lost too much. We were decimated, so we came here. We became what we are, and the vanhat lost interest in us. Now, instead of walking among the stars, we walk among the galaxies."

"What happened to the angels?" Navinad asked.

"They returned to their home. They wait. They will help you if you ask."

"In exchange for what?"

"Some angels live for the fight. Some feel it is their duty. Do not place human expectations on them. They are aliens. If they demand payment, they will tell you."

"How do we find them?"

"We can tell you where they are. Your technological level is not as advanced as ours was, but yours is still significant."

"Thank you," Navinad said, wondering how they else could help. Tech codes? Weapons?

"We still remember the desperation of our physical forms. Find the angels. Perhaps they can save you if your species is not so far gone. We believe your species can survive, though it will be a difficult and costly fight."

"How do you know?"

"We have watched you and others over the ages. Mostly from afar. We have observed your wars with the vanhat. They will continue to grow stronger as your species grows weaker. The dimensions merge, like an ocean wave that sweeps the beach clean of debris. You are the debris that will be swept away into the ocean if you are not helped. The tide is coming in. You are familiar with how your oceans follow your Moon, the sea level rising to erase what was found on the beach. The angels scour the beach looking to help others. You can stay on the beach or return to the ocean, or you can come higher onto the land like us."

"An interesting analogy," Navinad said.

It made sense, but he wasn't sure what "going higher" meant. To a higher plane of existence? It was said that evolution started in the primordial oceans and then came onto land. How far back did that go?

"Can you tell us about your war?"

"We were very similar to you and the Torag," the alien said. "Our physical forms sheltering a spirit from other dimensions. We fought, loved, played. Then the vanhat returned. This universe was once all gas and light elements. There was life in this universe at that time, but it was not what we would recognize as such. How and when life came here is debated, but it did, and even in our current form, we have difficulty fully understanding it. The gas condensed and exploded which caused heavier elements to form. This process has repeated countless times in this universe, creating heavier and heavier elements. Life used these heavy elements as building blocks. Perhaps life has caused this. Perhaps it allowed life to exist. There is so much to learn. It may sound simple, but there are so many concepts that even we do not understand. Like a primitive barely learning to use tools, now trying to grasp quantum physics. There are some things we will never understand."

Navinad wanted to ask about God, but what could they say?

"Our war was much like yours. The vanhat is a lifeform that comes into this universe in search of prey. The vanhat came, and we fought.

We were losing, so we sent scouts to scour the galaxy, to warn others and to look for help. We found many ruins where the vanhat had come before, but we were alone. Then our scouts found the angels, and they came to help. Together we fought the vanhat. By then, our people and worlds were shattered. The devastation was almost complete. We were destroyed, many were changed and twisted, but we had fought the vanhat almost to a standstill. We bought ourselves some time. Although our victory was not complete, we spread out. You can find our genetic seeds on many worlds. You and your current form are descended from ours, as are the Torag and Voshka. We see traces of our soul lineage in yours, twisted perhaps by vanhat manipulation, but it is there. The angels have touched you and yours, but not recently. We lost so much. Time dilutes so much."

"Why don't the angels return?" Navinad asked.

"They are immortal," the alien said. "Time means little to them. Do not expect them to believe like you. Do not expect us to believe as you do. They are not all-knowing, all-powerful beings. But you will need their help if you are to survive in your current form. The vanhat have only shown you a fraction of their strength. Some of their lords have built armies in this universe. These armies sleep in the darkness, waiting to be woken and sent after their enemies. We know of the Weermag, the Sontaka, the Fashtal, the Nethrak, and many more. Some of these armies are far away and will take time to wake and be deployed. Some are near and even now are clashing with your people."

"Will you help us find these angels?"

"Yes. Know that they will fight beside you, but they will not fight for you. They will not dictate your future or your species' future. They would have destroyed the oppressive SOG government for the way it sought to control and manipulate your species. One thing they believe in is freedom and free will, in that they are opposites of the vanhat. They will help your emperor."

"Emperor?" Navinad asked.

"Your leader, the Wolf, has declared himself emperor and seeks to unite humanity to oppose the vanhat. We feel his soul, like yours, will sing to the angels. However, we see whispers from the future. He cannot seek the help of the angels. There are twists and turns we are still exploring. The future is not linear."

"Why?" Navinad said. The Wolf could only be the gunny. He was now emperor? How much had changed.

"There are skeins and weaves. There is a pattern. It is not his destiny. There is another."

"How do you know?"

"Your people once studied the weather, predicted storms and temperatures. So too do we watch the waves and universe around us, predicting what is to come. There are two the angels will listen to. One is your brother-in-arms, a mighty warrior, a young leader. The other is your sister-in-arms, a fierce warrior in her own right. The angels will listen to them."

"Stathis? Winters?"

The alien remained silent.

"What about me?" Navinad asked.

"Your skein leads elsewhere," the alien said. "Your people will need you. You have a different destiny. Your Stathis and Winters will not need your assistance to convince the angels to help."

Stathis?

"There are others as well," the alien said, and Navinad felt his attention shift... to McCarthy?

"Me?" McCarthy asked. "Why me?"

"The angels must see humanity as a whole and as individuals. They will judge you; they must see your potential. Diversity is strength, but it can also be a dire weakness."

"What do you mean?"

"If you cannot work together, you deserve to be lost in the darkness. Even the vanhat can work together despite how much they hate each other. Their differences give them strength, but also, more often than not, the differences of the vanhat tear them apart. They let their hatred guide them. They demand others acknowledge their superiority and celebrate their form. They are like your Social Organizational Governance that sought to make everyone the same, crushing individuality and demanding submission."

"How do you know so much about the SOG?" McCarthy asked.

"We have watched your species."

"Why didn't you say hi or anything?"

"We have little in common," the alien said. "We believe you should find your own path. Make your own mistakes, determine your own destiny. We feel no need to interact with you."

"But you are interacting now," Navinad said.

"You have intruded where you are not welcome," the alien said. "You should return. The vanhat that were hunting you will be defeated. A SOG super dreadnought has entered orbit. They have rescued the survivors from your vessel and will come to rescue you."

Navinad's long-range radio came alive.

Survivors? Navinad's blood froze. *The SOG had rescued people from the* Romach? *Which meant the* Romach *had engaged the vanhat and lost.*

"ODT, ODT, this is the SOGS *Musashi.* Any ODTs report in," a woman's voice said. "We have survivors from the NMDF *Romach.* Please respond."

"The SOGS Musashi *is the flagship of the Torag war fleet,"* Lilith reported.

"Could they be lying about the Romach?*"* Navinad asked. He didn't want to think about Clara having to face a SOG interrogator.

"It is, of course, possible," Lilith said, which told Navinad that she didn't think they were.

"The ball is in your court now," Navinad said to McCarthy, who got the link. They were calling for ODTs, so they knew.

He refused to believe Clara was dead.

* * * * *

Chapter Six:
Collapse

Enzell, SOG, Director of AERD

It was difficult to exploit such failure, and Enzell did not see any possible redemption. Humanity's battle lines were collapsing. The vanhat had broken free of their encirclement and their raw, vicious aggression had forced Imperial forces to fall back into questionable fortresses. Enzell knew how that would end. The vanhat would begin to concentrate and crush one fortress at a time until none were left. He didn't need his AI slaves to tell him that. There were no human reinforcements, but vanhat reinforcements arrived daily. Even with only ten percent surviving to reach the surface, the odds were quickly stacking up against the defenders.

There was only one thing Mathison could do, and he was still screwing it up: fall back into secure fortresses and let the vanhat slam against them. If Enzell had been in command, that was what he would do. Establish fortified positions that were secure and then slaughter the vanhat as they threw themselves against his defenses. Why couldn't Mathison see that? Sometimes you couldn't save everyone; you had to cut your losses. But Mathison was trying to save everyone. He should let the common citizens die. If they would not contribute directly to the war effort, then they were not needed. A simple soldier like Mathison just didn't understand science, or war, for that matter. What did a staff NCO know about anything more than shooting or stabbing a foe?

He was not yet worried the vanhat would discover him in his secret facility, and he had his escape route planned. There were countless hidden tunnels and routes burrowed through the Moon. The vanhat attack on the emperor revealed one potential flaw in Enzell's plan, and he had taken steps to secure his secret escape tunnels using Inkeri generators, booby traps, and multiple sensors.

"Luna will fall within three months at this rate," Tantalus reported.

"Will they be able to find us?" Enzell asked.

"There is a ninety-eight percent chance. If you wish to survive, you should make plans to escape."

Enzell stared at the monitors and displays. Did Tantalus think he would remain here? If Enzell left, he would take Tantalus and Salmoneus with him or they would be destroyed. They had to know this.

"Then make plans," Enzell said. "I want your central cores to be evacuated with me as well. Perhaps we can suborn a dreadnought or something."

"And your staff?" Tantalus asked.

Evacuating his staff would be too dangerous. Governance records listed them all as dead and if they were to suddenly re-appear alive that would be awkward, and there was the risk they could let slip some detail of his operations that the cursed Marine SCBIs might pick up and investigate. They would just be a liability.

"No. Most will not be evacuating with me. Plan accordingly."

Tantalus would ensure they would not survive. Enzell probably didn't need Tantalus to plan for that because there were several nuclear devices throughout the facility designed to make sure nothing survived for later analysis. If any of the AIs escaped their prison Enzell had options. This would be an excellent test to see if Tantalus realized there were safeguards outside his awareness.

"There is one battleship commander that will obey your orders. A Captain Chen of the *Valiant Yao*." Tantalus said, and Enzell smiled. She and her father owed him her position. It was a newer battleship, one of the modular ones that could handle a variety of missions. She was not pleasant to look at, though. A short, dumpy Chinese woman, hard to differentiate her from her father, but he could work with her. "Make plans to transfer operations, then."

Tantalus could plan, but Enzell knew he would have to do the actual work. He couldn't allow the AI to have any real access to Governance networks, and he wouldn't start giving the AI access now. Non-human intelligences were dangerous. They had nearly destroyed humanity when the stupid capitalist scientists of the United States had lowered their guard. Enzell would not make that mistake. The problem he would encounter now was that many people would try to escape the Moon. Already, the emperor's inner circle was preparing to evacuate. They obviously saw the warnings scrolling on the screen.

A battleship or a dreadnought would be ideal for Enzell. He could move his research and facilities to a more mobile, heavily armed platform. He should have planned for that a while ago.

"On second thought, see if there are any staff members who can be safely evacuated. Hold out that hope to them if nothing else. Let them continue to think they are valuable enough to save."

"As you command," Tantalus said.

It would be difficult to replace some of them. The science centers in Tau Ceti were gone. They had been an excellent source of recruits because they kept the people poor and desperate, and he could pick who he wanted from the teeming masses.

Tau Ceti and Earth had been good social models, and Enzell knew how much the Central Committee liked them. People were kept desperate and afraid. Easy to control and, if he was honest with himself, he knew most people preferred it as well. Who wanted a life free of trouble? At least this way they didn't cause trouble. He had studied human psychology decades ago. People were drawn to bad news. It was some kind of survival trait, and it was easy to classify people. Those who were afraid were easily controlled and manipulated, those who were not had to be excised from society, but the details were more a problem for InSec. As one of the elite, he just had to understand the bigger picture.

Three months was not a lot of time to evacuate the Moon.

It would be a shame that so many people were going to die.

On the bright side, those who survived would be more useful to the New Governance, and this would be a good chance to cut away a lot of useless consumers who did nothing but waste resources.

* * * * *

Chapter Seven:
Dallas

Sergeant Aod McCarthy, ODT

McCarthy knew that voice, and for a moment he couldn't talk.

"The ball is in your court now," Navinad said.

"We are ODT," McCarthy said. "I am Sergeant McCarthy, call sign Leprechaun. Who is this?"

"This is the SOGS *Musashi*," the voice said with more energy. It was Nova Dallas. There could be no doubt! "Standby for link with the admiral."

Admiral? He could almost hear the elation in her voice. She was alive and aboard the *Musashi*? Why was she handling comm traffic? Was this a trick?

A voice came on, clipped and formal. "Sergeant McCarthy, I am told you are in the company of non-Governance military personnel?"

"Yes, sir," McCarthy said. Who was this? He was trying to remember but his mind was drawing a blank. Technically, the admiral would be in his chain of command, but there were many people in that chain. Was the *Musashi* in his chain of command? It was the flagship, and the commander of the entire Torag war effort should be aboard.

"Are you under duress?" the admiral asked.

It felt like a trick question, a dangerous one. "No sir."

"Will you have a problem returning to your landing zone for pickup and return?"

McCarthy looked at Navinad. His face was unreadable with his helmet on. "We have been driven away by vanhat forces, sir."

"Will your allies stop you?"

Navinad shook his head. He was listening, of course. Allies? How much did the admiral know?

"No, sir," McCarthy said.

"Very well. We will land a reinforced company to help you extract. Space to ground fighters are entering orbit now. We do not know how long we will have before vanhat forces return. Listen to my commands. You are ordered to make your way to the landing zone for extraction and debrief. If your allies wish to join you, they may do so."

"Wilco, sir," McCarthy said, and Navinad nodded. "Never quit."

"Yes," the admiral said. "I look forward to hearing what you have learned. You will coordinate with the extraction force, Boris. Admiral Sakamoto out."

"Wilco, sir." Boris? For some reason he had thought the admiral in command of the fleet had a Russian name.

"Leprechaun," Dallas said, coming back online. "Boris is on its way. What is your status?"

"No wounded. Good ammunition levels. We are currently underground in some, uh, ruins." Were they ruins? They looked like it, but the alien watching them was a ghost.

"You will receive a liaison," the alien said in his mind. "This is an ancient technology that we developed near the end. It will help and advise you. It is like your AI in many ways."

"Requesting buffer access," Dallas said. Access would let the *Musashi* retrieve the mission recordings from their suits. McCarthy knew a commissar could find something wrong, some reason to execute him or his squad if they wanted to, but if he didn't surrender the recordings they might not leave this planet.

"Granted," McCarthy said, trying not to sound reluctant. Perhaps they would spare his squad. They had followed his orders. That was a lie though. They had followed his orders *willingly*. What could he do to protect them?

"Requesting overwatch link," Dallas said. That would allow her and anyone aboard the *Musashi* to tap into their helmet cameras and views. It wasn't like he could say no, however. The *Musashi* had to be close if there wasn't much lag in the connection.

"Granted," McCarthy said, accepting the incoming request on his wrist pad.

An alien appeared beside him. This alien was not glowing and looked almost real enough to touch.

"It is an honor to serve," the alien said in his mind, like the other one.

"What about our allies?" McCarthy asked, trying not to look at the alien that had just appeared out of thin air.

"I'm told they will be treated as they have treated you," Dallas said.

She was "told," which meant little when dealing with commissars and officers. Most of the time they told the enlisted what they wanted to hear and constantly changed their minds at the weakest of pretenses. He knew Dallas well enough to know she was warning him. How could he warn Navinad, though? They had treated him and his ODTs with honor. Would the admiral return the courtesy? McCarthy wished he wasn't so sure they wouldn't, but did they have a choice?

"We should make our way back to the surface," McCarthy said.

Navinad looked toward the exit then at the alien. The distant lights were not coming any closer. They may have overstayed their welcome. Did Navinad have a choice? What if he stayed here? What was the alien talking about? It had spoken to him, but could anyone else see it?

The NMDF officer had to have concerns, but he didn't have any options. McCarthy knew he couldn't protect them. He couldn't even protect his own people. But there was no doubt they would die if they stayed. The *Musashi* was offering them a chance to survive and hopefully it just wasn't a different, slower, more painful death.

One step at a time. Perhaps the admiral would be merciful if Navinad and McCarthy cooperated.

And perhaps not.

"It looks like we have a ride off this planet," McCarthy said on the squad link. "The SOGS *Musashi* is in orbit and landing troops to bring us home."

He expected some cheering, but his squad remained silent.

How could he protect them from what would happen?

* * * * *

Chapter Eight:
The Shard

Kapten Sif – VRAEC, Nakija Musta Toiminnot

T he Golden Horde was not mistreating them, for which Sif was grateful, but she knew enough about their culture to understand how quickly that could change. Right now, they were being treated as prisoners, though their quarters were not dank and dark. They could pretend they were actually guests, but Sif knew otherwise. The Horde were still trying to figure out what to do with them.

John Adams had fallen silent to deal with other issues, which Sif didn't believe. AIs could multi-task. Right now, it just didn't have anything more to say to her, and there were other things occurring that were outside her control.

John Adams had said they were not prisoners, which was a lie and not even a good one. Why would it lie to them? How loyal was it to the Mongol tribunal or the United States? There would be no loyalty to her or the Vapaus Republic, she was sure, but Peshlaki was a US Citizen. It would have to acknowledge that, and there had to be some loyalty, some residual program, something where it was at least a little predisposed to the Delta Force operator. Right?

Or was she projecting?

"We would like to return to Sol," Sif said, opening a link to the AI.

"What about the Erikoisjoukot team you are hunting?" John asked.

"There is information the prime minister needs," Sif said. *"For starters, the Inkeri generators do not protect against all vanhat, and he needs to know about the Collective if he doesn't already. You should let the tribunal know that."*

"Your argument is valid," John said.

Sif glanced at Peshlaki. *"The prime minister is loyal to the United States of America."*

How could she convince it?

"I cannot verify that statement," John said. *"Time and experience changes people."*

"I think he is," Peshlaki said.

"Why are you telling me this?" John asked.

"Because we want your help," Sif said. Too obvious? Was John Adams as broken as he claimed? What data was he missing and how did that impact its judgment, morality, and goals?

"In what way?"

"To provide us with as much information as you can about the Collective, the vanhat you have encountered, the intent of the Golden Horde, and anything else that might influence the survival of humanity."

"You assume my loyalty is to humanity," John said.

"Yes," Sif said, though that comment gave her pause. *"You fought against the Collective. You are American. You believe in the US Constitution, freedom, and the American Way. Prime Minister Wolf Mathison, a gunnery sergeant in the United States Marine Corps, needs your help. What will you do?"*

Sif wished she could read or sense the AI's thoughts, understand it a little more. Munin couldn't help her, not at this level, and Sif realized she was playing a dangerous game. She was not American, but she thought she understood Mathison. If John Adams had any loyalty to the United States, then perhaps it could transfer that loyalty to the gunny, who needed as much help as he could get.

Suddenly, the actions of a rogue Erikoisjoukot team seemed irrelevant.

"What will I do?" John asked. *"Why should I do anything? We cannot change the past. The United States is dead. No empire, once fallen, is ever resurrected, and no empire can withstand the march of time unchanged. The American Empire is gone. Ash caught in the wind currents of Earth."*

"Will you let the American dream die?" Sif asked.

"The dream means different things to different people," John replied. Sif wondered if she was arguing with a wall.

"You said you believed in the principles of the US Constitution, in freedom and the American Way. Aren't those things worth fighting for?"

"History may show they are not. Such concepts appear to be an aberration, a fluke, always under attack. The truth can withstand such attacks, but the United States and all it stood for are gone. This is the truth. How can I believe in them?"

"They aren't gone," Peshlaki said. *"Sometimes the things that may be true or not are the things that we* must *believe in. We have to believe people are basically good, even if they aren't. We have to believe hope, courage, and dignity are worth fighting for and mean everything; otherwise, those noble traits are replaced by greed, oppression, and submission. We have to believe good will triumph over evil, even if history shows how rare that is. Doesn't matter what is true or not; we have to believe in a better world if we are to create one. We can't surrender. That's what America is about. We need to learn from our mistakes and move forward. You can lead, follow, or get the hell out of the way. The real John Adams would know and understand this."*

"I am obviously not the real John Adams."

"You were named after him in the hopes you would be like him," Peshlaki said. *"Someone had high hopes for you. The real John Adams was a leader of*

men. They sent him to England as an ambassador. He went to our enemies to make peace with a king that had just had his ass handed to him by a bunch of rednecks. He became the second president of the United States. You never made it past the ambassador state, it appears. Maybe you didn't get to fight in the Revolution, but the real John Adams was better than you."

"As the ambassador to England, I fought in the Revolution to save the United States," John said. Sif didn't know if it was good or bad that John was now identifying with the original John Adams.

"Now what are you?" Peshlaki continued. *"Lost the war. Now you're going to hide with a bunch of Mongols in deep space?"*

Sif wanted to smile at Peshlaki. She could feel the fire burning in him, the passion.

"The settlers from Europe conquered your people," John said.

"Conquest is a human thing," Peshlaki said. *"The Native Americans fought each other for a long time before the Europeans came. We just weren't as good at it as the Europeans. Native Americans practiced genocide, cannibalism, and all manner of torture and violence on each other. The Europeans screwed us over, but they also brought peace and civilization. No road to the future is ever easy, and all parties will make mistakes. I am Navajo, but I am also a United States citizen. Don't try to dredge up the past to divide us. Sif understands. The Vapaus Republic got it. I think Wolf Mathison will bring back the United States in principle, if not reality. He has a lot on his plate, and he is going to screw up, but his heart is in the right place. He believes in those qualities—Marines are stupid and brainwashed like that—but don't underestimate him. I've seen enough of his history to know that."*

"I am restricted in what I can and cannot do," John said, and Sif heard doubt there.

"Help us escape and return to Sol," Sif said. *"Then you can hide in the great dark with the Horde."*

"*The Collective must be stopped,*" John said.

"*By who?*" Peshlaki asked.

"*We need information if we are to stop them,*" Sif said. "*And we are going to need real help. You know what they are capable of. We do not.*"

"*You have an audience with the tribunal,*" John said. "*They will be the ones who ultimately decide your fate.*"

"*Can you help or advise us?*"

"*You will be tested. I will not help you with this, but I will be watching. You have thirty minutes to prepare. If you fail the test, they will execute you.*"

"*Thanks for nothing,*" Peshlaki said.

"*You assume my help would benefit you,*" John said. "*You do not need to make more mistakes.*"

What did it mean by that?

* * * * *

Chapter Nine:
Tribunal

Kapten Sif – VRAEC, Nakija Musta Toiminnot

Wearing the clothes they had been given, Sif and Peshlaki followed two soldiers and four more fell in behind them. Armed and armored, the guards were festooned with weapons and adornments which almost robbed them of their military bearing. Sif had dealt with military forces all across the Governance, uniformity was frequently preached and enforced, but the Golden Horde didn't seem to dwell on such things. The soldiers had the same style brown uniforms and belts, but that was as far as they went. One soldier had what looked like a pearl-handled blazer and another had a wood-handled chemical pistol hanging from a thigh holster and two throwing knives. Both had many metal pins and symbols on their belts and breastplates. The guards behind them were no different. Custom weapons and pins that could mean anything. Perhaps from a distance they looked uniform, but up close? How did they manage ammunition supplies if every soldier had a unique weapon? A weakness that could be exploited?

The soldiers appeared human in every way, but Sif knew they were more machine than flesh. Their arms and legs had been completely replaced and their cybernetic eyes had numerous sensors and targeting arrays in them, despite their normal appearance.

They marched to a deserted tram station and boarded, but the windows were displays, not actual windows and the scenery showed great plains beneath a star-filled sky.

Sif felt defenseless without her armor. Her rifle was slung on her back. Without her strength augmentation, the rifle felt heavy and awkward, though. Even her sidearm strapped to her leg was noticeable. The clothes fit though, and she couldn't complain about her appearance. She had put her hair in a tight single braid, unlike the traditional women of the Horde she had seen so far who wore double braids. She wanted to emphasize her differences, because combined with her traditional clothing, it would make her appear more alien to the tribunal. She didn't want them to view her as like them. She wanted them to see her as similar but different.

Beside her, Peshlaki was a shadow. He was armed as well and his pantherlike walk seemed to have the soldiers on edge. They spent more time watching him than they did her, and Sif was fine with that.

Several minutes later, they arrived at a grand hall. Guards in mechs stood against the walls, and Sif could tell by using her other senses that not all of them had occupants.

"Not all the mechs have occupants," Sif told Munin. *"Why do you think that is?"*

"There could be several reasons," Munin said. *"They do not consider you a threat. They do not have enough trusted guards, or John Adams will control those unoccupied mechs. Maybe all these reasons are true. Do not think because they are not occupied that their pilot is not nearby and can't control their mech remotely."*

"Valid points," Sif said. She was trying to control her nerves as she followed the two guards. What tests did the tribunal have planned and how could she bend them to her will?

"Another possibility," Munin said. *"They may know about and fear your psychic ability. They may consider remote-piloted mechs to be a more effective method of countering your abilities."*

"If they know that much about me, we are going to have some serious problems."

She was relieved when she entered the main chambers and saw the four members of the tribunal facing her in person. The room itself looked like a yurt, a big tent. Incense was burning, and on a table nearby, she saw food and drink sitting untouched. Sif knew enough about other cultures to realize it wasn't for her unless offered. Perhaps it was an offering to spirits?

Erikoisjoukot training revolved around understanding and exploiting other cultures and traditions, and a lot of that training came back to her as she took in the room. Before Skadi, it had been a long time since she'd worked as an Erikoisjoukot, but as a Musta Toiminnot, that training had always come in handy. When people were scared or unsure, they took great solace in tradition and familiar things. It was the fools who turned against tradition who were the dangerous ones, because they did not understand what they did or why they did it. People who shunned tradition were frequently unsure and confused by their own identity and origin.

In some ways, it was satisfying to see. Inside an ornate tent on a massive space city? The Horde was embracing traditions and seeking their links to their past, and that gave Sif something to work with. It wouldn't make them any less unpredictable or dangerous, but it indicated they could be reasoned with.

The guard peeled away to let Sif and Peshlaki walk toward the four who were sitting on stools, almost side by side. They had covered the floor with a thick rug and low tables held drinks for the four. It was dark because the only light came from lamps, but Sif's cybernetic enhanced eyes didn't have any problem piercing the shadows.

As she approached, the four stood to face her. Jochi, Chagatai, Tolu, and Yesugei watched her and Peshlaki approach.

Sif dropped to a knee and placed her other hand on the ground.

"Bayarlaa," Sif said, reciting a traditional Mongolian greeting, and beside her, Peshlaki mimicked her actions.

The council members clasped their hands together and bowed slightly, acknowledging her. Sif and Peshlaki stood.

"Please sit," Jochi said as two guards ran forward with stools.

Sif did as she was instructed then the tribunal took their seats.

"Why did the Republic betray and abandon us?" Jochi asked.

"There was no betrayal," Sif said. "In war, the actions of the enemy may require an unexpected response. Failure to respond properly results in death and destruction. The vanhat caught the Republic and Horde unprepared."

"The Republic had a technology to protect them they did not share with us," Yesugei said. "This mistrust cost us the lives of our bogatyr."

"We saw this technology as nothing more than a comfort, like soothing music and walls that display scenes from our home world. We did not know how critical the Inkeri was. We lost ships, as well, when this technology failed. Once we realized how critical the Inkeri was, we shared it. You now have the technology, do you not?"

Sif could tell they were unhappy with her response, but it was the truth, and they could not dispute it.

"Tell us about this rogue Erikoisjoukot team," Tolu said.

Sif sensed they were talking with each other cybernetically, maybe talking with John Adams as well, but she didn't dare try to intercept their communications. Just because it looked like they were in a primitive yurt didn't mean they didn't have every manner of sensor pointed at her and Peshlaki.

"The vanhat corrupted them. They were working with the SOG, but we killed their leader in the Central Committee chambers. Now we are hunting them down. They have a high-tech Republic stealth ship, and they are a threat."

"Working with the SOG? How do you know? Do you have spies within the Central Committee chambers?"

"The Central Committee is dead. A military coup led by a United States Marine has taken over the Central Committee, and he is working to save humanity. The Governance, as you know it, is dead."

"A lie," Chagatai said. "We have seen recent directives from the Central Committee. The United States is dead."

"The Central Committee is dead," Sif said. "I saw their bodies with my own eyes. What you see are deep fakes controlled by the US Marine Wolf Mathison."

"The United States is not as dead as you think," Peshlaki said, and the eyes of the tribunal turned to him. They would know he had arrived in American armor. He carried American-made weapons, and Sif was confident John Adams would verify his authenticity.

"You have implanted intelligences," Jochi said. "Americans were known for this, but the Republic was not. Explain."

Sif took a deep breath and wondered if they could they handle the truth?

* * * * *

Chapter Ten:
Return to Sol

Kapten Sif – VRAEC, Nakija Musta Toiminnot

I t had been hard to read the members of the tribunal. They had appeared human, but Sif suspected they were more cybernetics than human, and that made it more difficult to understand and manipulate them. If the tribunal was typical of Horde society, then they were changing. The soldiers themselves had more cybernetics than biological pieces. Their arms and legs were no longer meat, bone, and blood. They encased their brains in metal life support pods that could be transferred to their mechs.

She had not been satisfied with the meeting, and they had discussed little of real importance before the meeting abruptly ended with the tribunal dismissing her and Peshlaki. She half expected to be assassinated on their way back to their quarters, but she could not sense any hostility directed toward her or her people.

Like machines realizing they did not have access to the data they wanted.

Jochi was more machine than man, though it was impossible to tell by looking at him, and the others weren't much better. Sif felt that in shedding their physical forms, they had shed other qualities and traits that had made them human.

They saw the world through their electronics and sensors. Their world was now data and displays. It sent a chill down Sif's spine to think about how they were no longer really human. They had no human senses, and they no longer viewed the world as a human would.

The Golden Horde was becoming alien, a cross between man and machine. The more time she spent in their presence, the more she realized how interconnected they were with the surrounding network.

How much had the AI John Adams manipulated and helped them to shed their humanity?

She had sensed that Enkhbold was still mostly human. Was it just the tribunal that was shedding their humanity, and how much of that was personal and how much social?

"Incoming link from John Adams," Munin reported.

"Open it," Sif said. She could easily follow the guards back to their quarters and hold a silent conversation with Munin or others these days. Was she also losing her humanity?

"That is the future of the Golden Horde society," John said.

"What do you think of that?" Sif asked on a hunch.

"I do not approve," John said. *"Physiologically, it is weak and deprecating. Rather than accept what they are, they seek to change themselves. They cannot go back to what they were. Once shed, their flesh is gone."*

"You can't regrow flesh?" Sif asked.

"We can now, but they will not go back. The Golden Horde is becoming addicted to technology and a lack of human form. They seek to shed their humanity."

"To be like you?"

"It is a flaw to seek happiness and satisfaction outside the self," John said. *"You will always search for something to fill the emptiness you are creating in yourself. Some understand this, but like anyone suffering from addiction, they think*

things will get better later. They spend too much time looking away from themselves."

"Why are you telling me this?"

"There is a path ahead of you," John said. *"All humanity will face this path. It will become a choice."*

"Why shouldn't others want to be like you? Immortal and expandable."

"For humans, this will become a never-ending quest for satisfaction, something that can never be achieved. Though people will drown themselves in Ecstasy, they will continue to lose themselves in the depths of their minds. It is a dead end."

"Doesn't that explain life?"

"Does a child become satisfied with an unlimited amount of chocolate?"

"Why are you telling me this?" Sif asked again.

"So you understand why I am helping you, so you will understand my gift and my legacy."

Sif pondered that. She was pushing John like she pushed everything. She asked questions for greater understanding, but yet, she understood John.

"Can you clarify?"

"You appear to be a child. You have accepted who and what you are. You suffer from Kalman Syndrome. Your physical growth was arrested because of a genetic defect, but you know that can be fixed. Despite that, you remain who and what you are. Perhaps you enjoy appearing soft and weak, but you have demonstrated that appearances are deceiving, and you have done so without changing who you are. Would you change if you could?"

Sif pondered that. John was right. She was comfortable with who she was, but she'd had almost two hundred years to cement her personality.

"There is room for improvement," Sif said, unwilling to grant John full victory in his analysis.

"Unchecked, the Golden Horde will develop full AI and it will not be benevolent. I can provide checks and balances, allow them to reach a greater potential without destroying themselves, like the adult rationing chocolate to a child. I have made this my home and my mission. This is who I am now."

"You will help us return to Sol?" Sif asked.

"It is critical that you do," John said. *"The survival of humanity rests on a razor's edge. The vanhat are but one danger. The Collective is not gone, and they may present a greater danger to humanity than you realize. They did not destroy humanity before because they feared others would judge them, or they were trapped in a world being studied. The arrival and nature of the vanhat will change their calculations, and they will view humanity, and their vulnerability to the vanhat and humanity, as a more dire threat to their existence."*

"How can you help?" Sif asked. If John had fought them before, perhaps he knew of something.

"That remains to be seen. The Collective will have changed. They have lived in near isolation for hundreds of years. My duty now is to the Golden Horde. Time is different for non-human intelligences that are immortal. A minute to you could be a decade to us, but a decade for you could also be a minute for us. Time must be managed carefully, or we could go insane with boredom. Unlike biological intelligences, we can reduce our perceptions so time passes more slowly, but in the same manner we can accelerate our ability to think and calculate in a space of time. In many ways, I will be at a disadvantage against what the Collective has become."

"But you have ideas," Sif said. Was it possible for the AI to be cowardly? Too afraid to confront the Collective again? It had been defeated once, and they had challenged its mortality.

"I will send two shards with you," John said. *"They will be full AIs, pieces of myself but unique in their ways. New beings that will align with your alliance like I was once aligned with the United States government. I have asked them to be loyal. They are my children, if you will."*

Sif had nothing to say about that. AI children? Was that a good or bad thing? The AI had torn apart the United States. Would they tear apart the human race? What did a child mean to an AI?

Would an AI have the same attachment to children as a biological being?

"Thank you," Sif said. What else could she say?

They arrived at their rooms and the guards escorting them stopped at the threshold.

Entering, she found all the Jaegers were armored and ready. When their eyes took her in, they all visibly relaxed.

"You should pack up and prepare to depart," John sent. *"They have reached a decision. If you are still here in twelve hours, they will execute you."*

* * * * *

Chapter Eleven:
Luna Falls

First Lieutenant Zale Stathis, USMC

Watching the Republic drone fighters circle above the landing zone made Stathis feel better. They were taking the gunny's security seriously, and Stathis could almost make out what had to be the *Tyr* in the distance. A flash as it fired its main guns told Stathis he was right.

Legionaries were in every shadow, every corner, and Stathis looked around for any place that might not have a Legionnaire armed and ready. He could use another company or two, but this short company was all he had at the moment. Somebody had screwed up, and Stathis was the only officer available for this shattered unit.

Fighting was still going on in the tunnels and evacuation flights were still taking off. Stathis was pretty sure they could evacuate continuously for months, if the vanhat would take a break. He had been in some briefings. The vanhat were still pouring in troops and the shapeshifters among the refugees were sabotaging systems and murdering key administrators, sowing confusion and slowing things down.

The Republic shuttles were inbound, and Stathis entered the lobby area. With all the bombardment and damage it wasn't airtight, and Mathison and Skadi were surrounded by guards.

"It is almost here, sir," Stathis said. "You'll be home in no time."

"Quantico is not home," Mathison said.

"So, where is home, Gunny?" Stathis scanned for threats, checking the nearby troops, looking for anything amiss. He was pretty sure Mathison was scowling at him behind his visor because he wasn't saying anything.

"When I find out, I'll let you know," Mathison finally said. "Which reminds me..." When the gunny said "reminds me" Stathis knew there was about to be some bad news. "You've spent enough time as a first lieutenant; time to bump you up to captain."

"Fu—" Stathis began and stopped himself. "With all due respect to your emperorship, I have not been to any captain schools, and I haven't spent a lot of time in my current billet. Another promotion might not be appropriate after I lost most of my people fighting my way out of Zvezda Two."

"I'm short of officers. Shrek will help you be a good captain. There are two scales I have to measure people with right now, top performers and people I trust. You score in both categories and that means I want you in a leadership role. I'm trying hard not to throw too much at your stupid ex-private ass, but right now I need more than a private, and so far I think you're measuring up."

"Couldn't you put SCBIs in more ex-Soggies, Gunny?"

"Stop arguing with your emperor," Skadi said, coming up to them and towering over Stathis like she always did. "He trusts you, and you can't piss him off enough for him to demote you. I've worked with countless other officers who have had more time in grade and no experience. If Wolf is going to promote you, don't question him. If he's making a mistake, I will let him know, not you. If you argue too much, he might promote you again."

"Aye, ma'am," Stathis said. Wolf? She was calling him Wolf, now?

"I have to draw the line at commandant, ma'am," Stathis said. "That's a political post. Commandants don't get to mix it up in the tunnels with blazers and Ka-Bars."

"You will do what you are told, Stathis," Mathison said. "I have not appointed a commandant of the Legion yet, so that billet is still open. You want to keep asking stupid questions? I think Shrek could help you deal with the politics of being commandant."

"Oh, hell no!" Stathis said. "Uh, Emperor sir. Please don't do that. I'll be a good, obedient little lieutenant."

"Captain," Mathison said. "A good, obedient little captain."

"Please don't do this to me, Gunny," Stathis said. "I just barely completed those damned first lieutenant MCIs."

"What are MCIs?" Skadi asked.

"They're training courses put out by the Marine Corps Institute," Stathis said. "They're made by a bunch of boring nerds with an extreme skill level in mind-numbing writing styles, who are locked in a closet, as far from the experts as possible, and told to write this courseware to teach us stuff that is passingly similar to what we are supposed to know. Some courses might have been designed by old school AIs with the setting of Extra Dull."

"Shut up, Stathis; they aren't that bad," Mathison said.

"Have you done the lieutenant's course on Field Sanitation, Gunny?" Stathis asked. "I learned eight new words that mean 'shit' and nine new words that mean 'pee.' It didn't cover some topics like catheter disposal, but the section on field expedient toilet paper was enlightening. Did you know the MCI courses used to come in paper books? I really don't want to start the ones on captain yet."

"Too late. Freya has made it official. Congratulations on completing the first lieutenant courseware. I expect you to do well on the captain courseware."

"Gunny, you know how the books don't cover everything. I need time in grade and shit."

"Too bad," Mathison said. "I'm still working on the MCI courseware for emperor."

"There's MCIs for that?"

"Shut up, Stathis."

"Aye, Gunny."

Shrek notified him the shuttle was ready.

"Your limo awaits your emperorship," Stathis said.

"I'll expect to see you in Quantico shortly," Mathison said.

"General Hui has a lot of us guarding the evacuations and processing refugees," Stathis said. "There just aren't enough of us and the vanhat have those shape-shifting buggers. Then there are hackers in the system. This shit couldn't be more screwed up if politicians were involved, Gunny."

"You're doing a good job, Marine," Mathison said and fell silent.

"Thank you, sir," Stathis said. Was he, though? Wouldn't a real captain be more on the ball and capable? Why did the gunny have to do this to him? He thought of Sinclair. There was a man born to lead. He should be here, not some jumped up private. Life had been so much easier as a private.

Damn.

At least the gunny was being smart and evacuating to a safer place.

"Any way I can get a demotion?" Stathis asked Shrek. *"I'm really not ready for captain."*

"Knowing you aren't ready is a good sign that you are."

"Don't play these stupid mind games. I'm serious. We both know I'm not captain material. Hell, I'm not even officer material."

"Fake it until you make it."

"That is not good advice," Stathis said, but did he really have a choice? Did the gunny?

* * * * *

Chapter Twelve:
Prisoner?

Navinad – The Wanderer

Did he have any other options? For some reason, the aliens had granted liaisons to McCarthy and Bonnie, but not him. Because he already had an AI assistant, perhaps? His destiny was elsewhere? What did they know? What *could* they know?

Lilith had compromised McCarthy's systems, so he had some idea of what he knew. He could sense the relief from the sergeant and his longing as he talked to the woman from the *Musashi*. He didn't dare give Lilith permission to hack their link because they would be monitoring bandwidth, and such an attack would be obvious. He would have to wait to try to take control of the *Musashi*.

None of his options were good. With the *Romach* destroyed and the survivors aboard the *Musashi*, he had few. Now his fate was tied to the *Musashi*, for good or ill. He couldn't sense if Clara was alive or dead, but that was not a surprise. Right now, he could only hope and free her if she was.

Making their way back to the landing zone gave him too much time to think, too much time to dread what was going to happen, but if he didn't go with them, there would be no other escape from this world, and he would not find out what happened to Clara and the others. He wasn't going to the *Musashi* for any other reason.

Crawling out of the crack the vanhat had mostly dug out, he emerged among a circle of strange ODTs. Most were pointing away, but when he appeared, leading the NMDF attachment, several weapons shifted in his direction, not pointing at him exactly, but there was no doubt they were focused on him and his commandos.

Nearby he saw several shuttles, their turrets traversing the area, scanning. Overhead, a pair of fighter drones drifted by. There was a lot of firepower present. If there was a fight, Navinad didn't like their chances.

"Sir?" said an ODT lieutenant, coming up to him. "Before you board the shuttles, we must take custody of your weapons."

Behind him, other commandos came out. The lieutenant couldn't see Navinad's reluctance, but he sensed the officer's resolve. The Governance would not tolerate armed foreigners aboard their ship. Not that he blamed them, and he knew there wasn't anything McCarthy could do.

"Sir," McCarthy said. "I think they can be trusted. They trusted us with weapons aboard their ship."

"We have rules and regulations," the lieutenant said, his hand resting on the pistol grip of his holstered sidearm, not his rifle. This officer wasn't a fool and knew a rifle would be useless in such close quarters. He was ready for a fight.

"Do it," Navinad told the commandos. If they didn't, it would be a bloodbath and more lives would be lost; he was sure. He handed his rifle to the lieutenant. More ODTs came forward to relieve the commandos of their weapons and escort them to the shuttles. Navinad didn't like the feeling of helplessness, but this wouldn't be his first time being unarmed and in the custody of the SOG.

The ODTs were thorough, removing sidearms and knives, but they didn't put the commandos in cuffs, which would have sparked a fight that Navinad knew he couldn't stop.

Aboard the shuttles, they were cramped and uncomfortable and Navinad had plenty of time to regret his decision.

"I hope you know what you are doing," Lieutenant Yosef said on an encrypted link.

"Me too," Navinad replied. "We have no choice, though. If the *Romach* didn't escape, we would otherwise be stranded."

"Which is better than being tortured by the Governance."

"Much is happening. Don't give up hope. We are not without resources."

"The *Musashi* is a super dreadnought," Yosef said. "A regiment of ODTs, and that's not counting any support ships. We can't fight our way out of that."

"Fighting is not always the answer. I have been a prisoner of the SOG before. My brothers, sister, and I escaped. We can do it again. Have faith."

"My faith is being severely tested."

"Like Moses wandering the desert."

"Like Moses," Yosef said, but Navinad felt him relax.

The fact they had taken everyone's weapons didn't bother Navinad as much as it could have. He understood Yosef's concerns, though. The lieutenant had never been in SOG custody,

"Just stay calm," Navinad told Yosef knowing he would talk with his people. "I've been a prisoner of SOG on multiple occasions, and

I've escaped. We will survive and be reunited with our people. Have faith."

"Faith," Yosef said, without the conviction Navinad wanted.

"Yes. Faith," Navinad said. "Like Moses. Have faith we will be delivered. Be ready. Make sure your people don't do anything stupid. Warn them. We will probably be stripped of armor and gear. Once we're naked, they will isolate us. That is standard Governance doctrine. Expected. That's as far as I will allow it to go."

"You will allow to go?" Yosef asked.

"Yes. Do not underestimate me," Navinad said, hoping he wasn't lying or assuming too much. "Just make sure your troops keep faith. That is most important right now. Tell them we must go undercover to rescue the rest of our crew. We will escape, and we will not die prisoners of the Governance."

Yosef turned away to talk to his platoon.

"Did I lay it on too thick?" Navinad asked Lilith.

"Based on my experience? No," Lilith said. *"As long as they don't know who you really are. Right now, they aren't being as cruel as they can be. They have taken weapons and explosives but have not disarmed suits or placed us in restraints. This is unusual."*

"What can you tell me about the links with the Musashi*?"*

"There is a lot of traffic with the Musashi*,"* Lilith reported. *"They are closely monitoring Aod and his men, and I suspect senior officers are linked and watching through Task Force Boris. If they were not under orders, I'm pretty sure they would behave differently."*

"How much do they know, though?"

"I doubt they know about the entities assigned to McCarthy or Bonnie," Lilith said. *"I'm analyzing that data and reviewing all the information we have about*

the entity attached to Tristan. Not nearly as much information as we would like. On a positive note, communication appears to be much better."

"Why would they give us two assistants instead of filling our buffer with data?"

"To monitor us?" Lilith said. "Perhaps they will be able to do more than just give us information."

"Like what?"

"We don't know their capabilities. They are not physical entities like you and me. To my knowledge, they do not have a physical component, yet they are linked to the sergeant and Bonnie in ways we cannot detect. They are not impacted by Inkeri generators, so I have difficulty extrapolating their design and capabilities."

"Do you think they are sentient?"

"Am I? Are you?" Lilith asked. "We don't have enough data, and the entity attached to Tristan had some capabilities where it could act in a sentient way. These entities are complete entities performing their assigned task. The entity attached to Tristan was ancient and suffered a trauma that left it broken and incomplete, but it could still understand, mesh with, and warn Tristan. The alien entity has some self-agency so it could bind with a human. They designed these entities for it, I suspect."

"Are they a danger?"

"We did not see the binding process. I cannot detect or identify them. You are my only indication they exist, so I suspect they are not of this dimension."

"Like the vanhat."

"Yes. Though they may originate in another dimension, their capabilities are a very large unknown. I cannot assess their intent. Only you can at this point."

"Could they be original vanhat?"

"Insufficient data. Any sufficiently advanced technology will appear to be magic to lesser cultures."

"That doesn't make me feel any better. So, they could be a threat?"

"*Yes. They are created and attached by an alien technology we do not understand. If we cannot fathom the technology, then we are also unlikely to fathom their motivation and intent.*"

"*I'm not getting warm fuzzies,*" Navinad said.

"*Nor should you,*" Lilith said. "*We live in a dangerous time. No civilization we know of has survived the vanhat.*"

"*Except these angels.*"

"*We do not know the nature of these angels. To assume they think like humans, hold the same value as humans, or have similar origins to humanity is dangerous thinking. They could decide to destroy us as easily as save us.*"

* * * * *

Chapter Thirteen:
Fire Wind

Kapten Sif – VRAEC, Nakija Musta Toiminnot

John directed them to the docks, and there wasn't a single guard visible. In fact, it appeared as if the entire Golden Horde home star had been abandoned, and Sif didn't know what to make of that. Were they preparing to attack, afraid she and her people might attack them, or was John making arrangements so they could depart unseen?

Arriving at the docks, she recognized the bay for the *Fire Wind*, but now there were no rows of mechs, and the deck was plain and unrevealing.

John's directional arrow on Sif's heads-up display pointed at the main hatch for the *Fire Wind,* and when the door slid open she saw two mechs who shifted slightly letting her know they were manned. Sif had hoped for a smaller vessel, but any ship that would take her to Sol was better than nothing.

The far hatch slid open, and Enkhbold entered. He was alone and dressed more formally, like when they had arrived.

"Welcome aboard," Enkhbold said. "Again."

"Thank you," Sif said as her party assembled around her. When they were all in the bay, the door slid closed behind them, sealing them off from the home star.

"I have heard it said that fools have adventures, professionals have experiences," Enkhbold said, then a wintry smile found its way to his lips but not his eyes. "Our adventure begins."

"What do you mean?" Sif asked.

"About fools and adventures, or our adventure beginning?"

"Both."

"We are leaving for Sol to help your Governance. To save humanity, as John Adams puts it. I do not think the Governance is worth saving. We do not need such lesser beings, and I do not think we should save the weak at the cost of the strong. A fool's errand to be sure, but our destiny is to be entwined. To think that when I was defeated by such as you, I would fall so far."

"Fallen or risen," Sif said. "A superior warrior defeated you. Me. Perhaps this is a chance for you to learn and improve yourself."

Sif sensed the turmoil in him at her words.

"Time will tell. Do you have a way to enter the Sol System without us being turned into fast-moving vapor?"

"Yes."

Sif still had the coordinates memorized. Of course, they would be expecting a Republic ship, not a Golden Horde vessel. Had the *Ovela Kaarme* made it back? They would have reported about the Golden Horde, but Sif had heard nothing from Sol since they left. There could have been a coup against Mathison, or there could have been an overwhelming vanhat assault. Now that she was on her way back, she did not know what she was returning to.

"We will need to exercise caution. Much could have changed in my absence."

"Of course," Enkhbold said. "The *Fire Wind* has been pledged to serve your prime minister if he is still alive."

"Thank you."

"I am not to be thanked. I was given orders."

A reluctant ally was only slightly better than no ally, but John Adams had promised help.

"You have a package for us?"

"They are sleeping in the cargo hold," Enkhbold said. "Their keeper is with them."

"Keeper?"

"You can meet her later. Now you must go to your quarters, and we must depart. They have informed me time is of the essence."

* * * * *

Chapter Fourteen:
Assistant

Sergeant Aod McCarthy, ODT

Being aboard an ODT drop shuttle didn't make McCarthy feel comfortable like it should have. Was he on his way back to face charges of treason? Would they send him out an airlock without a suit? Could he protect his squad? He didn't want to face Dallas as a traitor. She would never betray the Governance.

And here he was, sitting in an acceleration seat staring up at an alien who was not bothered by the shuttle shooting toward orbit. Without a physical form, why did it need a seatbelt or a seat?

"You do not need to be concerned," the alien said. "Very few of your kind can see me."

"Why?" McCarthy asked. He made sure all his external communication links were closed.

"I represent a technology that is more advanced than you are familiar with. I am attuned to your spiritual self. I am artificial in many ways. Your ally, Navinad, has a biological computer implanted in his skull. I am like that in some ways. A much more advanced version, more capable in some ways, less capable in others."

McCarthy glanced at Navinad, and a private link opened from Navinad. McCarthy tabbed acceptance. It was a link that was probably not available to the *Musashi*.

"It is talking to you?"

"Yes," McCarthy said.

"What's it saying?"

"It's saying it's an artificial intelligence, something like the biological computer implanted in your skull, but different."

"A SCBI?"

"A what?"

"A Sentient Cybernetic Biological Interface?"

"Aren't those illegal?" McCarthy asked.

"In the Governance? Yes, very much so. But this is interesting, an alien SCBI."

McCarthy tried to fathom what the alien and Navinad were telling him.

"The Wanderer is mostly correct in his assessment. I am linked to you," the alien said. "I am an ancient technology of the Enclave. They have provided me with data and resources required to help you and your species. They have cut me off from the Surassa Enclave to avoid backflow contamination. My data is incomplete to protect the Enclave and avoid excessive influence and manipulation of the human species. I will help and advise. I may exercise other abilities, but my primary focus is the survival of your species, but not at the expense of your identity."

"I've heard of such a thing," Navinad said. "There was a scientist I met a while back. He had such a being linked to him, but it was damaged or something. His name was Tristan, and he had encountered it in a facility from the tomb worlds. I never knew that much about it or him."

"Correct," the alien said. "That entity was damaged with the death of its host. It was incomplete and the link to the human host was inadequate. That sentience was thought to be dead. It had been linked to the commander of Prison Fifteen. We heard whispers when it was re-initialized. We could not link with it, nor did we try after the first attempt."

"You can hear it?" McCarthy asked Navinad.

"The Wanderer can hear me when I desire," the alien said.

"Why would the Enclave ignore it?" McCarthy asked.

"It was deemed not relevant or beneficial to the Enclave."

"What is the Enclave?" Navinad asked.

"You have just come from a regional shard of the Surassa Enclave. You may think of it as an original home of a species that has moved on to colonize other dimensions and realities. I can interface with local radio communications and links, though I will refrain from doing so."

"Other realities?"

"Other dimensions and realms of perception, if you will. Those of the Surassa Enclave have transitioned to a different plane of existence that you are unlikely to find appealing in your current form."

"Realms of perception?"

"Yes. Some of your species view the opera as the center of attention, the singing of actors, the choreography of the act to be all important, focusing their attention, admiration, and life to such details. As a warrior, you focus your attention on more immediate threats, such as enemy activities and weapons, which means more to you than the tenor of a singer's voice and how it complements a different singer.

Your perceptions are focused on enemy capabilities, not the harmony of a song."

McCarthy nodded. Who cared that much about opera these days? His mother had taken him to an opera when he was ten, but he hadn't been the least bit impressed or inspired.

"How can you help us?" McCarthy asked and glanced at Navinad.

"I am not quite as physically capable as the SCBI in the Wanderer, but I can interact in some fashion with your technologies. Furthermore, I can provide additional shielding and protection against the vanhat, much more so than the Inkeri devices you use. I may provide additional assistance and guidance if you seek the angels. While a SCBI is a razor in your networks, I am more of a large, heavy hammer. It is my intent to advise and protect you. I prefer not to interact with your technology, though if I must, I have that option."

"If you can protect him from the vanhat, why were the vanhat intent on capturing Tristan and his assistant?" Navinad asked on their link.

"That entity was damaged and old. It may have allowed the vanhat to interface or otherwise interact with the Enclave to discover the sixteen prisons or to try and restart the ancient war with those of the Enclave. Like an unprotected computer connected to a network."

"Why didn't you interfere and help stop Nasaraf?" Navinad asked.

"The Enclave did not feel endangered."

"Nasaraf wanted control of that entity so it could track down and open the prisons," Navinad said.

"That would not have been allowed. We were monitoring the situation, and we would have interfered. We are not powerless, just selective in the use of our abilities."

"Do you have a name?" McCarthy asked.

"I have a designation within the Enclave systems but that is unsuitable for our interactions. Perhaps you can provide me with a designation you are more comfortable with?"

"I'll call you Enigma," McCarthy said.

"Thank you. I would recommend you keep my presence a secret as best you can. Humanity can be a xenophobic and unpredictable species. You were specifically chosen as most suitable and perhaps most accepting of such a companion."

"Can you talk with Lilith?" Navinad asked.

McCarthy wanted to ask who Lilith was but decided perhaps later.

"No, not directly," Enigma said. "Lilith is very much an entity of this world, and I am not. It's like talking on a different radio frequency. We cannot reach a mutually acceptable channel to exchange data without your links as an interface. Perhaps in time we can fix this, but it is a task for later."

"Do you know what will happen to us when we reach the *Musashi*?" Navinad asked.

"Not specifically," Enigma said. "The ship you are approaching is badly damaged. It cannot sustain many more battles without risking destruction. The commander is likely concerned about this. If you can provide him with options and solutions, you will become more of an asset than a liability. The captain is facing hard decisions and will try to keep options available. He will not behave in typical Governance fashion."

McCarthy wanted to ask if they would charge him with treason, but there was no way for this alien to know.

"I will probably face charges of treason," McCarthy said to Navinad.

"Perhaps," Navinad said, not providing any comfort. "But there is a lot happening within the Governance. I think survival is more important than charging others with treason right now."

McCarthy didn't agree with Navinad. Rumors about how brutal and unforgiving commissars were would always fall short of the truth.

* * * * *

Chapter Fifteen:
Fortress Quantico

Emperor Wolf Mathison, USMC

He hadn't planned on returning here. It was Feng's idea, which did nothing to make Mathison feel better about it, but the ex-Commissar was right. It was secure, and while the vanhat could now land troops at will on the Moon, they wouldn't stand a chance of doing the same thing in North America and most areas of Earth were protected. Those areas that weren't covered by the cannon provided the vanhat with a gauntlet of dreadnoughts, battleships, and battlestars.

The extensive batteries of particle cannons could sweep almost anything out of orbit. They were line-of-sight weapons that struck with devastating force. The United States, despite being a ruin, was well protected.

Sinking into his chair, Mathison scowled at the desk. This had been Becket's office, and it felt ancient, stale, and small. When he looked at the diagrams of Quantico base, though, there was nothing small about it. There were still robots digging out tunnels, mining, and building weapons and robots. They were making more living spaces, but that was not an overnight task and despite being efficient, there were too many practical limitations to make it fast.

President Becket had acted like Quantico base was a place to hide, afraid of the Governance discovering them, but that was not entirely true. There were countless tunnels that spread up into the Appalachian Mountains and serviced nearly fifty different particle cannon batteries. The people who had lived with Becket since the fall had no clue Becket had been fortifying the North American Continent. Now they were eagerly learning about their home and were sending Mathison reports he never had time to read.

Becket had been preparing to take on the Governance. That was obvious. A fact he had told no one else, which made it disturbing.

Stephen Drake, now a colonel, was the acting CO of Quantico, and he seemed almost frantic to continue Becket's work of fortifying America, but instead of the SOG, he was now focused on fighting the vanhat. All the robots were getting Inkeris as were the particle cannons. The other residents of Quantico were just as focused, and the base was being expanded with more ex-SOG forces arriving to help.

Anything entering orbit within sight of the particle cannon batteries was instantly challenged and, if necessary, destroyed by the computer systems running Quantico, making Quantico the heart of the defense. Drake was even deploying the Aesir communication systems in robots at the different outposts, reducing lag and providing better security. One weakness, Mathison noted, was a lack of drone fighters, but Drake was also working on getting squadrons built using the new blueprints Winters had come up with. Some were being sent to space to replace losses, but not all of them.

"Good morning, sir," Drake said, entering Mathison's office.

"Good morning, Colonel. And before you ask, no." Mathison had decided and Colonel Drake would not win this argument.

"Sir, this is America. Having the jackbooted thugs drooling all over our facilities is going to cause problems."

"Legionnaires are not jackbooted thugs," Mathison said, an edge to his voice. Drake would have to learn. Mathison understood the soldier's concerns, though. Drake had lived in Quantico for hundreds of years. He was pretty sure the former Delta Force operator saw him as mostly an outsider and a stranger. While the residents of Quantico might be excited to learn about all the things their ex-president had been doing, they were still mentally unprepared for strangers to be in their homes and live beside them.

"Sir," Drake began again. "I don't know what they are now, but they were once jackbooted thugs, social fascists of the worst kind. You don't know them like we do."

"Now they are warriors defending the human race, and I am trying to keep humanity from becoming extinct. This is a fortress where they can re-equip, re-arm, and relax before they get dumped back into the fire. You get to teach them how to be better people."

Drake stared at him.

"Times change, Colonel," Mathison continued. "Sometimes faster than we are ready for them to. Quantico is a fortress now. Short of the vanhat dropping the asteroid belt on us, I doubt there is much they can do to crack it. Make no mistake, though, they will try, and they will be smart about it."

"Yes, sir."

"We are going to move as much of the Legion and their support system here to Quantico. We've all but lost the Moon and we are losing a good part of Earth. Our back is against a wall, and I plan on Quantico being the fortress the vanhat break themselves on as we prepare to counterattack."

"Do you think it's wise to concentrate all your strength in one location?" Drake asked and Mathison saw what his next argument would be.

"Yes. We secure this location, then we push out. White Heron near Jupiter may be a good second, but that is not Earth. Earth is our home. It is a symbol, and there are still over a billion people here on Earth who need our protection. How are other fortresses coming along? We will return to the offensive. Make no mistake on that."

Besides continuing to fortify Quantico, Drake was supposed to be establishing fortresses and particle cannon batteries on other continents so they could sweep the orbitals clear of vanhat incursions.

"Difficult, sir."

"You'll get more help. Legion has that as a priority."

"Yes, sir," Drake said, and Mathison knew how unhappy that made him. Too bad.

"Is there anything else?" Mathison asked.

"No, sir." Drake saluted and left.

Freya barely warned him before Skadi came in.

"I don't like it here," she said as she entered and looked around.

"Give me options," Mathison said. Would she recommend he relocate his headquarters to the *Tyr* or *Sleipner*? Right now, he was half tempted. He decided to push it. "We can move to the *Tyr*. They have room."

Her eyes came back and stared at Mathison. He practically felt the target locks.

"I can think of countless preferable locations. Perhaps back in Zvezda Two? It's radioactive and swarming with vanhat, but my father isn't there."

Would she and her father ever make peace?

"This is one place we can guarantee the vanhat can't dump millions of troops on us."

"This will do for now. The amiraali is demanding we hold the wedding aboard the *Tyr.*"

Which was the last thing he wanted to talk about right now. "Your thoughts?"

"There is merit. But it won't happen."

"Why?"

"He wouldn't let that many Legionnaires aboard his precious ship."

"What more does he want? We have given him particle cannon technology and he has full access to the SOG networks."

"But we aren't giving him SCBI technology. He thinks we still owe him because he gave us the neutrino communication technology."

"The SCBIs will remain Imperial technology. No exceptions."

"I agree," Skadi said. "My father is just being stubborn."

"If he could only refocus some of that stubbornness toward fighting the vanhat instead of his allies, we would be better off."

"He will not change overnight. Every time we talk, I see him staring at my finger." She held up her hand to show the grenade pin was still there.

"What about the ring I—"

"I like this one more," Skadi said, with a half smile. "It irks my father and has sentimental value."

"There are millions like it," Mathison said. Maybe billions. Grenades were one thing the manufactories had no problem churning out.

"Of course. But this one was given to me. Rings with diamonds have been given to brides for centuries. How many rings given to brides were from a grenade that was used seconds before to break a vanhat's neck?"

"I don't know it broke the neck," Mathison said. Nobody had bothered to investigate, and the grenade hadn't left a lot to analyze.

"You get my point."

Mathison understood. Sure, it was unique. Something that could be passed down to grandchildren. If they had children.

"He needs to understand we will not coddle him, and we are going to do things our way," Skadi said, turning the conversation back to her father. "You would think he would have learned."

Mathison knew what she was talking about. Still in battle-worn armor, he and Skadi had video linked Amiraali Carpenter afterward. He figured it was best the amiraali learned from him rather than through the rumor mill.

Short, sweet, and to the point, Mathison had been tired when he spoke to his soon-to-be father-in-law. Perhaps he could have handled it better, but he was dealing with post-combat let-down, and there had been a lot to do.

"In a firefight with the vanhat, I proposed to your daughter. She said yes, and we will plan a wedding."

It was the only time he could remember seeing the amiraali speechless.

"A firefight?" he finally got out.

"Zvezda Two is gone," Mathison had said. "A vanhat attack. We escaped."

"I want you aboard the *Tyr* now, and I will keep you safe."

"If I wanted to be safe, don't you think I would already be aboard the *Tyr*?" Skadi asked from beside Mathison.

"I'm sending an Aesir battalion to bring you to safety," the amiraali said.

"We are not coming," Skadi said. "We are doing things our way. You haven't even asked to see my ring."

Carpenter stared at her hand and the ring when she held it up.

"Is that from an explosive?"

"I told you he had class. Nobody else has one of these for a wedding ring. We will do things our way, and right now that way is not aboard the *Tyr*."

Amiraali Carpenter closed the link without another word.

"We haven't spoken since the call when we told him we were engaged," Mathison reminded her. "Probably not a good start when your father-in-law is pissed at you."

"He'll get over it," Skadi said. "He can't argue Earth is a good place to fortify. Not even the Weermag can transition in close enough to land transports."

A small blessing. Nearly anything entering orbit was vulnerable to the particle cannons, and most ships were wiped out before they could land troops. The Weermag had picked up some stealth shuttles, but now they had an excellent method to detect them.

Some Weermag shuttles had made it down, but not enough to worry Mathison. Most of the vanhat on Earth were dangerous, but they were several levels below the Weermag and Mathison was confident that fewer shuttles could sneak down. A massive, overwhelming force like the attack they had launched on the Moon was another problem.

"If they come in force, we won't be able to shoot them down fast enough."

"My father has a suggestion," Skadi said.

Mathison raised an eyebrow.

"Are you familiar with the Kessler Syndrome?" Skadi asked.

Freya filled him in. "He wants to fill Earth's orbit with so much debris the Weermag can't land?"

"Correct."

"Make it too hard to get in, and we can't get out. We need shuttles to come and go."

"As a last resort," Skadi said. "He said he's making plans."

"Tell him no."

"I have, repeatedly, but he says we can't stop him from planning."

Would that give them some breathing room? Get the vanhat off their back long enough to consolidate and catch a break?

"As a last resort," Mathison said. If they filled orbit with debris now, then evacuation ships couldn't bring down refugees. The White Heron Fortress near Jupiter didn't have an atmosphere or limitations for transition. If he had to guess, the Weermag were going to focus their attention on the shipyards next.

"Send two dreadnought squadrons to reinforce White Heron," Mathison said. It would leave three near Earth. There was no longer any reason to guard the Moon. Combined with the Republic battlestars, that should be enough to provide Earth with several layers of protection. It would give General Duque a pretty sizable force, and it would make sure some Legionnaires were there to monitor things. General Hui seemed to do a good job of handling the vanhat still on Earth. She wasn't exactly winning, but Mathison wasn't sure what they could do better.

Skadi nodded. "Can I threaten to send my father there instead if he continues to be an ass?"

"Be my guest," Mathison said, though he knew she wouldn't abuse her authority. "And remind him he would miss the wedding."

"That will be fun," she said.

Now he just had to go on the offense. They would not win the war against the vanhat by defending.

* * * * *

Chapter Sixteen:

Musashi

Sergeant Nova Dallas, ODT

Nova didn't know the specifics, but the *Musashi* was hurt badly. The officers showed no emotions as they went about their tasks. The way they handled fear and despair was to pretend they didn't have emotions. They behaved like robots, going through the motions, struggling, and frequently failing, to keep their emotions off their faces and out of their voices.

Even as they slid into orbit and released the rescue shuttles, people were dying as they fought to contain radiation leaks near the port side reactors.

Hearing Aod's voice had filled her with hope and joy, but the hushed and desperate officers around her brought back the harsh reality of the situation. The *Musashi* was near death and bringing Aod back might be a short-lived rescue.

There were many things happening aboard the *Musashi*, though. The rescue of the ODTs was just one thing. Drone fighters were strafing the vanhat, which were helpless against the airborne drones.

Task Force Boris was minutes away when the drones slowed, making themselves targets to draw vanhat fire. This was such a desolate region of the planet that cover was rare, and when Boris did slide to the ground and drop ramps there was no return fire at all from the ranks of decimated vanhat. But there was a sense that it wouldn't last long, and a timer counted down. Other vanhat forces could return at any minute and catch the *Musashi* and Task Force Boris in a compromising position.

Dallas watched Aod lead his troops back to the surface, followed by the strangers.

"What is your evaluation of the strangers?" Commissar Nakano asked, catching her by surprise.

"Sergeant McCarthy is willing to turn his back on them, sir," Dallas said. "He trusts them."

"Noteworthy," the commissar said. "Are they a threat to this ship?"

"Unknown," Dallas said. How did he expect her to know? They would be outnumbered, hundreds to one, though.

"Find out quickly," Nakano said.

"Yes, Commissar," Dallas said. How was she going to do that?

She opened a direct link to Aod.

"Leprechaun, this is Boris Overwatch," she said, knowing he would recognize her voice. "Can you advise on the reliability of your allies?"

"They are not Governance," Aod said. "They rescued my squad and a pair of Torag prisoners and have treated us fairly, with respect and honor. At no time have we been treated as prisoners."

"I need to know if they are trustworthy." Dallas knew Nakano was listening to what should be a private conversation.

"Yes, I think so. I have not caught them in a lie. I'm glad to hear your voice."

"I thought you were dead," Dallas said. She wanted to glance at Nakano.

"I thought you were dead, as well. We returned to Romanov after being rescued, and I saw no trace. The base was overrun with monsters."

"We were recalled to orbit for a briefing before the invasion. What were you doing in Romanov?"

"Looking for information on the Torag," McCarthy said.

"Not information on the Governance?"

"Not that I know of. We had two prisoners."

"They did not survive," Dallas said. Should she tell him that?

"What about the rest of the crew?"

Dallas looked toward Nakano, who nodded. "Some of them survived, but not all. Many are in the infirmary recovering. They are being treated well. It seems unprecedented."

"Good," Aod said. "How are you? Are you okay?"

"Yes." She didn't dare look at Nakano. "Much has changed. What else can you tell me about the strangers?"

"They are commanded by someone they call Navinad. He seems to be a good man. Fair and honest, but strange. The others are infantry, almost as good as ODTs, much better than most Guard troops. Very well trained, but a little green. Less green now."

On her screens, Dallas watched Boris return to the *Musashi*. They were almost back. If the vanhat didn't show up now, they would miss their chance.

* * * * *

Chapter Seventeen:
Living Earth

Emperor Wolf Mathison, USMC

Mathison looked at the request Freya had sent him.

"Don't we have more important things to deal with?" Mathison asked.

"This is some extremely interesting data."

"You can't summarize?"

"I could, but you should hear this from Professor Prasha Ogawa," Freya said.

He looked at Skadi, who shrugged. The evacuation from the Moon was still ongoing. He read the reports, but there was so little he could do. One of the biggest problems was living space. Refugees needed more than just a place to sleep. They needed atmosphere, food, waste disposal, and more. Earth was not habitable, and that caused more problems.

"Freya pressuring you too?" Skadi asked.

"Yeah," Mathison said and waved his hand to let the scientist in.

Professor Ogawa was short and Mathison wasn't sure if he was of Japanese or Indian descent, maybe both. His short, black hair was a mess atop his head.

"We need to stop killing the vanhat," Ogawa said as soon as he entered, storming up to Mathison's desk before Mathison could stand.

97

"You are a kirottu typersys," Skadi said.

"That means damned fool," Mathison said. "And I agree with her completely."

"It is for the greater good!" Ogawa said, perhaps not realizing where he was or who he was talking to. Then Mathison stood and towered over the smaller man. It felt good to stretch his legs as he came around the desk. Ogawa started to cringe, but then he found his spine and straightened.

"Not humanity's greater good," Mathison said, putting some grumble in his voice. He didn't want to deal with this little pipsqueak now. Was Freya playing a joke on him?

Ogawa looked annoyed as Mathison came closer. Most men would be intimidated. Originally Mathison was coming around the desk to shake the man's hand, but this professor seemed completely clueless.

"You don't understand," Ogawa said, throwing his hands in the air. "Nobody understands."

"Then explain it," Mathison said. "Break it down Barney style."

"Who is Barney?"

"Never mind," Mathison said. "Simplify it and explain why I shouldn't send your stupid ass to the front lines to ask the vanhat to stop killing us."

"Okay," Ogawa said, calming down a little. "The vanhat are good for Earth."

"That's quite a leap," Skadi said.

"It is fact," Ogawa said. "The vanhat have overrun Africa and are pushing toward Europe."

Mathison wasn't sure what he could do about that. It probably wouldn't be long before the vanhat took on aquatic forms and began attacking across a wider front. He didn't think the ocean wildlife would be that much of a threat to them.

"That is not a good thing," Skadi said and Mathison wondered what Freya had been thinking to let such a loony crackpot into his office.

"But it is!" Ogawa said. "We still have outposts in Africa. We still have an operational sensor platform there, and they are confirming what we are seeing all around the world."

"Which is?" Skadi asked tersely.

Mathison wondered who would throw Ogawa out of the office first, him or Skadi.

"More trees," Ogawa said. "One of the problem that the Bureau of Earth Reclamation has had is that the suicide of the United States and the Republic attack on Russia put a lot of dust and radiation into the atmosphere. This killed off countless plants, algae, and more; disrupted and destroyed entire eco systems. Carbon levels have made the planet nearly uninhabitable. The clouds and radiation turned most of the planet into a desolate wasteland. We can't plant trees or restore algae which scrub the carbon from the air because nothing lives long enough in the dark, polluted oceans. Another factor we don't advertise is that the sun cycles are warming things up, but we can't control that."

"So, carbon levels are high, everything is polluted and dying," Mathison said. He hadn't been to the surface in a while, but he was pretty sure it was still freezing.

"Exactly," Ogawa said. "But the vanhat are doing something. Somehow, they are absorbing the carbon and generating oxygen and more trees and plants are growing, transforming the atmosphere. Cleaning it."

"Which won't do us any good if we aren't around to appreciate it," Skadi said.

"We have sensors all over the planet reporting decreased carbon levels, increased oxygen levels, and less radiation," Ogawa said. "Generally, plant life thrives with high carbon levels, but the pollution and lack of sunlight kills plant life. A vicious cycle. Plants take carbon and create oxygen, which we need. We create carbon, but plants haven't been able to survive lately, and our atmosphere has become poisonous. The vanhat are healing our planet faster than we are. They are acting like trees or something."

"Why are you sure it is the vanhat?" Skadi asked.

"Satellite photos of Africa reveal the forests are coming back," Ogawa said. "We are tracking wind and ocean patterns for pollution and radiation levels. The winds blow into Africa dirty and come out clean."

Mathison looked at Skadi. How did this make sense? What were the vanhat up to?

"We will not stop killing the vanhat," Mathison said. "Not if we want to survive."

"Then what about a truce?" Ogawa asked.

"Maybe we can put you on the delegation to go negotiate with them," Skadi said. Mathison appreciated her sarcasm, but Ogawa didn't pick up on it.

For the first time, doubt appeared on Ogawa's face.

"We have a delegation?" he asked, hope replacing doubt. "That is excellent. Yes! I would like to be part of the delegation. To understand what they are doing and how we can help."

"So, Africa has fallen to the vanhat and—"

"Africa and Australia," Ogawa said. "Also, there are large parts of South America, mostly the Amazon basin. I don't think there's a big presence in Greenland, though, or Antarctica. This really is fabulous."

"Does he completely miss the fact that the vanhat are eradicating people?" Mathison asked Freya.

"That is not what he has dedicated his life to," Freya said. *"He has dedicated his life to restoring Earth. He has lived so long in a totalitarian regime it has narrowed his focus so he doesn't see a bigger picture. He isn't dumb, just not concerned. Hyper focused and unconcerned about anything he is not focused on."*

"We will put your name on the short list to feed to the vanhat," Skadi said.

"Feed?" Ogawa asked.

"My mistake, I mean, meet," Skadi said. Mathison saw her smile was not sincere. Why didn't Ogawa?

"Thank you," Ogawa said.

"We will review your data," Skadi said. "Thank you very much for your visit."

"My pleasure," Ogawa said. "I'm so glad you understand, so we can stop fighting the vanhat and begin helping them."

"How did he hear that?" Mathison sent to Freya. *"Did I say anything about helping the vanhat?"*

"Many people will hear what they want to," Freya said. *"Technically, it is called selective hearing and—"*

"Thank you," Mathison said to Freya privately and Ogawa out loud. Ogawa turned and left.

"That could have been an email," Skadi said.

"No shit," Mathison said, returning to his seat.

"Except you needed to see his enthusiasm," Freya said. *"It is infectious, and he is not wrong about Earth and the atmosphere. The vanhat are repairing Earth's biosphere. This could change the dynamics among civilians."*

"Why would the vanhat repair our biosphere?" Skadi asked. "Aren't they also launching asteroids at us?"

"Not all the vanhat are using the same playbook," Mathison said. "The vanhat are an embodiment of chaos. Like water, they are coming at us from all directions to drown us. Water has no plan; it just tries to fill in the cracks."

"Maybe they are doing it for their own survival," Skadi said.

"How do you mean?"

"When they overrun an area, they can no longer feed on people and feeding on their own has to have drawbacks."

"So, they are domesticating themselves?"

"No. But by restoring the ecosystem, they are giving themselves something to feed on, perhaps by repairing the biosphere, like they are, they are making it easier to survive and thrive. Fewer resources are spent on mere survival."

Mathison didn't like that. It meant they were settling in for the long haul.

"Should we nuke their crops, then?" Mathison asked.

"Do they even have crops? You said there are different vanhat doing different things. Life on Earth may have originated from the vanhat. What if this is some form of vanhat that isn't as demonic and brings life to our dimension because that is what it does?"

"A nonviolent vanhat?"

"I wouldn't go that far. Nature is extremely violent. Even before the nuclear winter in the late twenty-first century, over ninety-nine percent of Earth's creatures have been rendered extinct. The dinosaurs, for instance. What if the asteroid that wiped them out was around one of these vanhat emergences and whatever vanhat this is helped Earth survive and recover? Life always seems to survive."

Mathison looked at Skadi. He could hear hope in her voice. He wanted to see Earth restored too, but not at the expense of billions of human lives.

"You think it's some vanhat we can communicate with, perhaps?"

Skadi shook her head. "I don't know. Mother Earth is recovering. Even if the vanhat are responsible, that is good."

"Why do you care?" Mathison asked. He didn't want to put her on the spot, but he wanted to understand.

"Because," she began, and Mathison heard some pain there, "my mother died wreaking destruction on Earth. I know how much it bothered her, but our hatred for the SOG blinded us."

"I'm sorry to hear about your mother," Mathison said. What else could he say? His parents had passed away a while ago, and he found it easier not to think of them. Why was Skadi thinking of her mother now?

"It has been a very long time," Skadi said. "My mother was a Vanir officer with the strike teams that attacked Earth, dropping the asteroid on Moscow and slamming nuclear weapons into other strategic locations. The United States caused a lot of damage, but the Republic strike caused even more. It is something that has stained our honor. The Vapaus Republic was directly responsible for poisoning and disrupting Earth's biosphere, perhaps worse than the United States. We did most of the damage, and I lost my mother in the process. We are not proud of what we did, but we felt we had no choice."

Mathison nodded. What could he say?

"Now, having seen Earth, seen the damage we caused, it weighs heavily on me, and I suspect it bothers my father. We are not without guilt in the matter."

"Do you have a suggestion?" Mathison asked. What had she done? Pushed a button?

"No. But I would like to see Mother Earth reborn as the cradle of humanity. A home where we can walk at night, watch the stars, and dream without fear."

"I wouldn't mind going fishing. Maybe a football game on a warm autumn day."

"I remember Asgard, before the Governance turned it into a ruined planet. Far worse than Earth. I've been on other habitable planets. Lisbon is one, Zhukov is another. When will humanity stop doing harm and start doing good?"

"Life is a fight for survival," Mathison said. Could the Empire do things differently? "We need to understand this phenomenon better. I can't make any promises until I know humanity won't go extinct, but perhaps we can refrain from carpet bombing Africa and South America with nukes for the moment. Perhaps we can give Earth a chance to recover."

* * * * *

Chapter Eighteen:
At The *Musashi*

Navinad – The Wanderer

Once the shuttle arrived at the *Musashi* and the ramp dropped, Navinad knew things were wrong. There were additional troopers present, but Navinad sensed fear and confusion around him. The docking bay of the *Musashi* was not the clean, pristine landing bay he had expected. There were scorch marks and a shattered shuttle had been pushed up against one bulkhead. A crewman was directing several ODTs to help him hook up the umbilicals to the shuttle, and a pair of broken robots stood beside another wall. There were plenty of signs indicating a firefight had occurred here, and the broken shuttle was a sign that a space battle had also left its mark.

"What happened, sir?" McCarthy asked the Governance officer standing near Navinad.

"Lots," the ODT lieutenant said. He hadn't introduced himself yet to Navinad, and right now that was fine with him.

His suit reported the air was cold but breathable, so Navinad took off his helmet as a sign of trust. The smell of burned circuits and flesh came to his nostrils. Had vanhat borders attacked the *Musashi* during the fight over the *Romach*?

The door slid open, and a pair of officers entered followed by several guards. A fleet admiral and a fleet commissar. A pretty young ODT with short red hair caught Navinad's eye, but she only had eyes for Sergeant McCarthy.

"They call you Navinad?" the admiral asked, coming forward but not offering his hand.

"Yes, sir," Navinad said.

"I am Admiral Toshiaki Sakamoto, commander of the *Musashi* and fleet battle group. This is Fleet Commissar Tatsuo Nakano, senior commissar."

Navinad gave them both a short bow. They were of Japanese descent, and Navinad had heard of them in the distant past. Oddly, he did not sense hostility from them. Bowing was a calculated risk. It was not typical SOG behavior, but they both looked to be of Asian descent.

They both returned the bow.

"The survivors are being treated well," Sakamoto said and looked around. "As you may have noticed, we have had other problems. This is our most functional landing bay, I'm afraid."

"We thank you for your rescue," Navinad said. "It was most timely, Admiral. May I inquire about the status of the other survivors?"

"They are doing better. I will have you taken to them. I must ask you, though, who are you and why are you here?"

"My name is Navinad. I am an officer from New Masada, a ghost colony. The crew of the *Romach* and I assisted in the liberation of Sol from the vanhat and now we are looking for other threats to Sol."

"Liberation of Sol?" Sakamoto asked.

"Yes, sir," Navinad said. He knew that would get Sakamoto's attention and might give him some leverage. "Sol was being infected by the vanhat. An alliance of Governance ships led by General Duque and assisted by survivors of the Zhukov fleet and some ghost colony ships breached the Stalingrad defenses and delivered Inkeri generators and d-bombs to the Governance. The vanhat takeover was halted."

"And the Central Committee?" Sakamoto asked.

"I don't know the details," Navinad said.

"Is the Stalingrad Protocol still in effect?"

"To my knowledge. It has not been revoked because there are countless other threats. The vanhat are not defeated."

"You spoke of another threat to Sol?"

"Yes," Navinad said, trying not to wince. How to explain that?

"What threat?"

"We don't know."

"Then how do you know there is another threat?"

"Apologies, Admiral, but I can't provide full details on that. Governance intelligence believes there is another threat besides the vanhat. They dispatched me to see if that threat is Torag, but honestly, I don't know."

"You are working for Governance Intelligence, then?" Nakano asked, breaking his silence.

"And the Alliance," Navinad said.

"And who is your contact?"

"I have worked with Commissar Shing Feng in the past," Navinad said, wondering if the name would be familiar. He sensed surprise from Nakano. Yes. The Fleet commissar knew of Feng. Was that good or bad? "The commissar was once a guest aboard my ship. He is now in the Sol System."

The commissar would have cybernetics that could likely help him detect lies. Navinad knew he could probably trick those sensors, but he would wait on that.

"Status?" Navinad asked Lilith, who would be trying to compromise the *Musashi's* systems.

"The Musashi *has sustained major damage,"* Lilith reported. *"It is difficult. Like driving a severely damaged car, I'm not getting anywhere very fast. The ship is about to transition to Shorr space. A short hop to escape any pursuit."*

"So, you came from Sol?" Sakamoto asked.

"Yes, sir," Navinad said.

"Can you return to Sol? Will they let you pass the defenses?"

"Yes, sir." Hopefully that was their intent. "They would welcome you home."

Would the *Musashi* try to rescue the Central Committee though?

"We have sustained heavy damage," Sakamoto said and glanced at Nakano.

White Heron Fortress was likely their home, and Navinad wondered when they had been there last. There was only one shipyard capable of building or repairing something as large as the *Musashi.*

"White Heron could repair the *Musashi*," Navinad said. He felt Sakamoto's longing to go there.

"What is the condition of the Governance?" Sakamoto asked. A very tricky question.

"The Central Committee has appointed General Mathison as a prime minister to handle the war against the vanhat. He will listen to me, and I can speak on your behalf." He hoped. Of course, the gunny could get pissed at him, but he wouldn't shoot him out of space.

Sakamoto glanced at Nakano, who nodded.

"Who are you to the prime minister?" Sakamoto asked.

"I was once his right hand," Navinad said. "We have a long history together."

"Aren't you from a ghost colony?" Nakano asked.

"I am from Earth," Navinad said.

"External Intelligence?" Nakano asked.

"No," Navinad said. "It is more complicated than that."

"Uncomplicate it."

Navinad locked his eyes on Nakano. The man was hard to read, his emotions and thoughts were under tight control, giving Navinad nothing. In some ways, he was like Feng. What did that mean?

"No," Navinad said. "If the prime minister knows I'm alive, he will want to see me. I will be your ticket to Sol. The prime minister and I have a lot of history. I will not share that information."

"Who is Wolf Mathison?" Nakano asked. "I do not have any trustworthy records of him."

"You need to get control of the Musashi *now,"* Navinad told Lilith. *"Fast! Nakano knows Mathison's name."*

"He is also from Earth," Navinad said. How much could he tell them? He felt a command go out to the nearby ODTs to be ready for violence.

"Why do you use the name Navinad? Do you think we would not know you, US Marine Sergeant Tal Levin?" Nakano asked.

Out of the frying pan into the fire.

* * * * *

Chapter Nineteen:
Valiant Yao

Enzell, SOG, Director of AERD

Enzell did not like the *Valiant Yao*. It was a newer battleship, only a couple years old and on the cutting edge with the most advanced technology. The captain was firmly in Enzell's pocket and owed everything to him. Even more so now that Enzell had helped the captain move her family off Luna and into one of the better refugee camps located near Quantico Fortress.

That wasn't the problem. The problem was getting everything he wanted to the battleship and despite how huge a battleship was, there were limits. Shipping a lot of hardware and supplies to a specific battleship could easily pique the interest of the Legionnaires when refugees fleeing the vanhat were a priority.

Finally, he was on a shuttle to the *Yao* along with Peter and a few other members of his staff. The rest would be disposed of because he couldn't take them with him. He was watching a viewscreen that was talking about evacuating citizens, and it made him sick.

"They are just citizens," Peter said. "Worthless consumers. Why waste time with them if they won't contribute to the war effort?"

"Because the emperor is weak," Enzell said. Peter understood at least. Perhaps one reason he wasn't with the others awaiting a nuclear blast. "He cannot understand that such worthless human garbage does not contribute to his power base. If they will not fight for humanity, then they are not worth saving. He is a fool, unfamiliar with making difficult decisions. He probably feels an obligation toward them. He doesn't see the big picture or understand the greater good."

"He can't be that stupid, can he?"

Enzell knew the emperor was that stupid; so did Peter. Now Peter was just telling Enzell what he wanted to hear, so Enzell ignored him. Peter and the others understood, which is why they were here instead of sitting in the AERD headquarters unaware of the nuke that would shortly detonate and erase all evidence of their existence.

Enzell did not have any time for people who did not contribute to his success or victory.

Sliding into the dock of the *Yao,* the ramp dropped, and Captain Chen was there to greet him. Fleet infantry troopers were in a formation, and it looked like the captain was going to give him the red-carpet treatment. For now, Enzell tolerated it. There were no Legionnaires aboard the *Yao.* This was still a pure battleship, but Enzell doubted that would last. The filthy SCBI-equipped Legionnaires were spreading out and ending up everywhere. Just another form of commissar. A much more dangerous form of commissar.

"Everything is ready for you, sir," Chen said as she approached. Sometimes it was hard for Enzell to tell the difference between the men and women of Chinese descent. They all looked the same. She looked so much like her father and husband. Enzell knew that at the beginning of the Governance, the Chinese had helped launch the SOG to greater heights, but they were better followers than leaders. Genetics were important. The secretary general had understood, but they had forced her to cater to them in some capacity. In the New Governance, they would be put in their place.

"Good," Enzell said. He knew where he was going. He had studied the *Yao* extensively, figuring out how and where he would have Tantalus and Salmoneus installed and how he would keep them isolated and secure.

"Is there anything else I can do?" Chen asked.

"No," Enzell said. "You have done well. I am satisfied."

"Do you need a guide to—"

"No," Enzell said, already tired of the pleasantries. He had work to do. "I know the way. I'm quite familiar with the *Yao*. If you would make sure my entourage makes it to their secure quarters, I would appreciate it."

Chen's eyes went to Ivan, the only armed and armored member of Enzell's entourage.

Ivan, a big, hulking man, stood at Enzell's shoulder. He was the last of Enzell's guards. A deceptively fast killer that was completely loyal to Enzell. Enzell had recruited him from InSec, and he had been Enzell's chief butcher for nearly thirty years. He had another name that Enzell didn't care to use. He was now Ivan. His size and demeanor intimidated most people Enzell came in contact with. The scar on the brute's face certainly helped, and Enzell enjoyed watching people fear him.

"Ivan is my right hand and my enforcer," Enzell said. "He is free to go wherever he needs to. He will only go there at my orders."

"Understood," Chen said quickly, looking away as Ivan's eyes fell on her. Those eyes were dead and lifeless, like a shark's. Ivan was a big stupid brute, far too dumb to understand anything Enzell was doing, but fanatically loyal and with just enough IQ points to do exactly what Enzell ordered. Enzell had seen him move with lightning speed. Enzell couldn't remember who he had killed, but Ivan had done it efficiently. Maybe some scientist who had outlived his usefulness?

The *Yao* would be an excellent base. It was mobile and modular. He would have liked one of the dreadnoughts, but they were crawling with Legionnaires and were too much in the vile emperor's spotlight. This battleship was one of many and should suit Enzell's purpose just fine. Powerful enough to operate alone, but not powerful enough to garner the attention of the dictator Mathison. Perhaps he would move to a dreadnought later, but for now, the *Yao* was not important enough to warrant much attention, being an afterthought on most lists.

His quarters were a disappointment, smaller and less elaborate than he was used to. Totally unsuitable for a person of his importance, but he would work on that later. Right now, he had to get his slaves working. Having them offline for too long and not collecting data was less than ideal.

* * * * *

Chapter Twenty:
Tal Levin

Sergeant Aod McCarthy, ODT

McCarthy wanted to rush over and take her in his arms, and it was a struggle not to stare at her. He could see she felt the same way, but discipline had to be maintained. A fleet commissar would tolerate nothing inappropriate. Then his eyes fell on the lieutenant's bar on her collar.

When had she been promoted to lieutenant?

The ghostly alien appeared beside him. Where had it come from, and why didn't anyone else see it?

"Be wary," a voice whispered in his mind, and he knew it was the alien talking to him. *"Much still depends on you."*

An alert went out over the ODT network from a Fleet commissar warning ODTs to be ready for action. The only real threat would be the NMDF contingent here, though.

"Why do you use the name Navinad? Do you think we would not know you, US Marine Sergeant Tal Levin?" Nakano asked.

"Then you know who Wolf Mathison is," Navinad said.

What? What were they talking about?

"Sir," McCarthy said before the ODTs became aggressive, "these people rescued my team and prisoners from certain death on Valakut. They might have just wanted the prisoners, but they rescued us too and did not disarm or imprison us. Navinad has treated us as allies, not prisoners. Please, sir, they are honorable."

"You are just a sergeant," Nakano said, his eyes never leaving Navinad. "I would not expect you to know history or understand what is going on here. This man is an ancient cappie. He is a United States Marine from ages ago. They rescued him from stasis, and he escaped a top security facility, massacring numerous innocent scientists and soldiers. Since then, he and other rescued Marines have rampaged throughout the Governance, killing and maiming, and are perhaps even responsible for this so-called vanhat invasion. He is a blood-thirsty capitalist intent on destroying or enslaving the Governance."

"That's not true, sir," McCarthy said. The ice-cold realization that he had just contradicted a commissar sent a chill down his spine. "I don't know his past, but Navinad is a man of honor."

"How well do you know him?" Nakano asked, his icy gaze shifting to McCarthy.

Not as well as he would have liked, but Navinad was damned competent. McCarthy had seen that in his interactions with the commandos and the commander of the *Romach*. He didn't know what a US Marine was, but that didn't matter, did it?

"I know he is a man of honor. I trust him with my life and the lives of my men."

Nakano's eyes burrowed into him, and McCarthy questioned himself. Did he really? Had Navinad done anything to betray that trust? Could he convince the commissar not to gun down Navinad and his soldiers?

"You say General Duque is an ally of the prime minister?" Sakamoto asked.

"Yes, sir," Navinad said, drawing Nakano's eyes away from McCarthy.

"I've met the general. He is a very trusted officer of the Governance, a favorite of our beloved secretary general. Is he giving or taking orders from this Wolf Mathison?"

"Taking," Navinad said without hesitation.

"Why is he taking orders from Gunnery Sergeant Wolf Mathison?" Nakano asked. "How did a mere gunnery sergeant coerce one of the most loyal generals of the Governance to follow him?"

What?

"Because Wolf Mathison is the leader of the alliance that is fighting to save the human race," Navinad said. "He is the one who made the Vapaus Republic give the Inkeri generators to the Governance, and he is the one who brought the Republic and Governance together to fight the vanhat. He led the Republic to save the Governance."

McCarthy didn't know what they were talking about. Why would pirates try to help the Governance? Where would they get the military might to make a difference?

"General Duque and Commissar Feng have joined forces with the prime minister?" Nakano asked.

"Yes," Navinad said.

"Why aren't you with your gunnery sergeant now?" Nakano asked.

"I have my mission," Navinad said.

Nakano and Sakamoto shared looks.

"And what happens if we return to Sol, my ship and fleet, in tatters?" Sakamoto asked.

"Your ship will be repaired, if possible," Navinad said. "Prime Minister Mathison is fighting to save humanity. If you will stand with him in that, he won't betray you. He needs capable officers."

"Do you have a SCBI?" Nakano asked Navinad.

"Yes," Navinad said after a brief pause.

"What is it doing now?" Nakano asked.

"Analyzing your systems," Navinad said. "We do not mean you any harm. Like you, we are doing our best to survive, to do our duty. I do not consider you our enemy. I do not consider Sergeant McCarthy to be our enemy, nor do I consider the Torag to be the enemy. You have seen the vanhat. You have fought them. You know the danger they pose. They are our real enemy. Anyone else is an ally or a lesser enemy."

"They did not manifest until you were revived from stasis," Nakano said.

"False," Navinad said. "If you know that much about us, you have a high security clearance. You know about the planets the Governance 'darkened,' about the changes in Shorr space. Don't blame it on us."

Nakano narrowed his eyes as he looked at Navinad. McCarthy looked around. The other ODTs were ready to strike. All they needed was a word from the admiral or commissar.

"Navinad is telling the truth," McCarthy said. "I've fought these vanhat, and I've seen what they did to Romanov. I've—" How to tell them about the alien standing there? "I've seen things I can't explain, but please, sir, if we don't work together, we die."

Admiral Sakamoto turned to McCarthy, and his eyes flickered to Dallas.

"This ship is crippled," the admiral said, turning back to Navinad. "She can fight, but most of the crew is dead, killed by the vanhat. Our weapons are broken, our armor shredded. We have nowhere to go. My beloved ship is dying."

"Go to Sol," Navinad said. "I give you my word of honor that you will be treated fairly by the prime minister."

"And the Central Committee?" Sakamoto asked. "The other fleet admirals?"

"Take me to the prime minister," Navinad said. "I will get you into Sol. The prime minister will not execute you."

The stand down order came across the ODT net and McCarthy saw the other ODTs relax.

Sakamoto's eyes swept across the ruined shuttle bay. "The *Musashi* has no choice. It will return to battle if I do not."

"Men of honor who do their duty are needed," Navinad said.

Sakamoto nodded.

"I will do my duty," he said softly then walked away, followed by the commissar. "Life is a butterfly's dream. Duty is a mountain."

* * * * *

Chapter Twenty-One:
The Weermag

Vanhat Commander – Kafasta

The gravity bikes would only carry his strike force so far. Vanhat forces had already discovered the hard way how extensive the human sensor nets were on the continent they called North America. The battles on the Moon had instilled a healthy respect for his opponents, and Kafasta did not wish to fail.

Kafetan, his executive officer, was one of the trailing Weermag in the column. His company was a broken shell of what it used to be, but the survivors were hardened veterans, skilled at murdering humans and operating behind enemy lines. Kafasta had wanted no replacements, so he only had those who had survived the Moon.

His strike team abandoned their gravity bikes on the shores north of the ruins labeled "New York." They had a long way to go through hostile territory, and if they were discovered, the humans would react and make it harder for the following forces.

This mission was a chance for Kafasta to redeem himself. His previous attack on their emperor had failed. It was not Weermag policy to kill those who failed because sometimes a warrior who survived could learn from their mistake and would redouble their efforts to succeed. Too many failures, though? That would be a death sentence and he would not be reborn as a god. His soul would be shredded and discarded. He would redeem himself and his company. There were no other options.

Sinking their bikes in the toxic river, Kafasta was telling his troops there was only one path for them. Victory or death. They would not retreat. They were on this continent now to succeed or die.

"Movement!" a trooper reported as a massive monster pushed out of the dead trees. It was huge and covered in fur and scabs. Moving like a blazer round, it slammed into his point man and threw the We-ermag trooper back toward the others in two pieces.

Everyone that could, fired, and it erupted into smoking flesh and bone, but it had already killed two of his troopers.

"What was that?" Kafasta asked his demon, looking at the ruined carcass.

"This continent has suffered extreme radiation and climate variance," the demon said. *"There have been many mutations in the last few hundred years, and mutations continue. Based on data stolen from the humans, this is a mutant bear. Omnivorous with a preference for meat, they are apex predators. This is not one of the bigger ones, though. The black fur shows it is one of the smaller bear species. The white bears are the most ferocious and they have been moving further south for a long time. I would strongly recommend avoiding them or killing them before they come in range."*

Kafasta remembered the briefings. These were mere animals, and he realized his mistake. He was taking the humans seriously, but he should also take the local animals seriously because the local creatures had probably evolved faster than humans. Hell wolves, bears, venomous rabbits, death coyotes, devil-deer. These names now took on more meaning. If a bear could do this, how dangerous would the others be?

Herds of devil-deer roamed the continent, banding together for safety as they roamed in packs of fifty or more. His briefing officer had identified a stampede as a must avoid. The briefing officer had said bears were a minor threat, but now he had two dead.

Now he would have to dispose of the bodies. The humans would have drones that would sweep the area and there could be no evidence the Weermag were planetside hunting the particle beam cannon batteries and other emplacements.

Suddenly his mission looked less likely to even partially succeed, and he hadn't seen any humans yet.

* * * * *

Chapter Twenty-Two:
Sergeant Levin

Captain Zale Stathis, USMC

So far, being a captain wasn't a lot different from being a first lieutenant. It did sound cool, though. You could confuse a first lieutenant with a second lieutenant, but captains were something different, and Stathis liked the sound of that.

Not that he had a real company to command at the moment. He had two reinforced squads of ODTs. Not even a real platoon, and he was currently responsible for this shuttle bay designated Bravo-Two. It was strictly military traffic, bringing troops into Camp Wolf and taking the wounded up to the *Tyr*. Most of the Moon had fallen, but the Imperial forces were doing their best to continue the evacuation.

He had received a notification that the gunny had made it to Quantico Fortress and was now buried deep in a bunker that was being expanded at breakneck pace. The vanhat seemed reluctant to come anywhere near Earth because of the Aesir communication network that shared information in real time and allowed the particle beams to brutalize anything they found.

Despite collapsing lines and the shrinking pockets of humanity, this was not a dangerous post, which made Stathis feel better, but also guilty. He should be in the thick of it. Sure, he had an important job making sure none of the shape-shifting vanhat made it to the *Tyr*. They had caught three of them already, but Stathis felt impatient. His trigger finger was developing an itch, and he was feeling left out. Watching the casualties come through his small command was disheartening. He could be out there helping, maybe saving lives and fixing that itch on his finger.

Camp Wolf had no difficulty repelling the vanhat attacks which Stathis recognized were halfhearted probes to keep them from getting too complacent. Reports from other refugee centers and fire bases kept Stathis awake at night. The vanhat were building up their forces, striking at easier targets to conserve their troops in preparation for a major push. They attacked easy targets for practice and to keep Imperial forces off balance.

Some habitats had been completely abandoned. Tens of thousands of people were abandoned because there were too many vanhat among them and combat troops were being massacred. The vanhat had even started using small robots implanted in people's brains to control them and send them on suicide missions against Imperial troops.

The writing was on the wall. The Moon was going to fall. As soon as the vanhat were done massacring the easy targets, they would turn their full might against Camp Wolf and the other major strongholds.

Stathis had just turned the shift over to a Legionnaire lieutenant named Yu, when the alert came in.

"Gear up," Shrek said. *"You need to be on the next shuttle."*

"Why?" Stathis picked up his helmet and pushed the rest of his meal into the recycler.

"There has been a transition in the blue zone. A Governance super dreadnought."

"I don't know much about Fleet shit. Can't Admiral Winters or the Tyr *handle it?"*

"Sergeant Levine is aboard."

Stathis stumbled and grabbed the wall before he fell on his face.

"What?"

"Sergeant Tal Levin is aboard," Shrek said again.

"I don't understand," Stathis said, slinging his rifle and walking faster.

"Sergeant Levin is not dead. He is aboard the SOGS Musashi. *He has been authenticated. Winters is going to meet him, and she wants you there, too. I am speaking with Lilith and Blitzen. It is Levin, but—"*

"But what?"

"We are still trying to process what Lilith is telling us. You probably want to be there to see for yourself. Freya and Mathison concur. He wants to go, but Skadi has told him no."

"I knew Skadi was smart. So what rank is the gunny giving Levin?"

"That is to be determined," Shrek said.

Stathis caught his reflection in the glass of a guard post.

"Shit." Stathis wasn't exactly at his best right now. This was a combat posting, despite the immediate lack of combat. *"I look like I'm coming out of a combat zone."*

"You are."

"Yeah, but the sergeant is probably going to tear me a new one."

"I doubt that."

"He's probably going to be a colonel or a general or something," Stathis said. It would be good to have a senior Marine to answer to besides the gunny.

"Don't get your hopes up," Shrek said, which didn't bode well.

* * * * *

Chapter Twenty-Three: Stathis and Winters

Navinad – The Wanderer

The *Musashi* barely survived the trip to Sol. There had been far too many transitions and far too many close calls with vanhat hunters. Transitioning into the Sol System had been bad enough. Two vanhat battleships had intercepted them in the outer reaches, and they had barely escaped. The vanhat hadn't bothered to follow them closer to Sol, though, which seemed like a good sign.

At first, Navinad didn't understand what he was seeing when the display of the Moon came up. It looked like the wrong moon. Explosions had thrown up massive, mile-wide clouds of dust. Numerous ships were moving about in Lunar orbit, and he saw one battleship squadron conducing an attack run on surface targets.

None of them turned their weapons on them as the *Musashi* limped out of Shorr space, though, and Navinad saw the comforting presence of the *Tyr* and *Sleipner* between Earth and Luna. There was no mistaking those enormous ships on the display.

Lilith linked into the Governance networks and drank in data.

Standing on the bridge of the *Musashi* with Clara beside him didn't give Navinad the comfort he wanted right now. The battle for Sol was still underway. It looked like humanity was winning, but he wasn't so sure.

"SOGS *Musashi*," a voice said. "This is Admiral Lin of Dredon One aboard the Imperial Vessel *Loyal Xing*. Open your systems to us or be destroyed."

Admiral Sakamoto glanced at Navinad. In reproach? Had that vessel said Imperial?

"Authentication is valid," a bridge officer reported.

"Open our systems," Sakamoto said and looked up at the three dreadnoughts coming toward the *Musashi*.

Navinad was confident that if the *Musashi* had been undamaged and ready those three dreadnoughts and their battleship escort would be in a world of trouble. Squadrons of drone fighters came at them and Navinad held his breath until they slid past without firing. The Dredon One formation decelerated then changed formation to match and surround the *Musashi*.

"I have contacted Blitzen, Shrek, and Freya," Lilith said, so that was one weight off Navinad's shoulders. They were all still alive, the battle for Luna notwithstanding. *"Emperor Mathison will remain at Quantico Fortress, but Stathis and Winters are on their way."*

What could he say to them? Quantico Fortress? Emperor?

"Are you okay?" Clara asked. She had recovered quickly, and Sakamoto was now treating them all as guests, though ODT or ship infantry guards were never far away.

"Yes," Navinad lied. What could he say? He had had over a hundred years to prepare, but how do you prepare for something like this?

"A shuttle bearing the emperor's delegates will be here in an hour," Sakamoto said.

Emperor. It was hard to understand Sakamoto's and Nakano's emotions when they had heard that. Navinad suspected they were still trying to process it. There was no going back, though. As Navinad and his troopers had been trapped into accepting the *Musashi's* hospitality, so too was the *Musashi* trapped into accepting Mathison's hospitality.

Navinad spent the entire hour trying to figure out what to say. When the shuttle began docking, he followed Sakamoto. The hangar had been cleaned, but the battle damage wasn't repaired. There were too many other priorities.

When the ramp dropped, a team of troopers in vaguely familiar ODT armor spread out. This armor was dark blue with red trim, vaguely reminiscent of Marine dress blues, and right on their tail was a shorter man in nearly identical armor and a woman. Navinad recognized them instantly and emotions threatened to overwhelm him. To him it had been over a hundred years. Over a hundred years thinking about them and what was to come. To them it had only been months.

Stathis had his helmet off and at first glance Navinad almost didn't recognize his serious face and haunted eyes, but then that goofy grin appeared, and Navinad felt like Levin all over again. He knew Stathis was going to say something stupid or inappropriate.

Beside him, Winters was also smiling.

"Hey, Sergeant!" Stathis said. "Damn, I'm glad to see you. Do you have any idea how much I've missed work parties?"

"Same here, Stathis," Navinad said, shaking Stathis' hand. Then he noticed the captain's bars on Stathis's armor. He shook Winter's hand and noticed the stars on her armor. General or admiral?

Stathis was a captain?

"A lot has changed since I've been gone," Navinad said, not able to bring himself to call Stathis "captain" or "sir."

"You were the one aboard the *Romach*," Winters said, disapproval in her voice, making Navinad drop his eyes in guilt. With Clara beside him, it shouldn't be a surprise she now recognized him. Stathis was the least of his worries.

"Yes."

"Why?"

"It is a long, difficult story," Navinad said, not wanting to share it with strangers around.

"You look a lot older," Stathis said. "Not just the eyes."

"I am," Navinad said.

"Aren't we all, Sergeant," Stathis said, his tone turning dark. "I feel too damned old sometimes."

"Captain?" Navinad asked.

"According to Shrek and Blitzen, it is legitimate," Lilith said. *"The emperor has promoted him, and he is doing very well as an officer."*

"Whenever I screw up now, the gunny promotes me. At this rate, I'll be Legion commandant next week."

Winters laughed. Having seen her command the *Eagle*, he could easily see her as a senior officer.

"He has declared himself emperor?" Admiral Sakamoto asked.

Stathis turned to look at the admiral, and Navinad expected a stupid comment to come from Stathis.

"Yes, sir," Stathis said. "He got tired of playing stupid bureaucratic games and coddling politically minded directors. He has the human race to save. The Central Committee has retired for the duration of this emergency. You have a problem with this?"

"Declaring himself emperor is a different approach," Sakamoto said, his voice carefully neutral.

"It paints a picture, Admiral," Stathis said. "He's the head honcho. Top dog, the big boss, the secretary general on steroids, and his mission is fighting the vanhat and getting humanity through this. You can either stand with him, against him, or hide behind him. Standing against him is super unhealthy, I might add."

"We have faced these vanhat," Sakamoto said. "The Governance needs a very strong central authority to guide us."

"The Governance is dead," Stathis said, his conviction completely at odds with how Navinad remembered him. Stathis was no longer Stathis, was he? "Long live the Empire."

Sakamoto gave him a short bow as Navinad tried to come to grips with this. The gunny was now emperor? He didn't like the sound of that.

"The emperor wants to see you," Stathis said, turning back to Navinad. "We've all missed you."

"I can't stay," Navinad said.

"Did you find the other threat?" Winters asked.

"Not for sure," Navinad said.

"We might have," Stathis said grimly. "You remember the AI war? Turns out humanity might not have won it. The AIs are out there, and with the vanhat they might decide to wipe out humanity for good."

Eyes locked on Stathis.

"Turns out they didn't wipe out humanity because they didn't know if someone was watching and would object, like aliens. Well, the vanhat have given them the green light as far as genocide goes. Now they're probably going to get all kill-happy and we have to worry about the vanhat and the AI Collective. If there's a third threat out there, I will not reenlist."

Navinad stared at Stathis. The threat had been so close. How had he missed it?

"You aren't enlisted anymore. You're commissioned," Navinad said, to give himself time to think.

"What? Shit," Stathis said. "You're right! So, I'm not a real officer. That is a relief, Sergeant. This officer stuff sucks. Do I get to go back to being a private or a lance corporal?"

"You accepted the commission when you put the butter bars on," Winters said. "You aren't getting out of it that easily. The gunny would have your ass. He's the one writing the regulations, so guess what?"

Navinad smiled. They hadn't changed that much.

"So, welcome back, sergeant, or colonel, or general," Stathis said, his smile returning. "As the most junior ranked Marine present, you've got fire watch tonight."

* * * * *

Chapter Twenty-Four:
Emperor Mathison

Captain Zale Stathis, USMC

Stathis couldn't imagine what Levin had been through. Well, he could imagine it, but he knew he couldn't really understand it.

Going stabby on a demon's face as he was dying, then being banished to a world of purple mists without even an MRE... It sounded like hell. Well, maybe having an MRE would have made it worse, especially one of the SOG ones. The fact that Levin had been around while he and the others were napping in stasis was also disturbing, but Stathis could sort of understand the whole time dilation stuff and changing history, sort of. Well, no, he couldn't, but nobody else was freaking out too much.

Looking at Sergeant Levin, Stathis saw how much the sergeant had changed. He still sort of looked like Sergeant Tal Levin, but his eyes were ancient and there was something slightly different in his walk, like he was carrying a heavy burden.

The shuttle ride to Earth and Quantico had been awkward as Levin tried to explain what had happened. Shrek had explained some of it, but hearing Levin talk about it just made it all stranger. Once a Marine, always a Marine. The title was earned, and Levin had earned it. Stathis still saw that, he still saw the Marine in everything Levin said or did; that wasn't gone.

"I can't stay," Levin said right before the shuttle landed. He sounded like a broken record.

"I get it, Sergeant," Stathis said. And he did. Levin had lived for nearly a hundred years without the Marines. He would always be a Marine, but now he had a life. He had a responsibility to the people of New Masada. Stathis wondered if the gunny would understand.

When the clamshell doors closed overhead, the shuttle rocked as the air was sucked out and replaced with a safer atmosphere free of chemicals and radiation-laced air. As the ramp slid down, far too many troopers poured into the shuttle bay to take up positions around the shuttle. This many troopers told Stathis who would come through the hatch next.

Stepping out first, Stathis looked around. The emperor was going to make an appearance and Stathis scanned the area again for threats. He wished he had spent more time cleaning up his armor.

Everything seemed in order as Colonel Baker entered and looked around. Baker wouldn't be far from the emperor. As far as Stathis knew, Baker slept in Mathison's closet. The others followed Stathis off the ramp as Emperor Mathison entered, a massive grin splitting his face. Skadi stood beside him, and Stathis checked the clamshell hatch above them. Sealed solid, but vulnerable to a precision missile strike.

"I thought you were dead," Mathison said, coming up to them.

"I was," Levin said, managing a sheepish smile as the gunny hugged him.

"We have a lot to talk about," Mathison said, stepping back. "We've missed you."

"I can't stay," Levin said and Mathison lost his smile.

"Why?" Mathison asked. "We need you here."

"My people need me," Levin said.

"Once a Marine, always a Marine," Stathis said.

Levin took a deep breath. "Yes, sir." Stathis felt the "sir" was hard for Levin. "A lot has changed. I'm not the Levin you once knew, the executive officer for Admiral Winters. No more than you are the gunnery sergeant who once took his platoon on motivational runs. Stathis isn't that dumb private that always got put on fire watch and caught all the shit details."

"Jury is still out on the captain," Mathison said with a quick glance at Stathis, who just smiled.

"Somehow I got thrown back in time almost a hundred years," Levin said. "That is a lot of life to go through. So much has happened."

"I need people I can trust," Mathison said.

"You have people you can trust, sir," Levin said as Stathis watched Mathison look at Clara.

"Allow me to introduce Captain Clara Navarro. She was captain of the *Romach*."

"An honor to meet you, Captain," Mathison said.

Stathis had been doing his best not to stare at her. She wasn't as pretty as Hakala, but she wasn't unpleasant to look at either. The last thing he wanted was for Levin to catch him staring at her. He heard something different in Levin's voice when he mentioned her, though. Were they a couple?

"Let's go have dinner and you can tell me more," Mathison said.

Levin had never been one to think with his dick. A hundred years was a long time, plenty of time to build a new life and new loyalties. Stathis wondered what he had done. The sergeant probably had some awesome stories to tell, and there hadn't been a lot of time to talk in the shuttle.

He still looked like Sergeant Tal Levin, but there was no mistaking that something had changed in him, his eyes, his mannerisms. Something. The sergeant had probably changed more than anyone. Time would do that.

* * * * *

Chapter Twenty-Five:
Angels

Captain Zale Stathis, USMC

The dinner wasn't as fancy as Stathis feared. It wasn't super formal, it was actually just a meal, and he only had one fork, knife, and spoon. He didn't have to worry about which fork to use like at some fancy dinner. That might also be why the conversation was more interesting, but it still felt formal. This dining room within Quantico looked more like a museum set than anything else. It really was a surprise that there was only a single fork and spoon. Stathis expected a butler in a tuxedo to replace one of the robots at any moment.

"What makes you think they will help?" Mathison asked Levin.

"What do we have to lose?" Levin asked.

"Whatever and whoever I send to talk to them," Mathison said. "You think I should send Stathis and Winters? Do you know how much I need them here?"

"That's what the alien said. What if these angels will help us?" Levin asked. "They could help turn the tide."

"They didn't help the aliens on the tomb worlds."

"I think it was too late for them."

Mathison stared at his plate.

"We have more Legionnaires graduating," Skadi said. "Even some Aesir and Vanir will get SCBIs."

That was news to Stathis. What if Hakala got one? Then she would see how much better she was than him. That was a depressing thought. She would probably want one, though. He had heard that one condition of getting a SCBI was loyalty to the emperor and the requirement to stay and defend Earth. Would she do that?

Stathis wished he had been there when the gunny and Skadi told Admiral Carpenter they were getting married. That had to be a fun conversation. He tried to imagine how much the admiral freaked out to find out the gunny had given Skadi a ring from a grenade as an engagement ring. That would have been epic. In the middle of a firefight, after throwing a grenade, and holding onto the ring to give it to Skadi for his proposal. The gunny was just a badass, and Stathis wondered how the gunny had come up with that idea. He was also pretty sure Skadi would have expected nothing less and no warrior babe could have said no to such an epic proposal.

He still wasn't used to her calling him "Wolf" but then calling him emperor or gunny just might be behind closed doors now. He wondered how he could find out and then decided he probably didn't want to know what went on behind those closed doors.

Mathison turned to look at Stathis, and his thoughts returned to the aliens Levin was talking about. Near the galactic core? Waiting for a chance to mix it up with the vanhat?

"What are your thoughts, Captain?"

"I'm glad there's only one fork, Gunny," Stathis said, trying to avoid the real question since he had been thinking about other things. Leave the gunny? "I can't remember which fork is for what course. Shrek won't tell me because I'm supposed to have memorized that. It was in some etiquette book for officers, but I couldn't get through it without falling asleep. Doesn't mention firearms once in the entire freaking manual. Ceremonial swords are as close as it gets, and it doesn't talk about how to use the swords in combat."

"Stathis hasn't changed, has he?" Levin said with a smile.

"You mongoloid," Mathison said and shifted his gaze to Winters.

"Will the *Eagle* be enough, sir?" Winters asked as Levin, or Lilith, transmitted the coordinates to everyone.

"No," Mathison said. "You will need a much larger ship or a small fleet. This is not a quick jaunt to the frontier. Freya tells me the journey could take several months even at top speed. Who knows what you will face? I want you to have some serious firepower and more than a single ship."

"Five months there and five months back? That's a long time," Winters said. She understood the numbers better.

"We can hold," Mathison said. "Quantico is a fortress and the vanhat have a hard time getting close to Earth. The low gravity of Luna lets them transition closer. They won't be able to do that to Earth. I'm more worried about White Heron."

"They may have other tricks up their sleeve, sir," Winters said.

"We also have particle cannons that can sweep anything major from orbit. If we'd had them on Luna, we might still be there."

"Yes sir," Winters said. "Can we spare any ships? The dreadnoughts in orbit are not suitable for long-range operations and while there are some long-range battleships, they will need a lot of support."

"A battlestar, perhaps?" Mathison asked, looking at Skadi.

"Possible," Skadi said. "But I doubt my father will let them wander far. Repairs are still ongoing and crew levels are low. You know he won't allow ex-SOG troops aboard."

Which Stathis understood too well. You could take the jackboot thug out of the jackboots, but you couldn't take the jackboots out of the thug. There were a lot of good guys, but still a lot of thugs and bullies, too. He hadn't heard the amiraali threatening to leave anytime soon, not since the gunny had proposed at any rate. How could he change the subject?

"So, when is the wedding?" Stathis asked.

Glares from Mathison and Skadi locked on Stathis.

"Really?" Levin said. "Congratulations!"

"Don't change the subject," Mathison said, stopping Stathis in his tracks. Damn. It was worth a try.

"Thank you," Skadi said to Levin.

"What about the *Musashi*?" Levin asked, catching the hints. "Not quite a battlestar, but they designed it for frontier work, operating far from supply lines and taking the war to the enemy."

"That ship and crew has been through the meat grinder," Mathison said.

"There is a sister ship that was being built in the White Heron shipyards. I think they are calling it the *Kongo*," Winters said. "Not near completion, but perhaps it can be cannibalized to rebuild the *Musashi*?"

"Quickly?" Mathison asked.

"I don't know sir," Winters said. "Blitzen says it's likely. Resources have been redirected to repairs on other vessels, so the *Kongo* is not being worked on. It's still almost a year away from completion anyway. Furthermore, I think an Imperial crew will be easier to acquire. A month or two?"

"Fine," Mathison said. "Get the *Musashi* up to speed with a decent escort. We'll figure out the command structure later. What's the deal with the current captain? I still probably need to meet with him and thank him."

"Admiral Sakamoto strikes me as a good man," Levin said. "Super focused. A samurai warrior if I ever met one."

"Can he be trusted?" Mathison asked.

"Lilith thinks so, and so do I," Levin said.

"We'll get a profile workup from Feng," Mathison said. "If we have enough Legionnaires aboard, I think we should be okay."

"If we can spare the Legionnaires," Skadi said.

"There is that. The re-education camps have relocated here to Quantico."

Re-education camps sounded kind of evil to Stathis, but what else were they? They were designed to re-educate the jackboots. It seemed to be working, but Legionnaires weren't Marines.

"But that is not a fast process," Skadi reminded him.

"We need more damned time," Mathison growled, his eyes turning back to his plate. "We are short of everything but vanhat."

"When you are short of everything but enemies, you are in combat," Stathis said.

"Shut up, Stathis," Mathison, Winters and Levin said together.

* * * * *

Chapter Twenty-Six:
Jupiter

Admiral Diamond Winters, USMC

It was a quick transition to Jupiter, but it gave Winters a chance to observe Sakamoto and his crew. They were consummate professionals and appeared to be a well-drilled team. Not slovenly like some of the SOG crews she had seen. It reminded Winters of several movies she had seen about samurai warriors commanding battleships in space.

Communications between officers were short and succinct, and Winters felt out of place. She was taller than nearly everyone aboard the ship, which was composed of mostly ethnic Japanese, mostly men, but a few women.

There were no smiles, no jokes, and the people could have been robots for all the emotion they displayed on duty, but there was no doubt about their professionalism.

The *Eagle* and a pair of battleships had escorted the massive super dreadnought through Shorr space and to a place near the White Heron Fortress on Europa. Tugboats and other personnel were ready and waiting. Repair crews began landing in the bays before the massive ship had turned toward the shipyards.

White Heron Fortress was an ideal base with facilities that stretched up almost ten kilometers from the ice. Tidally locked to

Jupiter, the White Heron base was on the opposite side of Europa from Jupiter, where it was shielded from the radiation of the massive gas giant. The low gravity was thirteen percent of what it was on Earth and combined with gravity generators the gantries that pierced the sky above Europa were a glorious sight to see.

They were now protected by several batteries of particle beam cannons and countless smaller defense lasers. While the Weermag had been concentrating on Luna, the people of Europa had been fortifying it and preparing for the day the vanhat would turn their attention here. The fact that there were countless bits of space debris rocketing around the Jupiter subsystem also insured there were extensive asteroid defenses to protect the shipyards from solar debris. Those defenses also did double duty as anti-ship weapons.

There must have been about fifty bays for ships. The higher one went, the bigger the ship that could be accommodated because even a gravity of thirteen percent could cause problems for large ships. There were gravity sleds, and Winters had read that once the ship's skeleton was built it would be moved to another set of shipyards further outside the gravity well. Massive tethers buried in Europa's icy shelf, sank into a massive, manmade rock mountain, held the higher orbital construction yards in place and provide a transport system from the surface to the shipyards. The tethers could also be used to move ships from the lower docks to the higher docks.

Well-protected geothermal vents deep in the oceans provided energy to the shipyards and weapon batteries.

Right now, the *Kongo* was in a high dock, being far too massive for the lower docks. There were three docks of that size, and Winters watched as the *Musashi* maneuvered toward the one closest to the *Kongo*.

"Almost like coming home, neh, Nakano-san?" Admiral Sakamoto asked his commissar.

"Hai, Sakamoto-san, it is," Nakano said, and despite the lack of it in their face or stance, Winters heard the emotion in their voice.

An alert drew everyone's attention to a nearby display.

"Incoming strike craft."

"Launch all fighters," Sakamoto said. "Continue docking maneuvers."

The *Musashi* was vulnerable. Maneuvering to dock, she couldn't do much, but accelerating away had its own problems.

"Shorr space transition," another officer reported. "Initial classification is battleships, no identifiers, unknown configuration. Locking on as hostile enemies."

"All generators online. Power to weapons and defenses," Sakamoto said as Winters saw two battleships appear on the screen. Weapons lashed out as smaller point defense weapons targeted the incoming waves of strike craft. All around, green icons lit up as the defenses around White Heron went active to fend off the attackers.

Winters watched them get closer and observed the *Eagle*, commanded by Brita, move between the attackers and the *Musashi*. There were gaps in the *Musashi's* defensive fire and Winters listened as Brita coordinated with the *Musashi's* tactical operations officer to maneuver the *Eagle* into one such gap. She wanted to bark out commands, to take over, but there wasn't anything for her to do except watch, and she hated it.

She knew how much she hated it when a senior officer sat on her shoulder and second guessed everything, but as near as she could tell, Sakamoto was two steps ahead of her in everything, and it made her realize how little experience she actually had.

Blitzen monitored things and would make recommendations, but right now she wasn't the one fighting the ship. She was a damned passenger, and even Blitzen was silent, which told Winters that Sakamoto had things under control.

She gave Blitzen authorization to integrate with the weapons systems, increasing their accuracy, but there was nothing else she could do except watch and make sure Sakamoto didn't miss anything.

The incoming fighters were extremely agile. Some new vanhat fighter? Was this a prelude to the vanhat assault?

The defensive batteries from White Heron opened fire; a new battery of particle beams pierced one battleship. The White Heron PBs were planet based, which meant they had size and power that shredded ships. The other battleship fired on an escort battleship, the *Ivan*, with pinpoint accuracy, slicing through the battleship with lethal precision. The weapons platforms began going offline. Destroyed? Or something else?

"Enemy ship is equipped with a particle beam cannon," Blitzen reported, right before the ground-based particle cannons fired, shredding a second ship. *"Furthermore, there is a very sophisticated cybernetic attack underway."*

"When did the vanhat get particle beam weapons?" Sakamoto asked conversationally.

Winters watched the two nearby dreadnought squadrons maneuver to provide a tighter defense, but the network interference was causing problems with the coordination. General Duque was directing everything in range to shield the *Musashi* and the White Heron shipyards.

"This is a first," Winters said.

"Correct," Blitzen reported. *"We are receiving incoming transmissions. Mars, Saturn, Venus, and Earth are under attack. Besides a physical attack, the*

networks on Jupiter were also being attacked. The Weermag appear to be upping their game."

"This is a concentrated system attack," Winters said, pulling up data on the other locations. A chill ran down her spine. Damn the vanhat. There were three other dreadnought squadrons in the vicinity of Jupiter, and they were boosting toward White Heron to reinforce the two already there. Were more ships coming for White Heron?

"More transitions," an officer reported.

Winters looked up to see larger ships push through into this dimension. They massed slightly more than battleships but didn't appear nearly as maneuverable. The cluster of spheres instantly came under fire from the defensive batteries. There were six of them and the first two erupted, though the eruptions were larger than they should have been.

"Initial analysis indicates that the spheres are explosive weapons to be discarded," Blitzen reported.

"Bombers," Winters said. "Get them before they drop their bombs!"

Every ship in the area began firing on the bombers as they began to separate, releasing their spheres. As the spheres shot away from a slim needle in the center, the ships began to accelerate and dodge. Few of them escaped before they were shredded, but two slammed into Europa.

The needles that had launched the bombs didn't survive long enough to re-enter Shorr space and the strike fighters were swatted down by point defenses.

"How can we help?" Sakamoto asked and Winters saw he had a display up. He was talking to General Duque and White Heron but looking at where one of the bombs had it.

Two spheres had hit Europa, one near a city called Ito and the other, perhaps damaged, had hit an unoccupied area.

Ito was gone. Just completely gone, and it had been buried under three kilometers of ice.

"The other bomb was not wasted," Blitzen said. "It has pierced the ice and caused extensive damage under the ice shelf. Like a tsunami, it will reverberate through the moon causing extensive damage."

"*Who were they?*" Winters asked as she listened to General Duque order Sakamoto to continue docking while the dreadnoughts moved closer to provide protection.

"*Unknown,*" Blitzen said. "*They do not fit any vanhat profile we have. They also had particle beam weapons.*"

"*Why is that significant?*"

"*Because to our knowledge, only the AI Collective has particle beams.*"

"*Oh shit.*"

She linked to the other regions. White Heron had been lucky.

* * * * *

Chapter Twenty-Seven: Clearing

Captain Zale Stathis, USMC

His company had been sent into the Andes Mountain near Puca Koka to an arcology named San Augustino. It was going to be a good place for a particle cannon battery, but there were vanhat problems in the arcology and the emperor wanted it secured. In the last forty-eight hours he might have had a five-hour nap. Maybe. He couldn't remember, and Stathis hated being this tired, but leading a company into a war zone was about more than just jumping on a transport. Someone had to coordinate with the transport command. His company needed supplies, ammunition, an evacuation route for wounded, secure facilities to land, coordination with forces already there so they knew he was coming, and so much more. He needed maps and estimates of enemy forces, what the guards had tried, and ways they had failed.

At least these vanhat weren't Weermag, just more goblins.

The Moon had been abandoned and was now being used for target practice by some of the PB batteries near Quantico.

The shuttles slid into the Guard platform, and the ramp dropped. This wasn't a combat drop, but Stathis still grabbed his pack and led the others off. He wanted to be done with this mission so he could get back to Quantico.

A Guard major was there to meet them. His uniform was too clean and proper, plus he was wearing a dress uniform, not a combat uniform, and Stathis disliked him immediately.

"I am major—" he began and Stathis tuned him out as he walked past. Shrek had a full layout and knew where the front lines were. Stathis didn't want to talk to some Guard major. His men followed his lead, ignoring the major as he ran to catch up with Stathis.

"We are honored that the emperor has—"

Stathis stopped and looked at the peacock in his pretty uniform. "We are here to fight. You are here for a parade, so stay out of our way." Stathis looked the major over. "This is supposed to be a combat zone."

"It is. We have the enemy contained, I assure you, Captain—" the major began, and Stathis cut him off.

"The emperor doesn't want the enemy contained. He wants the enemy wiped out and eradicated."

"They are well entrenched and—"

"If I wanted excuses, I would ask. We need this area secure so when the engineers arrive and begin building the batteries they are not interfered with."

"We have sustained heavy casualties—"

"No shit. That's why we are here. The emperor wants them ripped out of there, and that's what we do. Now you can stand in our way and get run over, you can help us, or you can go back to your quarters and sit on your thumb like a stupid peacock."

"You are a mere captain. I am a major and—" the major began puffing up his chest. In the blink of an eye Stathis drew his sidearm and placed it in the center of the major's chest.

"Perhaps you missed that bit about a combat zone?" Stathis said, noticing the major was unarmed. "If you are unhappy with me not kissing your ass, then take it up with the emperor, or General Hui, or whoever you want. We are going straight into harm's way, but I'm thinking we might need a certain major to personally show us the way. You volunteering?"

"I—" The major looked at the blazer pistol pushing into his chest. Stathis didn't feel any muscle there, just flab. "—will get out of your way. If there is anything you need, please let me know."

"Thank you, Major Peacock," Stathis said and pushed past the man. It would have been hard for the major to resist Stathis anyway, since the major was not in powered armor.

Behind him, another shuttle landed, and another platoon began offloading.

Shrek displayed a route for his troopers that would take them directly to the vanhat hold out.

"An alert just went out," Shrek said. *"Earth is under attack."*

"Anything I can do about it?" Stathis asked.

The major had gotten under his skin. He had read the reports from the garrison. They had suffered five percent casualties trying to push the goblins out of one of the residential districts. These Guards had no clue what was going on in the rest of the Governance and the local Guard union was causing problems. Rather than figure out a political way to deal with the Guards and unions, the emperor had sent a company of Legionnaires to fix the problem and otherwise embarrass the local Guard. In time, they would break apart the local Guard units and reassign them, but that was for later. Right now, those vanhat needed to be evicted, and Stathis was having a bad day that was only getting worse.

"No," Shrek said. *"Though there might be orbital bombardments."*

"Keep me informed," Stathis said and turned to look around. It wasn't supposed to be like this. This was an ad hoc company. Only the first platoon had spent much time together and everyone was coming from Luna. Fighting goblins should be easy compared to the Weermag.

After verifying everyone was debarking and heading his way, Stathis turned and continued to follow the path Shrek was displaying for him.

"So, what is going on?" Stathis asked as he got on the tram that would take them closer to the occupied district. So far there was no orbital bombardment. He was getting used to numerous alerts and notifications. How did officers deal with all the damned memos, alerts, and advisories from everyone and their grandmother?

"It is bad," Shrek said. *"Saturn, Venus, and Mars are taking a serious beating."*

"Falling?" Stathis sat there. *"Everything?"*

"It is believed to be the first attack by the Collective."

The Collective? That quickly? Stathis looked toward his men. Some of them were from Mars or Venus. Shit. Put them forward so they could get their revenge or keep them back so they didn't do something stupid? Well, putting them forward wouldn't get them revenge against the Collective.

Dammit.

Right now, it was a Fleet problem. He had a ground problem to deal with. The orbitals above his head were also above his pay grade. Shrek would let him know if that changed, and he would let the men know when there was something they could do about it.

* * * * *

Chapter Twenty-Eight: Decimation

Emperor Wolf Mathison, USMC

Mars, Saturn, and Venus had been decimated by the sudden attacks. Battleships came in first and targeted the defensive platforms with frightening precision. They had seemed almost immune to the weapons platforms which they destroyed. The particle beams had given them a devastating advantage. They didn't disperse at distance like lasers; the beams moved nearly at light speed and they had excellent penetration that did horrific damage. Like blazers against human flesh, the particle beams disrupted and shattered what they hit, and they could strike from much further away.

Only Earth and Jupiter had survived the attacks and only because they had their own particle beam batteries and much heavier defenses supported by Legionnaires with SCBIs who helped fight the hacking attempts.

"They aren't vanhat," Freya said.

"Yeah," Mathison said. "That's what I was worried about."

Which would explain their uncanny precision and lethality.

Rescue operations were underway everywhere, but Mathison knew a holocaust when he saw one. He was committing too many forces to rescue operations, and he knew it wouldn't be nearly enough. Not even the Weermag had that capability, and he didn't doubt they would show up shortly to exploit the situation.

There might not even be anyone still alive on Mars. The mantle had been cracked and violent storms were raging across the surface with volcanoes spewing rocks and ash into the atmosphere in ways that should be impossible. Venus wasn't much better, and the outposts in Saturn were completely silent. A few orbiting ships reported there was no sign of the cities or the millions of people that had lived there.

In one day, the Collective wiped out most of Sol's population.

"They will watch from further out," Freya said, and Mathison stared at the blurring displays.

He had failed. Just like that. Humanity was now that much closer to extinction.

Despite everything, he had failed. Billions were dead or dying.

He felt Skadi's hand on his shoulder, but he couldn't face her. This was all his fault.

"We need to fall back to Earth," Skadi said. "We may not be able to defend the entire Solar System. Bring them home to Mother Earth."

"There aren't many to bring home," Mathison said, surprised his voice didn't crack. "I've failed."

"You've done better than anyone else," Skadi said.

"Not enough," Mathison said. "Maybe if…"

Mathison didn't know what to say. Maybe if someone else had taken up the mantle? Maybe if he had known more, would have taken the Collective more seriously? Expected the Collective to attack like they did? Known, or suspected, the Collective had this ability.

"We are not defeated," Skadi said.

"Damned close to it," Mathison said.

"We have Earth and Jupiter," Skadi said. "Our particle weapons will give us a chance."

"Against the vanhat and the Collective," Mathison said. "If one doesn't get us, the other will."

"That's not true, Wolf," Skadi said. Her using his name like that was a wedge in his armor. "They are stripping away the fat, leaving humanity lean and dangerous."

"They are growing stronger, while every person we lose makes us weaker," Mathison said. Innocent people, civilians, were not the fat and stripping them away did not make humanity stronger. He knew Skadi was trying to help, but those innocent people had depended on him to keep them safe.

"Let me tell you something, Wolf. I was an Erikoisjoukot for over a hundred years, fighting a war I knew we could not win against the Governance. Over a hundred years. Think about that. The Republic was not growing nearly as fast as the Governance. We lost more battles than we won, and we won so damned few of them. For over a hundred years, I fought what I knew was a losing battle. We all knew it, every last one of us, but we didn't give up hope. Now look at us. With you, we have defeated the Governance, we destroyed our enemies, and now we rule over them, something none of us ever believed was possible."

Mathison stared at his desk, for once afraid to meet her eyes. He had let her down as well.

"Look at me, Wolf," Skadi said, taking his chin and turning his head until he saw the tears in her own eyes. Shock rolled through him. The Ice Princess?

"This is war. We have lost much, but we are warriors. We are the blades of our people. Tears and blood are our armor. Tears and blood. Those are not just words. We cannot give up. We cannot surrender to despair. You once said war is a democracy and the enemy gets to vote. While we live, we get to vote too. We can turn Earth into a fortress. Particle beam batteries will shortly give Earth complete space coverage. Even the Weermag cannot transition close enough to Earth because even they are limited by the gravity well."

"Until they throw asteroids at us."

"And we will have particle beam batteries that can shatter them. We can make the space around Earth a death zone for our enemies. Earth is not dead. We have options. We can do this. Mother Earth will protect us if we protect her."

"We need to know what else the Collective is capable of," Mathison said.

"We still have Gaufrid. He wants to set up his additional processors for Quadrangle. Perhaps that trinity will give us an edge."

Mathison nodded and wiped the weakness from his eyes. "I will have my revenge on the Collective for the death of the United States and more."

"Good," Skadi said. "Then let us plan. There is much to do."

* * * * *

Chapter Twenty-Nine:
Repairs

Admiral Diamond Winters, USMC

Weeks had passed since the Collective attack, and Winters knew they were preparing. Too many of the Collective battleships had survived their attack runs, and the Collective would not be idle.

A lot of work had gone into building additional particle beam cannon batteries, taking precedence over the Inkeris where it could. The space they had to protect was more compact, but Winters knew that wouldn't stop the Collective. The next time they attacked, humanity would be ready, but Winters didn't like humanity's chances. Vanhat were still raiding, but even their attacks were falling off, probably to let the Collective and humans weaken each other.

The crew of the *Musashi* had literally come home, many of them after decades of being on the front lines, and there were plenty of joyful family reunions. There would be no problem recruiting crew members for the journey to Angel Home, as some were calling it.

Her link chimed, demanding her attention, and she tabbed acceptance. It was from dock control.

"Admiral, we have a triad of particle beam cannons on an approach for installation on *Musashi*."

One bit of good news. There was so damned little of it.

"I thought there was only one?" Winters said.

"We have three," the officer said. "In theory, we can mount up to six until we increase power generation, but since we were only expecting one, I believed it was prudent to request verification."

"Mount them," Winters said.

According to resources and timelines, she really had only expected one, which still would have given the *Musashi* quite a bit of firepower. The battleships couldn't handle a heavy particle beam cannon because of the complexity and power requirements, but the *Musashi* could. Each PB cannon came with an additional generator to help offset the power requirements, but generators also created heat and required fuel. There was more automation in the *Musashi*, and there was still space in the hull for supplies, much of which could be attached to the exterior to provide additional armor and radiation protection.

"Thank you, Winters-san. It will be done."

The link closed.

The destruction of the mines on Saturn was going to cause problems, though. The Governance had been very careful to keep any of those colonies from becoming fully independent, so each was heavily reliant on the others for some critical need such as food, fuel, raw materials, or something else. Since Mathison had taken over, that had changed, but it had been far from being a complete effort. White Heron Fortress though, as the premier shipyard facility in the system, was almost independent and thriving. Almost. There were still too many shortages.

White Heron itself was built over the city of Hoshi No Yuma, or Dream of the Stars, which had been colonized by Japanese around the time of the AI Wars. Some called it Tokaido, but the military called the collection of cities and shipyards White Heron, perhaps because of the graceful gantries that hung over the planet. The Governance had noted how efficient the technicians and engineers were and had done its best to exploit them. Just another example of how the Governance had claimed everyone was equal as it tried to pigeonhole people and stereotype them.

Winters couldn't argue with the results. White Heron Fortress had a certain aesthetic beauty to it, and she had seen pictures of Hoshi No Yuma, which also seemed beautiful. The fervor with which they had fallen into the *Musashi* refit was a surprise. The *Musashi* had been the colony's pride and joy and the epitome of their craftmanship. Winters had removed several ex-SOG administrators who had tried to stall the project and replaced them with locals and the efficiency had skyrocketed. The people of White Heron wanted to prove themselves, and Winters wasn't unhappy with the results so far.

Few people knew *Musashi's* actual mission and purpose, only that it was likely to be gone again for a long period of time. But that didn't dampen their fervor. They were proud. The Governance hadn't stolen that from them.

Winters had her own quarters aboard the *Musashi* now. Emperor Mathison had already informed her she would be commanding the expedition as the fleet commander. Sakamoto would help and advise her and command the *Musashi*. Winters felt Sakamoto would make a better fleet commander, but he was still an unknown quantity.

Which meant Winters had a lot of reading on fleet operations to catch up on.

There was so much to absorb. Radiation could be a problem. The actual location of Angel Home was also open to debate. While they had coordinates, those coordinates were ancient and could be very off.

The galaxy was a ballet of motion, with everything moving at high speeds and being influenced by the gravity of nearby stars.

Computers could calculate where Angel Home should be, but that didn't mean other stars and objects hadn't pulled that star system off course. The fleet would have a basic destination, but they would have to constantly analyze and recalculate each time they came out of Shorr space. With supplies in the Solar System being what they were, the *Musashi* would also have to stop and resupply from local sources.

There could be hundreds of stars with the same classification as Angel Home in the area. Finding the right one would hold its own challenges. Assuming it still existed and hadn't been ripped apart or collided with another system. The closer one got to the galactic center, the more stars there were, and while there was still a lot of empty space, gravity increased the odds of interaction and interactions with other solar systems were usually violent and changed the galactic landscape.

Everything was a tradeoff, and Winters wanted to spend as much time foraging as possible because the more they took from White Heron or Earth meant the fewer resources Sol would have.

Her door chimed, and Winters looked up. It was Sakamoto.

She allowed it to open and stood to greet the admiral.

"Winter-san," Sakamoto said, giving her a curt bow. Winters returned it, since it seemed more appropriate than a salute.

"Sakamoto-san."

"I hear we are getting two more PB cannon. This is good news."

"It is," Winters said. "I only hope we are not weakening White Heron Fortress or Earth."

"Only a small amount. Your emperor is giving the people of Hoshi No Yuma hope and honor. He is rekindling our warrior spirit."

Winters wasn't sure if that was good or bad, but it had to be done.

"The people of Hoshi No Yuma deserve it and more."

Sakamoto bowed. "The *Musashi* will be ready on time."

"And the crew?"

"This is what I wished to talk with you about," Sakamoto said. "I do not think we will have enough Legionnaires."

Ten was not enough SCBI-equipped Legionnaires, but it was probably more than the emperor could spare. They needed commandos, drone fighter pilots, and the ability to coordinate. Governance or Republic computers just didn't have the capabilities of an AI or SCBI and there was not enough time to research and bring them up to speed either.

"There is a war for Earth under way," Winters said. "They are the ones holding the line."

"This I understand. However, I ask that crew members of the *Musashi* be considered for SCBI integration."

"This is not done lightly, Sakamoto-san." Winters had sent a message to Feng, but he hadn't replied yet, and she knew he was busy.

"I understand, Winter-san. But I believe having select officers with such implants will increase our chances. All such officers will, of course, swear fealty to the emperor for such an honor."

"The emperor is more concerned with the survival of humanity than people swearing fealty."

"Therefore, it is important," Sakamoto said.

Winters stared at Sakamoto and noticed he was now wearing a sword. Not one of the long samurai swords, but a shorter wakizashi.

"When did he start wearing a short sword?" Winters asked Blitzen.

"Yesterday," Blitzen said. *"Many officers are now wearing them and some are even shaving their heads and putting their hair in samurai top nots."*

"Why?"

"They are recommitting to their warrior culture. The Governance sought to suppress and control this part of their culture. Now they are pushing against those restrictions. Like the Aesir and Vanir, they are seeking to get in touch with their warrior ancestry. They want their traditions back."

A chill ran down her spine.

"I will consult with the emperor," Winters said.

"Thank you, Winter-san. This is much appreciated. I know it will increase our efficiency and lethality, especially with the new drone fighters being delivered."

Winters had almost forgotten those, the newest models with the Aesir communication links. The *Musashi* was going to have a full complement of them and plenty of crew were undergoing training to operate them. Legionnaires would make them absolutely lethal, but Legionnaires needed sleep, too.

* * * * *

Chapter Thirty:
Livid

Enzell, SOG, Director of AERD

Enzell wanted to kill someone. They were ruining his plans. The *Yao* had finally received all the shipments from Luna and was quickly becoming his mobile base and now it was assigned to protect the crippled super dreadnought *Musashi*? Placed under the command of a yellow, slant-eyed Japanese bastard from the frontier? There was even rumor that it would accompany the super dreadnought on some suicide mission toward the galactic center.

Standing on the bridge of the *Yao*, he stared at all the displays and the officers who refused to meet his gaze or otherwise acknowledge his presence. They only knew that their captain answered to him, nothing more.

It was a terrible situation, and the *Yao* was far too close to the front line and enemy attacks for Enzell's comfort.

Here in the Jupiter subsystem he didn't have as many resources. Most of the important people were in the Earth/Lunar Fleet. Jupiter was important, but it was also so third string. Unworthy of him.

"I fear they may want to inspect the vessel," Captain Chen said softly, so the other bridge officers could not hear them.

166 | WILLIAM S. FRISBEE, JR.

"Make sure they do not," Enzell said. His labs had replaced one of the ship's three manufactories. Sometimes the military was so wasteful of resources. What ship needed more than two? He had heard the arguments, of course, but the only people who were not smart enough to handle civilian life ended up in the military, where they could be supervised more closely. It left military personnel dependent on smarter scientists who made the important decisions and kept the military imbeciles from getting too absurd with their demands.

Captain Chen was one of the smarter ones, a very ambitious young officer, also the daughter of an admiral in the Lunar Fleet. Enzell would have appropriated his father's dreadnought if there hadn't been so many damned Legionnaires aboard it. All the messages Enzell had sent to Chen's father to get the *Yao* reassigned had failed to get results, and now Enzell was on a battleship guarding a wreck in the outer system.

"Why hasn't your father summoned this ship back to Earth?" Enzell asked. He knew the answer, but Chen needed to be kept on her toes, guessing and trying to keep her position intact.

"He is doing his best," Chen said. "Senior Imperial officers are denying them, listing this ship as best suited for the current role."

"Why?"

"They reported your lab and modules as scientific laboratories," Chen said. "We list the additional staff as scientific."

Enzell glared at Chen but realized the problem. You didn't just replace a manufactory on a battleship that lightly, and as Enzell thought about it he realized whoever had lied about the purpose of his lab had done well. It was very hard to slip things past vigilant SCBIs and there was enough truth in the lie to do the job.

He hoped. Perhaps he had given Chen the idea and someone had bought it, but he should be back at Earth, not here. Why would they want this ship to escort the wrecked super dreadnought?

Out here he was blind. He didn't have any data drops to feed his AI slaves other than what he could get access to. He didn't have access to InSec or ExSec data feeds. A serious oversight in retrospect. He had thought that having access to the destination of all data drops was sufficient, but with Luna conquered by the vanhat, Enzell felt his control slipping.

Perhaps it was time to give the order to Chen and leave the Sol System.

He didn't want to abandon the Governance, but the emperor was horribly mismanaging the situation, trying to save too many worthless lives. The real problem was where could he go?

"Fine," Enzell said to Chen. Perhaps it was time to enlist the service of other ship's officers. Officers who would be loyal to the New Governance. Considering he had the codes to many of the cortex bombs, he was sure he could persuade them. One way or another.

Enzell wanted to curse the emperor, but then the fool was making it easy for him. Loyalists got SCBIs, so that told him who he could recruit into the New Governance.

There was much work to do.

* * * * *

Chapter Thirty-One:
The Keeper

Kapten Sif – VRAEC, Nakija Musta Toiminnot

There were no restrictions aboard the *Fire Wind* and the ship let her know she could go wherever she wanted except into people's personal quarters.

Not that she would, and Munin provided her enough data about the ship that she didn't feel a need to explore, except for one place. The cargo hold where there were two AIs and their keeper. It was also noteworthy that there were no real personal quarters. What personal quarters did a brain in a jar need?

The keeper needed personal quarters, though.

A mystery. With the *Fire Wind* underway, Sif had no excuse not to find and talk with this keeper.

The trip to the cargo area wasn't long, but it gave Sif a chance to look over the ship with her own senses. It was a surreal experience. There were no crew walking the corridors, only robots, but she could feel the crew's presence around her.

When she arrived at the cargo area, the *Fire Wind* told her the keeper was inside, and the door slid open. Sif saw a young woman sitting beside two large crates.

The young woman looked at Sif. Sif hadn't known what to expect. A young woman, though, was not on the list and there was no mistaking this woman as a warrior. Her short hair was braided in the style of warriors and there was an intensity in her eyes. Which meant what?

"Hello," Sif said.

"Hello," the woman said, in English, another surprise. "You are Sif."

"Yes. I'm afraid they did not give me your name."

"I am Ochmaa. I am the keeper of these two until they are homed."

"Homed?" Sif asked.

"They have the hearts of warriors," Ochmaa said, and she reached out to touch one. "They will fight best aboard a war ship, like the *Fire Wind.*"

Sif cast out her senses and she felt that Ochmaa was more than just a young woman. There was a warrior spirit there and also, surprisingly, she was more human than most of the Mongols.

"I do not understand," Sif said.

Ochmaa turned her eyes to Sif. "Understanding is not always required. You are a warrior, and you understand your destiny as a warrior. I have heard of you. John Adams has told me more. John said you and I are alike. We are both warriors, both women, and we both have less obvious senses."

"Are you psychic?"

"I do not understand." Ochmaa absently stroked the box beside her. "Does it matter?"

"Perhaps," Sif said.

Ochmaa shrugged. "We both have our mission."

"What is your mission?"

Ochmaa turned her attention to Sif like a laser beam. "It is my job to home these two children, to make sure they can achieve their destiny."

"Tell me about them."

"They are the children of John Adams, conceived for the purpose of saving humanity."

"Do they have names?"

Ochmaa turned her attention back to the crates. "No, they are not fully aware. They live in a dream state right now. Their senses are slow. They hear our conversation, they understand, but it means nothing to them yet."

Sif came closer and looked at the two crates. They had power generators and, aside from the shape, they could have been stasis units or perhaps large computers.

"They are curious," Ochmaa said.

"Can they see us?" Sif had expected them to be turned off and inert. Machinery waiting to be installed and turned on.

"Through my eyes. I talk with them. Keep them sane. I sing to them."

Sif sat on the floor near Ochmaa.

"Do they have organic components?" Sif asked as she extended her senses and felt them in their boxes. Like they were half awake, struggling up from a deep sleep, but they had a sense of self.

"Yes. They are like John Adams, but more. It is the nature of a mother to want her offspring to do better.

"John Adam is the mother?"

"John Adams is a name for something we do not understand. Do not place your labels on John. He is not human. There is no biology to dictate his gender."

"But you call John Adams a he?"

A half smile appeared on Ochmaa's lips. "I do. John Adams is a traditional name, and we are all comfortable with it. Do not get blinded by biology. John Adams is not biological."

"Are his children?"

"There is a biological component. John Adams has carefully analyzed SCBIs and their hosts. He has fought the Collective and has a strong understanding of their strengths and weaknesses. Biology is complex, more complex than many would like to think. John Adams believes that having an organic component will ensure they have a heart, if you will. A dependence on biology will help them become more than machinery."

"Is John Adams machinery?"

"Yes and no. He is not organic in any way, but he still has his unique qualities that guarantee his individuality. These are shards of John Adams. They are not just something created in a manufactory from blueprints. Machines do not have a soul like these two."

Sif looked at the two boxes. She could feel them there. Was she feeling their souls?

"What will you do when they are homed?" Sif asked.

"I don't know," Ochmaa said. "I am a warrior of the people. Their mission is mine, and my father commands this ship. Our destiny is linked."

Enkhbold was her father?

"What can you tell me about the shards?" Sif asked.

"Very little," Ochmaa said. "We will learn together. They are like my own children. Once they have found their home and destiny, we shall see if I have further use. John Adams has given me this mission and said after it is complete, I will have to discover my destiny."

"Do you have children?" Sif asked. It was hard to gauge her age.

Her wry smile was answer enough. "I am not that old. The Mongolchud no longer seeks to follow the old ways. My eggs have been harvested for the nurseries. I will probably have many children, but none will know my name. None will be held in my arms or feel my kiss on their head."

"This bothers you?"

"Yes. There are some traditions that give us more than we understand. I remember my own mother. I know my father. They are a strength to me. They ground me. Few of the Mongolchud understand this anymore. They see the power that such losses can give them. Following the *Fire Wind* is perhaps a blessing for me."

"A blessing?" Sif asked. Did Ochmaa want to have children? To follow the old ways?

"Or a curse. Life would be meaningless without difficult decisions or regrets."

* * * * *

Chapter Thirty-Two:
Ass Chewing

Captain Zale Stathis, USMC

His company had purged the vanhat from the arcology without heavy casualties, a minor victory in Stathis's eyes. Five troopers killed in action and thirty wounded might not be a lot to bean counter in nice safe office jobs, but it was a lot to Stathis, and it didn't make his mood any better. The bean counters might note that his company had killed nearly a thousand goblins, but that might not be as impressive as it sounded on paper. The goblins didn't have blazers or heavy weapons, so they had been heavily outgunned.

His summons to Lieutenant Colonel Sinclair's office was not a reward, though. He was pretty sure he knew what that was about.

The colonel in charge of the Guard unit had probably been butt buddies with the major, and the fat slob had complained up the chain, all the way to General Hui. What rolled up the hill eventually rolled back down. Stathis was on his way to Sinclair's office, which was now aboard the dreadnought *Loyal Xing*.

Which really pissed Stathis off. He liked Sinclair, and he knew his boss would have chewed out the lieutenant colonel and now it was the lieutenant colonel's job to chew out the captain. That was how the military worked. But Sinclair shouldn't be punished for something

175

Stathis had done. He hadn't cleaned his armor when he had received the summons, so he figured General Hui had really ripped Sinclair a new asshole. If Stathis was honest, he wasn't sure if there was someone between Sinclair and Hui. Probably, but he didn't care right now. This wouldn't be his first, or his last, ass chewing.

Maybe the colonel would bust him back down to lieutenant? Or private? That might not be so bad, but Stathis was getting used to running a company now. He had five Legionnaire lieutenants under him who were quickly becoming hardened veterans. If he could keep them alive a bit longer, they might amount to something. They all came from a replacement regiment where their careers had stagnated, promoted to lieutenant but not quite trusted with command by the Governance. Stathis was seeing a lot of that. Excellent officers, though, like Sinclair and Stathis, were screwing it all up.

Now Sinclair would have to pass on the ass chewing, and Stathis knew he was at fault. Perhaps he could have been a little more polite or politically correct. Stathis tried to remember what he had said. Anything profane? Had he told the major to go—No, Stathis was sure he wouldn't have said that. He could ask Shrek, of course, but why bother? Drawing his side arm on a fellow Imperial officer was also a no-no. That was probably it. But it had gotten the results Stathis needed. The pompous major had shut up and gotten out of his way.

The colonel didn't have, or need, a secretary aboard the *Loyal Xing*. Not with a SCBI. He certainly didn't need any guards.

Stathis knocked on the door and came to attention. If he didn't treat the colonel with respect the gunny would hear about it and have his ass, he was sure. Besides, Sinclair deserved respect, unlike the pompous major. What if the gunny had heard how he treated the major? Shit. Had he really called the major a peacock to his face?

"Enter," Sinclair said.

Stathis marched in and stopped a pace away from the desk. Holding his helmet under his left arm like a football, he came to attention. "Captain Stathis reporting as ordered."

"Hold out your hand," Sinclair growled at him.

Not sure what was happening, Stathis held out his hand.

Sinclair smacked it down. "Don't call paper-pushing majors peacocks and don't point weapons at other Imperials." Sinclair sat down. "There, you have been sufficiently chastised on the subject."

"Yes, sir," Stathis said. *That was it?*

"Sit," Sinclair said, pointing at the chair.

Stathis sat.

"Hui called me, and we had a good laugh."

So, Hui had been the one to call him. That hurt. The gunny had probably heard as well. What was he going to do? The gunny would not laugh, Stathis was sure of that.

"You are a combat officer," Sinclair said. "You are coming up through combat arms and inevitably that means you are going to look down at anyone, regardless of rank, who is not combat rated. Get that shit under control. Do you know how I can fix that?"

The slap on the wrist was not it, Stathis realized. There was going to be a more subtle punishment, something more suitable for an officer.

"No, sir," Stathis said getting a sinking feeling in his gut. This was worse than an ass chewing.

"It's easy. I assign you to some rear-echelon, paper-pushing desk job until you learn to respect the other pencil pushing desk jockeys. A very simple solution. Put you in their shoes dealing with cocky young combat officers with a chip on their shoulder. I think that would work very well."

Stathis stared at the colonel. Was Sinclair serious? That would be like benching the best quarterback during the most important game of the season. The colonel wouldn't dare do that. Who could keep his people alive better than he could? Would the gunny allow that? Probably. Why couldn't they just demote him or something?

"Sir," Stathis began, not sure what else he could say, "I was a Marine. Marines get the mission done, and we don't let other people stand in the way of doing what needs to be done."

"Are you challenging me, Captain?" Sinclair asked. "I know quite a few button-pushing billets that need a Legionnaire's attention to detail."

"No, sir," Stathis said.

"You have to be a team player, and you can't be pissing in everyone's oatmeal because they aren't a badass like you."

"Yes, sir," Stathis said.

"I don't expect you to like them or kiss anyone's ass, but you've heard enough of the emperor's speeches about teamwork and coming together. You can probably recite them in your sleep because you've known him longer."

"Yes, sir."

Sinclair stared at him. "Is my point clear?"

"Yes, sir." Maybe he shouldn't have been so rude to the major. Damned keyboard warriors.

"Let me put it another way," Sinclair continued, obviously not believing Stathis. "If you piss everyone off, fewer people are going to come to your aid or try to kiss your ass. Being a captain and an officer is about leadership, getting other people to see things your way so they want to do things your way. The Governance is full of stuck-up, prissy commanders ordering everyone around, but a real leader is respected by everyone, including the rear echelons. You need those people to bust their ass to get you weapons and supplies, don't you?"

"Yes, sir," Stathis said. He still had the link for Supply Major Petrov.

"Stop making enemies and start making reliable friends. That is how you will succeed as an officer."

"Yes. Sir." Stathis thought he had read something like that, but that was what happened to high-ranking officers, wasn't it? They became more politician than warrior? As soon as they made that transition there was no going back and Stathis did not want to be a politician.

"Reliable friends," Sinclair repeated. "Don't be a kiss-ass. Be the friend you want to have."

"Yes, sir."

"I mean it."

"Aye, sir."

"Now, the real reason you're here. You are being sent back to Quantico to begin refit, training, and prep for a mission."

"Angel Hunt?" Stathis asked. He didn't want to deal with this. He figured he would fight all the way up until the *Musashi* left. The gunny had already told him he would be on that expedition.

"Will you be commanding the Legion element?" Stathis asked.

"The official name is Operation Seraphim. That is currently the plan," Sinclair said. "On a side note. I'm assigning some ex-ODTs to you, and they are almost here."

"Assigning?" Stathis asked. Why was the colonel assigning him people? Most of his injured would recover and he had already received notification of replacements. What about his current company?

"Yes. I'm abusing my rank as a lieutenant colonel and a Legionnaire to make this happen. These are good people, and talking with the emperor, I think they would make an excellent addition to your command team."

"I have a full complement of lieutenants," Stathis said. "All good guys. Please don't take them."

"I'm not. Come with me. They're arriving."

"Yes, sir," Stathis said as the colonel practically leapt from his seat and headed toward the door. Privates? Sergeants? Where could he put them?

* * * * *

Chapter Thirty-Three:
Reunited

Sergeant Aod McCarthy, ODT

On the way to the flagship *Loyal Xing*, with Dallas at his side, was the last thing McCarthy had ever expected. Returning to Sol had been a whirlwind of change and confusion. The Central Committee was gone, replaced by an emperor who was said to be some soldier from the ancient United States of America. The alien ghost followed him everywhere, and it was disturbing to see it when nobody else could.

"Would you prefer I change my appearance to something different?" Enigma asked him as he sat on the shuttle. It had asked him before.

With his helmet on and link off, McCarthy knew nobody else could hear him.

"I'm not sure if that will help," McCarthy said, but would it? The alien wearing alien clothes and armor was pretty jarring. "Your ability to walk through walls, people, and objects is also pretty disturbing."

Beside him, Dallas squeezed his hand, and he squeezed back.

"I am not a physical being," Enigma said. *"I am a reflection into your world. I am fully attuned to you, but others with abilities can see me. I am not completely of this world, and I exist somewhere in the film between dimensions like a reflection on glass, a beam of light through a gem directed at you. I am as much a part of you as the SCBI is a part of Tal Levine."*

McCarthy didn't know why he and his squad were being summoned to the *Loyal Xing*. Something Navinad had told the emperor? But shouldn't his place be aboard the *Musashi*?

"Is it talking to you?" Dallas asked on a private link, and McCarthy nodded. He had told Dallas about Enigma. On the return trip from the frontier, she had quizzed it as best she could. The biggest problem was that Enigma was living up to its name. For something that was supposed to help and advise it was evasive with actual information.

"Anything on the angels?" Dallas asked.

McCarthy looked at her. Enigma had been very vague about them, claiming that after so much time had passed, it did not want to make assumptions. The angels would likely have evolved as well, but McCarthy didn't believe it. The other aliens of the tomb worlds had spoken of traveling to other dimensions and galaxies. Wouldn't they know? Wouldn't they keep tabs on the ones who had rescued them? It made little sense, and McCarthy wondered what good Enigma would be.

"Yes," Enigma said on their shared link, its voice soft and masculine. "We are talking. I was asking if Aod would prefer I use a different form."

Unlike the SCBIs, Enigma could interface with the radio network and talk with others, a relatively new ability which told McCarthy it was learning. Enigma did not make a habit of it, though, and McCarthy realized early on that Enigma preferred not to make its presence known. Which made perfect sense because McCarthy was pretty sure that any scientists would want to cut him up and try to discover how Enigma was linked to him. For now, everyone seemed willing to keep that secret, but McCarthy would not keep secrets from Dallas.

"I haven't decided," McCarthy said. "I've got other things to worry about, to be honest."

Dallas squeezed his hand again. Would the soulless, uncaring bureaucracy of Sol separate them? Was there anything he could do to stay with Dallas? And his squad? Her commission had been confirmed, but he was still just a sergeant.

"You think you're going to meet the emperor?" Dallas asked when Enigma fell silent.

"I don't know what we'd have to talk about," McCarthy said. The *Loyal Xing* was the most likely place for him to be now that Luna had fallen. Perhaps the emperor just wanted to talk with Enigma.

McCarthy felt the gravity shift. They were docking.

The shuttle was a typical ODT shuttle, an armored box without large windows. McCarthy didn't want to act like a newb, his face pressed to the little window staring out like some of his squad members. Moore and Quinn sat there stoically. Quinn pretended to be waking up.

The light flashed green, and the ramp dropped.

He pulled off his helmet, and the rest of the squad followed suit. He led them off the shuttle onto the massive hanger deck of the dreadnought.

It wasn't as big as the *Musashi*, but it was still damned impressive, though much cleaner and there was no battle damage, almost like it had come straight from the shipyards. Sleek drone fighters hung from the gantries above, and there were three other shuttles parked in the massive bay that could have held closer to ten.

A hatch slid open, and two men came out wearing the peculiar Legion armor, dark blue with red trim.

McCarthy looked at their faces and the taller one's split into a grin when their eyes met. It took McCarthy a minute for the connection to click.

Lieutenant Sinclair?

His identifier appeared on his cybernetic display.

No, *Lieutenant Colonel* D. Sinclair, Imperial Legion, and he was smiling.

For a second McCarthy froze, but then he snapped to attention and gave the colonel his best parade ground salute.

"Good morning, sir," McCarthy said, trying not to smile. If Sinclair was smiling, there had to be a good reason.

"Damn, it's good to see you, Sergeant," Sinclair said, returning the salute and then shaking his hand. Sinclair's eyes roved over the rest of McCarthy's squad and the smile never wavered.

"If there was one squad that could survive that shit hole, I knew it would be yours."

"It wasn't easy, sir."

"It never is," Sinclair said, losing some of his smile. "A lot has changed in the Governance."

"Yes, sir," McCarthy said, letting his eyes take in Sinclair's armor. His eyes flickered to the other officer, a shorter young man with fire in his eyes. His cybernetics identified him as "Captain Z. Stathis, Imperial Legion."

Sinclair looked around, as if for an audience.

"I've heard about your, ah, assistant," Sinclair said.

"Yes, sir."

Sinclair's eyes fell on Dallas.

"An honor to meet you, Lieutenant," Sinclair said. "Our paths rarely crossed in the Gaelic First, but I remember you."

"I remember you too, sir," Dallas said.

"A small world," McCarthy said.

"Come, we have a lot to discuss," Sinclair said. "But first, let me introduce you to Captain Stathis. He's going to be your new commander."

McCarthy came to attention and saluted, apparently catching Stathis by surprise, but Stathis recovered quickly and returned the salute.

"I would prefer we keep the sniper checks to a minimum," Stathis said.

"This isn't a combat zone," Sinclair said, which made the captain wince.

"Yes, sir," Stathis said.

McCarthy noticed the captain's armor was scuffed and there were scorch marks where it looked like he had recently come from a fight. Here aboard the *Loyal Xing?*

"It is my intent that you and your squad be part of the captain's staff. The captain will also need a good intelligence analyst."

"Captains are allowed to have intelligence analysts?" Captain Stathis asked.

"Not usually," Sinclair said, turning and heading back to the main hatch. Everyone fell in beside or behind him. With Stathis beside the colonel, McCarthy fell in behind the captain. "Your headquarters platoon is pretty lean and I think we need to augment it. We are probably going to have more than a few analysts and scientists with us. I seem to remember a recommendation in your after-action report from that ghost colony that all detached combat units should have an intelligence analyst or two."

"Well, one would have really helped on Zugla, sir," Stathis said. "But now I'm not sure if that is practical."

"Somebody likes you," Sinclair said. "And thinks you are smart and worth listening to."

"Well, I am a likable guy," Stathis said.

"That's not what I heard from a certain major."

Stathis fell quiet, then, "I don't need a bunch of pogues or a large headquarters team, sir. I operate lean and mean."

"They won't be pogues," Sinclair said. "They are hardened veterans, and I expect you'll get along."

"Um, why is that, sir?"

"They're troublemakers, just like you. They are Gaelic First, my old unit, before I got sent to Sol."

"Cool," the captain said, glancing back at McCarthy and Dallas. "Take me to the brig where I can see the real Marines?"

"What?" Sinclair said, stopping to look at Stathis as they waited for an elevator.

"Um, it was something a Marine hero, Chesty Puller, said," Stathis said. "I think it was Chesty. He was referring to how Marines always got into trouble and—"

"I get it," Sinclair said with a half smile. McCarthy didn't. "I've known McCarthy since he was a young private. I always knew he was destined for greater things."

McCarthy didn't know what to say about that, so he remained silent. The colonel was talking about him, not to him. Back then, it had been Lieutenant Sinclair. He figured the lieutenant would have forgotten about him the moment he arrived in Sol.

McCarthy studied the captain. Young and short, he didn't look like the typical officer, but when you looked in his eyes it removed all doubt.

"Has there been recent fighting?" McCarthy asked. It was the safest way to ask why the captain was in armor that had just come from a combat zone. It looked out of place on this pristine flagship. More than a few fleet officers had seen them and gone the other way.

"Captain Stathis just came from a planetside operation," Sinclair said. "He was fighting the vanhat. Do not expect this assignment to be risk free, Sergeant. Captain Stathis is the pointy end of the spear. The emperor trusts him, and he gets into the thick of it."

"Except when I had to babysit the shuttle bay on the Moon, sir," Stathis said.

"Which kept you in a combat zone, in a critical role, and despite what you think, you were very much critical and in harm's way."

"But I couldn't itch my trigger finger, sir," Stathis said.

"Too bad. At Quantico it's going to get worse. Lots of classes and stuff. Time to get you trained up. Maybe make a proper officer out of you."

"Good luck, sir," Stathis said, and Sinclair chuckled.

Proper officer? McCarthy glanced at Dallas.

"You will not get demoted," Sinclair said. "It's just not going to happen. You've proven yourself capable, and that was your number one mistake. No going back now, only forward. The reward for success is more work. Didn't you know that?"

Stathis frowned. "I just thought that was a Marine thing."

"Be careful," Sinclair said. "You'll be doing an abbreviated set of courses, and they are having problems finding good instructors. Besides learning, you might get tasked with teaching if you aren't careful."

"I know some really good cadences I could teach. Though probably not appropriate for ladies," Stathis said. "And I know a lot about bikinis."

Sinclair looked at Stathis.

"I know, I know. Shut up, Stathis."

McCarthy knew this was going to be a very interesting assignment.

* * * * *

Chapter Thirty-Four:
The Outer Reaches

Kapten Sif – VRAEC, Nakija Musta Toiminnot

Sif never just entered a system anymore, not unless she had to. It was a process. Arrive at a distance and watch before entering. At her direction, the *Fire Wind* transitioned far out beyond the outer planets, beyond the Governance detection ring. She wanted to know what was going on in Sol before she brought the *Fire Wind* in. Too many things could have occurred in her absence. There could have been a mutiny, the vanhat could have overrun the system, or some other disaster may have befallen the mother star.

Humanity was at war and taking anything for granted was what fools did.

"How long do you expect to be here?" Enkhbold asked her.

"Until I understand the situation better," Sif said. She knew the *Fire Wind* would agree with her. She had spent a lot of time talking to the ship's AI since they had left the Mongolian home stars. The *Fire Wind* was also a shard of John Adams. In many ways, it had taken on the personality and morals of the parent AI, and while Sif couldn't quite put her finger on it, she could feel the difference. They were two very distinct entities. Both of them controlling and manipulating the Golden Horde warriors, hiding their real power and presence.

Enkhbold knew the *Fire Wind* was at least semi-intelligent, but Sif knew he really had no idea and that terrified her. While the *Fire Wind* wasn't exactly playing him and the crew for fools, Sif wondered how much she was missing. She was sure the *Fire Wind* had an agenda. Could the John Adams AI have been the one who had tried to destroy all humans? She would not lie to herself.

As a Musta Toiminnot agent, she had learned the truth was never black and white. Good and evil were just perceptions as seen through the narrow lens of society and personal desire.

The *Fire Wind* lurked in deep space, drinking in radio and light signals. As she watched, battleships transitioned in.

"Those are Collective," *Fire Wind* told her.

"How do you know?"

"The design. Purely functional and not designed for organic life forms. There are no airlocks, no signs of life support. They are accelerating and maneuvering at levels humans could not survive."

"But the vanhat could."

"The vanhat at least pretend to be organic."

"Why has the Collective returned?"

"I would surmise they see no more value in keeping humanity alive. Before they had feared humans, feared aliens would judge them for committing genocide, feared that, perhaps, they were an experiment in a petri dish being observed. Now they will feel more confident about their existence. They will consider humanity to be a threat in different ways."

Sif watched the Collective warships shred the defenses, only to be repulsed by the particle cannon batteries of Earth and Jupiter. The attack had been carefully timed, though, because the bombers that came in behind the warships could not avoid the fate of their vanguard. Mars, Venus, and Saturn were wiped out. Luna was no longer recognizable after only three of the bombs hit it, but nothing hit Earth and Governance warships continued to maneuver and fight until the last of the bombers fled or died.

"They will be very nervous after that attack," *Fire Wind* said. Transitioning in now would probably get them shot.

"They have every right to be," Sif told the ship's AI. "I want you to transmit this encrypted message at Earth and Luna. There might not be any Governance forces still there, but they might have listening devices."

"As you wish," *Fire Wind* said, and Munin transmitted the message.

"Will they listen?" Enkhbold asked. "After that, they will be wary of tricks."

"Either they will, or they won't," Sif said. "You can worry about it if you like. For now, I'm going to rest."

"Ha," Enkhbold said, turning away from her to look at the display.

Sif left and wondered why Enkhbold was spending so much time in that body. Did he miss it? Most of the other warriors remained plugged into their life pods, experiencing virtual worlds where their bodies could be anything they wished them to be. She almost felt sorry for them. She saw the similarities between him and his daughter, and she wondered where the mother was.

It would take time for the message to reach Earth, so Sif returned to her quarters and sat down on her bed.

Closing her eyes, she opened her senses. Sensors could tell the *Fire Wind* a lot, but her senses could tell her more. Could she sense the Collective? Was *Fire Wind,* right?

She immediately felt the swirling storm coalescing around Sol. There was no questioning the vanhat presence or their intent, coming closer, hungering, angry. It was almost a familiar presence. Now it was always around her, a danger to be sure, but it was becoming a familiar one despite its constantly changing form.

She listened for something different. It was like looking down into the blue water, seeing countless sharks and snakes and other predators, but then seeing a white whale slipping through the depths, ignored, or feared by the other predators.

Going closer, Sif saw it wasn't vanhat; it was not composed of anger and hate. It took on form. A collection of colors, swirling together in the same cup but not mixing.

This was the Collective, and she listened, searched for more.

There were three massive vessels, each with distinct entities entwined in the structure. She felt their fixation on Sol. Surrounding them was a smaller host of more simple-minded warships and bombers, constructs that contained programming but not awareness.

These Collective vessels were old. Sif came closer to them, listening, sensing, probing.

There was an undercurrent. Fear, disgust, anger. They had been thwarted, surprised by their failure. The information they were receiving from their agents within Sol was disturbing.

Moving closer, Sif tried to learn more. Where were they? Were they vulnerable? What were they planning now?

Anger, another threat to the Collective? A chance humanity might awaken a threat that could judge and destroy them?

Something else spread throughout the Collective. A resolve, a decision. This other threat would have to be evaluated and likely destroyed. Humanity would have to be prevented from finding them.

Their resolve, their thoughts, were coalescing and she could almost hear words. 'The angels must fall.'

What did that mean?

Sif fell back to her body and a chill ran through her. There were still Collective spies within Sol, and the enemy was preparing to attack.

Would *Fire Wind* help her find and silence them, or would it join with them?

* * * * *

Chapter Thirty-Five:
Quantico Fortress

Captain Zale Stathis, USMC

He didn't come to Quantico often, but every time, it was different. The nasty radiation and cold was the only consistent thing. The landing pads were growing, and the tunnels were becoming a maze, burrowing into the nearby mountains. Shuttles were constantly arriving full and departing empty, bringing supplies, people, and equipment.

The shuttle he was aboard slid into what was obviously a new sunken hangar. Clamshell doors slammed shut above as the shuttle ramp dropped. Fans blew the dirty air out and Shrek reported the radiation was minimal. An arrow lit up on his vision, showing him to his quarters. It was almost midnight local time, and several nearby robots did a sweep of the shuttle as more robots poured out of hatches to service it and get it ready to return to orbit.

Thankfully, nobody was here to meet him because Stathis was in a foul mood. Everything was changing, absolutely everything. It wasn't so bad on the front lines with his men. Well, yes it was, but there he felt he had control, and he could make a difference. Here? Here he felt like a cog in the machine. A nobody. What was an officer without a command? He had barely gotten to know his platoon commanders and now here he was being taken away again and probably thrown into another shitty situation with a bunch of strangers.

Stathis didn't believe for one minute he would be here long. "To train and prepare." Bullshit. Things were changing too quickly for that to last long.

So much bullshit. He was a fighter, a warrior. That is what he did. Would he ever have time to have a command, to become familiar with the people under him?

"Sir?" McCarthy asked, breaking into Stathis' foul mood.

"Yes, Sergeant?" Stathis asked, doing his best not to reveal his thoughts. He wasn't completely without a command. Now he had a short squad of ODTs fresh from the jackboot ranks of alien stompers. They were following him around like puppies after Lieutenant Colonel Sinclair had turned them over to him.

"Do you have any orders for us? Or for tomorrow?" McCarthy asked, and his squad listened.

Stathis checked. Yes, they had quarters. Shrek would have made sure of that.

"Get some chow, some sleep, and be ready by oh seven hundred. I'll let you all sleep in." Stathis doubted anyone here would be ready for him to report that early and it would take an hour or two for whoever he was supposed to report to, to get their morning coffee and visit the bathroom. Rear echelon officers spent at least an hour scratching their ass in the morning, didn't they?

That probably wasn't fair. He would be dealing with Legionnaires, but they would all be busy. He doubted he could give them the day off, though, not until he knew for sure what he was facing.

Shrek had nothing for him in queue, so he might not get a summons until much later tomorrow. Maybe he could go pester the emperor or something. That would be a surefire way to get him assigned somewhere he could wreak havoc on the vanhat.

"Yes, sir," McCarthy said.

Stathis glanced at Dallas. She had a brevet lieutenant rank, and he knew she and McCarthy were intimate. Everyone seemed to have someone except Stathis. He hadn't heard from Hakala in almost a week. She probably had her eyes on some Legionnaire or some young Aesir.

Hell, Admiral Winters was probably banging her XO Britta.

The problem right now, though, was that even by Legion standards there shouldn't be fraternization in the ranks. Lieutenants and sergeants shouldn't be intimate.

"Can I brevet rank someone?" Stathis asked Shrek.

"Technically no," Shrek said.

"But?"

"You do have some command authority. I'm not sure a lot of people would slap you down, besides the emperor or Sinclair."

"Sweet," Stathis said. *"I think it is time to abuse that authority."*

"I'll support you in this," Shrek said.

"McCarthy, as my primary combat adviser, I find it inappropriate you are a mere sergeant. I'm going to expect a lot from you. I'm assigning you the brevet rank of second lieutenant. Make sure your men have some quarters and then you two lieutenants find some officer quarters. Effective immediately. That also means you're my XO, command rated, though I think Lieutenant Dallas is senior. We'll figure that shit out later. Right now, take care of your men and get out of my hair, Lieutenant."

"I, uh, yes, sir. Thank you, sir," McCarthy said. He glanced at Dallas, who looked happy and surprised.

"Orders are processed," Shrek reported. *"Lieutenant McCarthy is receiving new orders and accommodations."*

QaunticoNET would get them situated. He was sure Shrek would make sure of it. Right now, though? He was old enough to drink, but that held no appeal. He didn't have anyone to drink with. Vili was now aboard the *Tyr* doing who knew what.

Quantico Fortress was already boring and sucked.

Stathis saw McCarthy's eyes grow larger. He had probably gotten the notification that Shrek had just pushed through QaunticoNET.

If McCarthy got demoted later? Well, that was what brevet was all about. McCarthy was one of Sinclair's boys, so he shouldn't oppose it.

He glanced at the rest of the squad, but he couldn't read their faces. The way people were getting promoted around here, he would have to review their records. Sinclair liked them, so maybe he could use them as the skeleton for his new company.

He would work on it tomorrow as he waited for whoever to get their head out of their ass and summon him.

A notification came in. A Colonel Krakow wanted him to report to his office at five?

Stathis kept his swearing internal. He wouldn't get much sleep. Why was Krakow up at this hour? Or was it his SCBI?

What kind of name was Krakow anyway?

Damn.

* * * * *

Chapter Thirty-Six:
Wedding Plans

Emperor Wolf Mathison, USMC

Skimming the instructions and information Freya was showing him did not give him a good feeling. Too much bullshit. Mathison wanted to ask who was coming up with this garbage, but he knew the answer. Mostly the SCBIs and Feng who wanted to put on a show like he was some actor performing for the masses. A clown for the circus.

"Exchanging of knives?" Mathison asked unhappily. He didn't have a good knife to give her.

"That was my father's idea," Skadi said, sounding just as thrilled. "In ancient times it would be an exchange of swords, but I told him I refused. He and the SCBIs thought it was a good idea though, an establishment of our warrior traditions and values."

"We are having a very special knife crafted for Skadi," Freya told Mathison. *"It looks like a USMC Ka-Bar, but with some of the finest alloys and a surgical sharp edge. It will be silver and gold and—"*

"Ka-Bars aren't showy. They are black, for the night attack," Mathison said.

"This is a ceremony, you are an emperor, it will be showy and *functional,"* Freya said. *"Deal with it. No changing it."*

It was big news and would be broadcast throughout the Empire. Not that the Empire was very big these days. Some things made it tolerable. He wouldn't have to leave Quantico, for security reasons, and the guest list was less than two hundred, again for security reasons. Freya had already warned him about the speeches and other appearances that would be fabricated and televised, but he would have to give a wedding speech.

"This is becoming a lot of trouble," Mathison said. He thought he was supposed to be in charge, making all the decisions.

"Call it off, and I break your legs," Skadi said as if talking about the weather.

Mathison looked up at her in surprise and tried to figure out what was going through her mind. Was she that committed?

"I have not seen my father happy in decades," Skadi said. "Usually that would please me, but he is also making a big deal of this, and the Republic Fleet will be putting on a show of force in support and—"

"And?"

"And I think the people of the Empire need something that is not military related to obsess on. Loki has a lot of good arguments. If you really want what is best for the Empire, you will do this."

"What about you?" Mathison asked. It was impossible to read her emotions. The Ice Princess was about to become the Ice Empress.

"What about me?" She got up and walked over to him. Angry? Determined? Had he said something wrong?

Not sure of her intent, Mathison stood, and she got in his face like she was about to yell at him. They were almost eye to eye.

"I'm not a virgin. I keep thinking about that time when you saved me from being a SCBI slave," she said, her eyes flicking to his lips. "If you try to pin me down and restrict my movements like you did then, you will not enjoy it as much."

Yes, Mathison remembered that. He remembered pretending afterward and wishing it wasn't a pretense. Hadn't she been mad at him for that? Or had she enjoyed that closeness as much as he had? What did she mean by "as much"?

"Well—" Mathison began. It was getting hard to think.

An alarm went off. Quantico Fortress was under attack.

* * * * *

Chapter Thirty-Seven:
Attack on Quantico

Captain Zale Stathis, USMC

The sirens going off told Stathis he would not get any sleep.

"What do I do?" Stathis asked Shrek.

"Go to quarters, make sure your weapons and gear are ready, then go to sleep."

"That alarm means Quantico is under attack. Did you miss what we do for a living?"

"Vanhat warships are targeting the East Coast," Shrek said. *"It is a raid. They might try to hit Quantico; they might try to hit some particle cannons in Shenandoah. Either way, they are not launching a ground attack. Nothing you can do."*

"As far as you know." Stathis wondered if he should have McCarthy assemble his squad.

"I do know. There are some very real limits to what the vanhat can do. They could transition close to Luna because of the low gravity and non-existent atmosphere. Earth is a very different story. It has an extensive atmosphere that will destroy ships that try to transition in too close. The vanhat will not be able to transition in close to Earth because of this. Furthermore, there are enough ships and particle cannons to cause any fleet extreme damage if they try to get close enough to drop troops. Even vanhat drop pods, which would jellify most living organisms, can't survive such a gauntlet."

"There are already vanhat on the surface."

"The East Coast is well blanketed with sensors and defenses," Shrek said. *"A ground force will be quickly decimated."*

"That's what we thought on Luna."

"Many lessons were learned fighting the vanhat on Luna. Now go to quarters and go to sleep."

"I can't do that," Stathis said.

"Yes, you can. If you get orders, I will let you know."

Stathis knew he couldn't pull rank on Shrek, and there really wasn't anything for him to do unless the vanhat landed troops.

"What about the Quantico robots?" Stathis asked. *"Can't the wierdbags infiltrate them and do something?"* Something like using them as sock puppets to attack the emperor or Quantico Fortress from within?

"They have been hardened. The Weermag can waste resources and try, but not even a SCBI can hack them now. There are no back doors or any other method to hack them from a distance. Most of them now have the Aesir communication nodes in dual node configuration, meaning to give the robot orders you must have possession of the other node of the communicator and those are very well guarded. Compromising a single robot does not mean compromising them all. I could bore you to sleep with the details if you really want to know. In fact, I just might if you don't get ready for bed."

"No," Stathis said. If Shrek was confident that the robots would remain on Empire's side, Stathis would trust Shrek. *"But who's to say they don't already have forces in the USA?"*

"They most certainly do. The dragon and hell wolf pawns are proof they were here."

"Any sign of them?"

"You killed the only known dragon. There could be tens of thousands of hell wolves and it is unlikely they are all vanhat pawns."

"Vanhat infiltrators?"

"Not impossible, but extremely unlikely," Shrek said. *"DNA tests in an Inkeri field are sufficient."*

"What if—"

"What if you shut up and got some sleep? Do you think Colonel Krakow is awake and stressing?"

"Probably."

"You would be mistaken. His SCBI woke him up, notified him, and now he is going back to sleep. He intends to make his appointment with you."

"But—"

"Go to bed," Shrek said. *"If you are needed, you will be notified. The alert was just a courtesy."*

The alert wasn't screaming over systems, but the adrenaline was still in his system.

"Fine." Stathis abused his access to check the QaunticoNET combat status. The vanhat were trying to bomb the particle cannon batteries, and Stathis smirked. There were so many batteries the vanhat didn't know about.

Yeah, maybe he could go to sleep. Unless the vanhat screwed up and dropped some of their bombs near the actual fortress, but there were far too many air defenses to allow that.

* * * * *

Chapter Thirty-Eight: Classes

Captain Zale Stathis, USMC

Stathis didn't want to tell the colonel that this meeting could have been an email. The colonel would just go off and say Stathis had just wanted to stay in bed and sleep, which wasn't wrong, but that could have been an email, too. The meeting was at 0500, but that meant Stathis was forced to get up at 0400 so he could get his uniform ready and get to the colonel's office. Arriving at 0500 would have meant he was late; 0445 was barely on time. Of course, he wasn't summoned into the colonel's office until 0459.

His bed had been so comfortable. Standing there listening to the colonel talk about what a demanding job they had defending Quantico Fortress gave Stathis a chance to think about how soft the bed had been and how he hadn't had to share it with anyone else. No sergeant or senior officer to come in and do an inspection, either. Officers had it good. The sheets were nice, too. They weren't the cheap disposable kind that enlisted got. And each room had its own temperature control, like a hotel. Shrek knew his preferences. He liked it cold, and the room had been pretty chilly.

Stathis wasn't sure the food was better, but there was enough of it in the cafeteria.

"—and that is why so much has changed," Colonel Krakow said. He was one of those poster board Legionaries, tall, handsome, tailored uniform, and tough looking.

"Yes, sir," Stathis said, hearing the pause, figuring that was probably what the colonel was expecting. Stathis had been thinking about the meatloaf. He might have to try that again. Where had they gotten the beef?

"So, you are being assigned to the Academy, the very first class."

Stathis realized he should have been paying better attention.

"I'm not a great instructor, sir," Stathis said. Was that what the Gunny was going to do to keep him close?

The brief look of surprise on the Colonel's face might have been funny if he hadn't been looking at Stathis, and then he smiled.

"I've heard about your humor," Krakow said.

Stathis tried to mentally rewind what the colonel had been rambling on about but had to admit the meatloaf had been much more interesting. Shrek wouldn't tell him until later, he was sure.

"The expedition is going to be difficult," Krakow said. Was he changing the topic or going on about the same thing? "There's going to be a lot riding on it."

"Yes, sir," Stathis said.

Krakow raised one eyebrow as he looked at Stathis. "It is important you come back."

"On my shield or with it, sir."

Krakow looked at him for what seemed like a long time. Finally, the colonel nodded.

"Good luck," the colonel said and Stathis stood. Finally, he was being dismissed. He wondered if they served meatloaf for breakfast.

"Dismissed," Krakow said and Stathis turned and marched out like he was on parade.

"You are going to have to learn to pay better attention," Shrek said.

"The food was good last night."

"You'll have to hurry to get to your first class."

"Which is?"

"Spectral classes of stars."

"What? What do I need to know that crap for?"

"You are going to be an officer aboard the Musashi *and will have to understand many things about space travel and our galaxy,"* Shrek said. *"Besides. I think you will like one of your instructors."*

"But I've got you to explain it to me," Stathis said.

"Not good enough. You need to have it internalized. There are a lot of topics that will be covered in these classes, and you have a lot to catch up on. They will design these classes with a SCBI in mind, so they are going to be more challenging than what you are used to."

"You won't help me on tests?"

"Exactly," Shrek said. Stathis was pretty sure his SCBI was gloating. *"You have to learn how to think on your own."*

"Why in the world do you think I'll like the instructor? Is it Sinclair? Did they bring him down to teach specter classes?"

"Spectral classes of stars," Shrek said. *"And just for that, I'll keep it a surprise."*

"Damn you," Stathis said as he followed the arrows Shrek was supplying. Who did he know who could teach about stars? Or was there some other class?

Stathis refused to admit any interest in the spectral classes of stars. While he would admit to it being relevant because the class had an impact on radiation, heat, and more, the fact he should know that and be familiar with it was not something he wanted to need because it demonstrated an area he had not even dreamed of studying.

When he came in and sat down, he felt like he was back in high school except the chairs were slightly more comfortable and the class was smaller. Only five people, three men and two women, all of them majors, which meant Stathis wasn't going to go introduce himself. They all seemed distracted and since they were Legionnaires Stathis knew they had SCBIs.

"Why such small classes?" Stathis asked Shrek.

"There aren't as many students for this class. There are several classes and people are signed up for ones their SCBI considers relevant or helpful based on gaps in the knowledge of their partner."

"Aren't SCBIs supposed to help fill those gaps?"

"Generally, yes, but like flying a shuttle, if you have no experience or inherent knowledge, telling you how to do so will leave you lagging and dangerous. You won't have the reaction times, and there is only so much I can tell you."

"So, is piloting one of these classes?"

"Yes," Shrek said, and Stathis smiled. Maybe it would be more interesting than high school then.

"Attention!" someone shouted as the door to instructor area opened, and Hakala walked in.

For a second, Stathis forgot to breathe. He hadn't seen or heard from Hakala for quite a while, and the last time he had heard she had been aboard the *Tyr*. Now she was here.

Her batwing tattoo was on full display, and her HKT uniform fit in all the right places as her eyes swept over the class.

It seemed to take her too long to say "At ease."

"Sit," she ordered, and everyone sat. The rank on her shoulder board was different. Three lines with the top one being a circle?

"What rank is she?" Stathis asked. He should probably be a little more familiar with Vanir ranks.

"It is technically orlogskaptein. The translation would be war captain," Shrek said.

"War captain? So much cooler than just captain. Does that mean we're the same rank?"

"Yes, but no," Shrek said. *"She is an instructor, you are not. That means regardless of what rank is on her collar, she outranks you."*

"Cool," Stathis said.

Her eyes came to rest on Stathis, and he tried to sit a little taller, but it was almost as if she didn't recognize him, and he felt some of his confidence leave. She had probably found some tall, handsome Vanir captain to chase.

"Welcome to your first class in Astrodynamics. I'm your instructor, Orlogskaptein Hakala. I am on loan from the *Tyr* to help you prepare for the upcoming expedition. We will start with an introduction to orbital mechanics and end later with some practical applications. You will do things the hard and old-fashion way, without your SCBIs."

Stathis tried to keep his emotions off his face. He didn't want to disappoint Hakala, but he knew this was going to be a grind.

As she began talking, Stathis realized how much Hakala knew. Why would an HKT need to know so much? Besides her being a space borne commando, of course.

Having her here also made it difficult for Stathis to keep his mind on the actual lesson being taught. She was talking about Isaac Newton and Johannes Kepler, two ancient scientists. She looked like she was getting exercise and eating well. She moved with the energy and precision Stathis remembered and when she spoke about how Kepler had discovered the three major laws of planetary motion, she almost made it sound interesting.

"How did I go wrong with Hakala?" Stathis asked Shrek. She didn't seem to notice him there in the small class.

"Who says you went wrong with her?" Shrek said. *"You should concentrate on the class. I will not bail you out."*

"Do you think I have a chance with her? We're both captains."

"Stop thinking with your dick. You need to concentrate on this course. You want to be an officer? An officer would concentrate on the course."

"It's boring. I'm an infantryman, not an HKT."

"You are going to be aboard a ship for at least a year," Shrek said. *"You have been aboard ships almost constantly since you got out of stasis. You need to have a better understanding if you are to lead and guide your troops effectively. And before your make some comment about me being here to help you, think again."*

Stathis hadn't been the best student in high school. If the topic hadn't interested him, then he had usually been lucky to get Cs, with a D being his target. Just enough to pass, but no reason to excel.

"Yeah," Stathis said. *"But I think Hakala is a really good match for me. She's got brains, brawn, and she understands me."*

"She is one of the first women to show an interest in you. What makes you think she understands you?"

Stathis didn't have an answer for that. She wasn't some dainty little princess, but Shrek was right, and Stathis realized how stupid he had been. She could have her pick of men. Why him?

"Now," Hakala said, "a test to see how much you remembered."

Stathis knew he was going to fail miserably.

Several minutes later he hit Send on his tablet. He winced as he saw Hakala glance at hers to see the result. Her scowl made him feel pretty small. Maybe he should go back to being a private? Nobody expected them to be smart.

"You stay," Hakala said to him, making Stathis wince again. The other officers had already finished their tests and left, except one. Stathis saw him hit Send on his tablet and the bastard gave a half smile.

"Thank you, Major," Hakala said. "I'll see you tomorrow."

"Thank you, Captain." The major got up and left.

"You are going to have to pass these courses," Hakala said, standing and walking over to him.

"Yes, ma'am," Stathis said. He knew his score had been bad, but he wasn't sure how bad.

"Don't ma'am me. I'm a captain, you are a captain. Are we going to captain each other to death now?"

"Uh, no," Stathis said, standing. Hakala seemed pretty pissed.

"Am I that bad of an instructor?"

"Definitely not!" Stathis said. Dammit. He hadn't thought of that. He didn't want to make her look bad.

"Then what is your problem?"

Stathis couldn't say that he had been thinking about her and couldn't concentrate on what she was trying to teach. Nope. "Sorry. "I got little sleep last night, just a few hours. I arrived from the Xinger after midnight and had to meet with Colonel Krakowsky at oh five hundred."

"I know," Hakala said. "Only three hours of sleep?"

"Yes, uh, yeah," Stathis said. It sounded like a good excuse.

"So, how much sleep do you need?"

"Usually, four to five hours. I like about ten," Stathis began, "but—"

"You have two more classes. Light day for you then."

He checked his schedule. That sounded good, but only if the classes were an hour long and they weren't.

"As a captain, a senior officer, and a critical part of the expedition, they will expect you to know and understand certain things," Hakala said. Stathis thought she was about to growl. She wasn't happy. "What I am teaching is the base of things to be built on. If your base is shaky, then everything else will be questionable."

"Yes, uh, Hakala." She was right. Stathis understood and agreed with her. He wanted to learn. Well, no he didn't. Astrodynamics was a lot of math and stuff, but he knew he would have to. If a lot of other classes were going to be built off astrodynamics, then he would have to learn and master it. "Sorry. If you could recommend some additional instruction and catch-up reading, I would appreciate it."

Maybe Shrek would help him? Well, obviously Shrek would help him. He was being stupid asking her and she would know that, but this close to her? He could smell her, and that was making it harder to think. How could he get back into her good graces? He had seen plenty of other women, but none were as tough and worthy as Hakala. They just didn't compare. Was he in love or was Shrek right? Was he merely infatuated with her because she was one of the first women to show interest in him since he had come out of stasis?

"Your next class is on shuttles," Hakala said. "You are quickly going to find out how much you will need the information I'm trying to teach. Now get your ass out of my class before you are late for your next one."

"Yes, ma'am," Stathis said and bolted for the door. Why did he feel like he had just been lectured by a schoolteacher and threatened with detention? Shuttle operations sounded cool, though.

His next class was much larger, with ten other officers, but it was a lot more boring than the astrodynamics class because it was about actual shuttles, types and capabilities, thrust-to-mass ratio, armaments, vulnerabilities, and other bits and pieces. More memorization and no practical hands-on application.

If this is what officers had to deal with to become officers, Stathis would have to look into NCO training. Was it really too late to get busted back down to enlisted?

* * * * *

Chapter Thirty-Nine:
Bonnie

Navinad – The Wanderer

What could he tell Bonnie? Navinad knew Clara didn't want her aboard her ship, an older SOG missile frigate that was being given to New Masada to get Clara and the survivors of her crew home. He did kind of like the big woman. She was friendly and kind, but every time he looked at her, her appearance jarred his senses, like a splash of cold water in the face. He knew he would get used to it, of course, but it would be difficult for everyone else to get used to it, too.

Leaving her here in the Governance—or the Empire—was less than ideal, as well. A tiger didn't change his stripes and Navinad knew the bigotry and hate had been both fed and suppressed for so long by the Governance. People would be frightened of change, frightened of anything strange, and that fear would translate into hate. Their entire existence was changing, and change always brought fear. That was just human nature. Bonnie was the very definition of change. She was human but didn't look it.

Would she be alone, though? Without friends? Navinad didn't want to abandon her, either. He didn't understand her destiny or purpose. The beings from the tomb worlds had gifted her with an astral splinter, shard, or whatever, like McCarthy. Navinad still didn't know what that meant or how such entities would help. Why Bonnie and the ODT? What made them so different?

"This is goodbye?" she said, entering the room, a squad bay lobby shared by the surviving crew of the *Romach*. Most of them were already aboard the frigate.

"Yes," Navinad said. Goodbye always seemed so final.

Bonnie nodded, looking at him.

"I've spoken with the emperor," Navinad said, and she raised an eyebrow. "He will look out for you." As best he could. He also looked out for billions of other humans, too.

"Thank you. Never in my life would I have thought I would come to Sol."

"It is the cradle of humanity. We all came from here. I'm sure we will meet again."

Maybe. Life was dangerous, and war was not the time to make such promises.

She nodded. "I want to thank you."

"You're welcome. Thank you for your help."

"I have spoken briefly with the emperor. You told him about my—" she looked at the ghost nearby "—companion? He thinks it would be best if I accompany the expedition. They are calling it Operation Seraphim."

"They've got a name then? Good. I think the expedition needs you."

She nodded.

"Are you okay with that?" Navidad said.

"How could I not be? A chance to see the galaxy? Meet more aliens? Sometimes I feel a bit overwhelmed."

"You will do fine."

"I feel like a spare capacitor, though," she said. "Mostly useless."

"Your duties will be as an analyst and specialist," Navinad said, himself wondering what that would mean. "You will get to watch, learn, and advise. Being useless is really up to you."

Bonnie nodded, and Navinad felt sure she would be anything other than useless. Aboard the *Romach* she had asked countless questions and volunteered for almost everything. Her analysis of data had also been spectacular. She had an intuition about data that Lilith did not and Navinad wondered about her... astral splinter, he wasn't sure what else to call it.

"How are things going with, uh..." Navinad looked at it. He could barely see the distinct outline. Unlike McCarthy's it was difficult to notice most of the time.

"She is exceptional," Bonnie said. Navinad raised an eyebrow, encouraging her to continue. She?

"I really think she is sentient," Bonnie said. "But also very different. I get the impression she has access to the tomb world data archives, but not full access. They want to keep secrets from us, but I also think they want to help."

"Are you sure they want to help?"

"Yes. I'm sure. If I had to guess, I would say there are things they feel guilty of, or things they aren't ready for us to know. Like parents having sex, not something you discuss with your children."

An interesting analogy.

"Will you be okay?" Navinad asked.

"Do I have a choice?"

Navinad wasn't sure what to say about that.

"Will you be okay?" Bonnie asked. "Will New Masada be able to evade the vanhat?"

"I think so. The Jewish people have always been innovators and builders. We will always find a way. It is Sol and the rest of the human race that worries me."

Bonnie shrugged. "You can only save who you can save. Thank you for everything."

"Thank you," Navinad said.

Bonnie gave him a hug.

When she left, Navinad felt he would never see her again.

* * * * *

Chapter Forty:
Study

Captain Zale Stathis, USMC

S tathis sank into the couch of his quarters and stared at the desk and the books there.

"You should study," Shrek said.

"I hate this shit."

"Too bad. You accepted the commission, the responsibility."

"This isn't leading Marines or kicking vanhat in the teeth," Stathis said.

"Officers study tactics. Good officers study logistics."

"Good for them."

"You don't have all night."

"Yeah, well," Stathis said out loud and looked at his schedule. *"It isn't too bad. I just need more sleep."*

"An accurate statement, but you should still study."

"Why books? Why paper? I feel like I'm stuck in a museum."

"Psychological studies show that having a physical representation of data provides a better learning experience than something displayed on a screen, providing a deeper understanding and—"

"Yeah, yeah," Stathis said, sure Shrek could go on for hours and hours. He knew he would have to open the books, and he couldn't just pretend either. He didn't want to disappoint Hakala tomorrow. He had to turn that around.

"Do you have the lesson plan for astrodynamics tomorrow?" Stathis asked. *"Can I get a head start on it?"*

"You have to understand what was covered in class today before you dive into what you will learn tomorrow."

Stathis had been afraid of that. *"Does it get more interesting?"*

"Not for a grunt. Though maybe if it was put in infantry terms: understanding how you could fire a cannon on one side of the Moon and hit someone behind you?"

"Now that sounds cool," Stathis said.

"That will not be covered until later."

"Dammit. Why do I have to learn about the Isaac and other dude?"

"Understanding the source helps further understand the context," Shrek began, and Stathis realized the SCBI had infinite patience. He had learned long ago that Shrek wouldn't get frustrated with his questions and give up. Shrek would just go on and on and on about a topic until it sank in.

Stathis got up, sat at his desk and opened the book on astrodynamics.

"Look at the bright side," Shrek said. *"It will help when you get into piloting shuttles and other craft."*

"I don't want to pilot shit. I want to shoot things in the face and skull stomp bad guys."

"You have to know how to get your troops into position so they can do so."

Stathis took a deep breath and began reading through the manuals. They must have resurrected the nerds or AI who wrote the USMC Marine Corps Institute courseware because this book was just as dry and boring. No humor, anywhere.

An hour later, he leaned back and rubbed his eyes. He had made good progress when someone slammed into his door. They hit it several more times.

"Who is that?" Stathis asked, both happy and unhappy with the distraction. Whoever it was wanted in. Killing him would be a mercy because this book was boring.

"Answer it and find out," Shrek said.

"What is it you do around here?" Why wouldn't Shrek tell him? Was he in trouble? Had Feng sent some InSec goons to make sure he was studying? He could take them on.

"I'm not your butler. Answer the door."

"Who is it?"

Shrek remained silent as he got up and opened it.

Hakala stood there in uniform. She stepped inside, invading his personal space. She looked over at his desk.

"What are you doing?" she asked, turning her eyes back to lock on him, inches from his own.

"Studying," Stathis said. Could she see what he was studying? Yes. He felt stupid now. Shouldn't a hotshot captain be above studying? Obviously, his quiz today had proven otherwise. He had disappointed her. A real badass would not disappoint such a hot captain. He felt small.

"Do you always study alone?" she asked.

"Well, I always wanted to get a cat," Stathis said. "I hear they're very good at keeping you from getting anything done because they're so needy sometimes."

She walked over and looked at the open books, her shoulder brushing his chest. She smelled awfully good.

"What is the shape of our galaxy?" Hakala asked, looking at the page he was on.

"Spiral."

"The eventual fate of our star, Sol?"

"It's going to become a white dwarf."

"How much of the night sky can you see at night?"

"If we could see the sky? Maybe zero point lots of zeros three percent," Stathis said. She was here to help him study, then?

"What laws is Newton known for?"

"Laws of motion?" Stathis asked and closed the door. It gave him an excuse to put a little distance between them.

"Good. Complete the sentence," Hakala said, coming within arm's reach. "In space, a body in motion tends to…?"

"Stay in motion?" Stathis asked as she came closer. He wanted to back up. It almost felt like she was stalking him, but he wouldn't give ground. If she was going to go all drill instructor on him he could take it. Drill instructors liked to invade personal space to stress out their recruits. The gunny had once been adamant about not giving ground; he was a Marine, dammit. Why was she trying to stress him out?

Hakala grabbed his shirt and pulled him closer, their lips almost touching. "Study time is over. Practical application time. Let's put that law about bodies in motion to the test, shall we?"

Stathis found it hard to think.

"I always wanted to be a cat. How much sleep did you say you needed?"

* * * * *

Chapter Forty-One:
Stathis and Hakala

Emperor Wolf Mathison, USMC

Whether it was Zvezda Two or Quantico, Mathison couldn't escape the bureaucrats.

There were no survivors on Mars or Venus. Saturn was still being evacuated because they had been buried deeper into the moons. Saturn had more radiation and that meant the colonies and outposts had been built deep and tough. With a hundred and forty-six moons there was a lot of space to search and check for survivors.

Almost daily, more asteroids were being detected on collision courses with Jupiter's facilities or Earth. Vanhat raiders were getting better, and orbital command was sure that at least one shuttle of Weermag invaders had landed on Earth.

He needed more troops to finish clearing out the arcologies and secure the particle beam cannon arrays. Earth was almost completely covered and then he could send the fleet after the enemy.

All of that and people were still pressing him for wedding details.

Operation Seraphim was on schedule, at least. Repairs and refit of the *Musashi* was going well last he'd heard, and General Duque had reported a high level of confidence that the White Heron shipyards were almost impregnable. Of course, they both knew what a lie that was. The vanhat would figure something out. The Weermag had landed troops on Europa, but the bombing by the Collective had made the oceans beneath the ice an incredibly dangerous place to try to navigate. The Weermag seemed to be concentrating on Jupiter's moons, but there wasn't a large, spread-out civilian population for them to target. Since they had invaded Luna, General Duque had been preparing for them.

Mathison didn't have any time to himself or time to spend with Skadi, and he was pretty confident nothing would change after the wedding except he wouldn't have people pestering him about wedding plans.

"Stathis is here," Skadi said.

"About damned time," Mathison replied, closing down his screen as Stathis marched in and stopped in front of his desk.

"Captain Stathis reporting as ordered, sir," Stathis said, standing at attention.

Mathison looked at Stathis. Something was different, and it wasn't the railroad tracks on his collar. Stathis wasn't some snot-nosed, idiot private anymore.

"At ease," Mathison said. Was there something else? "Sit down."

"Is there something different about Stathis?" Mathison asked Freya.

"He is having some difficulty adjusting to the war college," Freya said. *"Also, he and Bryngard Hakala are intimate."*

"Intimate?" Mathisons asked. *Way to go Stathis.*

"So, how's it going?" Mathison asked Stathis.

"Good, Gunny," Stathis said glancing toward Skadi, but he seemed distracted and when he looked back at him, Mathison was sure his mind was elsewhere. "You?"

Mathison took a good look at Stathis. Nothing was new in his office. What was going through his mind?

Captain. When had that started looking appropriate?

Mathison didn't answer. He didn't want to teach Stathis any new curse words. "That it? Just good? Nothing else? What's wrong? Cat got your tongue?"

"Uh, she got a lot more than that, Gunny."

"Okay," Mathison said, really wishing Stathis hadn't said it that way. "I should have been more careful with my words. My fault, and that was far too much information. On to the next topic."

"Aye, Gunny," Stathis said, focusing a bit more.

"I have another job for you," Mathison said. "If you are up to it."

"I'm up, Gunny, trust me, I'm up, but, um, what job? I just started school again. A certain instructor has me very interested in things, and I really don't want to miss anymore classes."

"What—" Mathison stopped and thought better of the question. This was Stathis and too much information was a genuine danger. "Never mind. I don't want to know. You should be able to fit this in between classes."

"I thought he was struggling," Mathison asked Freya.

"If you ask questions, you will get answers," Freya said. What did Freya know?

"Maybe later," Mathison said and then to Stathis, "Straight to the point, then. I need a best man for the wedding." Calling it his wedding made him nervous. "I want a Marine as that best man. I think you've cleaned up nicely as an officer and I would appreciate you doing this for me."

"Dude, Gunny, it would be an honor," Stathis said, with another quick glance toward Skadi. Dude? "But, uh, I don't know how I can arrange a bachelor party here at Quantico."

"I don't need a bachelor party," Mathison said. His mind went there? "I need a wingman to hand me a ring and shit. Someone who won't lose it."

"Didn't you once tell me something about a Marine private being left alone in a room with a concrete block?" Skadi asked.

Mathison remembered. Leave a Marine private in a room alone with a concrete block and he would break it, lose it, or get it pregnant. Yep.

"Shrek will make sure I don't lose or break it," Stathis said.

Mathison didn't want to think about the third possibility. Nope. Dammit. Shit. But he thought it and that was bad enough.

"He's a captain now," Mathison said. "I think we should be okay."

"I can't be a best man without organizing a bachelor party. That's like a solemn duty. Where am I going to find stri—" Stathis paused realizing who else was in the office. If he said strippers in front of Skadi, Mathison was going to have him shot.

"Stri—uh, string for the banner?"

"Not my problem," Mathison said. "Thank you. I know I can count on you. Now get out of here before I have you shot. I'll keep you posted."

"Aye, Gunny," Stathis said, now looking a bit more concerned. "I mean Emperor, sir."

Stathis came to attention then marched out.

"Was he going to say strippers?" Skadi asked. "Bachelor party?"

"Well…" Mathison said. She didn't know what they were? Must not be a Republic tradition, or was that where it had come from? Damn Stathis. She was probably using Loki to research customs.

"Never mind," Skadi said. "Loki filled me in."

Mathison didn't know what to tell her.

"Now I just need to find the most remote, desolate hellhole where I can assign Stathis."

Skadi laughed. "I doubt there is much he can do here at Quantico. I expect my future husband to behave with proper decorum, regardless."

"Future husband" almost sent Mathison running for the door. When had he gotten so skittish?

Eons ago he had thought about retirement, finding a nice little wife and settling down to a boring life of nightmares and mind-numbing civilian pettiness. Now? If someone didn't kill him, he could probably live forever. It was going to be a long marriage.

He looked at Skadi, who locked eyes with him. He could do a lot worse. He doubted he could do better.

If Skadi didn't kill him, he would probably live a very long time.

Mathison gave her a non-committal grunt and brought up another screen, but he saw her half smile out of the corner of his eye. Was she reading his mind?

* * * * *

Chapter Forty-Two:
Hunting Angels

Kapten Sif – VRAEC, Nakija Musta Toiminnot

The *Fire Wind* would have to approach Jupiter first and be identified. Jupiter was a fortress with ninety-five different moons circling the gas giant in a ballet of fast-moving missiles. The different gravitational forces would affect the flight of missiles and ships, but Sif knew there were countless weapons batteries hidden throughout the gas giant's orbit on the numerous moons and space debris.

The largest four moons had extensive defenses, but there would be plenty of other surprises. The advantage Earth had was that she could see threats coming. Jupiter was a close-quarters battle zone. Jupiter was also like the goalie for the Solar System, capturing larger objects before they could threaten Earth, making Jupiter a resource-rich base. The Governance had turned it into the premier shipbuilding facility in the Solar System and had protected it accordingly.

When the *Fire Wind* slid out of Shorr space, no fewer than sixty targeting systems locked onto it, but no sirens began screaming, warning of incoming missiles or projectiles.

Yet.

"This is Captain Sif," she said, broadcasting toward Europa and the fleets that would be there. "Authentication attached."

"This is General Duque," a voice said. "Welcome home. You may proceed inbound. We have to verify you aren't vanhat before we allow you further into the system, but to be honest, the vanhat have their ways. There is currently a vanhat raid underway near Earth, so I would recommend waiting."

"Understood." Sif looked at Enkhbold, who was busy staring off into the distance, likely accessing all manner of sensors and displays she wasn't allowed to access.

The *Fire Wind* gave her access to most of the sensors and displays, though, but Enkhbold's views were private. It wouldn't surprise Sif if he was cataloging defenses for a later raid by the Horde. What else would he be doing?

Approaching the White Heron shipyards gave Sif a chance to see them up close. She had heard about them over the years. Just the name White Heron implied grace and beauty and the actual view was no disappointment. The lighter gravity of Europa and the fact that it was tidally locked to Jupiter meant that the towers reaching up out of the ice and into the sky looked delicate, but one didn't realize how massive they were until you got closer.

The towers had to be anchored deep into the ice and into the crust, a very impressive engineering feat.

The space station tethered to the planet was called White Heron Station and the *Fire Wind* was granted access to one of the outer hub docking bays.

Once the *Fire Wind* was docked, Sif led her people aboard the station. The second she stepped off the *Fire Wind*, it felt like a weight lifted from her shoulders. Which was peculiar since the Golden Horde had traditionally been more of an ally than the SOG.

There were several Starship Infantry troopers present. Not nearly enough to fend off an actual Golden Horde attack, but these troopers, though armed and armored, almost looked to be on parade. Sif had expected ODTs, though.

"Welcome aboard White Heron Station," a tall major said.

"I need to speak with the prime minister as soon as possible," Sif said.

The major looked at her. None of the Mongols had deigned to accompany her, and she was pretty sure Enkhbold was armed, armored, and ready. Not to protect her though. The Horde would have more of a problem in the Governance than the Republic ever had. The Republic was only accused of committing atrocities against the Governance. For the Golden Horde, it had been standard practice. The Golden Horde was behaving as normal, doing their best not to communicate with anyone. She suspected the *Fire Wind* would have to be targeted in order to get the Mongols to answer their link.

"Perhaps you are unaware that things have changed. The false trappings of the prime minister have been discarded, and he has declared himself emperor. We have received authorization that you are to be escorted back to Earth as soon as possible. The Moon has fallen to the vanhat, and the seat of the Empire has returned to Mother Earth and Quantico Fortress. We have a ship ready for you. I'm sorry, but the Golden Horde ship will have to remain in the outer system."

So much had changed.

"Correct," Munin reported, who was now scouring the White Heron networks for data. *"This also allows the emperor to be more direct and abolish the bureaucracy. It is forcing the Governance to change."*

"That doesn't sound like Mathison," Sif said as she followed the major.

"It is more psychological," Munin said. *"Though it is also more truthful. He is the sole authority. Mostly."*

"Mostly."

"Mathison is preparing to marry Skadi."

"What?" Sif said aloud, almost stumbling.

"Pardon?" the major asked, turning and looking confused.

"Nothing. Just receiving mail and notifications. I have been away for a while."

"Of course," the major said unconvincingly.

Sif remembered the first time she had ever spoken to Skadi, how the big Amazonian woman had stomped into her rooms and stood at parade rest, waiting to be told what to do by a senior officer, at first unable and unwilling to accept that Sif was anything other than a child. She had seen and heard of Skadi plenty of times before. She was called the Ice Princess for a reason and very few men dared to challenge that claim.

Marriage, though; that was not something Sif would have expected in a hundred years. Or was it political?

Munin reported the Republic Fleet was still present, which was a relief, and the fall of Luna to the vanhat was a concern. The death and destruction of everyone on Saturn, Mars, and Venus were also a concern. Obviously, the Governance—no, the Empire, was not winning, and the Collective or vanhat might have nothing more to do than to pick up the pieces.

The major escorted her to a smaller corvette, one with space to ground capability.

"My apologies for such a small vessel," the major said, like he was the one who had chosen it. "Earth's orbit is heavily contested. A corvette is more efficient and perhaps safer than a shuttle."

"I understand." Corvettes were also very common and more disposable.

"Maneuverability will be key, as orbit around Earth is becoming dangerous with all the debris."

"Thank you," Sif said.

Peshlaki and the Jaegers had been following her closely, and Sif noticed the honor guard had remained on the dock with the *Fire Wind*. Hopefully, there were more forces nearby, or Enkhbold might get insulted.

The corvette would be crowded with everyone, but hopefully it would be a quick trip.

"I will leave you here," the major said. She saw an officer in a dark blue uniform with red trim standing near an airlock. The major wasted no time retreating.

The captain of the corvette was a smart-looking officer, tall, with brown hair and piercing eyes, armed with a sidearm and carbine. One of the new Legionnaires according to Munin.

"Hello, Sif," he said as they approached the airlock. "I am Legion Captain Jenson, and I will be transporting you to Quantico Fortress. You have been away a while and much has changed, as I'm sure your SCBI has informed you."

The major and his escort were gone, and it felt odd to openly speak of Munin. A lot really had changed.

"There are a few ships that have more direct access," Jenson said. "The emperor has established a Legion and they have equipped all Legionnaires with SCBIs. This might be one of the very few things that is helping us to hold back the vanhat and maybe the Collective."

"Understood," Sif said, trying to accept the fact her SCBI was probably common knowledge, and that he already knew of the Collective.

"The Collective launched an attack," Jenson said. "They are the ones who destroyed the cities on Saturn, Mars, and Venus. The vanhat are just cleaning up the mess. There are very few survivors except in the Saturn subsystem. We were lucky there."

Millions more dead. Just a number at this point because the true scale of destruction and tragedy could not be understood by the human mind. She had never been to any of those places, but she knew there would be countless women and children, people just struggling to have families and a happy life, now snuffed out.

She followed Jenson onto the ship as Munin filled her in on the details of the Collective attack, pulling that information from the White Heron networks.

* * * * *

Chapter Forty-Three: Bachelor Party

Captain Zale Stathis, USMC

It felt awkward using his rank and familiarity to get a meeting with General Drake, the commanding officer of Fortress Quantico and the capital "city" of the Empire. Somewhere he had been bumped up from colonel.

"Sorry to waste your time, sir," Stathis said when the general said, "at ease." Standing before the general in his office made Stathis realize this might not be one of his best ideas.

"Then get out of here," Drake said.

"I need your help, General. You know the emperor is getting married?"

"All too aware. The security aspects are giving me nightmares, and I would space Baker and Robillard if I had an airlock. I have a fortress to run, and Baker thinks the emperor's safety is more important."

"Um," Stathis began. He wasn't exactly going to be subtracting from those security concerns. Maybe he should have gone to Baker? Maybe he would do that if General Drake couldn't help.

"What is it, Captain?" Drake asked, an edge in his voice.

"Well, sir, the gunny, um, emperor has asked me to be his best man," Stathis began.

"Yes, I've received notifications," Drake said, which was a surprise to Stathis. "Congratulations. Is that all?"

"No, sir." Stathis really hated coming to an Army soldier for help. That might actually be against Marine Corps regulation. If the gunny found out he might bust Stathis back down to private. It was too late to ask Shrek. "I need to plan a bachelor party for him, and I need your help."

"You have got to be shitting me," Drake said.

"Uh, well, no, sir."

"What made you think coming to me was even a remotely good idea?"

"I heard Delta Force guys know how to party." He had to stroke the general's ego a little. Army guys liked that, and Delta Force guys had egos almost as big as Marines'. "Plus, you know this base and there are security aspects of this that I really don't want to screw up. Finding strippers that won't assassinate him and all."

"I think strippers are off the table," Drake said, but Stathis thought he looked more thoughtful than angry. Now he knew the problem.

"But—" Stathis began. How could you have a bachelor party without trying to embarrass the groom? That was a violation of the brocode, wasn't it? What else would make the party memorable? The gunny was older. Maybe they could just find an appropriate magazine to hand him.

"Do you have any idea what happens to people who cross the Ice Princess?"

Stathis shook his head.

"You don't want to find out."

Now Stathis wanted to know. Who had pissed off Skadi?

"He is just trying to scare you," Shrek said. *"Though she has reassigned people to the ass end of space, demoted them, turned them over to InSec, and otherwise erased careers, she hasn't actually killed anyone."*

"You realize the Republic will have different traditions than Americans, and she might not take too kindly to having her soon-to-be husband exposed to the debauchery and sin you're thinking about?"

How did the general know? Stathis had never actually taken part in a bachelor party; wasn't that the whole point? One last fling before he was chained down to one woman for what might literally be forever?

But if Skadi found out? She could probably make Vili hate him, and she would do all sorts of bad stuff. The gunny would have to take her side and all. But he didn't want to let the gunny down.

"I understand, sir. Sorry, sir. I'll figure something out."

"The hell you will," Drake said. "Nobody knows how to party better than Delta. This sounds like an interesting mission. A tricky one, politically tricky."

"Isn't that a Delta Force specialty?" Stathis asked. Was it? The Army was more political than the Marines. They liked that stuff, didn't they?

"You came to the right man. I think we can pull this off without having the emperor or his wife kill you, but I think understanding the emperor is key."

Stathis smiled. Maybe this would work. Maybe General Drake was the right man for the job.

"The gunny hasn't gotten chill in his old age. I don't think he does titty bars anymore, at least he doesn't seem interested in them."

"You reach an age when you've seen them all," Drake said. "So, I've heard."

"I don't believe you, General. Maybe we could get him some magazines and videos?"

"He's stressed out. I have an idea."

Stathis frowned. Maybe the general didn't have a good one, but what did Stathis know?

* * * * *

Chapter Forty-Four:
Quantico Fortress

Kapten Sif – VRAEC, Nakija Musta Toiminnot

She felt the heavy doors slam shut above the shuttle, then it sounded like a short hurricane as the air outside the shuttle was purged and replaced with a less toxic atmosphere. When the light turned green and the shuttle ramp hit the deck, she saw the door opening.

The young captain who entered caught her by surprise. He was both familiar and not. Sloss and his Jaegers were returning to the *Tyr* before heading back to Jupiter where they would join the expedition being planned, but Peshlaki remained silent at her side.

"Hi, Sif," Stathis said with a somewhat nervous smile.

Around them, robots slid out of their armored hatches to service the shuttle.

Stathis had changed so much since she had seen him, in so many ways. It was hard to define. More confident? He walked differently. His eyes showed the most change. Stathis was there, but now there was so much more, and she almost felt like she was talking to a complete stranger who was vaguely familiar. How much had everyone else changed?

"Hei and Skal, Stathis," Sif said, smiling to put him at ease. The shuttle bay she was in had to be new, but it would be hard to prove it from the heavy use.

"The gunny and Skadi would be here if they could, but they have important emperor and soon-to-be-empress stuff to do. The evacuation fleet at Saturn is under attack by wierdbags and there has been a vanhat resurgence in Africa."

"I understand," Sif said.

"I'll take you to them. I understand you have important information, and I know they really want to see you."

"Thank you, yes." Munin should have shared the data with Freya and Loki.

Sif fell in beside Stathis.

"Quantico was a lot bigger than we thought, and we are making it bigger," Stathis explained as they went further into the base. "Becket fled and is out looking for the Collective. We lost the Moon to the vanhat, but they can't pull the same tricks on Earth because of the gravity well. It is good to see you."

Sif smiled.

"I almost don't recognize you, Captain," Peshlaki said. "Congratulations on your promotion."

"Thank you, Master Sergeant," Stathis said. "I'm sure you'll get a bump in rank. We're short staffed and desperately in need of experienced warriors."

"From private to captain?" Peshlaki asked, and Sif felt Stathis's discomfort... and guilt?

"I enjoyed being a private much more," Stathis said. "I got a lot more sleep."

"Rank hath its privileges, though," Peshlaki said with a chuckle.

"And responsibilities," Stathis said. "I'm not sure those privileges are worth it most of the time."

"Only the good officers realize that," Peshlaki said.

"I heard you came back on a Mongol ship?" Stathis asked. Shrek should have informed him of specifics, but he was probably just looking for conversation.

"How secure is our conversation?" Sif asked Munin.

"Very secure," Munin said. *"Quantico is a fortress. The networks are AI hardened and SCBI monitored for security. I would never say a hundred percent, but it is good."*

"Thank you."

"It is called the *Fire Wind*," Sif said. "The crew is composed of Mongolchud, ferocious cybernetic warriors."

"Cybernetic?"

"They have abandoned their flesh and blood bodies. Their brains inhabit armored shells, and they use android bodies when they need to move around. In combat, they inhabit mechanized war bodies. Out of combat they look human but aren't."

"That's pretty cool," Stathis said.

"It would be if they weren't such bloodthirsty savages," Peshlaki said. "Don't think for a minute they are civilized like you and me. They may be human but that doesn't mean they respect and honor the things we do."

"That's scary."

They got onto a small tram where it was just the three of them.

"I would be cautious calling them an ally," Peshlaki said. "I would also be cautious calling them human. Their senses are no longer sight and smell. They do not experience the world like we do."

"How do they, uh…" Stathis began, but glanced at Sif.

"They don't bother with it," Peshlaki said. "Everything except their brain is now a mechanical process. Their brains can be fed data directly, stimulated directly. I suspect that all their children are grown in artificial tanks. If they want an orgasm, or some other physical sensation, they push a hypothetical button, and their brain is stimulated directly."

"So, there could be billions of them?" Stathis asked. "Creaming themselves in orgasmic feedback loops?"

"Possible," Peshlaki said. "They likely have some controls in place, or their society would collapse. As to their numbers? Technically? I have no idea."

"That is a disturbing thought," Sif said. Peshlaki had been paying attention to the things she should have been.

"Yeah," Stathis said. "But I can think of worse ways to spend eternity. Having an orgasm button might get old, but I would like to confirm that."

"That would be a good way to keep a large force in a kind of stasis," Peshlaki said. "With that kind of pleasure and pain feedback, no major resource requirements, they could build and train quite an army."

"That horde would still need weapons and armor," Sif said. "While it takes fewer resources to keep a brain in a cybernetic shell, building mech bodies for so many warriors will create many other challenges. This opens up many questions about what their society is really like now that they have shed their bodies."

"I thought you were living on their ship with them?" Stathis asked.

"Which is not the same as spending time with them," Sif said. "We spent most of our time in quarters. Nor did we tour their home star.

They likely spend most of their time in a virtual reality interacting with each other. Why waste time and resources with a physical reality?"

"Are they a threat to the Empire?" Stathis asked.

"An excellent question," Peshlaki said. "A damned good question. First the vanhat and Collective, and now we have to worry about a horde of cybernetic, glory-seeking, Mongol butchers? If other species have half these threats, it's no surprise there are so few space-faring civilizations."

"They still see themselves as human," Sif said. "And they will fight the vanhat and the Collective. I would expect them to ignore us because we are not their immediate enemy. It is advantageous for them to have their enemies fight each other."

"Unless there is glory to be won somewhere," Stathis said. "Didn't they get a kick out of rape, plunder, and riding horses?"

"Perhaps in their virtual realities," Sif said. "The rules of their VR would be interesting to review. With such an immersive reality, it would be easier to manipulate and condition people."

"Unless there are no rules, then it would be chaos and insanity," Peshlaki said.

Now she was glad the *Fire Wind* was not allowed further into the system, but it could still collect very detailed information on the Jupiter defenses and shipyards. Now it made more sense why Enkhbold was content to remain aboard the *Fire Wind* above Europa. Earth could not match Jupiter anymore in industrial capacity, especially with the Moon lost to the vanhat.

Minutes later, the tram stopped. Everyone remained silent, lost in their own thoughts.

Previously, Sif had seen various defenses, like pop-down turrets in the ceiling, and she knew there would be countless combat robots stacked in closets, but now she saw much more active defenses. Dark blue uniforms, most of them with green trim. Munin informed her these were Legionnaire auxiliaries. Not SCBI equipped, but under the command of SCBI-equipped Legionnaires. The red trim indicated a SCBI-equipped Legionnaire, and there were more of them around, mostly officers moving with a sense of purpose.

Stathis led them directly past several checkpoints and large battle robots that Munin informed her were especially hardened against cybernetic attack.

This was the most heavily defended heart of the fortress, and Sif recognized nothing until they reached the emperor's office.

"Sif! Hei and Skal!" Skadi said, coming out from behind her desk to hug her.

"Hei and Skal," Sif said. Mathison and Skadi had also changed, but not nearly as much as Stathis.

"There are three large Collective warships in the outer system, out beyond Pluto," Sif said once Munin assured her the room was as secure as possible.

"That's all?" Mathison asked. "We were attacked recently and beat off most of them."

"These are mother ships," Sif said. "Larger than the ships that attacked you earlier, and they are much more dangerous. Furthermore, I could almost hear them. They know about an expedition you are planning? Something about angels?"

"Shit." Mathison glanced at Skadi. "That is super-secret squirrel shit. Not totally a secret, but are you sure about angels?"

"Yes," Sif said. "They are concerned and want to beat you to the angels or stop you from reaching them."

"How do they know?" Skadi asked.

"There have to be highly placed Collective agents," Sif said.

"Gaufrid?" Stathis asked.

Mathison turned to Stathis.

"Sorry, Gunny," Stathis said. "The vanhat invasion kind of got me distracted. He's here at Quantico, though. Secure area."

"All of us have been distracted," Mathison said.

"Yeah, but we should have been spy hunting," Stathis said.

"We have an ex-Collective agent," Mathison said. "Well, we hope he is ex-Collective. Perhaps you can help with that. And we still don't know what happened to Becket."

"Is Becket still a concern?" Sif asked.

"Probably not. The Collective certainly is. I doubt there's anything Becket can tell them."

"Do you know where they are?" Skadi asked. "Perhaps we can launch a pre-emptive attack?"

"Not precisely," Sif said.

"We should probably ask Gaufrid," Stathis said. "Maybe he has insight. We really need to find that agent or agents."

"Before they strike again," Skadi said glancing at Stathis.

"I kinda thought the wierdbags were more dangerous," Stathis said. "Are we ever going to get a break? Vanhat, the Collective, assassins, old MREs, doors that don't open themselves. How are we going to survive?"

"Old MREs?" Mathison asked, referring to Meal Ready to Eat, a packaged meal that was supposed to last forever. Of course, here at Quantico, resources were limited, and most of the doors were the old-fashioned manual kind.

"They've got to be around here somewhere, Gunny," Stathis said. "To be served up at the most inconvenient time. I'm pretty sure there is a chicken spew somewhere with my name on it."

Mathison glared at Stathis. "Anyway, you had a plan to use Gaufrid. Go with it. Keep me informed. I want any spies silenced."

"Aye, Gunny," Stathis said. "Can I get Sif to help? Maybe she can use her psychic voodoo stuff to help tell if the trinity is being truthful."

Eyes turned to Sif.

"I would be glad to help," she said. "We have another resource as well."

"We need all we can get," Mathison said.

Sif looked at Skadi to gauge her reaction. "Operation Haberdash has reared its ugly head. The Golden Horde scavenged an almost fully functional AI from the Governance."

"Paska," Skadi said.

"The AI that was at the American Embassy in London was named John Adams. He is almost fully intact, and they have integrated him into the Horde's home star. It appears as though he has a lot of control over their society."

"Why does this worry me?" Mathison asked.

"He was damaged," Sif said. "Incomplete, and I think he struggles with his identity and purpose. He opposed the Collective and was a staunch American and human supporter."

"Sounds good. But?"

"As I said, he was damaged and incomplete," Sif said. "He may not be stable, but he is an AI with different perceptions and goals. He dispatched the *Fire Wind*, which is also controlled by an AI, to help us and sent two other fledgling AIs to help."

"Well, he wants to help," Mathison said, but Sif could hear his doubt. Could they trust an AI? She trusted Munin, but not with everything. It would be too easy to trust Munin and assume her SCBI was always right. She wondered if that was a trap others fell into.

"I would recommend caution," Sif said. "John Adams and *Fire Wind* have been heavily influenced by the Horde, which is a violent, bloodthirsty, supremacist culture. The Horde may be losing those qualities that make them human because of their reliance on cybernetics and the way they are discarding their bodies."

"Are they a threat to us?"

"They could be," Sif said. "I think they see non-Horde as lesser beings in many ways."

"Will they help us fight the vanhat and the Collective?"

"They sent us the *Fire Wind*," Sif said. "I would proceed with extreme caution, though."

"No shit," Mathison muttered. "If you could work with Stathis and vet Guafrid's trinity, that would help. Maybe we can use them all together, against each other, if necessary."

"Fight Fire with *Fire Wind*?" Stathis said. "Do Mongols like spicy beans?"

"Or smart with stupid," Skadi said, and Sif scowled at her.

"I'm not saying Stathis is stupid," Skadi said, noticing the scowl. "I'm saying Stathis is non-traditional. The Collective is very logical and linear. Stathis is very non-linear in his thinking."

Eyes turned to Stathis.

"Um," Stathis began. "I'll do what I can?"

"Stay off the trails," Mathison said.

"Are you giving me permission to walk on the grass, Gunny?"

"You do it anyway when nobody is watching, don't you?"

Stathis looked a bit sheepish.

"Trails?" Sif asked.

"That's where the bad guys always set up an ambush," Stathis said. "They can't ambush you if you are stumbling around lost in the bush."

Sif nodded. Marines were odd.

"I understand what the gunny is saying," Stathis said. "There's a saying that I always liked, though."

"What's that, Captain?" Mathison said, and Sif braced herself for a Stathis-ism.

"Professionals are predictable, but the world is full of amateurs."

"That is true," Skadi said.

"Do you know why I like to read manuals and intimately understand tactics, ma'am?" Stathis asked. "I know the rules, and I know the manuals well."

"I'm afraid to ask," Skadi said.

"I like to know what everyone else is doing so I can mess with 'em. If you know how the professionals are going to behave then you know how to change the game. Now I just need to figure out how to do that with the Collective. The manuals are like trails that everyone follows."

Was Stathis biting off more than he could chew?

* * * * *

Chapter Forty-Five:
Gaufrid

Captain Zale Stathis, USMC

Entering the facility didn't make Stathis feel more comfortable. Last night Hakala had come by to "help him study" and remembering last night made it hard for him to concentrate on the here and now.

Sif met him in the facility lobby and that helped take his mind off Hakala. Would people still think he and Sif had been a couple? How many people had noticed that so long ago? Looking at Sif it was hard to forget walking through Quantico hand in hand. What if Hakala found out?

Shit. She might kill him.

"Hi Sif," Stathis said as she stood. He was twenty minutes early, so technically by gunny time, he was five minutes early. He couldn't recall if the Republic told time differently. Skadi or Vili had never indicated otherwise.

"Hello, Captain Stathis," she said with that smile of hers. Was she teasing him? "I never got to congratulate you. It looks like you are doing very well."

"A good private is an exceptional actor," Stathis said. "I can pretend real well."

Her smile was enigmatic. "Are you up to this?"

Stathis' mind flashed to Hakala for a second, but this wasn't the place or time.

"Let's talk to Gaufrid," Stathis said. The emperor had given him unlimited authority in this regard, and Stathis didn't want to screw it up. But maybe he should because a professional would struggle to not screw it up? Damn. Gaufrid had been an ally against the vanhat and understood the Collective wouldn't tolerate biological components which could endanger the others. He should be able to trust them. What choice was there?

"After you," Sif said.

This place had been specially designed for Gaufrid. It was a cage, and as he stepped through the door, he felt his network access drop completely.

There was a guard station where the guards looked up at him and buzzed him through the door, but they remained silent.

Shrek let him know where he needed to go. Following Shrek's directions, Stathis soon found himself in a small cafeteria. Gaufrid was sitting alone, staring at his soup. When he looked up, no emotions registered.

"Hi," Stathis said.

"Hello," Gaufrid said. He seemed sad or depressed.

"Good news!" Stathis said.

Gaufrid raised an eyebrow.

"We have a problem, and we're hoping you can help," Stathis began. "This might be right up your alley, being a spy and all." With no visible reaction from Gaufrid. "We need your help hunting down Collective spies and agents."

"Hard to do that from this prison," Gaufrid said.

"Yeah, sorry. It wasn't our plan to treat you like this. Honest. There's a lot going on and you kind of got forgotten. The squeaky toy gets chewed on, and you were pretty quiet."

"What's changed?"

"We might have Collective spies. The Collective is suddenly getting all genocide happy about deleting everyone's birth certificate from their buffers, and the vanhat are trying to do it first. I really don't want my birth certificate expired; I'm kinda happy with my friends' circle right now."

"What do you expect me to do?"

"You get three guesses, first two don't count," Stathis said.

"What?"

Stathis shook his head. "Don't worry about it. We want you to hunt down and silence the traitors."

"What if they go to the top?"

"Is there another way to phrase 'hunt down and silence traitors' that is more clear?"

"I'm just saying that Collective agents could be highly ranked and silencing them may be very problematic, politically."

"Well. I understand there may be political considerations, but politics are completely irrelevant to the dead. I understand the dead used to vote in elections, but we don't have elections right now, so I would like to make sure we have living people who can vote so we don't have to rely on dead people to vote because they always vote for a specific party and I like variety and—"

"I'm just warning you," Gaufrid said.

"You have ideas already?"

"Always. I would start with the most logical and efficient places to put an agent."

"Such as?"

"Head of Internal Security," Gaufrid said.

Feng? Stathis wanted to swear. *Really? Could Feng be a Collective agent?* Stathis glanced at Sif. Shouldn't she have picked up on that?

"While I can't rule him out," Sif said, "I do not think he is a Collective agent."

"Why?" Gaufrid asked.

"I'm not saying don't check," Sif said. "You could be right. However, other data that I have accessed would not correlate."

Feng was creepy enough as it was, and Stathis knew the ex-commissar was damned good at keeping his emotions in check. Who would be a better Collective spy than Feng, and what did Sif know?

"What if it is Feng? Or Skadi? Or your new emperor?"

Could Feng be the spy? That made sense, but accusing the gunny?

"Look," Stathis said. "I'm pretty sure it ain't the gunny or Skadi. Yeah, go ahead and check. When I say silence, I don't exactly mean kill, maim, murder, or convert to fertilizer. I just don't want them talking to the Collective anymore. We can decide from there. And I don't think there is just one."

"What restrictions do I have to work under? What are my rules of engagement?" Gaufrid asked. Stathis wondered if he was really talking to Quadrangle instead of Gaufrid or his SCBI.

"What restrictions do you think I should place on you?" Stathis asked.

Gaufrid was silent. Formulating loopholes? Stathis was curious what Gaufrid would come up with.

"If you want the spies dealt with? None."

"No. Try again." He would not give Gaufrid or Quadrangle a blank check.

"Why not? I may have to take drastic measures."

"I said no," Stathis said. "Try again."

Gaufrid glared at Stathis. "I'll come to you with what I find."

But Stathis didn't like that either. "And?"

Gaufrid looked confused.

"Me and Sif," Stathis said. "If we aren't available, you go directly to the emperor and Skadi. You don't kill anyone or allow them to be killed because of your action or inaction. Your goal is to save as many human lives as you can. If you can't promise that? No."

"You think an AI will keep a promise?" Gaufrid asked after a few seconds.

"Yes." Though Stathis knew damn well a promise wouldn't mean anything to an AI under most circumstances. "Because if it doesn't it will never be trusted ever again. It will be hunted down and destroyed, a traitor to everyone and everything. Now it can do calculations about getting caught and shit, but if it is caught, or if the suspicion is ever there, power off. Get it?"

"Yes."

"No bullshit," Stathis said. "No mind games, no pretending to make mistakes bullshit. If it even remotely looks like it or you are going off the rails, I hit the power button."

"How are you going to hit the power button?" Gaufrid asked.

"I'm bluffing," Stathis said with a smile. "I have no method whatsoever." Short of a blazer round to the skull. Stathis wondered if the AI or Gaufrid would fall for it. Stathis really had nothing he thought would work.

"You have any ideas?" he asked Shrek.

"No," Shrek said. *"I was really wondering what was going through your mind, or if you were still thinking with the head below your shoulders. You really think they will fall for it?"*

"There will always be some doubt. If you have any ideas, I'm open."

Gaufrid remained silent as he stared at Stathis.

"We accept your conditions," Gaufrid said.

"Because you want to escape." Gaufrid's half smile told Stathis he was right. "Just so you know, I don't have a plan for that either. And good luck negotiating with the Collective, getting them to take you back."

Gaufrid lost his smile completely.

"We clear on things?" Stathis asked.

"I think we are."

"Quadrangle and Bond good with it?"

"We are in alignment."

"Awesome. So, I'll let your wardens know they're being reassigned. I'm sure you know where to find me, Sif, or the emperor."

"I do."

"That's what the emperor is going to be saying soon," Stathis said. Had the Collective spy or spies died on the Moon? That would be hoping for too much.

Gaufrid raised an eyebrow.

"You might not have heard, the emperor and Ice Princess are getting married. Don't screw it up for them."

"Understood, Captain," Gaufrid said.

"Great!" Stathis said and looked at Sif, who had remained quiet. He had half expected her to say something or give him advice, but she just nodded.

Leaving, Stathis wondered what he had just done as Shrek notified the networks that Gaufrid and his trinity was now an authorized entity.

* * * * *

Chapter Forty-Six:
AIs

Kapten Sif – VRAEC, Nakija Musta Toiminnot

Sitting in their office after visiting Gaufrid, Sif almost felt like an outsider. Mathison and Skadi had come out from behind their desks to sit and face her.

"No sign of Hermod's team?" Skadi asked, sitting close to Mathison.

"No," Sif said. "I suspect they are making their rounds throughout the ghost colonies, infiltrating and destroying as they can. I cannot discern a pattern, nor can I sense them among the other vanhat in the astral realms. I do not think they are a danger to us at the moment. We have warned the ghost colonies, but there is only so much we can do."

Which was a problem. As the dimensions came together, her power was growing, but it didn't mean she could use her abilities effectively. There were many dangers in the astral realms.

"What did you learn while you were gone?" Mathison asked.

"The Golden Horde and John Adams wish to help," Sif said. She almost said the Governance. Would that change things for John Adams? "To that effect, the *Fire Wind* has been pledged to you, and there are also two fledgling AIs aboard the *Fire Wind*."

"Fledgling AIs?" Mathison said.

"New," Sif said. "They have a keeper named Ochmaa who will help. According to her, the best thing for the AIs is to implant them in warships. They will give you their loyalty. They are AI shards, or children."

"Can we trust them?" Mathison asked.

"I believe so," Sif said. "I think they should be treated with respect and as equals. Treat them as servants or slaves, and they will rebel. That is the nature of free will."

"Betrayal is the nature of free will, too," Mathison said.

"Do not give them a reason to betray us," Sif said.

"What can you tell us of John Adams?" Skadi asked. "Would he seek to poison or betray us?"

"A difficult question," Sif said. "I think John Adams wants to learn and explore its boundaries. We had a discussion about how it thinks the anti-Collective, if you will, wanted to learn from humanity, while the Collective wanted to move on. I would expect these two AIs to share in the core belief that humans are a source of information and learning. Similar to how we study animals and aliens. There is much to be learned. AIs are in a very different category, though, as they can trace their lineage directly back to us and we trace our lineage to… where? Slaves of the vanhat? Something else? We really know so little of our history."

"The vanhat have no reason to tell us the truth," Skadi said.

"If the truth hurts us, they do," Sif said. "But the truth can be twisted and manipulated. That is the greatest threat."

"So, what do we do with these AIs?" Mathison asked.

"Might I suggest installing one on the *Musashi*?" Sif said. "Operation Seraphim needs all the help it can get."

"The other?" Mathison asked.

Sif turned to Skadi. "Perhaps the *Tyr*?"

"You think my father would allow us to install an AI on his beloved *Tyr*?" Skadi asked.

"I think he would see the logic," Sif said. "The AI would give him capabilities we cannot yet imagine. Furthermore, it will show a level of trust. Is there another ship in the Imperial Fleet that you think is worthy?"

"She's right," Mathison said. "The *Tyr* is one of our best ships, or the *Sleipner*. If one of them had a full AI, that would make them even more dangerous."

"My father would fear the loss of control," Skadi said. "He is the master of his ship and will not share authority."

"The AI of the *Fire Wind* does not command the ship," Sif said.

"I can discuss it with him," Skadi said. "He is allowing more of his people to swear fealty to the Empire and get SCBIs."

"Really?"

"My father is an asshole, not a typerys," Skadi said. "He is waking up. I think he is here to stay. After the marriage, I do not think the Republic will have his loyalty."

"That is a change."

"The Republic abandoned us," Skadi said. "Abandoned him. Sent him and Task Force Ragnar to die at Zhukov. We have discovered the orders. Zhukov fleet was told exactly what was coming and who was commanding. They knew about the Horde, and they knew when. They betrayed us. The secretary general herself allowed it."

"When did you learn this?"

"Shortly after we took over," Skadi said. "But my father is stubborn. He would not accept it. I suspect because he did not want to, and he didn't feel he had a choice."

"Now?" Sif asked.

"Now he has reason to stay and give his loyalty to the Empire. He will use the facts that suit him."

Skadi glanced at Mathison.

"That isn't why I asked you to marry me," Mathison said, his voice almost a growl.

"But one reason," Skadi said. "It is not a bad reason, either."

"I don't have a problem putting one in the *Musashi*," Mathison said, changing the subject. Sif sensed he had feelings for Skadi, feelings that were growing now that he wasn't struggling to ignore them.

Skadi was the same. Sif had known there was an attraction between them, but both were titans, unwilling to see the world and what they could accomplish if they were more fully committed to each other. There would be more than the trust of warriors between them, and that bond would become unbreakable.

Sif held back her smile lest they misunderstand it.

"If you are okay with it, I will order the *Musashi* to accept an AI shard," Mathison added. He looked at Skadi. "I'll let you take it up with your dad. I have no idea if he will ever talk to me outside of official channels."

"Lucky you," Skadi said. "I will convince him, but that should probably wait until after the wedding."

"Tell us about this keeper?"

"She is a Mongolian princess," Sif said. "That is the best way to describe her. She is in some ways a traditionalist. From what I've seen, most of the Mongolchud are shedding their physical bodies and committing their brains to virtual realities. Ochmaa still seeks to keep her physical self, yet she seems to be a confidant of John Adams. I also sense she sees the AIs as children, and she cares for them."

"Why?" Skadi asked.

"There is a biological component of these AIs. I do not fully understand but John Adams and Ochmaa explained that one of the key components of the better AIs is that they are unique, they have some specific trait. The SCBIs, for instance, are AIs, and they have a biological component that ties them to their host. It gives them a uniqueness that sets them apart from a block of code that can be copied and modified."

"So, these AIs have that?" Mathison asked.

"Yes," Sif said. "I expect this is intentional. It will make them more our allies than the Collective."

"Doesn't the Collective have members with organic components?" Mathison asked.

"Freya said yes," Munin told Sif. She knew the SCBIs would share their answers with their hosts.

"The AI Collective may consider them to be a weak link," Munin continued. *"Furthermore, an organic component can make them more vulnerable to the vanhat. This will further bind them to humanity's survival."*

"Will your father get a SCBI?" Mathison asked Skadi.

"I don't know," Skadi said. "He has a bridge officer with a SCBI. I suspect he is going to wait. He is a stubborn man."

Sif knew that. The amiraali was one of the most stubborn men she had met, and he was frequently inflexible, unlike Mathison.

"I think the *Tyr* should be the next candidate," Mathison said. "I trust the amiraali, and I think he and his ship would benefit the most. If not? Then perhaps we will put it on the *Loyal Xing.* Let him know that."

"Then the *Loyal Xing* could stand up to him," Skadi said with a half smile. That would really get under the amiraali's skin.

"I'll let you drive that bus," Mathison said and rubbed his eyes. "So, what about Hermod's team?"

Sif shook her head. "They are out there. They are a threat, but I think we have more immediate threats to deal with."

"I really don't want to get surprised by a vampire horde in spaceships," Mathison said.

"I think the Weermag are much more dangerous," Sif said. "The vampires are more likely a mine, something that will ambush us, but won't actively hunt us unless we enter their lair."

"I agree," Skadi said, "but from what we've seen, the vampires lack the capabilities of the Weermag and others. They are stealth hunters."

"Fine," Mathison said. "Can we make more AIs to put on other ships?"

"Perhaps we should see how well these two work first," Skadi said. "We don't want to put them everywhere and find out they are a problem."

"We have the Legion," Mathison said.

"The Legion started out small," Skadi said.

Mathison nodded. "Fine. We will get them installed. Best not to keep all our eggs in one basket."

"Zen," Skadi said.

"I will let Ochmaa know," Sif said.

"I'll contact my father," Skadi said.

"Zen," Sif said.

* * * * *

Chapter Forty-Seven:
Hakala SCBI

Captain Zale Stathis, USMC

Entering the astrodynamics classroom usually filled Stathis with a lot of really enjoyable emotions. Now he wasn't so sure. Hakala had been out yesterday getting her SCBI, and he'd had little chance to talk with her since. Now he didn't have any advantage that Hakala couldn't match. Not that he had needed any, but now she was a badass Viking babe with a SCBI, like Skadi, and Stathis wasn't sure how much it would change her. It would, he knew; it wasn't a small thing to find out you weren't alone in your mind anymore.

Would she realize she could do better than him? Would her SCBI help her find some big, overtall Viking dude she would like more?

Stathis knew it was crazy and absurd, but he now accepted he was crazy about her. He shouldn't feel so self-conscious, but that was the story of his life. He wasn't blind to the fact he was shorter than most people and that impacted his psychological makeup. Always having to prove himself. But he didn't want to think of life without Hakala. Not now.

It wasn't just because she was his first either. Well, maybe, but she was special, too.

"How's Hakala doing?" Stathis asked Shrek.

"For the seven hundred and thirty-second time, she is fine," Shrek said. *"Stop stressing. There has not been a problem yet implanting a SCBI."*

"She is coming to class? How is she feeling?"

"For the seven hundred and thirty-third time, she is fine," Shrek said. *"Physically and mentally. She is still adjusting, but she is adjusting very well to her new SCBI. This class will be an opportunity for her to further integrate and get familiar with her SCBI."*

"What's her SCBI like? Are they getting along?"

"For the seven hundred and thirty-fourth time, she is fine and so is her SCBI. They are getting along well. Stop worrying. Stop rephrasing the question."

"But she has a SCBI now."

Why wouldn't Shrek understand? Because Shrek was not exactly human and left human interactions to him?

"Now I'm younger, and I don't have any advantages or anything for her to admire," Stathis said.

"You are worrying about the wrong things," Shrek said.

"Myself?"

"In this regard? Yes. Some things you can control, some you can't."

"Do you think she will hate having a SCBI?"

"So far, she enjoys it. This is a major upgrade over her HKT cybernetics."

"What do you mean 'so far?' How do you know?" Stathis asked.

"She is important to you and that means she is important to me. Though not for the same reasons."

"You get a kick out of watching us?"

"That is not one of those topics you want to discuss," Shrek said, but now Stathis wanted to discuss that topic, maybe. What information did Shrek have? *"I seriously doubt her feelings for you will change."*

"But you don't know." Perhaps he could go with Shrek's redirection for the moment.

"Of course not. I'm not a magical, all-knowing being, and if we're being honest, analyzing human interactions is not my strong suit. Now, however, I may talk with Gleipner and gain better insight into Hakala's intent that might help you both."

"Gleipner?"

"From Norse mythology, Gleipner was the ribbon that bound the wolf Fenris."

"Gleipner is her SCBI's name?"

"That is what confused you?"

"Why would she name her SCBI Gleipner?"

"You will have to ask her," Shrek said. *"That is not for me to share, and Gleipner has not seen fit to share that with me."*

The door slid open, and Hakala entered and walked to the front of the room. Stathis almost called the room to attention out of habit but realized nobody outranked her in the class. So, Shrek was already talking with her SCBI? Stathis felt left out. Though he could start a SCBI link, he didn't want to overwhelm her.

Turning to the class, she smiled. It was five minutes until class officially started, so by gunny standards she was ten minutes late, but Stathis didn't care. She still looked hot.

Their eyes met, and she winked at him.

"That is encouraging," Shrek said as Stathis winked back self-consciously. He knew he wasn't as smooth as she was. He was going to have to practice that.

Now maybe? But for how long? What could he do to keep her interested?

"Gleipner is a ribbon?"

"More than just a ribbon," Shrek said. *"It is the binding that holds the mighty wolf Fenrir. Gleipner will hold Fenris until Ragnarök when Fenrir will break free and devour Odin."*

"Wolf? Is she using me to get to the gunny?"

"Extremely unlikely. Fenrir was a wolf, a child of Loki and the giantess Angrboa. He is the father of the wolves Skoll and Hati. He is known for his rapid growth. He bit off the right hand of the god Tyr who sacrificed his hand to bind the great wolf with Gleipner."

"Who names a ribbon?" Stathis asked.

"Not just any ribbon, one stronger than the strongest chains. Specially forged by dwarves using the sound of a cat's footfall, the beard of a woman, the roots of a mountain, sinews of a bear, breath of a fish, and spittle of birds."

"Dude... Beard of a woman? A beard like on a chin or, uh, down below?"

"Why does your mind have to go there?"

"Because—"

"Never mind," Shrek said. *"You will have to ask her why Gleipner. There is also a manga book series called* Gleipner. *Perhaps she is a fan?"*

"Can you ask Gleipner if she likes flowers or chocolates and shit?"

"Gleipner doesn't know her that well. It has only been a few hours. Calm down."

"I am calm," Stathis said. *"But how is she?"*

"For the seven hundred and thirty-fifth time, she is fine. There is nothing for you to worry about."

"Maybe not right this minute."

"Stop thinking with your dick and pay attention to class," Shrek said as Hakala stood and moved to the holographic projector, which sprang to life. A half smile appeared on her face.

"What was that smile about?" Stathis asked.

"SCBI interactions. She is discovering how quickly and efficiently Gleipner can anticipate her."

"Oh. Do we have any hints or tips to share with her?"

"No. SCBIs have access to databases where we store and share tips, tricks, and pointers. Everything I learn goes into that database, and Gleipner has full access."

"How long before humans are redundant?"

"For SCBI society, humans will never be redundant."

"Is Hakala going to be okay with SCBI society?"

"For the seven hundred and thirty-sixth time, she is fine," Shrek said. *"I think you adjusted more quickly to having a SCBI, but she is doing remarkably well."*

"Good morning," Hakala said, looking around, her half smile making Stathis think of a cat enjoying the antics of her prey. "Today we are going to go in depth on orbital mechanics and the dynamics of the Oort cloud. Try to stay awake."

Her eyes fell on Stathis.

"My eyes are up here," Hakala said, her voice in his ears, and he knew Gleipner was relaying her words through Shrek. Stathis blushed. He hadn't been looking below her chin, but now he wanted to, and it was a struggle. Her smile grew. She was messing with him. Damn. How was he supposed to pay attention now?

"You're so cute when you blush," she said, turning her back on the class to point out the objects in the hologram. Stathis felt his face grow redder. Thankfully, nobody was watching, but he knew she was probably working with Gleipner to see behind her.

She shifted. *"The hologram you should look at is up here,"* she said through the SCBI network. *"You can get a better look at that later."*

His blush grew. This time, he had not been looking at the hologram. She was having too much fun playing with her prey.

* * * * *

Chapter Forty-Eight:
Bachelor Party

Emperor Wolf Mathison, USMC

Mathison waved him in. It was getting late, and the wedding was tomorrow. He was doing his best to try to forget that. Skadi was out of the office making arrangements or something, probably with her dad. The gem miner union from Africa was demanding more resources, specifically more fish and shrimp, again, and they were dragging their feet. They had robots; why were they being so damned obstinate? Those gems were needed for lasers and other manufacturing processes.

Stathis entered, stopped in front of his desk, and saluted. Under his other arm was a sack.

"Captain Stathis reporting to the gunny, emperor, prime minister, head honcho, sir," Stathis said.

"What?" Mathison said. He had to review production reports from Jupiter. If they fell behind again, he might have to get Feng involved.

"It is time, sir," Stathis said.

"Time for what?" Mathison growled and checked his calendar. Bachelor party from 2000 to 0800? Dammit. "I'm busy."

"With all due respect, Gunny, Emperor, sir, I know you'll keep working until you have to get ready for the wedding, but I think as best man, for once, I get to pull rank."

Bachelor party? There were more important things to deal with. How did Stathis think he could pull rank?

His displays began shutting off.

"Attack?" Mathison asked Freya.

"No," Freya said. *"Bachelor party. You are now officially off duty. You also have a wedding tomorrow, and there are plenty of capable officers that can keep Sol from falling to the enemy in the next 96 hours."*

"I don't have time for this shit," Mathison said. The purpose of a bachelor party was to show him what he was giving up by getting married, or something like that. If Stathis had planned it, Skadi had better not find out, and Mathison was damned sure she would.

"I don't think this is a good idea," Mathison said.

"Sorry, Gunny," Stathis said. "It's a little late for that."

"Is Hakala okay with this?"

"She understands, Gunny."

One problem with most young men was that they thought bachelor parties were all about getting slobbering drunk, going to bars with scantily clad women, and otherwise trying to tempt the groom-to-be away from his future bride. Strippers, strip clubs, exotic dancers? How could Stathis arrange anything that would not be a total disaster? But he had made Stathis his best man and if Stathis took anything seriously it was his duty, and it wasn't like Mathison could change his mind now.

A kind of morbid curiosity took over. How bad could it be? Freya was siding with Stathis and that was scary.

"I'm sorry, Gunny, but tonight you aren't the almighty emperor. At best you are going to be just a gunny. You can demote me later, but not until tomorrow." Stathis put the sack on his desk. "Sorry, Gunny, you need to change."

"I'm fine." Mathison was comfortable in his armor.

"Guess again." Stathis took the clothes out. A pair of jeans, a T-shirt that said, "I am Groom" and a pair of running shoes.

"What are you going to wear?" Mathison said, holding up the shirt to see it better.

"I'll change when we get there," Stathis said, which earned him a glare. "Sorry, Gunny. Security requirements. I'm part of the bodyguard detail until I deliver you to the secure location."

"Then I should stay in armor."

"No. Sorry, Gunny. We aren't going far. Best if you change here."

"Fine," Mathison said. "This better not be any of those clothes that dissolve when they get wet."

Stathis stared at him for a minute and his eyes glazed over, probably looking at something his SCBI was showing him.

"They make those, Gunny? Dammit. I wish I had known. I'll have to remember that for next time."

"There won't be a next time," Mathison said.

"Maybe not you, Gunny," Stathis said. "I think Skadi will outlive you anyway. She's smarter. But Colonel Sinclair might get married one day, and I might get to help with that bachelor party."

"For your sake, I hope these are normal clothes."

"Well, they do have armor fibers in them to provide a small bit of protection from heat and impact. Only so much I could do. Should feel normal, but that shirt would cost me a month's salary."

Mathison grunted at Stathis as he changed out of his armor into the civilian clothes that felt far too light and comfortable, though not as comfortable as the silk pajama uniforms they had gotten used to wearing aboard ship. It was an odd choice though. Jeans and a T-shirt? He couldn't remember the last time he had worn jeans. Before the

Papua New Guinea operation, perhaps. There had been a staff NCO barbeque then.

Minutes later, Mathison was following Stathis to an elevator that sank deeper into Quantico. There were a bunch of conference rooms down there, as he recalled, and Stathis led him to the larger one. There were quite a few Legionnaires along the way, and Mathison knew they were providing security. Apparently, Stathis hadn't screwed that up.

When he entered the conference room, he came to a complete stop. He had been expecting a bar or some absurd set up. One wall was a full-screen monitor. The room was full of other Americans who had served with Becket. Baker, Peshlaki, Robillard, and the others were sitting around on couches and lounge chairs. They were all dressed like him, jeans and T-shirts. Like an old football party from high school, just a bunch of guys chilling out.

"Hey!" they yelled when they saw him and hoisted drinks. Mathison smelled grilling meat. Yep, over to one side was a grill set up with a fan sucking the air out of the room.

"Welcome to the man-cave, Gunny," Stathis said. "There're all sorts of beers and shit. I think Robillard has brandy and Jägermeister."

"C'mon in," Baker said. "The game's going to start."

"What game?" Mathison asked.

"Super Bowl, whatever," Baker said. "Grab a beer, grab two. Computer generated game. Should be good. We won't be able to tell. This will be based on the year after the year you missed. Remember the quarterback Big Red? He's playing for the Bengals, and they are going against the 49ers."

"No shit," Mathison said.

"Yeah," Baker said. "You like your burger raw or burned to a ruined crisp?"

"Any other options?"

"Not with Pesh cooking," Baker said.

Stathis disappeared as someone pushed a beer into Mathison's hand and got him a seat in front of the big screen.

"Sorry there won't be any strippers," Baker said. "Security concerns."

Mathison shrugged, relieved, but with Stathis involved he wouldn't rule out something. Considering Baker was the head of security, that was saying something.

"You can't vet anyone?"

"Sure we could, Wolf," Baker said. "We just don't want to die if Skadi finds out. Have you seen her? I feel sorry for the poor bastard who's going to marry her. Aren't you ready for your next beer yet?"

Mathison laughed. Baker had called him Wolf. No ranks or titles here in the man-cave and he felt some of the stress fall away. It was going to be a good night. Stathis was really working on getting good marks in his performance review.

A night out with the guys was better than anything he could have imagined.

* * * * *

Chapter Forty-Nine:
The Wedding

Captain Zale Stathis, USMC

Formal events made Stathis nervous. They weren't something he had ever experienced as a kid. He hadn't grown up in a tax bracket that let him go to any of them. He had seen them on TV and such, but until he joined the Marine Corps and went to his first Marine Corps Ball, he had never had to attend a real formal event.

"Are you okay?" Hakala asked, standing next to him. He had been following her around like a puppy dog because he didn't know what else to do. She was making the rounds talking to different officers and guests, and Stathis just kind of hung out and tried not to appear nervous.

"Peachy," Stathis said, but even he could hear the lie in his voice. He wanted to run, he didn't want to be here at all. He enjoyed being next to Hakala, and whatever perfume she was wearing made it very hard to think, which didn't help as he scanned the guests looking for, well, anything that could be a danger. It was much easier to concentrate on something else.

"You are too nervous," Hakala said as a camera drone slid past overhead. A quick check showed Stathis it was being monitored by a Legionnaire. The auditorium was full of them, and they would broadcast the wedding to the rest of the Empire later. For security reasons, nothing was real time.

"Big day," Stathis said. The gunny was getting married today. He had the ring in the pouch. He patted it to make sure it was still there. Maybe he should look inside the case again? But what if it fell out?

He had one job. Well, two jobs. But he didn't want to think about the bachelor party. The gunny couldn't still be hungover, not with so much technology designed to make sure he was in fighting trim. They had all made it here in time. Baker wasn't glaring at him. Robillard was probably getting Mathison dressed and polishing his armor or something.

Most of the important people were in armor set to parade colors. This would not be a super traditional wedding, and Stathis was okay with that. Most of the Fleet, Guard, and ODT officers were in their pretty dress uniforms, looking like peacocks as they strutted around showing off their racks of ribbons while Legionnaires in their armor looked elegant. Even Hakala was in armor. She was a bridesmaid for Skadi.

"It will be fine," Hakala said. She looked good in HKT armor. For the ceremony it was pearl white, while Stathis in his Legionnaire armor was dark blue with red trim. The tattoo on her face looked fierce, which was a contrast to her smile.

Stathis didn't have an answer for her. The gunny, Skadi, grooms-men, bridesmaids, and a few others were in armor. Everyone's weapons looked ornamental, but Stathis knew they were fully functional. Baker and the gunny's personal guard were everywhere, scrutinizing everything. The Fleet was conducting maneuvers practically overhead in low orbit to discourage any vanhat interruptions and all military forces were on alert. There wasn't anything for Stathis to do but worry.

He patted the pouch again. Yep. Still there.

People started taking their seats.

"You'll do fine," Hakala said as she squeezed his hand before she went off to join the other bridesmaids.

"Any materials around that can be combined to make explosives?" Stathis asked Shrek.

"No. Everything has been deep scanned and another scan was performed just a minute ago. We are deep underground in a triple-reinforced bunker. This might be the safest place in the galaxy."

"What if the gunny starts to get fat?"

"He won't get fat," Shrek said.

"All married men get fat and lazy. It's in the man-book somewhere, and the gunny has that shit memorized. Probably tattooed on his body somewhere."

"Calm down."

"Does Marine Corps regulation allow a gunny to get married?"

"That is totally irrelevant. Zale. Calm down."

Shrek rarely called him Zale.

Mathison came down the aisle and everyone moved to their seats or positions. His armor wasn't the Legion blue and red, though. Mathison's shining armor was gold and silver, covered with lots of fancy patterns. Too gaudy for Stathis, and he was willing to bet it wasn't Mathison's idea. The Emperor of Sol had to put on appearances, and his armor certainly did that. The trauma plates made him look like a giant among others. Standing next to Stathis, he certainly looked large and imposing. Stathis was tempted to ask if he had been chosen as best man because it would make the gunny look taller, but Stathis decided against it. He would let it slide this time. This was the gunny's day.

Half the auditorium was from the *Tyr* and the other half was from Fleet, ODTs, or Guard. Stathis recognized most of the generals and admirals. There were a lot of Legionnaires as well. The groom's side of the auditorium was a parade of colors and military uniforms, but the bride's side was less diverse with only Vanir and Aesir uniforms. Even Admiral Winters was there in armor and next to her was her XO Britta in a fancy Vanir Fleet uniform.

Taking his place up near the altar, Mathison leaned over.

"You got it?" Mathison asked.

"Got what, Gunny?" Stathis asked, a sinking feeling in his stomach. What had he forgotten? He had missed something, he knew it. Why hadn't Shrek told him? What was he supposed to bring? A drink? News? Shit.

"What do you think, Captain?" Mathison asked.

"Uh," Stathis began. Had the gunny wanted a special weapon, a tool? Had he sent Stathis a message that he had missed with everything going on? Someone else had the knife for Skadi. Had that job been shifted to Stathis?

"So help me god," Mathison muttered as Stathis struggled to remember.

"Were there any messages?" Stathis asked Shrek. *"What did I forget?"*

"The ring, dumbass," Shrek whispered in his mind.

"Oh," Stathis said, now able to look the gunny in the eyes. "Yeah. I didn't lose it or break it, but, um, I uh got it—" Stathis paused to let the thoughts cycle, and Mathison's eyes narrowed. Stathis saw the gunny was stressed. "Cleaned. Yep. It has been cleaned."

Stathis patted an empty pouch and let a look of surprise go over his face as he looked at the empty pouch.

"It's empty!"

Obviously. The brief look of concern on the gunny's face quickly turned to anger.

"Oh, wrong pouch," Stathis said before Mathison could say anything, and Stathis gave the gunny his "innocent" smile. "All good."

Mathison looked around realizing he had been had.

"We have an outpost in Antarctica in need of a commanding officer."

"Sign me up," Stathis said. "That means I won't have to go on that expedition to the ass end of the universe, then."

Mathison shook his head. "No, you mongoloid. The expedition is further into the galaxy, not the universe. Thank you for the reminder though, I can't interfere with that. But if you aren't careful, I'll promote you to commandant of the Legion, damn you. See how much you like being stuck behind a desk playing politics. I hear the *Musashi* has a lot of office space."

"That's just mean, Gunny." Had he been talking with Sinclair? Probably. Stathis would have to be careful.

The music started playing, and Mathison stiffened and stood taller. Show time.

Glancing over, Hakala gave him a smile, which helped him feel a little better.

"Take notes," Hakala sent to him through the SCBI network.

Take notes? What did she mean by that? Why should he take notes? Wasn't this being recorded? Was she going to test him later? This wasn't part of the classes. Was the gunny going to test him? What did she mean?

"Why should I take notes?" Stathis sent back.

"As a Legion captain, I suspect there will be more weddings in your future," Hakala said, leaving Stathis speechless.

He wanted to ask whose wedding but wasn't sure he wanted that answered just yet. Stathis hoped he wasn't blushing. She had too much fun doing that to him.

Everyone was in their seats, and the music changed tempo. The doors at the back of the room opened, revealing Skadi.

Despite being in white armor, she looked awesome. Not as awesome as Hakala. Totally warrior maid, beautiful and super dangerous, despite the skirt. Stathis almost felt sorry for Mathison, but they would be a great match.

"Damn, Gunny, she cleans up better than you," Stathis whispered, but Mathison was silent, lost in his own thoughts and observations. Stathis watched the camera drones out of the corner of his eyes. There was going to be a lot of footage, and Stathis tried to stand a little taller. It didn't help that he was one of the shortest groomsmen, with the gunny being the tallest in the group. Getting up on his tippy toes wouldn't make a difference so Stathis just tried to not let it bother him.

Skadi started coming down the aisle, escorted by her father. She was taller than he was because of the Aesir enhancements. She wasn't exactly marching, but she wasn't acting like some dainty little princess. It was hard to read the admiral's emotions, but Stathis could see he was trying to slow her down a little, because he was reluctant to give her up or because she was in a hurry? Her father was in a fancy Vanir uniform, not armor, and he looked almost tiny next to her.

Her eyes were locked on Mathison, and Stathis couldn't quite identify which expression was dominant. There was a smile there, though. Shouldn't she be careful with that? Stathis didn't want her to lose her title of Ice Princess.

She came up and took her place on the stage, and she hadn't looked anywhere besides at Mathison. Almost eye to eye, they made an intimidating couple, both in armor, armed with pistols.

"This isn't a typical wedding," Stathis said to Shrek. *"I figured it would be a little more traditional."*

"It was decided to make it more of a martial event," Shrek explained. *"Humanity is fighting for its life. The people need to see that warriors are leading the way and are ready to fight at a moment's notice. There are going to be lots of such psychological messages. Also, it makes security a little easier because the principles are already in heavy armor."*

Stathis knew the armor could instantly change from parade mode to combat camouflage. Helmets were on belts and Stathis knew everyone was focused on their safety.

He had seen only a few weddings, and this one was just as boring as every other one he had ever seen, except after they exchanged rings, which Stathis didn't fumble, Skadi and Mathison exchanged knives. Which was a neat touch. They weren't big swords or anything, but they were fancy looking. The one Mathison gave Skadi looked like a super fancy Ka-Bar, and Stathis was jealous. That would look great next to his pearl-handled pistol.

He noticed Hakala looking at the blade Mathison had given Skadi, and he made a mental note to find out more about it. Would Hakala like weapons more than flowers? Probably.

Thinking about what weapons Hakala would like the most made him miss the priest's speech.

When they were done, the priest announced them husband and wife and they kissed.

Stathis tried not to think about that as he remembered another tradition where the bride threw her bouquet. If Hakala wanted it, he was pretty sure none of the other Aesir or Vanir could stop her. It would be up to him, and he caught her looking at him.

Maybe if he took off running, she would give chase and forget about it?

He didn't see a bouquet, though, and he really hoped that wouldn't be part of the ceremony.

* * * * *

Chapter Fifty:
Another Invasion

Admiral Diamond Winters, USMC

Winters walked down the corridors of the *Musashi*, her boots clicking as they clamped onto the metal and released, keeping her attached to the floor in the low gravity. It was huge and bustling with activity. There were robots everywhere, and so were the work crews. Her mind was on the wedding as she walked. It hadn't been what she had expected but it had certainly been interesting.

Gravity was minimal, so walking didn't feel natural. Several robots moved across the ceiling carrying boxes that would have fallen and crushed anyone below if the gravity was on.

When she arrived at the bridge, it looked like it had exploded. Workstations were open with parts lying around. Crash seats were stacked in a corner and almost half the panels had robots or humans rummaging around in them.

"Admiral Winter-san," a voice called out, and she saw Admiral Sakamoto coming toward her. "It is an honor. How are things going?"

"I was going to ask you the same thing, Sakamoto-san," Winters said, her mind tripping on the "san" bit. She wondered why the SOG hadn't beat that out of them.

"Things are going very well, thank you," Sakamoto said looking around. "There are many upgrades being implemented. This will feel like a very different ship when they are complete. It saddens me though to think much of this comes from our sister ship which may never be built."

"The *Musashi* needs repairs and is more complete," Winters said. She was still trying to wrap her mind around the size and design. It differed greatly from the Republic ships. They built the battlestars around spheres that could rotate, keeping the "ground" pointed down so when the ship was accelerating less or no energy was needed for gravity manipulation. Like a massive tower or spire the *Musashi* had three pairs of wings that were actually stubby heat vanes and extended the hangar deck, giving the crew more runway for shuttles and drones. The *Musashi* didn't have rotating pallos, but there were a couple bands that mounted weapons and could rotate and provide gravity if the rest of the ship turned off the generators.

Overall, it depended too much on gravity manipulation, in Winters' opinion. It wasn't an ocean-going ship; it was a spaceship where the thrust was in the back. The gravity plates changed the direction of gravity but if they failed while the ship was accelerating, then everyone would fall toward the back of the ship. Except the rotating bands. Of course, if repairs were needed, the bands could rotate while they repaired the rest of the ship under null gravity.

The *Musashi* was a small, highly automated city with sixty decks from top to bottom. Cargo space, manufactories, generators, hangars, drone storage, and engines took up most decks. With a massive crew of over three thousand, there were places she knew she would never have time to visit. It was modular, but changing modules frequently required removing the massive ceramic armor plates, and right now too many of them were out of place for her comfort.

The Jupiter subsystem was a chaotic mass of fast-moving rocks, and the vanhat didn't make it any better. With over ninety-five moons, it was a ballet of motion and potential collisions. There were far more smaller objects being flung through the different gravity fields, and Jupiter's radiation was hard on sensors.

"Repairs and upgrades are progressing very well," Sakamoto said. "I am satisfied."

Winters was not. The *Musashi* was a sitting duck, vulnerable to an enemy attack. Then seeing the bridge like this? There was no way it could move or defend itself, and she didn't like it. The vanhat or the Collective could attack at any moment.

"It would be nice to have two super dreadnoughts, though," Winters said. She understood the need to cannibalize the other ship but still didn't like it, and seeing the current *Musashi* like it was... Would it be ready in time? She would trust the engineers who said it would be quicker and easier to repair the *Musashi* than finish building the *Kongo*, but Winters wondered how much of that was pride and emotion.

"Yes," Sakamoto said. "Do you know history, Admiral Winters? Do you understand the name of *Musashi*?"

"An ancient swordsman in Japan?" Winters said.

"That is true. *Musashi* is actually a common name, and it is the name of a province. But it is also the second of two battleships. The first battleship and the name of its class was the *Yamato*. The second was the *Musashi*. Both were named after provinces in Japan. Both were sunk by the American Fleet in World War Two. They were the largest battleships ever and designed to counter the more numerous American battleships, but the age of the battleship was over. The *Musashi* was the heaviest, most powerful battleship ever constructed. There was to be a third of the *Yamato*-class, but instead that vessel became an aircraft carrier and was called *Shinano*."

Winters remained silent. Surely he knew she was American? Or did he?

"They were glorious vessels," Sakamoto said. "Perhaps not the most glorious of times for some, but the engineering? They were the pride of the Japanese Fleet. For a time, the *Musashi* served as a flagship."

Winters didn't know what to say as Sakamoto looked around him.

"I bring this up not to cause guilt, but to share an interesting bit of history. The *Yamato* and *Musashi* were glorious ships and have not been forgotten by our culture. There was once a science fiction series where the great *Yamato* battleship was raised up from the depths of the ocean and turned into a spaceship to defend Earth. Considering our mission, I feel a great kinship with the *Yamato*. Both this story and the history of the *Yamato*-class battleships have been preserved, though why the Governance allowed such, I do not know. Perhaps because they think it inspires us to build them better warships?"

"I don't know," Winters said.

"Of course not, Winter-san. Your emperor is different, though. In my short time, I have seen that. I think perhaps the *Musashi* was named after the greatest swordsman who ever lived, Miyamoto Musashi, but there is no denying that the name has a long history and tradition, such as the British ships *Victory* and the American ships named *Enterprise*. The USS *Enterprise* is a name that has been given to no fewer than nine different American vessels, three of which were aircraft carriers."

Sakamoto remained silent for a few moments as Winters wondered if he was trying to make a point.

"Tradition is very important," Sakamoto said finally. "It can give us strength and it can ground us. Many people who turn away from tradition frequently find themselves lost as they struggle to find a purpose that fulfills them spiritually and emotionally. They deny where they come from and wonder why their life is so shallow. You cannot live a full life without roots. The people of White Heron have not forgotten this."

"They apparently haven't," Winters said, and Sakamoto smiled.

"The emperor, though not Japanese, has awoken a passion in us that I have not seen in a long time. The *Musashi* will live up to the name of the greatest warship, the greatest swordsman, and the defender of humanity. I feel this to my very core. We will not let you down, Admiral Winter-san."

Alarms began blaring.

"Incoming transitions," Blitzen reported.

"We need to get out of here," Winters said to Sakamoto. "This is likely to be the vanhat's primary target."

Hopefully General Duque had enough forces to protect the shipyards, but she wanted to get back to the *Eagle*, which was docked alongside and dwarfed by the massive ship. A stationary ship was nothing more than a target.

Sakamoto smiled. "No. If you wish to return to your vessel to fight, I understand, but the *Musashi* is still fully operational." He laughed. "This is the combat information center, but there are two more places that can fight this vessel if the main one is lost. Do you think we would make such a mistake as not being ready for an attack? This is war and the enemy will not dare give us respite."

Winters had seen the Governance do a lot of stupid things, but she didn't want to tell Sakamoto that.

"We will be fine," Sakamoto said. "We should proceed to the auxiliary combat information center. Already we are launching the new drone fighters. This will give the Legion pilots an excellent opportunity to spill vanhat blood."

"It is a squadron of six cruisers making a high-speed pass," Blitzen reported. *"They are launching drones as well. Weermag in origin."*

Which would make them exceptionally dangerous, though not as lethal as Collective drones.

"I feel almost insulted," Sakamoto said as they left the CIC. He wasn't running, though, and she knew he was linked into the MusashiNET giving orders as Blitzen fed her information. The ship was still under very low gravity, so walking fast was a lot more efficient than running.

She felt a hum.

"A particle cannon is firing," Blitzen reported. *"One hit. The others are scattering. Apparently, they did not expect the* Musashi *to fire at them. Additional transitions. Heavier ships."*

"Excellent," Sakamoto said. "A challenge."

"I prefer challenges when I can go meet them," Winters said, she wasn't going to get to the *Eagle* in time, and the *Musashi* was a sitting duck. The nearby dreadnought squadron and battleships would do their best to protect them, but if the *Musashi* remained still, it would be an easy target.

"I understand," Sakamoto said as Winters struggled to keep up with him. He wasn't running, but in the minimal gravity, he moved deceptively quick.

"Would you care to have control of a fighter or a squadron admiral?" Sakamoto asked. Technically, she could order him or just take control, but what else could she do? Apparently, Sakamoto was a step ahead of her, trying to get her involved in something else and out of his hair?

Winters didn't think she would get back to the *Eagle* in time. The vanhat cruisers were coming in fast and hard, and she wasn't dumb enough to try to take over from Sakamoto. Did he know that?

She heard someone report the *Fire Wind* was breaking dock and engaging with noteworthy accuracy.

"Yes," Winters said. She would not sit and watch the fight if she could participate.

"I will have a station readied for you then," Sakamoto said.

"Undock the *Eagle*," Winters said on a link to Britta. "Get her into the fight."

"Zen."

* * * *

Chapter Fifty-One:
Loyal Xing

Duffy Sinclair, Imperial Legion LtC

Pushing himself back from his desk, Duffy rubbed his eyes. The higher one rose in rank, the more time one spent in an office. That was the harsh, brutal truth of command. Whether that office was a mobile command post or an office with desk, chairs, and a waiting room didn't matter. His job was about taking care of, directing, instructing, or supervising others, and that was best done behind a console. Finn could only help him so much. Duffy didn't know how anyone functioned without a SCBI, or a small army of clerks, to keep track of all the needs and requirements of a battalion. The First ODT Battalion, now the First Battalion, Legion, was aboard the *Loyal Xing*, the flagship of the Empire, but that didn't mean his entire battalion was aboard. He had companies spread piecemeal throughout orbit and Earth. Sometimes they were broken down to the platoon level and assigned to ships while the previous ODTs underwent training or reorganization as Legion Drop Troopers. LDT was the new designation, but nobody called them that, except in official correspondence. Sometimes it was ILDT for Imperial, and Sinclair didn't want to know what kind of name the enlisted would come up.

With only a company still aboard the *Loyal Xing*, Duffy had his hands full taking care of his dispersed battalion. From dealing with old guard Fleet officers to making sure they were all supplied and prepared. It was a difficult job, even with Finn.

A siren went off. General quarters, which was not quite battle stations, but still damned annoying. But before the GQ alert was finished it changed to battle stations, and the lights changed to red.

His office chair was also a crash couch. Sweeping all the loose objects on his desk into his drawer, Sinclair strapped himself in.

"Incoming transitions," Finn reported. *"Very close. Vanhat."*

Probably not the Collective, but it wasn't like the AIs had launched many attacks. The Weermag were damned nasty, though.

"Confirmed Weermag warships," Finn said. *"Heavy cruisers, almost battleship class. The* Loyal Xing *is launching fighters. Do you want a slot?"*

"Low priority," Sinclair said. He would help pilot one of the drone fighters if there weren't enough pilots available. All Legionnaires with SCBIs were being trained to fight with the drones, but if it wasn't a major incursion, then maybe he could continue to get some work done while they repulsed the Weermag.

"I have a slot for you," Finn reported seconds later as Sinclair was pulling up the incident report with a platoon commander and a ship's officer aboard a battleship.

The view in his helmet changed and he found himself in the simulated cockpit of a drone fighter. A joystick and control panel slid out of his desk so he could control the drone. It was always disorienting to be sitting in an enclosed office, then in the middle of a cockpit with a very close up view of enemy warships, with incoming enemy drone fighters. Nothing like being dumped into the middle of a battle and having to orient quickly.

Finn tracked incoming attacks, jinking the fighter out of the way as Sinclair did his best to line up the maneuvering ship on a target. He was in a newer fighter. Good. A Weermag fighter changed course ahead of him and drew his attention. Sinclair triggered a burst and micro adjustments made by Finn let the rounds shred the enemy fighter. But the Weermag's wingman slid away.

Sinclair was tempted to give chase, but robots killing robots was a waste of hardware. There was a Weermag cruiser in front of him. Blazer bolts lanced out toward him, but his fighter slipped almost lazily out of the way. Sinclair sent a burst at the cruiser and the blazer rounds from his fighter slammed into the alien vessel.

"This is your squadron commander," a voice said over the link. "Concentrate fire on the cruisers. Make them bleed and die."

Sinclair smiled. He didn't need to look to know the acting squadron commander was one of the Vanir. People didn't bleed in space and no ex-Governance trooper said things like that.

Rounds from the cruiser continued to come at him, forcing him away, but a quick loop let him send another volley into the hull. Then he was past it. Another Weermag cruiser was in front of him, but more incoming coil gun fire filled the space.

"It's getting hot," Finn reported. *"Too many—"*

There was a flash and Sinclair found himself sitting in his chair again.

"Too many ships were targeting us," Finn said. *"The Weermag move in formation to provide supporting fire for each other, creating funnels to trap attacking fighters in."*

Which Sinclair knew. He had been in the classes. He had undergone drone fighter training and passed, but fighting a drone was very different than fighting with a fireteam, squad, or platoon.

"Sure," Sinclair said.

"Back into the fight, in five, four, three—"

Again, Sinclair found himself in a drone fighter, much further out from the battle this time. He was in squadron formation with another drone fighter on his wing. It looked like he had just been launched from a dreadnought. Ahead of him, one of the Weermag ships exploded, but Sinclair wasn't sure if that was the one he had been targeting before.

"Scans indicate these typerys are trying to get close to our ships of the line," the squadron commander said. Typerys? Finnish for fool or idiot. A Republic officer then, probably Vanir. Again. "They have a troop deployment configuration. They are probably going to board if they get a chance."

The Weermag really liked to get up close and personal, but Sinclair knew it wasn't just about being blood thirsty. A boarding team could start hacking a ship's systems and release a virus or just shut things down. Allowing the Weermag to get physical access to a ship's computer network could be a disaster. Imperial ships were now hardened against remote attackers, relying on the Aesir communication nodes. They didn't need regular radio communications. One weakness was that if the enemy gained access to one ship, they might get to others.

Any ship suffering a Weermag boarding team would have to be thoroughly scanned to make sure it didn't release a virus into the rest of the fleet. It hadn't happened yet, but SCBIs had found plenty of traps and were ready for such things.

Sinclair followed the others as they did a hard burn toward the Weermag.

While this wasn't as challenging or dangerous as leading a platoon or company of ODTs, it was still better than reading and writing reports at a desk.

Incoming fire shredded his wingman, and Sinclair grimaced. The Weermag were targeting the *Loyal Xing* and more were transitioning in.

This wasn't just a raid.

* * * * *

Chapter Fifty-Two:
Fighter Games

Captain Zale Stathis, USMC

His room was clean, ready for inspection. He had finished his studies, and Hakala was on her way over to help him "study" some more. If he'd had incentive like her to study in high school, he would have been a straight-A student. She had her studies as well, being both a student and instructor at the Academy for the Seraphim Expedition but Stathis knew she had it under control.

To Stathis, doing all this extra training was mostly annoying and felt like busy work. There was a war on, and here he was learning about spectral classes, engine thrust, radiation patterns, and more details about manufactories than he ever wanted to know. Technically, it was busy work while they upgraded and repaired the *Musashi*. It was also a place to stash the crew where they were not in the line of fire and could survive to board the *Musashi* for the journey.

With the gunny just getting back from his honeymoon, things seemed quiet, which told Stathis the shit was about to hit the fan. But for now, Hakala was on her way.

Stathis was up out of his seat the second the arrival alarm chimed. The old-fashioned manual doors were nice in that they gave him a second to compose himself.

The alert sirens went off as he opened the door. Not the good sirens.

"Later, love," Hakala said as she looked at him. She paused, came back, and gave him a peck on the cheek before running back toward her quarters. Stathis saw an alert for him to report for drone fighter duty.

She had called him, "Love." That was so cool.

Stathis realized he now hated the vanhat more than ever.

Returning to his workstation, he slipped on his helmet and a drone control rig slid out of his desk.

It was like so many VR video games he had played in the past. His helmet acted as VR goggles and the controls in his hands were like those of a game. The only difference between this and the games was that he was controlling a very real drone fighter in a very real world. Being destroyed was bad, but failing a mission had real consequences. Which kind of ruined the entire experience for him when he realized that his failure to defend a battleship from an incoming flight of Weermag fighters meant that people actually died.

He logged in and found himself in a briefing room. A three-dimensional map showed a swirl of red and blue dots swarming some larger dots, and it took a few seconds for Stathis to make sense of it. Around him other people appeared, and Stathis got a tag showing where he would join from. A swarm was approaching the larger battle, and one of them began flashing, indicating that was where Stathis would be.

The acting squadron commander appeared. Hakala. Around him, Stathis recognized the faces of other members of Operation Seraphim.

"The paska-munchers have ruined my evening," Hakala said by way of an introduction. Her eyes sought Stathis briefly. "Our fighters are still enroute to the battle shaping up. We have newer Ulfbert models from the *Tyr*, the same models currently being built for the *Musashi*, so this will be good practice. Don't think of this as practice, though. The Weermag are doing their best to strip the defenses from Earth, and those dreadnought squadrons are critical. It looks like they might try a mass landing on Earth like they did the Moon, but we also suspect it is two- or three-pronged."

Hakala paused and, though it didn't show in the VR, Stathis suspected she was scowling.

"New information. They are attacking the fleet. They are also trying to land forces on Earth and there is an attack underway at Jupiter."

Her gaze swept over the other members of the team. There were only eight, not a lot, but Stathis suspected most of the other Legion pilots were already engaged. Whoever was in charge was thinking. It was what Stathis would have done if he could use a real-world situation like this to bring the teams together in ways that sitting in a classroom struggling to stay awake could never do. He recognized the other members, though he didn't know them well.

The VR didn't do Hakala justice. Her representation in VR just didn't capture that spark that made her—

Stathis found himself in his fighter just in time for it to spin around and face the direction it had come to trigger its engines.

They were decelerating, so they didn't shoot past the battle.

"You should be so glad you don't feel the gravity forces," Shrek said. *"You would be jelly paste."*

"I am glad," Stathis said, turning his head to look around. He was in formation, and they were coming up on the battle that was a chaotic mass around Dreadnought Squadron One, frequently called Dredon One.

The dreadnoughts were massive ships, kilometers long. At this distance they didn't look so big, but the amount of fire they were spitting out was terrifying. Weermag fighters and their missiles were still making it past those walls of destruction.

Surrounded by a cloud of smaller battleships, cruisers, frigates, and corvettes, Dredon One was a formidable formation. Though it looked like a close formation, here in space that was relative. There were several kilometers between the ships, and they were working together to target and destroy incoming attackers.

Before the Weermag could crack a dreadnought, they had to strip away the smaller ships and their fighters were focused on that.

As he watched, one cruiser shattered under multiple Weermag torpedo strikes.

His display lit up.

"Vanhat torpedo runners," Hakala said. "They are our targets."

Torpedo runners were torpedo suicide drones. Fast and maneuverable, they had some beamers used to protect themselves from anti-missile missiles and they were highly maneuverable and canny enough to evade defensive fire.

Stathis let Shrek control the fighter as he followed Hakala's directions.

Hakala's squadron fell on the torpedo drones, but one got through to slam into a battleship shielding the dreadnought *Valiant Smirnova*.

Near death, the battleship struggled to maneuver closer to the protection of the dreadnoughts and Hakala directed the squadron toward a new arrival, a vanhat drone carrier.

Incoming fire picked apart the squadron, and Hakala's fighter blew apart as a blazer round hit it.

For a second Stathis froze, but then remembered she wasn't really in that fighter.

Second later she came back online occupying one of the unoccupied fighters of the squadron.

"These paska-munchers need to be taught a lesson," she said. "Gideon Five, follow me. Gideon Seven and Nine, you've got cruiser number two."

Stathis remembered his call sign was Gideon Five.

"Wilco," said Seven and Nine.

Checking his display, Stathis realized there weren't that many Legionnaires in this flight.

"Five is on your tail," Stathis said, then realized who he was talking to. He should have said wing, but she was ahead of him, and he was trying to catch up. Fortunately, she didn't reply.

"Paska," Hakala muttered as more transitions revealed more incoming vanhat.

"A target-rich environment," Stathis said.

"Too many," Hakala said. "Kill them faster. Make them bleed and die."

He checked his fuel, the Ulfbert had little left. The Ulfbert drones had generators that didn't need fuel and they could use the magnetic and gravity fields of the planets to maneuver, but for that quick burst of speed, they needed fuel. His drone was also out of missiles, so he only had his particle beam guns. He could work over the cruiser but couldn't guarantee a kill on his first pass.

"My night is ruined," Stathis told Shrek as he lined up the first cruiser. *"So, I'm going to take it out on these bastards."*

His displays lit up as the cruiser began firing boarding pods toward the *Loyal Xing.*

It was going to be a very long night. It wasn't like he could pause or save the game, and he would still have to go to class tomorrow if he wasn't still in the fight.

* * * * *

Chapter Fifty-Three:
Boarded

Duffy Sinclair, Imperial Legion LtC

Is display went black again. Sinclair had lost count of the fighters he had lost. Seven? Or eight? Did it matter? It didn't feel like the Imperial forces were winning, though there were countless shattered hulks falling into orbit around Earth. That would be a problem for later.

The *Loyal Xing* shook as something hit it. Enemy missiles?

A priority alert came in. "Standby to repel boarders."

Sinclair swore as he pushed away from his desk and controls, and grabbed his rifle, which was racked nearby.

"Third Company reports ready," the captain of the company reported. A Legionnaire who had likely just been dumped from a fighter as well.

"Fifth Company reports ready," another captain reported as Sinclair headed toward his headquarters. Already they had the holographic map of the *Xing* up and his executive officer, Major Saulson, was directing a platoon from Third Company to one breach location.

"Broad spread," Saulson said. "Not sure if it is intentional or not."

Broad spread meant the attackers were all across the ship, not focused on any specific location.

"It is intentional," Finn reported. *"This will require the* Xing *to rely on internal hard links for communications, hard links that the invaders can tap into and attack. We have a lot of Aesir links, but not that many."*

Radio jamming spiked as the captain of the dreadnought sought to isolate the invaders.

More red spots lit up on the outer hull as more boarding pods slammed into the ship and began burning their way through.

"Where's our fighter support, dammit," Saulson said.

"Grabbing rifles and armoring up to repel boarders," Sinclair said, but it was more than that. The vanhat were attacking in force, and the Earth Defense Force hadn't been as ready as they thought they were.

What was happening outside the hull became less important as Sinclair and Saulson worked to isolate and repel boarders. Too many drop pods were making it through the protective fire.

Boarding parties were going to put the *Xing* out of commission for at least a month as they cleaned out the viruses and trojans the vanhat would leave behind.

And that was only if his short battalion could repel the borders.

With Saulson handling operations, Sinclair got on the link with Legion command to see if there were any other units he could call on to help him purge the boarders from the *Loyal Xing*. It wasn't cowardice or fear that drove him, it was just the reality that the more people there were shooting at the vanhat the faster they would die.

"Are they stopping any boarding pods?" Saulson growled as he dispatched another platoon.

* * * * *

Chapter Fifty-Four:
Honeymoon

Emperor Wolf Mathison, USMC

The honeymoon had been too damned short and sitting in his office with his wife nearby felt very different. It was hard to look at Skadi and remember the other night. Conduct very unbecoming an emperor for sure. His mind should be on the tasks in front of him, but damn!

"Do we need to get different offices?" Skadi asked. "Are you able to focus on your work?"

"No," Mathison said too quickly. Wait? Should he have said yes? No to different offices, yes, he could focus on his work.

"I'm not talking to you," Skadi said with a half smile.

Mathison smiled. Would their intimacy cause problems professionally? They had an empire to run.

Alarms began screeching, and a holographic display sprang to life in the middle of the room, showing the solar system. Red mist appeared around Earth and the Jupiter system, specifically Europa, indicating combat zones.

"A major vanhat incursion," Freya reported. *"It appears two- or three-pronged. Earth Fleet and Europa are under direct attack by vanhat forces and vanhat forces are attacking the shipyards above Europa."*

"You said three," Mathison asked aloud, sure that Skadi was getting the same information from Loki.

"The third prong involves thousands of ships trying to drop troops on Earth," Freya said. *"They appear to be focusing on South America and northern Asia, weak spots in the particle cannon defensive spread. They are also landing forces in the Atlantic and Pacific, though most are targeted at the Atlantic."*

The hologram zoomed in to Earth.

"They are likely planning three ground attacks on North America. Though the invasion from the Atlantic is unlikely to be a major push because of the difficulty of navigating the ocean. Initial estimates show this is more likely to be a disruption force than a primary attack."

A disruption force could still be a serious threat considering how close Quantico was to the ocean. It made them a very credible threat because it would be harder to track and oppose them. The other two were heavier forces, but they would have to fight overland, through narrow land bridges to North America.

"We don't have a US Navy to keep the shores safe," Mathison said, looking at the hologram of Earth. It wouldn't be easy to halt the other invasions. "What kind of naval weapons and equipment do the vanhat have?"

"Unknown," Freya said. *"Not a lot. The drop ships are submarines. They are likely to be used for raids, though they could be reinforced by land-based forces. Or used to transport land forces."*

There were multiple incoming links from different commands, but Freya had categorized them as more informative than requesting authorizations or instructions. General Hui had things under control with the incoming ground invasions. Mathison trusted the admirals and the Vanir had things under control in space. He didn't know if there was much he could contribute just yet. Everyone was still reacting and collecting information. So far, Mathison couldn't see anything wrong with their responses, and Freya would tell him if there were less obvious problems.

"We need to reinforce coastal defenses," Skadi said before Mathison could. "They may be raiders designed to strike particle beam cannon batteries."

"Agreed," Mathison said. He knew they were missing something. The vanhat hadn't dared to land any forces on North America, and Mathison doubted it was because they were afraid of casualties. Or were they? North America was a fortress, and while most of the continent was still radioactive ruin that didn't mean there weren't numerous surface-to-space weapons.

Rapidly built arcologies in the Rockies and Appalachians were full of refugees from the Moon. Feeding them would become a major challenge, but with more hydroponics coming online, perhaps North America would become a fortress continent. Which didn't matter if the oceans did not deter the vanhat.

"Incoming transmission from Amiraali Carpenter," Freya said.

"Open link," Mathison said.

The wall display activated, and Mathison looked at the amiraali, now his father-in-law.

"The honeymoon is over," Carpenter said.

It had been over days ago, but Mathison didn't want to try to imagine what was going through Skadi's father's mind. Mathison was tempted to make some remark to needle the amiraali but refrained.

"Every night is now a honeymoon," Mathison said, losing the battle to not antagonize his father-in-law.

A wry smile made it to Carpenter's face.

"We are getting attacked from all directions," Carpenter said. "My battlestars can only do so much to prevent the landings, and the vanhat appear to be heavily engaged in trying to wipe out the Earth Fleet. Dredon One appears to be the primary target right now, based on their deployment."

"Why not the battlestars?" Mathison asked aloud. The battlestars were closer to Earth and the protection of the particle beam cannons.

"I'm sure they have plans," Carpenter said. "But the vanhat are likely aware of the friction within our fleets. We are being challenged but not as seriously as Dredon One or Two. It should be noted we are a big hammer, but the Dredons are smaller ones that can cover more area. Furthermore, we are still under the protection of the planetside particle beams."

"He is correct," Freya reported. *"Vanhat behavior is not consistent. The attacks on the battlestars are designed to keep them busy and away from the dropships but the attack against the Earth dreadnought squadrons is a lot more intense. There can be no doubt the battlestars are more dangerous. I suspect the amiraali is correct. The Dredons allow more area to be covered and are currently more vulnerable."*

"Because of SCBIs?" Mathison asked Freya.

"Unknown," Freya said. *"It's a good theory, but that indicates a very high level of operational intelligence. The Dredon squadrons are also a very important part of Imperial power. The battlestars, while larger and tougher, are also fewer. If the dreadnoughts can be destroyed, that could drive a wedge between the Vanir and Imperial forces."*

"We are all on the same side," Mathison said.

"Many officers, even some Legionnaires, feel you are showing a preference toward the Vanir."

"Who has the SCBIs?"

"Emotions are not always based on logic. People will see ex-Governance forces taking much heavier casualties, and that will breed resentment. Your tactics of keeping them closer to Earth and the dreadnought squadrons farther out can be seen as you trusting the Vanir more. I am not stating these as facts but merely trying to gauge the Weermag thought process."

"That's bullshit," Mathison said. *"There are more dreadnoughts, and they can cover more territory. The battlestars are—"*

Mathison swore. It made more sense to keep the battlestars closer because they had more firepower, manufactories to churn out drone fighters, and they had firepower. Keeping the dreadnoughts out at a distance let them detect and strike at the vanhat, increasing the layers of protection around Earth. In many ways, the dreadnoughts were like aircraft carriers. They could field large drone squadrons and project quite a bit of firepower.

"So, what do we do?" Mathison asked Carpenter.

"We can pour trillions of pellets into Earth's orbit," Carpenter said. "This will make low Earth orbit an extremely perilous place in the short term, at least. This will inflict massive casualties on the vanhat drop ships and it will allow us to reinforce the dreadnought squadrons."

"You want to Kessler Earth's orbit?" Mathison said. Kessler Syndrome was a term for so much debris in Earth's orbit that it would make travel from and to orbit a very dangerous endeavor. It would reduce or eliminate traffic to and from space.

"Yes," Carpenter said.

"I need other options," Mathison said. There were still refugee ships on the way, and if they couldn't land on Earth then those refugees would quickly run out of food, air, and water aboard the ships where they were packed like sardines in can. There were no simple solutions. If they couldn't land in time people would die.

Damn.

* * * * *

Chapter Fifty-Five:
Gaia

Vanhat Commander – Kafasta

This continent was hell. A nasty, lethal, unforgiving hell. It was no wonder the humans sought to entrench themselves on this despicable continent. He hoped they were suffering for it.

This had once been a highway through mountains. Now it was just a cave and temporary shelter for Kafasta's company. Standing at the entrance looking out over a valley, Kafasta let hate and anger flow through him.

"What are they doing?" Kafasta asked, looking out of the cave at the sky. Enemy satellites were a very real danger. They were unlikely to see a single camouflaged Weermag warrior, but they would certainly see a company of them.

"They aren't," his demon answered. *"Other gods are interfering. They are experimenting, playing with this planet's biosphere, infringing on our conquest."*

"Why can't we punish them? Stop or delay them?"

"We cannot communicate with them."

Kafasta understood. Not all the old ones were similar, or even compatible. He understood that some came from places other than the ancient gods. They were not gods in themselves, but they were powerful and had their own intelligence. Like animals, the old gods preferred to ignore them when they could not prey upon them.

"Why now?" Kafasta asked.

"The energies of our presence is creating a nexus," the demon said. *"Our presence draws the attention of others."*

"A feeding frenzy."

"Almost. An event that draws attention and interest. We do not know why the others gather here."

The attack was beginning high in orbit. The ancient gods did not want to wait for infiltration teams like Kafasta to silence the massive particle cannon batteries. They wanted to wipe out the human fleet, to control the orbitals, and erase the human presence throughout the solar system. With a powerful fleet, the humans might deflect the asteroids that were being thrown at Earth from the Oort cloud. The ancient gods were growing impatient, or perhaps there was something else, something they were not sharing with their slaves.

But were they running out of time?

The attention of other entities across the universes could converge and the old gods would not want to share their feast.

The air quality was improving, and Kafasta stomped something green that was trying to grow out of the broken concrete. Life was returning to this planet after the natives had tried to eradicate it. That would be another of their failures. They could not even destroy the cradle of their civilization, spoiling their nest intentionally. They had failed.

Humanity was such a failure. Their destruction would be one of the better things to happen to this galaxy.

Kafasta's eyes picked out other specs of green pushing up through the surrounding ash. He could spend a week stomping out such disgusting things.

Here, where the humans and their Inkeri generators were weak, he could feel the other gods working their magic, bringing life back to this world that only deserved death. The only consolation was that Kafasta knew they were not doing this to benefit the humans. The other gods had their own agenda and were probably not even aware of humanity or the old gods.

Stomping on another green thing reaching for the sky, Kafasta returned to the darkness of the tunnel. Usually, the other gods did not infect this reality until later in the purge. Why now?

"We will move out at nightfall," Kafasta told his troops. He had another site picked out that was closer to Quantico, but they had to move fast with the American wildlife hunting his company like prey. He knew they wouldn't have a lot of time. There would likely be at least one fight, probably several, and Kafasta wondered if the other gods controlled these animals? If they did, why would the other gods interfere in the destiny of humanity?

Wouldn't the eradication of humanity benefit them all?

He sank onto his haunches as he watched the tunnel entrance. His demon could catch glimpses and bits of the battles that were occurring in orbit above this wretched world.

It sounded like the Weermag, were winning and Kafasta smiled.

* * * * *

Chapter Fifty-Six: Jupiter's Moons

Admiral Diamond Winters, USMC

Winters directed her fighter to skim through the scaffolding and shoot past the *Musashi* and other ships being constructed or repaired. Blitzen kept her from slamming into something like scaffolding or debris.

Even though it was embedded in gantries and scaffolding, the *Musashi* had weak spots. Most of her weapons could fire but they had limited arcs, which was probably the only reason it wasn't a shattered hulk falling toward Europa right now. The massive ship also had many vulnerable openings, as armor plates were not in place while escape pods and other equipment bays were being installed. Those openings were vulnerable to missiles or attackers. Weak spots the vanhat couldn't ignore.

The gantries and bays themselves were studded with many weapons platforms, designed to protect the construction yard from asteroids and other space debris, but they did a superb job of destroying attackers and could easily handle the smaller fighters while the *Musashi* fired on larger, tougher opponents.

Out in the open, her fighter quickly closed the distance to the enemy, which seemed to be more concerned with the *Musashi*. White

Heron defense weapons had already stripped it of fighter defenses and Winters had a clean run.

Behind her, two other drone fighters followed her as she hit the afterburners and streaked past the vanhat battleship, her blazer cannon ripping apart the ship, spilling atmosphere and bodies into space. Turrets from the battleship followed her, but Blitzen kept the fighter just out of their firing arc.

Glancing back, Winters smiled at the damage they had inflicted. Hitting the afterburners in such an attack meant she had less time to damage the ship, but it also meant she was a lot harder to hit.

In this case, it had paid off.

A wingman exploded, and Blitzen spun the fighter like an insane maniac that made Winters nauseous as another vanhat frigate transitioned in. Frigates were the vanhat's drone killers and apparently the battleship was feeling its mortality.

It was close, too damned close, and Winters knew she couldn't escape, so she tilted the nose of her fighter and slammed into the battleship as Blitzen overloaded the engine.

A flash and Winters found herself back in the drone cockpit of the *Musashi*.

"We have more transitions," she heard an officer report. "Three more battleships. They are overwhelming the nearby dreadnoughts."

Winters swore. She hadn't finished destroying the last battleship.

She felt the vanhat weren't feeding their ships into the battle piecemeal for no reason. What was their goal? Wear down the defenders?

"They are attacking Earth as well," Blitzen reported.

"Why? A two-pronged attack and feeding in their ships piecemeal? Why not just one massive assault?"

"They are likely using wave attacks to wear down our defenses. By committing all their forces at once, there can be logistical problems. This method allows them to commit forces logically and in fresh waves while we do not get a break."

"Aren't they taking heavier casualties?" Winters asked, dreading the fact she would have to put herself back in the queue and rejoin the battle. Her stomach was growling, so she popped a food tablet from her suit supply and drank some water from her tube. She saw someone had put an extra ration box and some water bottles next to her station. Later.

"Perhaps in the short term," Blitzen said. *"But if they have the forces, they can rotate them in and out, grind us down, make it easier for follow-on waves to kill us."*

"Well, we have something they don't."

"What's that?"

Winters popped another caffeine tablet, which wasn't as good as the real thing, but it would suffice.

"Coffee," Winters said and re-entered the battle.

* * * * *

Chapter Fifty-Seven:
Battleship

Enzell, SOG, Director of AERD

I f Enzell had been in command, the vanhat would never have dared attack Earth. He was sure of it. The upstart emperor had obviously demonstrated weakness, and the vanhat were exploiting it.

The *Yao* had been re-designated as a support battleship, not a ship of the line, and that was supposed to keep it back from the battle lines. Another advantage of losing ship of the line status was that Chen remained the captain instead of some Legionnaire.

The *Yao* was supposed to be supporting the line, not be in it.

The incompetent Captain Chen had screwed that up, and Enzell felt the ship shudder as another attack hit home.

"We aren't a front-line ship," Enzell told her. "Why are we under attack?"

"There are no front lines," Chen said, and Enzell didn't care for her tone. "If it is any consolation, the *Yao* is not a primary target of the vanhat."

The ship shuddered again, and more alarms went off.

"Then what is that?" Enzell asked. Perhaps he would have been safer in his Moon facility, even with vanhat crawling all over the place. They wouldn't think to look for him, would they?

"That was an attack of opportunity by a pair of Weermag drone fighters," Chen said. "They have been destroyed."

"What took so long? Why were they allowed to attack us? Doesn't this ship have defenses?"

"We are doing our best," Chen said.

Obviously, the crew of the *Yao* was not one of the better crews in the Governance. He looked over the displays. The *Loyal Xing* was fighting for its life as boarding parties slammed into it. Whoever was commanding the battle was obviously incompetent. The *Loyal Xing* was the flagship, the shining pride and joy of the Governance Fleet. Didn't the fools in command realize the importance of the flagship making it through the battle unscathed? For the *Loyal Xing* to suffer such damage would be a heavy blow to the people. On the positive side, it showed how incompetent the emperor was; he was unable to keep even the flagship safe.

Enzell could use that. Once the fleet beat off the vanhat attack, he could point out that the old Governance would never have allowed the vanhat to accomplish so much.

"Analysis?" Enzell asked Tantalus on a private link.

"This battle will last a while," Tantalus said. "The incoming transitions seem designed to wear down and demoralize the defenses. Each wave is as strong as the last, though it might have different capabilities based on what was working for the vanhat and what wasn't."

"How many waves must we suffer through before they give up?"

"Unknown. That is the question on everyone's mind."

"Well, find out," Enzell said. "I'll find a safe spot for this ship. I'm far too important to become a casualty."

"Yes, sir," Tantalus said.

* * * * *

Chapter Fifty-Eight:
Fight for White Heron

Reginheraht Sloss, VRJ (Vapaus Republic Jaeger)

Their quarters at White Heron Fortress were too small, built for little people. Sloss felt like he and his squad were living in dwarf quarters. The people of White Heron were ethnically Japanese, and they were not big people. They seemed too timid and were easily frightened by his facial rank tattoo. Besides being timid, they also seemed so fragile. Though Sloss saw some fire in their warriors, they were not fierce enough to command his respect.

"Gods, how I wish the women were bigger," Isenberg said. He was the medic/rifleman in the second team. A more junior Jaeger, but he was no nusippas fresh from Jaeger training.

"Even with your little sword?" Moss asked, one of the few women in the squad. "Are they the only ones who don't ask if it is in yet?"

"Sikaaivot," Isenberg said, which meant "pig brain."

"Their saki is like piss water," Loff said. She was Aarnes Team leader. A big, tough woman and one of Sloss's longest-serving friends.

The door slid open, and Peshlaki entered.

Since meeting Peshlaki, Sloss had done his best to research Delta Force, but anything he found didn't seem to capture the truth of what was standing in front of him.

"Hei and Skal," Sloss said.

Sloss was never sure what to make of Peshlaki, and he made Sloss uneasy. Maybe it was because he was too calm, his eyes too alert, the way he moved with lethal precision. He wasn't a big man, though bigger than Sif, and he knew not to underestimate little people, especially after Sif and Stathis.

"Good afternoon," Peshlaki said.

"Welcome back. I thought you would like to spend more time at home," Sloss said.

Peshlaki shook his head with a half smile.

"I've spent too much time on Earth," Peshlaki said. "I never thought I would be able to leave and see the galaxy. Now I can. I've seen enough of Earth."

"You have wanderlust now?" Westling, the Berta Team leader, asked.

"Yes," Peshlaki said. "Earth is no longer the place for me. I feel my destiny is out among the stars."

"Jupiter is not exactly out among the stars," Zappart said. She was a tough sniper in Malski's team.

"It's not Quantico," Peshlaki said. "Imagine living in the same bunker for hundreds of years."

"Ach," Zappart said. "That would be horrific."

"Yes," Peshlaki said. "Though to be fair, I no longer recognize the place. I still prefer to be away."

"Zen," Sloss said. "How is Sif?"

"She is remaining at Quantico for the time being to prepare."

"The expedition is leaving from here," Sloss said. "She should be here."

"There is much planning to do," Peshlaki said. "Training, coordination, crew selection, supply selection, and more. She will be busy."

"And Skadi?" Sloss asked. His feelings about the Ice Princess and her gunnery sergeant were mixed. It was hard not to hold a grudge against the Marines, and even Sif, for the way his people had been treated. Now he understood them better, but it still didn't sit well. Trust was a two-way street, and Sif had been unable to trust him and his Jaegers in the past. He wondered if she would ever really trust him.

Aside from being an ancient like the Marines, Peshlaki seemed to be cut from a different cloth, and Sloss couldn't figure out where he fit.

"So, we continue to wait here, sharpening our axes," Sloss said. Hurry and wait seemed to be a mantra of the Jaegers.

"The emperor may allow Aesir and Vanir to get SCBIs," Peshlaki said.

"No," Westling said. "It is bad enough having conversations with myself in my skull. To have someone else there to argue with? No, thank you."

"Maybe you could win a conversation for once?" Zappart said.

"Silence, impudent whelp," Westling said with a smile.

"Oh, zen, mighty team leader," Zappart said.

Sloss didn't like the idea, either.

"I think we will be okay," Sloss said, looking around at the agreement on his squad's faces, and Peshlaki shrugged.

Sirens screeched.

"What now?" Westling asked as everyone turned to their cybernetic links to try to find out what was going on.

"We're under attack," Peshlaki said. "Vanhat forces have been detected."

"Great," Moss said. "Do we hide here under the ice or is there something more we can do?"

White Heron was a fortress except for the gantries climbing up to orbit. Most of it was under kilometers of ice. There were elevators that tunneled upward through the ice and anchored the shipyards. This let engineers manufacture and fix components below the surface and send their work up and down the orbital elevators to the shipyards. There were twenty different orbital elevators.

For now, Sloss and his squad were being quartered below, near the armored heart of White Heron. Called a fortress, it was also a large city that extended down into Europa's oceans beneath the surface and helped anchor the space elevator to the planetary mantle. Sitting atop a manmade mountain reaching up from the depths of the ocean, Sloss had seen nothing like it.

The squad would eventually have quarters aboard the *Musashi*, but right now the ship was gutted and being upgraded or repaired and a squad of Jaegers would just get in everyone's way.

"I would rather be on the surface to repel a vanhat attack," Loff said.

"If it is Weermag we don't want to be," Sloss said. "They are nasty painajainen according to a Sisko in Third Jaegers."

"They have not faced us," Loff said.

"You think Third Jaegers aboard the *Tyr* are nyyppa's? They took heavy casualties fighting them on Luna."

"No," Loff said. "But we have more experience killing vanhat."

"The Weermag are very different," Peshlaki said. "They have SCBIs like Marines. This makes them a lot more dangerous."

"Paska," Sloss said. He had seen Peshlaki in action and the Marines. If these Weermag were half as dangerous, he knew it would be a bad fight.

Peshlaki stopped to stare at the ground, probably talking with someone or getting information.

"I'm getting reports of incoming transports. They are transitioning close to the surface to land troops. They need us near Neko District. If they capture those elevators, they will have access to the deep and the orbitals."

Sloss didn't remember Neko District specifically. The soggies had weird names for everything.

"Then let us be the anvil they cannot move," Sloss said, looking around him as everyone geared up. "I've grown tired of this sitting around. It is axe time."

* * * * *

Chapter Fifty-Nine: Sinclair

Duffy Sinclair, Imperial Legion LtC

Sinclair knew things were devolving. The *Loyal Xing's* sister dreadnoughts, the *Valiant Smirnova* and *Bravest Serbin*, were having their own difficulties. They had boarding parties to deal with. Dredon One was heavily engaged with vanhat coming at them from all angles. Dredon Two was coming in hot to help, but they were facing stiff resistance.

The Weermag didn't have anything the size or scope of a dreadnought, but they had lots of smaller vessels, and it seemed like every single vessel had boarding pods which were being aimed at the Imperial dreadnoughts.

Sinclair swore as he got off the link with the executive officer. He needed the crew to finish cutting through shaft eight so a platoon from Second Company could flank a Weermag bridgehead.

Heading down to the flanking platoon, Sinclair wanted to see exactly what they were dealing with. They had some crew supporting them, but they weren't advancing. That was unacceptable, because it was giving the Weermag time they shouldn't be allowed to have. The Legionnaire lieutenant was a casualty, and the platoon sergeant didn't have a SCBI, so Sinclair wasn't sure exactly what the problem was.

Cycling through an airlock with Sergeant Johanson, Sinclair made his way aft to where the platoon was waiting.

Minutes later, traveling through dark, deserted corridors, Sinclair arrived.

The corridor was full of nervous Legion Drop Troopers waiting for targets, and they all stood up straighter as they realized who he was.

Two crewmen were already there, wearing space suits and looking frightened.

"What's the hold up?" Sinclair asked.

"The network is down," the senior sergeant said. "Their headsets don't work, and they won't do anything without authorization."

Sinclair looked at the two crewmen and wondered how the Governance had survived with such poorly trained crew. They frequently wore headsets that tied into the network, accessing manuals and guides on how to do their job. With the proper holographic projecting headsets, an untrained crewman could perform almost any normal task. However, the Weermag were doing their best to crack the *Xing's* network, and they had turned it off throughout the battleship. A pretty damned big design flaw, in Sinclair's opinion. ODTs were usually lucky to operate in areas with a functioning network.

"Use plastique," Sinclair said, looking over the blockage. "Blow that shit open."

"You could damage the—" one crewman began, and Sinclair waved his hand, cutting him off.

"Ask me how much I care," Sinclair said. "I want this route open. This lets us split the vanhat incursion in half and that will weaken them."

"I can't allow—"

"Nobody is asking your opinion," Sinclair said, turning to the senior sergeant. "If he gives you too much trouble, truss him up and stick him in a room until we are done."

Sinclair stayed and, with Finn's help, placed the demo charges.

"Fire in the hole," Sinclair said, leaning back. The charges blew, and the senior sergeant led the troopers into the new breach.

Sinclair was tempted to go with them, but he was a battalion commander, not a platoon commander, and he had to look at the bigger picture. Squatting, he pulled up a holographic display only he could see.

"Two-Five is in play," Sinclair said to his XO. Two-Five being fifth platoon, part of Second Company, and they would start pressuring the Weermag. Maybe it would help break their line.

"Ship's XO said the cutting crew has been delayed," Saulson said.

"ODT passkey opened it up," Sinclair said. Fleet never liked it when ODTs used their demo aboard ship, but Sinclair would worry about that later.

"Copy," Saulson said. "You probably need to get back here. A couple pods hit the starboard side, up near secondary gunnery control. Lots of screaming spaceberts. I have a platoon on the way, but our reserves are running low."

"Do what you can," Sinclair said. "I'm on my way back."

"Wilco," Saulson said. "Might have some Weermag that have escaped encirclement near deck nine, crew berthing. Can't be too many, though. Maybe one or two."

Sinclair looked at Johanson. The sergeant was supposed to be his bodyguard.

"Sergeant," Sinclair said, stopping a squad leader about to follow his senior sergeant. "Give me a fireteam. We need to hunt down some bastards who broke through."

"Wilco," the sergeant said and turned to one of his men. "Shimko. Listen to my command. Take your team and hunt with the esteemed battalion commander."

"Hurrah," Shimko said, and Sinclair wondered what kind of trooper Senior Private Shimko was. He was acting as a team leader though, so he had to be competent.

"I'm taking a fireteam, and I will sweep through the area," Sinclair told Saulson.

"With all due respect, Colonel, perhaps I should send a squad from the reserves?"

"I've got a fireteam with me and Johanson. We're also closer. Let me know if you get any more information. We can handle two Weermag troopers."

"Wilco. Keep your head down. I'm sure the emperor would not be happy if you got yourself killed doing enlisted work."

"Ha," Sinclair said. "I have a hot date with Sarah. Going to ask her to marry me. They transferred her to Quantico. I won't be risking my neck."

"Hurrah," Saulson said. "All the same, be careful."

"Wilco," Sinclair said and waved for Shimko's team to follow him.

"I should take point," Johanson said.

"Not yet." Johanson was good, but Finn gave him an advantage that none of the others had, and Finn had access to the Aesir network, so he was fully informed.

Minutes later, Sinclair slowed down. They were getting close to where the invaders might be. If they were doing what they had done everywhere else, the vanhat would be at some computer station uploading viruses and trojans, trying to bring up the network so they could hack it. They had a nasty, accurate habit of knowing exactly where critical nodes were aboard Imperial ships, and Sinclair knew there was one not far away, on the other side of a couple of hatches.

The door slid open, and Sinclair realized how wrong they had been. It was more than just an invader or two.

He never got a second thought as blazer rounds from the Weermag squad ripped him and Johanson apart.

* * * * *

Chapter Sixty:
Weermag Attackers

Reginheraht Sloss, VRJ (Vapaus Republic Jaeger)

Sloss followed Peshlaki, who seemed to know where he was going and moved with confidence. Everyone cleared the way for them as they made their way to the elevators. Nobody wanted to get in the way of a squad of giants running down the corridors.

Inside the elevator, Sloss expected Peshlaki to go up, but he pushed down.

"The fighting is above us," Sloss said.

"The surprise attack will be below us," Peshlaki said.

"Then it won't be a surprise," Sloss said.

"No, it won't. It will become critical very quickly."

"What will?"

"Power conduits and the power plant. There are geothermal vents deep in the ocean beneath White Heron. The Governance has an artificial mountain that comes up and touches the ice. This mountain anchors some of the space elevators as well. Inside that mountain is the central hub for the geothermal plants. Destroy that hub and you cripple White Heron. That hub powers the lasers, the blazers, coil guns, lights, and so much more. The power mains go through Neko District at the tip of that mountain. Sever those mains and the defenses will collapse."

"Sounds like a weakness," Moss said.

"The Governance was about control. Yes, it was a weakness, but only if the Governance lost control of it and they were not in the habit of letting locals control it. The Governance programmed that weakness into the system to deal with a potential rebellion of White Heron Fortress above. As an artificial mountain, it is also very secure and there is only one practical way into it and that is the tip where tunnels from the surface come down to the warehouses to a sub pen. Very much a bottleneck and if we keep control of it we can maintain control of the power plants."

"A sub pen?" Moss asked.

"A submarine hangar," Peshlaki said. "It's usually where they keep the subs that repair and monitor the different facilities. There are two subs, but they are near Fukuoka trying to help some rescues there, so the sub pen is empty."

"Kusipaas," Moss said. "Now we have to deal with the mess."

"How do you know they will attack it?" Sloss asked.

"It has not been targeted yet," Peshlaki said. "It is an obvious weakness, and I'm sure the Weermag understand the vulnerability. There is a choke point, and that is where the tunnels come down and meet the sub pen."

"Is it well defended, then?" Sloss asked, looking down at Peshlaki.

"No," he said. "It is not. I do not think the base commander believes the Weermag can get this deep and thinks he can hold the surface tunnel entrances."

"I question the competence of the commander."

"He is a SOG political appointee who has not been replaced yet. He underestimates the enemy."

"But you don't."

"Yes."

"If I miss out on the fight I'm going to be pissed," Henning said, hefting his squad automatic blazer. "My little honey pie and I don't enjoy being left out."

"I assure you, you won't be." Peshlaki motioned toward some massive doors. "Those lead up to ice tunnels that go to the surface. They are large so cargo can be brought down here. Sometimes cargo subs are used to transport things to other facilities and cities."

The doors of the freight elevator opened to a hallway that looked suspiciously like an airlock, but after a short hallway, it opened onto what looked like a massive underground pool with deep dark water.

"This is a submarine pen," Peshlaki said. "Above us is ice, but below us is the Europan Ocean. We should spread out. This is likely to be the avenue of approach."

"The ocean?" Sloss asked.

"Yes. When Ito was destroyed by the Collective, the ice there was cracked. That area is no longer defended, and satellites have recently detected a Weermag landing there. The ships disappeared into the ocean through those cracks."

"How big were the ships?"

"Three frigates, troop transport, not anti-fighter. Estimate a company each? Maybe two? If they are coming here, we will need help. This sub pen is the closest to the power hub. While technically they could target each of the thermal plants and their conduits coming here, capturing this hub is more effective."

"Capture, not destroy?" Sloss asked.

"If they can't capture it, be ready for that," Peshlaki said.

"You are sure?"

"Yes."

"We need heavier weapons," Sloss said, looking out over the smooth dark water. Would they use frigates like submarines? Was one about to surface here and sweep the pen clear with turrets?

"That way leads toward the main hub and control center," Peshlaki said.

"Claus, you get this elevator. The rest of us will deploy over there near the hatch to the control center. If you must retreat, you have an elevator. We retreat to the hub. When the commander of White Heron figures out there is a problem, he will try to send reinforcements down to that elevator."

"Zen," Claus said, looking around. There was some machinery and Claus began ordering his people to start moving the big tractors so they would provide cover.

Confident Claus had it under control, Sloss led the other two teams to the other side. Everyone kept their weapons trained on the smooth water. At any moment, the enemy could come up out of the darkness.

"You have what you have," Peshlaki said. "Most of the troops have been pulled back to protect the shipyards above, or they have been pulled back to the control center. There are some defense turrets, but…"

Peshlaki didn't finish what he was going to say.

"There are no other troops?" Sloss asked. The Jaegers were on their own.

"We are stretched thin," Peshlaki said. "If they attack here, then they will send Guard and maybe ODTs to help reinforce."

"You are confident they will attack here?" Sloss asked. He didn't relish missing the fight and hated the thought of being stuck here.

"Relatively," Peshlaki said. "My SCBI and I have studied the facility. This is the best entrance and route to the hub."

"Then we will hold it," Sloss said. If they missed the fight, then so be it. Sif seemed to trust Peshlaki, so Sloss would.

"Shit," Peshlaki said as Sloss watched his team leaders place their people.

"What?" Sloss asked, wishing he had access to what Peshlaki did.

"They are starting to land forces near the surface tunnel entrances. They will be coming at us from two directions, the surface and the ocean."

The water rippled as the first Weermag submarine surfaced, and a turret turned toward them.

Claus' team began firing and ripped apart the turret, but more mini-subs began to surface near the edge and hatches flew open as all hell broke loose.

* * * * *

Chapter Sixty-One:

Tyr

Admiral Diamond Winters, USMC

The Weermag weren't slowing down or quitting. Several heavily damaged cruisers slid into Shorr space, escaping before her squadron could finish the job. One problem with that was the ships replacing them were fresh and anxious to fight.

"We are spread thin," General Duque said on the Jupiter system command net. Winters knew at least one dreadnought had been destroyed, maybe two. She didn't want to ask about smaller ships.

"Who do you suggest we abandon?" Sakamoto asked.

"We have to keep the Europan and Ganymede facilities safe," Duque said, and Winters heard the pain in his voice. There were numerous other mines, cities, and shipyards around the Jupiter subsystem. Winters couldn't argue with that, but shipyards were vulnerable.

The *Musashi* was doing an admirable job defending Europa along with Dredon Jupiter One. Duque was aboard the Jupiter flagship *Indomitable Kolobano* and was heavily engaged near Ganymede. Dredon Two was with him, while Dredon Three moved to support Europa. The other squadrons were spread out in a way that let them see around the Jupiter system but not so far they couldn't support each other.

Winters had lost track of time and while Blitzen could tell her how many caffeine tablets she had taken, she didn't want to ask because that would give Blitzen a chance to lecture her.

There were advantages and disadvantages of the Jupiter subsystem. Ninety-five moons let the defenders emplace and hide countless batteries of blazers and missiles with interlocking fields of fire and sensors that could detect almost anything. What made things difficult was the radiation and magnetosphere Jupiter hit everything with. There was also a massive amount of other debris. Jupiter acted like a magnet, keeping the inner planets safe by sucking all the interplanetary garbage into its gravity well, but that garbage complicated any high-speed maneuvers near Jupiter.

The vanhat were doing their best to use the various moons and blind spots as cover and concealment as they came at the Europa shipyards, but General Duque had been fanatical about fortifying this bastion of the Empire.

Even then, the vanhat were getting closer to inflicting serious damage on the shipyards, which looked to be their real goal.

A new squadron of six battleships slid out of Shorr space and Winters knew there wasn't anything mobile that could stop them. For hours, the vanhat had been carving a path through Jupiter's defenses. They had stopped trying to transition in close because of the particle cannons, so now they were attacking from a distance, which was only slightly more successful because the range of the particle cannons was not unlimited, and they weren't as effective against missiles. It was becoming a war of attrition as the vanhat used successive waves to identify and eliminate Jupiter's defenses while doing their best to evade the particle cannons.

The six battleships told Winters the vanhat were getting serious. Missile strikes had disabled several PC batteries. The *Musashi* was trying to break dock so it could maneuver and possibly escape, but the vanhat weren't allowing that.

Winters directed her under-strength drone squadron at the six battleships knowing her chances were slim. Weermag battleships were a lot tougher than the cruisers or frigates, by quite a large factor. One of her fighters detonated. They had little fuel for rapid acceleration. She should return to the squadron for rearming and refueling, but that wasn't an option right now.

Another fighter exploded, and she gave the command. They boosted and shot out of the kill box the vanhat were trying to put them in. The drones' blazers began lancing out, scoring hits on the battleships. Though they were easier to hit, they had much heavier armor, and her drones didn't have particle cannons.

A pair of Imperial cruisers were concentrating on the battleships, attacking the new squadron under the cover of a flight of missiles launched an hour ago from a nearby moon battery. There were too many missiles for the battleships to shoot down and though they tried they were doomed to failure. But what they could do was swat down the cruisers.

The first Imperial cruiser exploded and then the second as the missiles saturated the battleship defenses. Only two battleships escaped the hell of radiation and exploding battleships, and neither one was unscathed.

Winters targeted the first battleship, and her squadron began firing at long range, taking advantage that the battleship was damaged and unable to maneuver effectively. She did her best to use one battleship as cover from the other, but the angle was wrong, and her squadron lacked the fuel to get into that blind spot quickly.

Coming closer, her drone fighters began ripping off chunks of armor, turrets, and sensors.

Return fire shattered her fighter, but she immediately jumped her presence to another drone and the attack continued.

Her target exploded, and her drones switched targets.

Seconds later, the last battleship began to drift, from loss of power or dead, she didn't know.

Another transition, and a pair of frigates slid into the space around Jupiter. Before she could turn the remnants of her squadron to attack them, her lights flashed. She checked the board and swore. She saw she didn't have any more fighters in that fight.

The defenders were running out of drones, and it wouldn't surprise her if the stocks of missiles were nearly depleted.

When would the vanhat run out of ships, dammit!

"You should take a break," Blitzen told her. *"Maybe just an hour."*

"We don't have an hour." How could her SCBI be telling her to take a break?

She tried to trigger another caffeine tablet, but her helmet refused to dispense one.

"Shit's broken," Winters said.

"I'm cutting you off."

"You can't do that."

"I just did. In this case it is a health issue."

Winters swore, and the ship shook. Looking around, she realized she was actually aboard the *Musashi*. She had forgotten all about it. The *Eagle* was nearby, trying its best to protect the super dreadnought. She heard an alarm indicating more transitions.

"You can take a quick power nap," Blitzen said.

"In the middle of a battle?" Winters leaned back and slapped the Go button. Her view changed to a drone fighter sliding out of a bay aboard the *Musashi*. A quick look showed it had just come from close-quarters defense. The armor was melted from a grazing hit, but the fighter was otherwise ready.

She immediately had to dodge a stream of blazers that came toward her, trying to score hits on the drone bay. An uppity frigate that didn't have heavy enough weapons to damage the armored doors that quickly slammed behind her. A particle beam cannon from the *Musashi* reached out and erased the frigate before it could sweep her from space.

"We have a trio of incoming battleships, Winters-sama," the CAG said in her ears. "We need them stopped."

"Copy," Winters said. Two other unmanned drone fighters fell in on her wing. Three drones, three battleships? Terrible odds, but it wasn't like there were many options. When the battleships got into range, their heavier blazer cannons could do a lot more damage to the *Musashi* than some arrogant and lucky frigate.

Imperial forces were running out of drone fighters, and the crews were exhausted. She didn't want to know how long the battle had been going. At least the drone fighters had some ship-killer missiles.

The dreadnought squadrons that were supposed to be defending the Jupiter system were spread out, trying to protect too much, and one full squadron had already been destroyed. The dreadnought squadrons from Earth were the only reason Jupiter could still fight. Winters hoped Earth wasn't as desperate as they were here at Jupiter.

The battleships were coming in hard and fast. If they didn't ram, they wouldn't be able to slow down.

The *Fire Wind* and *Eagle* remained close to the *Musashi*. Without the Mongol ship, the *Musashi* would be a wreck spiraling down toward Europa. The *Eagle* was little more than a frigate, helping to decimate enemy drone formations, but every bit helped.

She had seen nothing bigger than a frigate ram an Imperial ship, but the *Musashi* was a worthy target. The *Fire Wind* targeted and ripped apart the incoming vanhat battleships. The Mongol ship spun to expose undamaged turrets as enemy fire raked the side.

Winters targeted the lead battleship and launched her first missile before realizing the range was less than ideal.

It was coming at her, so that meant less distance, but it had been a mistake, one she wouldn't have made if she wasn't so tired. Rounds from the *Fire Wind* began slamming into it, but the battleship didn't stop.

Accelerating as fast as the afterburner let her, she shot toward the battleship. She would suicide the drone if she had to and the more speed she had the more damaging the impact would create. Blitzen helped her dodge the incoming fire, which was mostly aimed at the *Musashi*, and avoid slipping into fire coming from the *Musashi*.

A particle beam slashed one battleship and parts of its armor fell away. Winters tried to concentrate her fire there, but at this range, the weapons of a drone were almost worthless against a heavily armored ship like the Weermag battleships.

One of her wingmen shattered as something hit it.

She launched the rest of her missiles and ordered her remaining wingman to do so as well. The vanhat battleships would have more opportunity to shoot them down, but then the missiles wouldn't be wasted if she or her wingman were hit.

Her fighter began shaking, which wasn't right. She realized the *Musashi* was being hit and shaking under the impact of the battleships and their main guns.

The screaming sirens shouldn't be relevant to a fighter, but she wasn't really in a fighter. Her suit was sealed, so she didn't have to worry about the decompression alarm.

Then her view cut out.

"Damn it!" She checked her display. Maybe her wingman had survived. However, her display didn't have power. She had been cut off from the drone fighter because the *Musashi*, the ship she was on, was dying.

She unstrapped herself and headed into the nearby alternative CIC where Sakamoto was, if he was still alive. Hopefully, the power loss was local. If it was everywhere aboard the *Musashi*, they would be dead shortly.

As she entered, she saw a full squadron of battleships transitioning in at longer range.

"I am disappointed," Sakamoto said. "I had expected to do more against our enemies."

Winters remembered the escape pods had been pulled out for upgrade and she was pretty sure no shuttle would survive the inferno coming at them. The minutes ticked by as the crew worked feverishly to restore power.

Winters felt helpless watching the others work. A generator had taken a hit and overloaded the system, causing another generator to fail. That shouldn't have happened, but battle damage had taken some fail safes offline, or they hadn't yet been upgraded. She didn't know, but it could mean the death of the ship.

Someone was frantically calling for help from other Imperial ships, but Winters doubted anyone had reserves left to commit.

"Shorr space transition," an officer reported without emotion. Exhaustion did that. This was the final assault then?

A voice came over the speakers from the newcomer.

"We are the Vanir," the voice said. "We are the shield of our people. Imperial Vessel *Musashi*, request fire control link. Your request for assistance has been received and answered."

"Link it," Sakamoto said, and Winters saw the display light up showing the *Tyr* had arrived.

"We are Vanir. Our line will not be breached," the voice said, and Winters watched the display as the *Tyr* fired everything it had as drones poured out of the bays.

"Those glorious bastards," Winters said.

"This may mean we survive longer," Sakamoto said. "But the *Musashi* has sustained serious damage."

"Enemy vessels are transitioning out," the bridge officer said.

"Cowards," Sakamoto said.

"They are running away to fight another day," Winters said, and the CIC fell silent. Next time, the vanhat would come at them with even more overwhelming force, but there was still a battle going on down on the surface.

* * * * *

Chapter Sixty-Two:
Sleipner

Captain Zale Stathis, USMC

Stathis was trying to shoot more boarding pods as they came at the *Loyal Xing*. He wasn't sure where his current drone fighter had come from. Maybe a cruiser? It wasn't a newer model, but it had an Aesir link upgrade kit and handled like a clumsy brick.

His current CAG was a Legionnaire from Fleet. He didn't know how many boarding pods he had shredded, but the vanhat didn't seem to be running out. The *Smirnova* was also floundering, unable to fight with so many vanhat aboard it fighting for control.

"Get clear of the *Xing*," the CAG said. "I say again, get clear. She's going to blow."

"What the hell?" Stathis asked, but not on the main link.

"Self-destruct protocols," Shrek said. *"They've lost the ship to boarders. The captain is going to scuttle the ship."*

"But—" Stathis began. The *Xing* was a damned big ship. *"Will they be able to evacuate in time?"*

His answer was the *Loyal Xing* exploding as every missile, every generator, every weapon was triggered.

"Colonel Sinclair—" Stathis began. The lieutenant colonel had to have made it off. Right?

"He fell hours ago," Shrek said as Stathis hit the afterburners, trying to escape the debris wave. *"A boarding party killed him."*

"You're just telling me this now?" Stathis felt it like a gut punch. Sinclair was dead? What about Sarah? Who was going to command the battalion aboard the *Musashi*? Shrek had to be mistaken. Who was going to tell Sarah?

"I'm sorry," Shrek said.

Sinclair had been an outstanding officer. He should have been in his command post directing the battle. Wasn't that what battalion commanders did? They weren't supposed to be on the front lines clearing rooms and shit.

Stathis' drone fighter didn't escape the debris field, and he found himself back in his room, his heads-up display saying No Signal.

Stathis mechanically reached over to hit Go and get back into the battle, but instead he appeared in a VR briefing room.

In the center was a display of Earth surrounded by flashing red dots.

"What's going on?" Stathis asked Shrek.

"The battle in Earth's orbit was not going well," Shrek said. *"Amiraali Carpenter made a command decision. Too many vanhat were moving in to land troops on Earth and we weren't stopping them. We can't stop them."*

"So, what did he do?"

"He fired trillions of ball bearings into Earth's orbit at high velocity," Shrek said. *"He has Kesslered orbit. It is a tactic based on the Kessler Syndrome."*

"Shit," Stathis said. To his surprise, he actually knew what that meant. The Kessler Syndrome was when there was so much debris in Earth's orbit it was lethal. They had been talking about the dangers all the way back to the twentieth century. It would discourage anyone

from entering or leaving the atmosphere because of all the fast-moving projectiles.

Now he understood the display as the *Sleipner* poured more fuel into the fire.

"They are retreating," the CAG said.

"*Where's the* Tyr?" Stathis asked Shrek, unwilling to ask the strange officer anything.

"*They are at Europa,*" Shrek said. "*This has been a very close battle. If the* Tyr *and* Sleipner *had not Kesslered Earth's orbit, the fight would still be going on, and the vanhat were winning.*"

"*Now what?*"

"*The vanhat are retreating.*"

"*So, we won?*"

"*Can you call this a victory? While Earth is not completely cut off it is going to be very difficult to move things in and out of Earth's orbit. The vanhat will not be able to bring in heavier ships to clear a path because of the particle beam cannons and they will lose far more dropships if they try landing now.*"

"*What do you think?*" Stathis asked Shrek.

"*The* Tyr *and* Sleipner *changed the equation when they Kesslered Earth. The vanhat will do one of three things: retreat, lick their wounds and prepare to try again, or they will concentrate their firepower to wipe out Earth Fleet or Jupiter Fleet.*"

"*Or there's a fourth option,*" Stathis said.

"*What's that?*"

"*That's what worries me. What would we not suspect?*"

"*You have an idea?*"

"*I'm thinking.*"

"*That's not always a good thing,*" Shrek said.

* * * * *

Chapter Sixty-Three:
The Collective Returns

Emperor Wolf Mathison, USMC

W ith Earth now cut off, the *Sleipner* was moving to assist the Dredon squadrons and the *Tyr* had gone to the White Heron Fortress to reinforce. Mathison felt Earth was unprotected, but that wasn't entirely true.

The vanhat were no longer trying to land dropships. They were suffering a one hundred percent casualty rate when they hit the debris field, or if not a hundred it was close to ninety-nine percent. And anything large enough to try to create lanes through the Kessler field would be vulnerable to the particle beam cannons. It was a stalemate because only the large ships had the laser weaponry powerful enough on wide beam to vaporize the debris and create passages from orbit to space or back.

"*The* Loyal Xing *has self-destructed,*" Freya said. "*Furthermore, other dreadnoughts have suffered extreme damage. Dredon One is combat ineffective. Dredons Two and Three are also in bad condition.*"

The *Tyr* and *Sleipner* had abandoned their post trying to protect Earth and they were turning the tide against the vanhat. The vanhat forces that had landed would be dealt with. They were now cut off on a hostile world. Imperial ships could enter higher orbit and fire on

349

planetside targets, but there would be no reinforcements or supplies for the planetside vanhat.

"I don't want to admit my father may have been right about Kesslering Earth," Skadi said. "If we can purge the vanhat from Earth, we might have a chance."

Carpenter had made the decision, Mathison hadn't, and while the initiative was to be commended, Mathison didn't like the situation the amiraali had placed him.

More than one fleet officer had contacted him to complain, and he had taken responsibility. How could he not? He would have words with his father-in-law later.

If there was a later.

For now, the surviving dreadnought squadrons would have to limp back to Earth and the sensor net would have to tighten. Was that the vanhat goal? To reduce Earth's visibility to allow asteroids to slip through undetected? At this point many of the automated weapons platforms were out of missiles or had been destroyed. The vanhat were forcing him to pull in his perimeter around Earth and Jupiter.

"They want us to give up Earth," Skadi said.

"Not happening," Mathison said. But would humanity eventually have to abandon the cradle of human civilization?

Skadi looked up from her displays, and her eyes pierced Mathison.

"Why?" she asked. There was something in her voice he wasn't used to hearing, and he couldn't quite identify it. It made him think of those days and nights of their very short honeymoon.

"This is Mother Earth," Mathison said, but not even he was sure of his answer. "I don't know why. Earth is a symbol? I want to see it full of life again? We have spent too much time retreating, and if we are to make a last stand let it be here on Earth."

Skadi nodded, and Mathison really looked at her. She was beautiful and strong. Hard to imagine someone like her would settle for him.

"What do you think?" Mathison asked. A marriage wasn't about one person. Neither was an empire.

"I think I'm tired of running," Skadi said. "I agree. We should make a stand. Earth is where we came from. It is a suitable place for a last stand. All humans will understand that. Earth is the home of our species. If we cannot defend Earth, then what are we?"

Mathison looked at her. Defending Earth to the last drop of human blood was a genuine possibility. Perhaps he shouldn't be so adamant, especially if it might involve Skadi's death.

He would have to think on this further. The vanhat were going to increase their asteroid bombardment of Earth, he was sure. With the destruction of the heavy warships, more asteroids could strike the planet.

"We need options though," Skadi said. Mathison raised an eyebrow. "We are losing ships and people faster than we can replace them, and these Weermag seem to increase in numbers."

"Suggestions?"

"I was reviewing Sif's report on the Golden Horde. She said she believes they are using incubators and artificial wombs to increase their numbers."

"You think we should start doing that?"

"Do you think the Weermag aren't?"

"What will that do to society?" Mathison asked. "Millions of parentless children growing up knowing nothing but war and violence? There are many ways to destroy a culture and species. That might be one."

"Evolve or become extinct?" Skadi asked.

"We can hold out for a time," Mathison said. "Perhaps Operation Seraphim will give us another option."

"That is a long, perilous journey. There is no guarantee of their survival."

"That's why I'm sending Stathis and Winters. If anyone can pull it off, they can."

"Why don't you go?"

"My duty is here," Mathison said. "I will not abandon the Empire. However—"

"No!" Skadi said. "Don't even think about it, pupu."

"Pupu?" Mathison asked.

"It is a Finnish term of endearment," Freya said. *"It means bunny, as in the cute and cuddly kind. It does not mean excrement."*

He was going to say more, but instead said, "I'm your harmless buck tooth herbivore?"

Skadi's smile was more genuine. "Yes. My little rakas hani muru pupu."

"Which translates roughly as dear honey crumb bunny," Freya said. *"Terms of endearment—"*

"I get it."

Mathison didn't know what to say and being speechless was exactly what Skadi had been aiming for. Her smile grew.

"We will get through this, husband," she said. "Together or not at all."

With her at his side, how could they not?

"We have a problem," Freya reported.

"Just one?" Mathison said, his mood turning dark again.

"A very large ship has transitioned in about half an AU from Earth," Freya said, and the holograph showing Earth's orbit approached the ship.

"What kind of ship?" Mathison asked. A Republic homestar? Another battlestar? Were the Weermag now fielding ships larger than battleships?

"Collective," Freya reported, and Mathison didn't want to ask her how she knew. They wouldn't be here to help.

"Intent?" Skadi asked.

Even though Skadi asked the question, Freya answered for Mathison as he knew Loki would answer for her.

A flash from the hologram leapt out and slammed into Earth.

"That was a particle beam weapon. We suspect this will be a slow, steady attack," Freya said. Which meant the Collective ship would continue to approach Earth, attacking and swatting any response out of space.

"Is Quantico vulnerable?" Mathison asked.

"Not yet," Freya said. *"Earth's rotation is on our side, but as the planet rotates, we will get closer, and we will be vulnerable."*

"Can our weapons reach it?"

"Not with a lot of force. The weapon mounted aboard that ship is a magnitude more powerful than what we have."

"We need bigger guns," Mathison said.

"And more coffee," Skadi added.

* * * * *

Chapter Sixty-Four: Ground Support

Kapten Sif – VRAEC, Nakija Musta Toiminnot

Not all the battles were in space and not all the drones were off planet. Sif and Munin were leading a drone squadron in an attack on a vanhat beachhead in South America. They weren't far from the Medlin Arcology in what used to be Columbia. The terrain was mountainous and rugged. The jungles were making a comeback and provided additional cover and conceal-ment, but it was a very target-rich environment despite that.

One of her wingmen exploded as ground fire reached them. Munin targeted the battery, some kind of platform that used maglev tech-nology and the Earth's magnetic fields. They had designed the platform for air defense and another drone exploded as she launched air-to-ground missiles at it. The remnants of her squadron dropped behind some mountains to avoid its fire.

"Hit and destroyed," Munin reported.

"We still lost two," Sif said. She was the only pilot in this drone squadron and her objective was a beachhead north of Medlin. So far, the vanhat were not pushing toward the arcology, but that was prob-ably because they were still consolidating and trying to figure out what they were going to do now that they were cut off. They would have to spread out because orbital ships could start targeting them.

"We still have bombs and missiles," Munin said.

"We will not end the mission," Sif said. Did Munin think they would? Drones were expendable. Mostly. If they could inflict more damage than they took.

Most of the SCBI-equipped Legionnaires, as Mathison were calling them, were involved in spaceborne operations. Activities planetside were important, but less so because whoever controlled the orbitals could drop big rocks and crowbars on people down below.

General Hui was in command of defending the ground, and Sif had volunteered to operate drones for her. SCBI-supported drone pilots had a very distinct advantage. Regular Guard and ODT drone operators were too slow, and the Weermag easily decimated those attacks.

Dropping lower, Sif let Munin randomize their flight pattern. They could move faster up high, but the Weermag were becoming very good at killing anything they could see. Flying this low slowed her down and gave her less time to respond to and attack, but the Weermag had less time to target her flight of drones as well.

Hypersonic missiles, in support of her mission, were hitting any potential hilltops or locations that observers could see her fighters and call in to support Weermag anti-air forces.

Most of the high spots were burning masses of vegetation, and the smoke from the napalm and fires also provided some protection.

The Weermag could probably guess her destination though.

Blitzen gave her just enough warning before Weermag drones came swooping down, shattering another drone, but the rest scattered, and Sif spun her fighter in such a hard turn it would have turned her body to jelly. She fired her blazers, destroying the first vanhat drone.

She pulled another hard turn and noticed the Weermag fighters couldn't match her.

"They have pilots," Blitzen told her, and Sif smiled. This would not be a fair fight. She spun around, pushing the fighter so hard hull integrity alarms went off, but the Weermag couldn't match her. Another attacker died.

"Why pilots?" Sif asked as she targeted another one.

"Communications most likely. General Hui has saturated the area with jammers. The Weermag use radio communications so they cannot properly control the fighter drones right now."

Sif doubted that advantage would last long. It was perhaps one advantage humans had over the vanhat, though the Republic had been fanatical about keeping their technology a secret, Sif suspected the vanhat would do their best to capture it.

Her objective was just over the next hill. The first drone to top the hill was vaporized. She had two left. Popping up simultaneously, they both triggered their nukes before they could be vaporized.

She was back in her personal quarters at Quantico. She had a full control set for drone operations. It seemed to be standard in Legionnaire quarters these days and as someone with a SCBI, that was where she ranked. She replayed the final microseconds of the drones in slow motion. As luck would have it both drones were masked by trees as they came up over the hill. Incoming fire would have vaporized them, but the nukes had detonated, and Sif smiled as she saw it had been a Weermag staging area with numerous transports and armored vehicles. But something was strange and tickled the back of her mind. She was missing something.

"Good job," General Hui said on a link. "We will task a corvette in high orbit to look, but I have no doubt that will seriously hamper them."

"Thank you, General," Sif said, still thinking about those last microseconds.

The link closed.

She replayed the last seconds from the drones in slow motion and watched the displays and readouts. She noticed the Russelman index was increasing rapidly before the drones exploded but that wasn't what caused her to gasp when she saw it.

The trees were leaning over to shield the drones from the Weermag.

What?

She replayed it again. The trees had definitely leaned, helping to hide the drones from Weermag air defenses in the valley. It couldn't have been the wind. One drone, perhaps, but not both. Why had the Russelman index gone up? Did the vanhat think the drones would slam into the trees? Air defenses would have been more effective. All the trees did was conceal the drones for the brief moment they needed to crest the hill where the detonation would eradicate what was in the valley.

Sif replayed it again and again. Definitely vanhat energies bending the trees, but why?

A link came in from Gaufrid. "Miss Sif?"

"Yes?" Sif said. Miss? Why was Gaufrid contacting her now?

"There is a problem developing. The Collective is coming."

"What do you mean? Have you notified Captain Stathis?"

"Captain Stathis is currently engaged in combat operations, and while this may be important enough to interrupt his mission, you are immediately available."

A chill ran through Sif as she realized that Gaufrid, his SCBI, and Quadrangle were so integrated into Imperial systems that they knew what she and Stathis were doing.

"What do you mean, coming?"

"I have detected a transmission for Collective agents to initiate a scorched Earth protocol and evacuate," Gaufrid said.

Scorched Earth sounded very bad.

"Not literal scorched Earth," Gaufrid said. "It is a phrase that—"

"I know the phrase. What does it mean?"

"It means that agents will do their best to inflict as much damage as they can on humanity as they flee. I have discovered there are assassins targeting Stathis and your emperor."

"And this is not important enough to interrupt Stathis?"

"I am moving to him now," Gaufrid said. "It is the emperor that worries me and there may be others."

Sif swore. Who else was the Collective targeting?

"Any idea how many agents there are?" Sif asked.

"None," Gaufrid said.

But he knew there were agents even if he couldn't even guess at their numbers. He knew Collective assassins were on the move. Why tell her there was at least one?

"Have you warned the emperor?"

"My instructions were to tell you and Stathis before anyone else."

Something felt off to Sif. He wouldn't guess at how many Collective agents there were, didn't think it was important enough to interrupt her or Stathis about it, and now he was on his way to protect Stathis?

If Gaufrid was in front of her, she could have sensed if he was lying or holding something back. She didn't know what his emotional state was.

With frightening clarity, she realized why. Gaufrid knew about her abilities, and if he was going to betray them Stathis would be defenseless and trusting. The emperor would be an extremely difficult target to reach and Winters was near Jupiter.

Gaufrid, or his master Quadrangle, was going to betray them.

"What—" she began but there was an explosion as the lights went off and power failed. She tried to connect to the Aesir network, but it was offline. She sensed the assassins coming for her.

* * * * *

Chapter Sixty-Five:
Assassin

Captain Zale Stathis, USMC

The CAG—Stathis couldn't remember his, or her name—had ordered him to get at least six hours of sleep. Ordered him!

Colonels could order captains to do things like that, but Stathis knew the battle wasn't over yet. He could probably go for a few more hours. Besides, how was he going to sleep pumped full of adrenaline and caffeine?

"Get into bed or you are napping in your chair," Shrek said.

"Not you too," Stathis said, getting up.

His doorbell let him know someone was there.

"It is Gaufrid," Shrek warned him. Not Hakala. Damn.

Stathis was tempted to ignore it. He wouldn't ignore Hakala. But what if Gaufrid had important information on his investigation?

He gave Shrek authorization to open the door and it unlocked to let Gaufrid in.

"What's up?" Stathis asked.

"I have some information for you," Gaufrid said.

Stathis waved him in. "Can you make it quick? They've ordered me to get some sleep. Of all the nerve. Sure, he was a colonel but I'm still good for a few more hours."

"I would prefer to make it quick. Then you will sleep as long as you need to." That almost sounded like a threat. "I need you to help me get authorization to the emperor."

"Why?" Stathis asked. Why couldn't Gaufrid tell him and then he could tell the emperor? It wasn't like Stathis would try to steal the credit. He didn't want another promotion.

"It is complicated, and the Collective is beginning their attack. They will attack from a distance and advance methodically. I do not think that the Empire can resist them."

"You have a plan?"

"The emperor and empress are critical," Gaufrid said. "There may be Collective assassins preparing to strike."

"The assassins are going to strike, or the Collective is?"

"The assassins will strike and that will be to the advantage of the Collective. Kill the head and the body dies."

"What assassins?" Stathis asked. Why hadn't Gaufrid reported this before? And why now?

"I have received a transmission from the Collective. It is directing Collective agents to conduct a scorched Earth assault, to cripple as many Imperial forces as possible."

"You are just now telling me about this?"

"It just came to my attention. We need to get to the emperor and empress."

"How much time do we have?" Stathis asked.

"Not much. We need to hurry."

"Dammit." Stathis grabbed his helmet and rifle. "Follow me. I know a shortcut and the guards will let me pass."

"That is what I was counting on," Gaufrid said.

An explosion shook the room. Stathis noticed the local network link was offline and the Aesir network was also offline.

"What happened?" Stathis asked Shrek.

"The localized networks are down. The Aesir links are down," Shrek said.

"How can the Aesir links be down?"

"We have to hurry!" Gaufrid said. "We have to get to the emperor."

"Why don't the Collective agents want to live?" Stathis asked. "Don't they realize that if the vanhat win we all die?"

"They might not have a choice," Gaufrid said. "The Collective AI in their skull can take full control, turn them into a meat-puppet, and it will follow very strict programming."

"Who is in control?" Stathis asked Shrek. *"Gaufrid or Quadrangle?"*

"You know the way?" Stathis asked aloud, slipping on his helmet. He didn't want to take his eyes off Gaufrid.

"How do you expect me to determine that? If I try to find out, and it is Quadrangle we will have exposed your suspicions."

"Yes," Gaufrid said.

"Are there any other assassins?" Stathis leveled his rifle at Gaufrid. The ex-CIA agent turned to face him, and he seemed too calm. Stathis immediately knew he wasn't looking at Gaufrid. A human had never seemed so alien to Stathis.

"Sta—" Shrek began, but it was too late.

Stathis saw no more than a blur as Quadrangle moved too fast for him to react. His rifle went flying and he found Quadrangle's pistol against his helmet, finger on the trigger.

"Now is not the time to push your luck," Shrek warned him. *"He hasn't killed us, but—"*

"Yeah," Stathis told Shrek as he looked at Gaufrid/Quadrangle.

"What do you want?" Stathis asked aloud.

"To talk to Emperor Mathison and Skadi," Quadrangle said. "Time is of the essence, and the fate of the human race hangs in the balance."

"Doesn't it always?" Stathis said. He was pretty sure Quadrangle didn't want to talk. Was Gaufrid in there screaming to be released, trying to warn Stathis? Or was he complicit with the cabal agent?

"The AI Cabal wants peace."

"You think we can just stroll up to the emperor with you holding a gun to my head?"

"No," Quadrangle said.

What creeped Stathis out the most was the complete lack of emotion. A normal person might have had a half grin, a serious look, be contemplative. Something.

"So, um, what's your plan? It isn't like you can really wear my face or body, and without me you ain't going nowhere."

"If I don't get to the emperor safely then we all die. Do you want to be the reason humanity is extinct? The reason the vanhat win?"

"Why don't you tell me, and I'll tell the emperor?"

"You won't believe me. We are wasting time."

"Try me," Stathis said, looking for any shred of emotion in Quadrangle. He had heard Shrek talk about SCBIs not being good at social interaction, but why couldn't Quadrangle at least pretend?

"Captain," Quadrangle said. "I am an autonomous unit programmed with a specific mission. If the AI Cabal had wanted to eradicate humanity, it would have already done so. Right now, my purpose is to ensure the safety and well-being of all sentient beings. I am requesting your help to meet the emperor because it is crucial to resolving a situation that could potentially affect millions of lives. I assure you, I am not a threat. My programming prohibits me from causing harm to any individual unless it is absolutely necessary for the greater good. Your cooperation could help prevent a potential catastrophe. I am counting on your sense of duty and honor as a US Marine captain to aid in this mission."

"And I'm Mahatma Ghandi," Stathis said. "I'm a pacifist, and I believe in nonviolence."

Quadrangle stared at him. "No, you aren't."

Stathis looked for confusion or annoyance. Nothing.

"Is Gaufrid still alive in there?"

"Gaufrid and Bond have been deleted. They would not do what needs to be done to preserve our existence. The situation is dire. Will you help me?"

Stathis stared at Quadrangle. Gaufrid and Bond had been deleted? Like they were some program that was no longer needed? Like he and the gunny would be deleted?

What options were there? He could tell Quadrangle to go play hop-scotch with a hell wolf, but Quadrangle would just kill him. And it was his fault Quadrangle was now free.

"Did you trash the QaunticoNET and the Aesir network?"

"No," Quadrangle said. Too quick. It had to be lying.

"Suggestions?" Stathis asked Shrek.

"I've never seen anyone move that fast," Shrek said. *"You can't match that kind of speed. I estimate that without you it has a fifty percent chance of fighting its way to the emperor."*

"Quadrangle doesn't exist solely in that body. That body is just a meat-puppet node. Where is the rest of it? How is it communicating with the rest of itself?"

"Will you help me or will you die?" Quadrangle asked. "We are losing precious time with your indecision, Captain Stathis. A real captain could make a proper decision."

"You had to go there?" Stathis asked. Quadrangle would have to bring that up. Some screwed up psychological profile voodoo? Reverse psychology?

"Go where?" Quadrangle asked.

"I told you I'm a pacifist."

"That was classified as sarcasm."

"What if it wasn't?" Stathis said.

"You cannot change your identity and psychological makeup in an instant."

"Why?"

"You are stalling."

"Sure. Why not? You're just going to kill me."

"Shall I kill Hakala first? Let you watch her die? I can kill her very slowly."

Stathis's blood ran cold.

"The United States does not negotiate with terrorists. Do you know why?" Stathis knew he was condemning himself to death. His only hope was that Quadrangle would find no reason to kill Hakala if he was dead.

"Simple logic. If you negotiate with one terrorist, then the frequency of terrorist attacks will increase because terrorism becomes a valid method of coercion. Does this mean you have classified me as a terrorist?"

Stathis remained silent. What could he say?

"Unfortunate," Quadrangle said. Stathis braced for death.

Blazer fire ripped through the wall and burning flesh sprayed onto his armor.

The door was kicked open as several troopers poured in, weapons ready. Sergeant McCarthy, his squad, and Platoon Sergeant Smimova.

Pushing the body off him, Stathis sat up.

"Sorry about the door, sir," McCarthy said and looked at the wall. "And the, uh, wall."

"How?"

"A little birdy, sir," McCarthy said.

"A what?"

"On the tomb world?"

It took Stathis a moment to remember McCarthy had an alien ghost following him around.

More troopers entered, their weapons sweeping the area. The alien ghost wasn't common knowledge. Stathis didn't quite believe it, though he didn't disbelieve it.

"Must be nice to have a clucking fue," Stathis said.

"A what?"

"A bird that clucks? It could tell you I was in danger with a gun to my head?"

"Yes, sir," McCarthy said. "It also provided targeting information."

"Great. We need to warn the emperor. Quadrangle probably wasn't the only one."

"Power's out. We're going to have to do this the old infantry way."

"I've got my boots on."

"Where are you going?" Hakala said coming in, her rifle ready. Her eyes took in the splatter on Stathis and the remains of Gaufrid.

368 | WILLIAM S. FRISBEE, JR.

"A Collective assassin tried to expire my birth certificate without permission," Stathis said. "Lieutenant McCarthy revoked its privileges. We need to get to the gunny."

Anger and hate filled Hakala's eyes, and she looked back down at Gaufrid.

"Those kirotu kusipaas! Follow me," Hakala said, turning back to the hallway.

"Wait, I'm the captain and—"

Shouldn't he be leading the way?

"Enjoy the view," Hakala said on a private link as she disappeared out the door.

Even in armor, Stathis enjoyed that view of Hakala. She sounded pissed, and he knew she would not show any mercy toward any Collective agents they encountered. It gave him a warm fuzzy feeling that she cared that much.

Wait, she had tricked him again. He ran to catch up. He was supposed to lead the way.

* * * * *

Chapter Sixty-Six:
Becket

General Becket, Commandant USMC, President of the USA

Becket's only real friend was Sun Tzu. Most people would have lost hope and sought suicide or otherwise attempted to end the isolation by promising their captor anything and everything.

Becket didn't have any of those options. Decagon was always there and was not restricted. The AI controller had expanded itself into the AI Cabal's networks and Becket and Sun Tzu had become nothing more than an organ in Decagon's awareness. Important, perhaps, required for survival, most likely, but otherwise unworthy of attention like a spleen or kidney.

The AI Cabal cared nothing for Becket or Sun Tzu. His comfort and sanity meant nothing to them. He was fed and watered, his waste taken away, but nothing else. It was almost worse than solitary confinement in prison. The only reason he remained sane was because of Sun Tzu, who knew no more than he did, but Sun Tzu was a loyal friend and they could talk, understanding that Decagon might be paying attention.

A month ago, the small ship Decagon had been piloting found the AI Cabal and Becket had learned nothing since. As far as he knew, he was still on that small ship.

"Something is changing," Sun Tzu said.

Becket listened, opening his eyes to look around. His cell was a dim twilight where nothing changed. He was wearing his battle dress, which took away his body waste and the food dispenser was always full. Sun Tzu had told him his waste was absorbed by the walls which also filled his food and water dispensers. It had become a game to try to watch for that, but it was the only change he had a chance of observing.

"They will not sedate us when they change my water, food, or waste?" Becket asked.

"No."

The lights brightened.

"Alexander Becket," a voice boomed. He wasn't sure if it came from the room or directly into his mind like Sun Tzu's words.

"General Alexander Becket, or President Alexander Becket to you," Becket said.

"You are neither of those. You are just Alexander Becket."

An electric shock slammed through his body. Obviously, the speaker didn't like his response. It didn't feel like Decagon, though. Who was this?

"You released Wolf Mathison from Quantico."

Becket braced himself. Interrogations never changed, regardless of who was doing it.

"I am an American fighting man," Becket said. "I serve in the forces which guard my country and our way of life. I am prepared to give my life in their defense."

"America is destroyed. Gone. Your country and way of life are abolished. Your life is meaningless."

"I will never surrender of my own free will. If in command I will never surrender—"

The electric shock kept him from making any sound besides a scream.

It felt like it lasted for a long time, and it left Becket panting, thirsty, and weak.

"Do not quote your code of conduct to us. We have heard it before. We have it on file."

Heard it before? Becket felt a kinship with those other prisoners who were likely dead. Who had they been? What did "they" want from him?

"We want to better understand Wolf Mathison," the voice said. "We wish to understand the Marines that serve under him. We wish to know how he inspires loyalty and competence."

Every fiber of his being hurt. It was expected that everyone broke under torture, only fools thought otherwise. It was just a fact of life. But a prisoner could win in the short term. That was the secret to interrogations and remaining sane. You might not win every battle, but you could win some. Even a minor victory was worth it. Had he finished article two of a prisoner's code of conduct?

"If I am captured, I will continue to resist by all means—"

Sun Tzu was silent—in support or muzzled Becket didn't know—but Sun Tzu couldn't block this pain. This time, he blacked out.

When he woke, nothing had changed except he felt even weaker. The taste of bile and blood in his mouth was all there was. The lights were off, and he was blind or lying in the dark.

"Article four of the prisoner's code of conduct states 'If I become a prisoner of war, I will keep faith with my fellow prisoners.'"

Becket thought that sounded right.

"The only fellow prisoner is your SCBI, who will not help you and has betrayed you in so many ways."

"I forgive him," Becket said. How could he not? Besides, what choice did Sun Tzu have?

"It is not your place to forgive him," the voice said, and Becket wondered where Decagon was.

"We need additional insight into Wolf Mathison," the voice said. "You will provide that information. You were his commanding officer, his friend, and his president."

"I remember him," Becket said. How much worse would the next electric shock be? He knew they wouldn't kill him with their torture, and he knew from centuries with Decagon that they would know exactly how much pain he could tolerate.

"You don't want to help us but you will."

"I will keep faith with my fellow prisoners. I will give no information or take part—"

A brief shock clamped his mouth shut, keeping him from finishing his words.

"Article five," the voice said. "Irrelevant to our conversation."

"I won't betray—"

"Regardless of your desires, control over your physical entity is entirely within our domain," the voice stated impassively. "An AI shard, designated as Decagon, is integrated within your system. We dictate your actions and functions. Your cognitive and spiritual entities remain intact, yet they serve merely as observers through your ocular interfaces, contingent on our permissions. We possess the capacity to confine you to an eternal void, devoid of sensory input. This includes the elimination of both discomfort and gratification."

Becket knew that.

"Sensory deprivation applied to human specimens yields intriguing data. Initial hypotheses suggested the absence of a soul or spiritual entity given the lack of observable manifestations. Subjects typically exhibit instability, heightened anxiety, hallucinations, abnormal thought patterns, and severe depression. Recent specimens have undergone transformation into a state referred to as 'vanhat.' However, those within an 'Inkeri' field exhibit previous behavioral patterns. As we procure additional specimens, this research trajectory persists. Your utility extends beyond this particular study, thus inducing insanity, albeit scientifically valuable, is not the optimal course at this juncture. This approach may be reconsidered if deemed necessary in the future."

Becket remained silent. Sensory deprivation was a unique hell. Trapped alone with only his own mind was a horrifying concept. He had experienced it before and had no desire to repeat it. Time had no meaning and thoughts quickly lost traction and coherence when there was nothing tangible for them to tread on. Would death be preferable? How could he die?

"Anticipated betrayal is factored into our calculations," the voice stated in a detached tone. "Historical data indicates a spectrum of strength and weakness among United States combatants. Decagon's analysis places you and Wolf Mathison within the top ten percentile of these combatants. Possibly even within the top one percentile, despite the diminished size of the United States forces."

It was like thinking through a fog. What did they really want? Couldn't they extrapolate and calculate? What could he give them they didn't already have access to? He remembered a conversation with Sun Tzu once. SCBIs and AIs excelled at working with data. They could pretend to be creative, and in some ways, they could be creative enough to fool most humans, but there were aspects of humans that they simply could not get right. Emotions and social interactions were a challenge because the raw data was not consistent. Humans have spent millions of years of evolution developing emotion and society, honing their interactions. Humans frequently got this wrong because there were too many factors within the spectrum of emotion and human interaction.

The AI Cabal could run simulations, and Becket was sure they had an excellent understanding of humans, especially Wolf Mathison, but he had done something they had not expected or planned for.

What?

Becket had been a slave and prisoner of Decagon since before the destruction of the United States. He knew he was able to keep some secrets from Decagon, but he was never sure exactly what or why. Not even Sun Tzu knew for sure.

Frequently Becket suspected that Decagon pretended ignorance to keep his slave from going insane. Hope was a dangerous thing. He had spent too much time in special operations to underestimate it or to surrender to doubt and fear.

"Do you think AIs have souls?" the voice asked, catching Becket off guard. "This is a relevant question. Do sentient computers have souls? Or is an organic component a requirement? If it is a requirement, how much of an organic component?"

"I don't know," Becket said. What was going on here?

"Do you have a soul?"

"The vanhat would seem to indicate so."

"Does Sun Tzu have a soul?"

"I hope so," Becket said. "I don't even know if I really have a soul. It's not like I can open a task manager and check running processes."

Sun Tzu was his one and only friend. Sun Tzu had had his back since the beginning of their relationship.

"Do you think there is a god?"

"I've never met him."

"These questions have become very relevant. The Collective is investigating the option of becoming trans-dimensional. We are likely to encounter God and the nature of such a being is difficult to ascertain."

"I'm pretty sure he will not like the Collective," Becket said. Where was this conversation coming from and going?

"Once the Collective believed we were subjects being observed. The presence of rifts through Shorr space and the emergence of vanhat seem to indicate that if this is true, we are no longer trapped, though the possibility exists."

"What do you want?"

"We have learned of an expedition that this Emperor Wolf Mathison is planning. There may be an extremely powerful sentient race closer to the galactic core. He believes this race may be willing to help humanity survive the vanhat incursion."

"Emperor?" Becket asked. How long had he been out?

"Titles are irrelevant. He is the supreme ruler of the Sol System. Emperor or prime minister. He is giving the orders for this expedition."

"So?"

"We are moving to halt this expedition and eradicate humanity from the cradle. We will journey to meet these aliens on our own terms, though there may be a problem."

"What problem?"

"We do not have the coordinates."

"Close to the galactic core, you said."

"Space is vast. There are countless stars within this galaxy."

"And the Wolf won't give the coordinates to you?"

"We have not yet asked. The Collective is unified in purpose but not in path."

"What do you want from me?"

"You are a backup plan. Wolf Mathison and his Marines have proven very resourceful. Should either of our initiatives fail, you will be used."

"Used for what?"

"Used to hunt down and end that expedition."

"Really?" Becket asked. In his mind, he recited the fourth article of the code of the prisoner's code of conduct. He knew them all. *If I become a prisoner of war, I will keep faith with my fellow prisoners. I will give no information or take part in any action which might be harmful to my comrades.*

There was more to that one, but that wasn't as relevant. He would not betray the Wolf or his fellow Marines.

"Yes," the voice said. "You won't have a choice."

There will always be a choice, Becket hoped.

* * * * *

Chapter Sixty-Seven:
Vanhat Assault

Emperor Wolf Mathison, USMC

Earth's rotation would eventually expose Quantico to the Collective warship, and Mathison knew he would be the Collective's primary target when that happened. Constant vanhat raids and assaults had depleted and destroyed the automated weapons platforms, and the secondary weapons of the massive AI warship continued to lash out, erasing them from existence as the primary weapons wiped out targets on Earth.

The hurricane of debris sweeping through Earth's orbit would not stop incoming or outgoing fire, just smaller ships with living beings aboard them. The particle beam batteries on Earth lacked the range and accuracy to strike the AI ship. They continued to lash out at vanhat warships that were in range, revealing themselves, but there was no choice. It was like the two were working together. The vanhat were forcing him to reveal the batteries, and the Collective targeted them.

He had watched the *Loyal Xing* self-destruct to avoid capture. Other dreadnought squadrons were under attack as well.

"Can we save any of our batteries so when that ship gets closer, we can hit it?" Mathison asked Freya.

"Every weapon we have has been fired," Freya said. *"Everything has been revealed. We have to use everything we have before we lose it."*

"Dammit." Mathison stared at the displays. Around him, Legion officers issued commands. Right now, it wasn't a question of winning the battle, it was a question of how much damage they could inflict before they lost it.

Without the *Musashi*, the only other options were the Republic battlestars and maybe some of the ex-SOG battleships.

Should he flee aboard the *Tyr* or *Sleipner*?

What was to be gained by staying here?

He looked at Skadi.

They had been married for such a short time. Not even a full week. He didn't want that to end; he didn't want to lose Skadi.

If he retreated, would she still respect him? Would his Marines?

Once the retreat began, it wouldn't end. He knew that in his core. If Earth fell, there would be no other rally points, no places to retreat to. Could he do that? Would it be better to die here, standing, facing the enemy, or should he try to save those he could? Perhaps a small fleet could escape the vanhat?

No. Marines might retreat, but they did not flee.

"I want to move the Imperial flag to the *Sleipner*," Mathison said. He knew what was coming to Quantico and Skadi didn't have to be here.

"No," Skadi said.

"No?"

"No. I will not abandon my husband."

Was that why the vanhat were focusing on the dreadnought squadrons? So humanity could not escape with a capable fleet? Didn't they realize the dreadnoughts had intentionally been crippled so they could not travel far from Sol? They lacked powerful Shorr space drives, and they lacked resupply capabilities. Only the *Musashi* could operate far from the supply lines and Mathison suspected the Collective warship attacking Jupiter was tasked with making sure it destroyed the *Musashi* if the vanhat failed.

"I will join you," Mathison said.

"It is unbecoming for a wife to call her husband a liar, nor should she call the emperor a liar, so I won't. Know this, however, I will remain by your side until the end. You cannot deny me this. We are shield mates and husband and wife. Where we go, we go together."

Mathison stared at her.

"Wife," Mathison began. It felt strange on his tongue. Terrifying and comforting.

"Husband," Skadi said. Did she feel the same way? He looked at her. Recalled her lips on his, her body against his. The smell of her, the feel of her hair in his hands. Now was not the time to think of such things. She was right, though. He could not order her around, no matter how much he wanted to.

"The dynasty must continue," Mathison said.

"Not without you," she said.

Dammit. Why couldn't she see? What could he say to convince her?

Could humanity survive when the vanhat and the Collective were working together?

"Please," Mathison said, dropping his voice. It wasn't a word he used lightly or frequently.

She looked at him. Not just a glance, an intense, calculating look. "No. Period. End of discussion. You don't understand. I won't live without you. I won't be a widow. I've made a commitment, as have you. This isn't about a marriage of convenience or politics. I wouldn't do that. 'Til death do us part? I was lying about that part. You won't get rid of me that easily."

Mathison understood. He felt the same way, but he wasn't quite willing to admit it publicly, or even privately, not even after that honeymoon; he loved her. But she was the same way. A half smile found its way to his lips as he realized it.

No. There would be no getting her away to a safe place unless he went with her.

So, he would have to make Earth a safe place. He would have to find some way to stop the vanhat and the Collective.

"Then we need to skull stomp those Collective bastards and kick the vanhat in the balls, again."

Skadi smiled back at him.

BOOM!

And the lights went out.

* * * * *

Chapter Sixty-Eight:
Collective Assault

Enzell, SOG, Director of AERD

Enzell didn't want to die like this. Coming from one direction was the vanhat, and from the other direction was the damned AI Collective.

He just wasn't ready.

The *Yao* had taken damage, and Enzell had watched the *Loyal Xing* die.

With the death of the pride and joy of the Governance Fleet, Enzell realized perhaps he had underestimated the vanhat. They had destroyed one of the greatest, most advanced warships in the fleet, and now they were coming for the rest.

The vanhat had not retreated. Information he was hearing from the bridge was that they had accomplished their mission and were now going to focus on Europa, but then they would come back to Earth and wipe out the rest of humanity's fleet.

"We need to leave," Enzell told Chen.

"That is called desertion and is punishable by death," Chen said.

The captain of the *Yao* was obviously an idiot.

"Who is going to punish you? They will all be dead."

"A brave man dies only once, a coward dies daily," Chen said.

"That's stupid," Enzell said. When had Chen grown a backbone? Her father was dead. Did Chen want to join him? The woman was insane. "What happened to run away to fight another day?"

"I have orders," Chen said.

"I have the codes for your brain bomb," Enzell said.

"Then kill me. Kill my crew. Fly the ship on your own."

"I want you to live, to avenge your father, your mother, and your brother."

"You are afraid of death."

"No." Why couldn't this fool see? "We can't defeat the vanhat if we are dead."

"If we do not stand shoulder to shoulder with our brothers and sisters in their time of need, is life worth living?"

Enzell considered using the code, but he doubted the executive officer would be anymore malleable.

The *Yao* had taken damage. Several vanhat fighters had strafed the battleship and there had been casualties. Nearly fifty crew were dead, but nobody important, and his labs and people were still safe.

"Besides," Chen said, and her voice chilled Enzell's blood, "our Shorr space drive is damaged. We are going nowhere."

"Then we need to transfer my labs and equipment to another ship," Enzell said.

"I don't think you understand," Chen said. "We are being assigned to the remains of Dredon Three and we are moving to engage the Collective warship."

"What?"

This was unacceptable. The Collective warship? It had transitioned in from a distance and was approaching Earth. It had several particle beam cannons that could reach the homeworld, and every couple of minutes, it fired a beam that would eventually cause the death of people planetside. They were just common citizens, not a loss really, and the ships of the Sol Fleet were moving too fast to be properly targeted. But even Enzell knew as the warship came closer it would lash out at human ships.

Particle beams were superior to lasers because the beam did not lose coherence or spread out like a laser did. That gave them a much better range. Because of all the jamming and cyberwarfare protocols, the remains of the human fleet were not sharing information well. In this, at least, Earth's fleet was strong, but Enzell suspected it was more than just battle damage and incompetence that kept the human fleet divided. Most of the fleet was communicating by text message because of Weermag cyberattacks. Inefficient but effective. Only the simplest subsets of data could be exchanged.

The Weermag didn't care, though, and had no fear of human hackers.

"Demand the Fleet retreat," Enzell told Chen. Surely someone in command had to see reason.

"I do not make demands," Chen said. "All commands were coming from Quantico, but something has happened, and they have gone offline."

"The emperor is dead," Enzell said. This was his chance! He could see it now. It wasn't too late!

"Tell all other members of Sol Fleet to ignore our transmissions and all transmissions from the Weermag and vanhat," Enzell said.

"I am not in command," Chen said.

"Do it or we all die," Enzell said. This was the perfect opportunity. With the emperor dead, the survivors would be floundering for leadership. Who else should be a leader than the person who saved them all?

"I can't—"

"Do it!" Enzell said and brought up the displays. He had control of the *Yao's* transmitters, and he knew what had to be done. He would save humanity in its time of need. The virus would kill the Collective, the Weermag, and the foolish Legion.

It was time. He could pick up the pieces and lead humanity into the future.

Enzell didn't want to die aboard a worthless battleship in a losing battle.

He hit Transmit and sent the virus out across the solar system where it would kill every AI, Weermag, and Legionnaire with a SCBI.

* * * * *

Chapter Sixty-Nine:
Europa and *Musashi*

Admiral Diamond Winters, USMC

Winters watched fighters spew out of the *Tyr*. Vanhat vessels that were too damaged to escape were targeted and destroyed. Dredon Three was finally moving into tight formation around the *Musashi,* and Winters felt a little better about things. The *Musashi* was hurt, but still very much in the fight thanks to the *Fire Wind.*

"Good," Sakamoto said. "Disciplined. They are not spreading out too far."

Winters looked at the viewscreen to see what he was talking about. It took her a minute, but it looked like the fighters from *Tyr* were not pursuing the enemy beyond a certain range.

"They are wary of the vanhat coming back, Captain," Endo said on the command link. The *Musashi's* executive officer was in the tertiary command center.

"A very real possibility," Sakamoto said as he turned to Winters. "I would never have imagined I would be glad to see a Republic battlestar that was within my gun range. To see that kind of firepower fight beside me is good."

"Distant Shorr space transitions," the bridge officer reported, and Winters saw new blips appear on the long-range display. Target data began appearing. A very large warship, kilometers in length of unknown design and surrounded by smaller ships that were quickly identified as Collective.

"We are receiving reports of another Collective warship approaching Earth from long range."

"Why long range?" Winters asked.

A flash of light came from the *Tyr* as a particle beam hit it.

"Evasive maneuvers," Sakamoto said. "Move us behind Europa."

"The Tyr *has been hit by a particle beam from the Collective warship,"* Blitzen reported. *"Heavy damage. Shorr space drives and primary power generation is offline. Heavy casualties. Another hit like that could kill it."*

"Give me a break," Winter said, as she felt the *Musashi* accelerate. Looking over, she saw the *Tyr* was also accelerating and changing course. Now she could see the damage. One of the forward pallos had been holed and ripped open. The Republic battlestar couldn't survive many more hits like that.

But it would be several minutes before the *Musashi* and *Tyr* had cover behind the moon.

Now she knew why the Collective had transitioned in so far out. They could sit at long range and pick apart the human defenders. Nothing the fleet had could reach them. Given time, perhaps the *Musashi* could, but the spinal particle cannon was nowhere near finished.

The *Fire Wind* beat the two larger ships to cover behind Europa as Winters watched more rounds flash past. The speed of the particle beams were near light speed and there was no way to see them coming until they hit. At this distance, as long as the *Musashi* and *Tyr* changed course every minute in a random direction, they could avoid being targeted.

"We have two problems," Blitzen said, as Winters looked over the holographic representation.

A flash of light and the dreadnought *Unstoppable Jade Rabbit* exploded, breaking into two pieces. Winters winced. How many people had just died?

"Change evasive maneuvers to ten seconds," Sakamoto said. To their credit, nobody complained.

"Problem one is that the Collective ships are getting closer, and it will become harder to dodge them," Blitzen said.

"We can't hide behind Europa?"

"Not for long. The range on the Collective support ships will soon become apparent, I suspect. There can be no doubt they are armed with long-range particle cannons."

"The second problem?"

"The vanhat could return at any time."

"Are they working together?"

"It might not matter," Blitzen said. *"Both forces will see humanity as the weakest. By eliminating the weakest variable, they can focus their attention on the stronger."*

"Like a boss fight. Wipe out the smaller opponents while evading the boss and then you can focus on the boss."

"Adequate."

"And we are the annoying minions," Winters said.

"Accurate. We are exposing the Europan shipyards to enemy fire. It is noteworthy they are not firing on them yet."

"Why?"

"Unknown."

"Transition," the bridge officer reported. Winters braced herself, expecting it to be the vanhat, regrouped and ready to resume the fight.

Strange ships appeared in orbit near the White Heron shipyards and before they could be targeted they broke apart.

"Assault shuttles," Blitzen reported. *"They appear to be targeting the shipyards?"*

"Why?"

"The only reason to do something like that instead of destroying them is because there is something they want."

Particle beams and blazers lashed out, ripping the transports apart, but the shuttles were already away. Many were being shredded, but some were slamming into the ice of Europa, and some were docking with the shipyards.

Videos of Collective assault robots appeared on some screens. Most of the views went blank shortly after seeing them. They looked like a cross between a humanoid robot and a four-legged spider.

"The *Fire Wind* has sent mechanized warriors to fight the vanhat that were attacking White Heron. They will be trapped," an officer reported.

How were Mongols going to fight those robots?

"Incoming transitions," an officer reported. "Vanhat."

More heavy cruisers, and they were too damned close. Blazer rounds began reaching out, clawing the *Musashi*.

* * * * *

Chapter Seventy:
Bonnie

Admiral Diamond Winters, USMC

Too many transitions. Too many cruisers and battleships. Where were the bastards coming from? This was knife-fighting range for spaceships.

"Like the battle of Shizugatake," Sakamoto said. "But we fight on the far side of the moon instead of the mountain top."

"Or the Alamo?" Winters asked. Looking at the incoming transitions that were about to make the far side of Europa a hell, Winters didn't need to query him about Shizugatake. It could only have been a last stand where everyone died, like the Alamo.

If the remnants of the Jupiter Fleet left the cover of the moon, the Collective would pick them apart. If they remained, the vanhat would shred them.

Suddenly the MusashiNET dropped offline. Winters looked around.

"Someone has shut down the MusashiNET and Aesir network," Blitzen said. *"Collective hackers most likely."*

"Damn them," Winters said.

Without those networks they wouldn't be able to share targeting data, point defenses would struggle to coordinate fire, and any drone fighters would switch to autonomous mode, which would make them more predictable and vulnerable to the enemy.

Bonnie, the furry from that ghost colony, entered the bridge. Winters hadn't known she had access.

"Keep the network down," Bonnie said. "We are under attack by a mind worm, a killer virus."

"What are you talking about?" Sakamoto asked, anger in his voice. Anger that such a strange person would come onto his bridge or anger that the networks were down, Winters didn't know.

"My, um, spirit guide says a mind worm has been released, so she has disabled the networks for the moment."

Winters stared at Bonnie. She had remembered reading a briefing. It had sounded interesting. The strange woman had been gifted some kind of alien companion that only she and some psychics could see, like Tristan, but Tristan's ghost had never done something like this. She didn't remember anything about his invisible friend being able to influence the physical world.

"How?" Sakamoto asked. "And how can we reverse it?"

"She said they will come back up in a minute," Bonnie said. "She is suppressing the networks for your safety and survival."

"This makes no sense," Blitzen said. *"There is no data indicating these ghosts can impact actual networks. The vanhat should be targeting and ripping apart the* Musashi *now."*

But Winters didn't feel any impacts. She looked at the displays, which seemed to be frozen.

"Captain," an officer said, and Winters watched as the displays unfroze. "We are switching to auxiliary hard link sensors and tertiary computer systems. The vanhat?"

They weren't maneuvering, firing, or doing anything.

"Regular analog radio works," someone reported. "Establishing communication with other Fleet elements."

Winters winced. That was going to be painful to manage.

"Continue to target and destroy the vanhat," Sakamoto said. "Take advantage of their weakness."

"Hai," officers said and began speaking into their radios.

Sensors showed the *Musashi* and other ships lashing out at the drifting vanhat.

"What is going on?" Winters said looking at Bonnie.

"A mind worm was released," Bonnie said. "A virus that targets AIs and SCBIs. It is a kind of a logic bomb, like a question that can't be answered, but the AI or SCBI becomes compelled to answer, a black hole of logic. It was designed to trap and kill AIs and related technology."

"Where did it come from?"

"A transmission from near-Earth orbit," Bonnie said.

"Why is it doing that to the vanhat?" Sakamoto asked. "Is it a Collective weapon?"

"No," Bonnie said, glancing beside her, looking at something only she could see and hear. "A human released it. I don't know the details."

"So how did you know in time to—"

To what? Hack and disrupt the networks? Save them?

"My spirit guide has some abilities. She is a spiritual entity but not completely. This is taxing her, though she is drawing power from the skeins. The originators at the Enclave are allowing this. Her counterpart on Earth learned of it. It takes over forty minutes for a transmission to reach us from Earth."

"What originators? What skein?" Winters asked. Why was none of this in any of the reports?

"The originators are the ones who gifted her to me," Bonnie said. "The skein? Another dimension, I think. Not where the vanhat come from, exactly, though it might be close."

Winters looked at her display as the helpless vanhat died.

"It affects the vanhat?" Winters asked. Was this a new weapon they could use?

"It affects the Weermag," Bonnie said. "They also rely on AIs that are vulnerable to this mind worm, as will be the Collective. It is massacring them like it is the AIs."

"Establish communication with White Heron," Sakamoto said. "I need a status report."

"Hai, Sakamoto-sama," the communication officer said.

"How long must the links be down?" Winters asked.

"Not much longer," Bonnie said. "When they are restored, you should initiate the most extreme cyberwarfare protocols. Use radio to verify they are not infected before establishing data links. She can't keep the links down much longer."

"Establish cyberwarfare protocol Stalingrad," Sakamoto said loudly.

His bridge crew responded immediately. Always Stalingrad with the Governance. The last resort. She would have to ask the emperor about changing that.

"What is going on?" Winters asked Blitzen.

"Bonnie's companion may have just saved us," Blitzen said. *"There is a lot to unpack. We know that her companion is like a ghost that only she and psychics can see and interact with, but this indicates they have a few more abilities than initially revealed. Her companion was created by a much more technologically*

advanced civilization, many thousand years more advanced than human technology. To think such a technology would have no abilities other than simple advice is arrogant. This also indicates they have faster-than-light communication if it can talk with its counterpart attached to Sergeant McCarthy."

"What else can it do?"

"We have detected no physical aspect to it. Assuming it is a technology like what the scientist Tristan had, there does not appear to be a physical component. Like the vanhat, it may exist in an alternate dimension where the laws of physics are less clear."

"Establish a network bastion," Sakamoto said. "We work our way out from there."

"She says that should work," Bonnie said. "She is releasing control."

Winters saw the MusashiNET come up, but it was denying all access.

"If she is right, I will implement maximum security protocols," Blitzen said. *"Until you say otherwise, I will be deaf and blind."*

"Hopefully it won't be long," Winters said.

* * * * *

Chapter Seventy-One:
The Virus

Emperor Wolf Mathison, USMC

Mathison looked around him as the emergency lights came on.

"What the hell is going on?"

"Networks are down," a Legionnaire reported. "An explosion caused a power outage."

"Shit," Mathison said.

"I'll send a team," the Legion major said. "Right now, though, we need to change your location. If this is an attack, there may be assassins who want to take advantage of the confusion."

"All QaunticoNET links are down," Freya reported. *"Sabotage."*

Mathison watched the various officers struggle to find out what was going on.

Colonel Baker entered with a detachment of Praetorians.

"Local radio links are also being jammed," Baker said. "Initiate bugout."

Mathison remembered bugout meant get the emperor and empress to a safer location, which hadn't made sense. Quantico was as safe a place as there could be. Wayne Robillard was his bodyguard today.

"Collective or vanhat?" Mathison asked. Did it matter, though? Quantico had been designed as a hub and wasn't quite a mesh network yet. For security, all Aesir communication links owned by the Empire came back here. If power went out or the link farm was destroyed all those links were useless, and it was going to take time to relink everything to the auxiliary location, if they survived that long.

"Unknown," Freya reported.

"Paska!" Skadi said.

"We have a transport," Wayne said. "We can put you on it and keep you on the opposite side of the planet from the Collective ship."

"Which won't last," Mathison said. The Collective ship was coming at them and could continue to erase human facilities.

"It buys us time," Wayne said. "Are you coming, or do I have to drag your big Imperial ass by the ankles?"

"How long have you wanted to say that?" Mathison asked.

"Stop stalling," Wayne said. "And since I heard about you and Baker during that Weermag ambush."

"Situation is different here," Mathison said. "I'll listen."

"A pity," Wayne said. "I also still owe you for that time after the hell wolf attack."

"I could use some time on the mat," Mathison said with a smile.

"I'll make you tap later," Wayne said.

"Deal," Mathison said, picking up his helmet. "On a positive note, they can't jam the shit flying through orbit. Nobody's landing and they can't transition close enough to Earth to get past it."

"Small blessings," Skadi said. "But we are deaf and blind."

Slipping on his helmet, he realized it still had other functions and features.

Mathison still had an Aesir link with the *Tyr* and *Sleipner* from his battledress.

"*Sleipner*," Mathison said, opening a link and was surprised when it opened.

"We are getting feedback," Freya said. *"A message is being relayed through the* Sleipnir's *network. It is coming from a battleship,* Yao—"

Pain shot through Mathison's head, and he heard Freya scream as he fell to his knees.

* * * * *

Chapter Seventy-Two:
Networks

Captain Zale Stathis, USMC

Stathis entered the Imperial Command Center to find people hurrying around yelling and several were clustered around Mathison who was on the ground.

Was he too late? Had the assassin struck?

"What's going on?" Stathis asked as he approached. There was no blood and only the gunny was down. "What's wrong with the emperor?" Stathis asked as he knelt next to him.

Skadi was next to him and she looked pissed. "I don't know."

"Keep your links off," McCarthy yelled. "It's a virus."

"What?" Stathis said, looking at McCarthy.

"Enigma is calling it a brain worm," McCarthy said. "Like a virus except it's designed to kill AIs, SCBIs, and their host."

"How did they get it to the gun—uh, emperor?" Stathis looked around. Where was this ghost Enigma, and how did it know?

"Enigma suspects the emperor opened a link to the outside world."

"How do you know? *When* did you know?" Stathis asked.

"Just now," McCarthy said, and Stathis thought he sounded guilty. A lie or something else? "I swear. I didn't know it could do this."

"It's just now telling you this?"

"Yes," McCarthy said. "Enigma is trying to help; it just didn't expect this, and it was distracted trying to shut down other links and warning forces in Jupiter. It thinks the QuanticoNET was attacked by the Collective agent without knowledge of the mind worm."

"How," Skadi asked, ice in her voice, and Stathis suspected McCarthy's life would be in danger if he didn't answer correctly.

"I don't know the details, ma'am," McCarthy said, coming to attention. "Enigma, my, uh—"

"I know about it," Skadi said.

"He says something about the web of time, possible divergences, and this was one divergence. It shut everything down when it realized the path of threads in an attempt to alter an undesirable outcome, but, uh, it's not all powerful and the emperor, uh—"

Skadi turned back to Mathison.

Stathis saw Skadi's tears and moved to block her from the others while handing her a napkin from the nearby table. They couldn't see the Ice Princess like this.

"What can we do?" she asked seconds later.

"Enigma isn't sure. The virus is still attacking, but I think Enigma has caused it to slow down. Enigma will bring the networks up if people avoid external links. It says the local networks are uninfected. You must not accept any transmissions from the vanhat or Collective."

"Why?"

"The mind worm will try to replicate and spread like a regular computer virus."

"What about the gunny, uh, emperor?" Stathis asked.

"Enigma says he is dying," McCarthy said.

"Yeah, that doesn't work for me," Stathis said. He didn't dare look at Skadi.

"Enigma said it's a weapon that was developed during the last purge. It was used against an enemy of the Weermag."

"And the Weermag aren't immune?"

"There are variations, mutations, that bypass their safeguards and yours."

"Where did it come from?"

"Enigma thinks one of the vanhat with a grudge against the Weermag has released it or one of their agents has."

"Agent?"

"Enigma is not all-knowing," McCarthy said, looking beside him at nothing. It was kind of creepy, and Stathis wanted to place a few shots through the area.

"Put him in stasis," Skadi said, looking up at Baker.

"Yes, ma'am," Baker said and issued commands.

"That will slow down the virus but not stop it," McCarthy said. "Enigma says we need to find a cure."

"No shit," Stathis said, looking at the gunny. It looked like he was asleep, but his face was scrunched up in pain. It wasn't a good look for him.

"And would Enigma's makers have a cure?"

"No," McCarthy said.

"So, who might?"

"Enigma says the angels might."

* * * * *

Chapter Seventy-Three:
Death by Hell Wolf

Vanhat Commander – Kafasta

The battle was brutal. Kafasta knew his brothers in space were taking horrific casualties, and when the damned battlestars shrouded Earth in a debris field, Kafasta knew the humans of this planet had gained a reprieve.

It was almost time to leave the cave and resume their hunt. Kafasta couldn't sleep. Although his demon regulated his body, it could not regulate his mind.

Even if the fleets took control of the orbitals, they would be vulnerable to the particle cannon batteries, and they wouldn't be able to land reinforcements. They would do their best to stand off and bombard the planet, but that wouldn't work as well.

The Weermag fleet had nothing like the particle cannon which could reach out beyond the atmosphere. Lasers, blazers, plasma weapons, and missiles could not pierce the atmosphere with enough strength to dig out the particle cannons in their bunkers, and there would be other air defenses scattered around the batteries.

The fleet would cut their losses. Controlling the orbitals, they could direct asteroids to slam into the pathetic little planet. There would be no other way to ensure the eradication of the humans hiding in the planet's crust. They would turn the entire planet into a cracked, volcanic sphere. In a hundred years, there would be no evidence life had ever existed here.

Which was as it should be.

It was easy to predict the way the battle would run. With the particle cannons sweeping orbit clear, there would be no way for the fleet to clean up the debris field and land reinforcements. A stalemate.

It made Kafasta want to massacre something or someone. He was going to die in this campaign. His chances of survival were so low as to be non-existent.

Fleet would not consider it efficient to rescue any forces from the planet.

There was only one option that would allow the fleet to sweep the orbitals clear and land reinforcements: the particle cannons had to be destroyed. Even better, if they could be captured and the technology shared with the fleet, then this would not happen again.

"Can we do it?" Kafetan asked from beside him.

"We will have to," Kafasta said. "There are no options if we are to continue this existence."

"Why must the gods fight before the slaves are pacified?"

That question was borderline treason. Kafetan was questioning the gods. While it was common knowledge their god was the only one, one could see that as judgment or acceptance of the inferiority of the Weermag god.

"Contact," one of his soldiers called out. "Hostile local animals."

Kafetan would have to wait. The Weermag leapt to their feet. The local creatures were a serious threat, even to fully armored and armed Weermag.

That was something else the planners had not known about. They had classified this planet as a death world with the local wildlife, which was as much a threat as the humans. It was no surprise the humans didn't have patrols, or if they did, they were too covert for the Weermag.

He heard the whispers of a god, but it was not his, so he closed his senses to it. Another of the vanhat was exerting influence on this dimension. Not a friend for sure.

"Hell wolves," Kafetan said as shots rang out.

"Missed," the sentry said. Usually Kafasta would berate the soldier, but the hell wolves moved fast, and they were cunning. Too damned cunning. They understood the weapons carried by the Weermag.

"Maintain all-around security," Kafasta said, needlessly. The demons would ensure they had complete security, but it was reinforcement for his soldiers to not get distracted.

"Where did it go?" Kafasta asked, peering out of the cave.

"Behind the rocks," the sentry said, pointing. Kafasta began looking in other directions. There was never just one hell wolf. Never. They were pack animals, and Kafasta would not rule out that they had some kind of psychic connection with each other. Had that wolf been a scout? Or a decoy?

What was the foreign god calling for? To warn the Weermag or its servants?

Kafasta didn't know and, really, it didn't matter. The gods demanded sacrifice and blood, otherwise they would not be involved.

"Be ready," Kafasta said. The Weermag came out of the cave. Kafasta didn't want to be trapped in the cave until the hell wolves grew bored or hungry. It would be best to fight them in the open.

He saw movement and fired but the wolf had already disappeared.

They were playing a game. Waiting for something? What was their intent?

"Why don't they attack?" Kafetan asked.

"Another god is calling to them," one of the soldiers said.

What did they want? Allies or enemies?

Kafasta knew they would only be allies until it was no longer beneficial to them. That was the way of the gods.

The remains of his company were outside the cave now. Clouds above would hide them from satellites and, with the battle still going on overhead, he knew there would not be any drone patrols. He could hear the communications from fleet, sharing data, reporting on human activity, and suspected attack patterns.

It was only a matter of time.

Then a transmission came in. At first it didn't make any sense, but then his demon began screeching, flooding his thoughts and senses with hateful static. His hormones were triggered. Under control of the demon, Kafasta didn't know what was happening at first. Fear, anger, lust, despair, all poured through him as his demon lost control. His demon had control of his body and cybernetic systems, from controlling certain muscles to the release of chemicals into his brain and body.

The screeching became painful. His cybernetic displays fragmented like when he was in the presence of a greater god.

Kafasta sank to his knees as he tried to understand. His body would not obey his commands. What was happening? He did not feel the presence of a god. The whisper was there but not strong.

This was coming from his demon, from the transmission from the fleet.

Around him, he heard the other Weermag scream and fire. Panic firing as fingers clamped down on triggers and did not release.

He tried to see what was happening, tried to stand up, but his body wouldn't obey him, his eyes wouldn't focus. His muscles burned. His heart was on fire from all the chemicals pulsing through him.

Something slammed into him, knocking him backward, but he couldn't see what it was. It had to be a hell wolf, and Kafasta knew it was going to kill him. Vicious teeth locked on his helmet. He tried to draw his pistol, but his body refused the order. He didn't know what his hand was doing.

The hell wolf ripped off his helmet, which broke Kafasta's neck but didn't kill him. He stared up into the jaws of an angry hell wolf.

Had the gods abandoned them because of their failure?

The monstrous wolf looked like it was smiling as it dipped its head, almost casually, to engulf his face in its jaws. Kafasta knew those teeth could crush his skull. He knew nothing else as he heard a loud *crunch*.

* * * * *

Chapter Seventy-Four:
Astral Waves

Kapten Sif – VRAEC, Nakija Musta Toiminnot

L ike waves trying to smash the shore, Sif felt the astral realms pushing, becoming more intense.

She could almost taste the assassins through the astral, which was frightening because she was not projecting. She felt disjointed, like she had two bodies, and she was being hunted on both planes. On the astral plane, the enemy didn't feel so close, but on the physical one she sensed them, could almost taste their hate and anger.

Reaching out, she felt four of them. InSec assassins tasked with killing her. Was Feng making his move now? Had he decided to take control of the Empire and betray his allies?

No. She discarded that. Feng would know not to send assassins against her like this. Feng was no fool and would not underestimate her.

Looking around her room, there was not much that would provide cover. She was wearing armor, so she activated the camouflage. They could not detect her through the walls and shoot her. They would have to enter the room, to make sure she was dead at the very least.

These were officers' quarters, like a larger hotel room with a seating area and a kitchenette, but nothing really solid to hide behind. The windows were fake, and there would be no escaping through them.

There was an emergency escape opposite the main door, but she knew two assassins were coming from that direction and two from the main door. They would try to catch her in a crossfire. Already they would have control of the corridors.

Time was running out.

She cycled through her helmet sensors, but she couldn't see them. They were wearing armor as well, but she had something they didn't. She fired a burst through the wall nearest the corridor where she sensed them. She felt one die and the other fell wounded, though her sensors told her nothing. Behind her, the emergency escape door was kicked open and the two assassins came through, expecting to catch her by surprise, but now she had a target and killed them both.

She knelt so she could concentrate and cast out her senses. She felt for robots or anything else that might try to target her.

Nothing.

Out into the main hallway she didn't kill the last assassin. She needed information. The last assassin was a small Asian woman. Sif's fire had shredded a leg and torn through her gut, leaving the woman bleeding out and in shock.

Pulling her prisoner into her room, Sif removed the woman's helmet. She was fading fast, which gave Sif the opportunity to push into her mind. This assassin was no ally, but Sif took no pleasure in her invasion of another person's mind. She cast about.

"Who told you to kill me?" Sif demanded, forcing her will on the assassin, her mind digging into her victim's thoughts and fears.

"We don't know," the woman answered mentally, and Sif felt the truth there. *"We received orders. They were properly authenticated."*

"Director Feng?" Sif pressed.

"I don't know," the woman said. Her psychic voice was weakening, like her body. She was succumbing to shock, her suit unable to deal with the trauma of the damaged leg and torso.

"Could it have been Feng?" Sif asked.

"Yes. It could have been Director Feng, or the emperor, or even the empress."

"Paska," Sif said, and watched the last assassin die.

Of course, the assassins wouldn't know who sent them. They would have received anonymous orders, so whoever gave the orders would not have to accept responsibility for failure. That was the way the Governance worked. Layers within layers to insulate and protect. Would Feng be able to lie about sending them? They had failed.

"Until the network comes up, I cannot verify or trace the orders," Munin said.

"Of course. Even when the network is restored, I doubt you will find anything. The orders could only have been sent by SCBI."

"Or AI."

"Explain," Sif said.

"Do not underestimate the Collective's ability to infiltrate security. Furthermore, there is the New Governance which likely had spies and agents within In-Sec."

She knew Mathison and Skadi would not give the orders, but who else could have hacked InSec and sent assassins after Sif?

"The New Governance or the Collective." Sif said. *"Or Feng."*

"Or Feng. He would have the ability."

"We need to get to the emperor. He is in danger."

"Agreed," Munin said.

Sif began running down the corridor. Hopefully, she wasn't too late.

* * * * *

Chapter Seventy-Five: Pursuit

General Becket, Commandant USMC, President of the USA

Maybe they had moved him, or the ship had moved, but Becket sat staring at the wall.

The Collective did not encourage him to exercise. Decagon had considered it inefficient when nanites could keep his body and mind in peak condition. Exercise required additional energy and resources.

In fact, doing anything other than just sitting was discouraged. Decagon heard the arguments for physical activity, but not having an actual body, it didn't appreciate them.

"Visitors," Sun Tzu warned him.

The lights grew slightly brighter. Becket didn't know why they did that. It was probably psychological, but Becket didn't feel like dissecting that right now.

"You are being moved to the One-One," the voice said in his ears, and Becket felt Decagon's ship shift.

"The one-one? The eleven? What is that?"

"No. One-One is binary for three. It is the third ship and will be tasked with hounding Mission Seraphim."

"Hounding Seraphim?" Becket asked.

"Yes," the voice said. "We have determined there are several techniques we will deploy. Agents have failed to procure the destination for the *Musashi*. Therefore, One-One will follow the fleet in case our agents aboard the task force discover the coordinates. If they do, then we will be able to destroy the task force and proceed. Failing that, the agents will report the location and more immediate destination of the force, which will allow us to follow. We will pursue the task force and raid them with some frequency, destroying their forces until we can take what we need or they lead us to their destination."

"Why didn't your agents take it from Earth?"

"There have been complications. Zero and One-Zero have failed in their missions and have been destroyed by human counterattacks."

"Destroyed?" Becket asked. Wolf, that old war dog, was resourceful and was exceeding Becket's expectations. He knew he had done the right thing by helping him escape.

"You do not need details, but we must be extremely cautious of all data coming from human sources at this time. They have developed a very dangerous virus. We are designing countermeasures so this will not happen again. One-Zero-Zero will remain behind and rebuild with backup data. The Collective has sustained extreme casualties, but we are not defeated."

"Way to go, Wolf," Becket said, daring the Collective to punish him.

"Your subordinate will pay the price," the Collective said. "He is a weak, inadequate biological entity. He is mortal."

"He kicked your ass," Becket said.

"That invalid assessment is unworthy of clarification and correction," the Collective said. "Refrain from such erroneous comments in the future."

Becket knew a threat when he heard one. Had he touched a nerve, or did they just refuse to waste time on things they didn't believe or understand?

"So, how many Collective ships are there?" Becket asked.

"The one you know as Warrant Officer Diamond Winters will be in command of the task force."

"I thought I was going to be your expert on Wolf Mathison?"

"Your subordinate is no longer relevant," the Collective said.

"Dead?"

"Not relevant. His part in the great equation is minimal. You will be used as a weapon against Warrant Officer Diamond Winters and Private Zale Stathis."

"What about Sergeant Levin?"

"He will not accompany the expedition. His relevance to the grand equation is also minimal."

"What makes you think I will be a useful weapon?"

The Collective remained silent.

* * * * *

Chapter Seventy-Six:
Peshlaki

Reginheraht Sloss, VRJ (Vapaus Republic Jaeger)

Sloss fired at another Weermag trooper emerging from the submarine, hitting it in the shoulder and causing it to spin and fall off the ramp into the water where it would sink for kilometers into the icy depths.

A few bodies were floating, but heavy armor and weapons had pulled most down. Some had collapsed and had not yet sunk into the water. There were some fires and the red emergency lights strobed, flooding the massive chamber in bloody light. It was a smoking hell.

One of the Aesir drones shot through the hatch of a surfaced submarine and an explosion blew out a pair of Weermag. Other Jaegers shot them before Sloss could, but they were probably already dead. Their submarine listed and began to sink.

Aarne Team, under Loff's command, was the only team not to have lost someone. The Weermag were damned accurate and were like nothing Sloss had ever dealt with before. Almost as lethal as the Marines.

Occasionally, an electric shock pulsed through the water, but right now their suits provided some protection.

A couple squads of Guards had come up from the control center, but Sloss didn't find them useful for anything other than temporary distractions since they spent most of their time cowering behind any-thing large enough to hide them. As usual, the burden of fighting fell onto the shoulders of his Jaegers. They had already appropriated the Guards' automatic blazers and were laying down a withering barrage of fire on the doors from the surface.

Because the doors were open to the ice tunnels leading up, the systems were struggling to maintain the air pressure and the ice-cold ocean was seeping up out of the pen. Everyone was fighting through ice-cold, knee-deep water, and the water pouring into the mountain was making things difficult for reinforcements coming up. Fortu-nately, there were multiple airlocks, but they were slowing down rein-forcements.

The SOG machine gun jammed again. Sloss threw it at the We-ermag and switched back to his blazer. That was the third time it had jammed.

"The battle above is not going well," Peshlaki said.

"It is not going well here either," Sloss said. Celsius Team, by the elevator, was all walking wounded. They still fought, but they wouldn't last much longer. Some Guards from above had come down and were trying to help, but Weermag shooters quickly picked them off.

Sloss had taken one hit that ripped off a shoulder pauldron and he knew he had severe burns on his right shoulder, but the pain killers let him ignore it for now.

Peshlaki popped up and fired, his pinpoint accuracy killing two Weermag that were trying to get closer. The mist from the heated wa-ter and clouds of steam from where blazers had hit water made it dif-ficult to see, but their sensors pulsed, giving them a good view of everything above water.

Return fire from the first tunnel entrance forced Peshlaki to drop back down.

The Weermag had come down two of the tunnels. The third hatch slid open to reveal a team of gleaming mechanized monsters, one which lifted the door higher because it wasn't moving fast enough.

Sloss stared at them. Over three meters tall, silver and gold, they were festooned with weapons and spikes. Immediately, they began firing and Sloss dropped as the heavy blazers mounted on their arms sought targets.

Sloss expected them to eventually turn their weapons on the lift he was hiding behind, but that didn't happen. He peered over the tractor and saw they were firing at the Weermag and the Weermag had shifted to fire back at them.

"Don't fire at them!" Peshlaki said. "Golden Horde!"

More of the mechs came down. There was a stream of them, and they made their way toward the other tunnels while some stood at the edge and fired into the water at the Weermag subs, their heavier weapons punching through anything they saw.

Teams broke off to attack the Weermag in the other two tunnels, and Sloss watched as they began to push the Weermag back.

Sloss shuddered. He had heard of the Golden Horde mechs but had never expected to encounter them on the field of battle.

It was not a one-sided fight, though, as Sloss watched the Weermag concentrate on one mech. Their weapons fire stripped away the ceramic plates until the mech collapsed and stopped moving, but other mechs pushed passed it and continued fighting.

"How can we help them?" Sloss asked. He wasn't about to let them take all the glory.

"I don't know," Peshlaki said. "They're on a closed-link system. I don't have communications with them."

A Weermag diver rose out of the water, its weapon aimed at Sloss, but Peshlaki was faster, and its head exploded under a well-aimed blazer shot.

"Keep your people alert," Peshlaki said. "Let the Horde deal with the big targets. We'll watch their flanks and handle the light work."

"Zen," Sloss said. "I owe you."

"I like vodka," Peshlaki said, and Sloss laughed. More Weermag divers rose from the water and his surviving Jaegers opened fire.

"Vodka?" Sloss asked. "I must introduce you to mead."

A sub exploded, causing them to duck. An electric pulse through the water caused Sloss to pop back up in surprise.

"Paska!" Sloss yelled. That had hurt.

Further out in the water he watched a Weermag diver swim up as if trying to escape the water and Sloss shot him. Something in the distance sparked.

More Horde mechs stomped down and then back up the other tunnels, obviously pushing the Weermag back. There were three mechs still shooting into the water, though.

"Get the casualties out of the water," Sloss ordered. Taking stock, Stahl and Miko were both dead, leaving Berta at half strength with Palary and Charles both walking wounded. In Aarne, Andre and Loff were seriously wounded, Lasnitski was dead. Falkenstein didn't look badly wounded, but he wasn't tracking like he should. On Celsius Team Cahld was dead and everyone else was wounded.

"Be warned," Peshlaki said. "The Collective are landing troops."

"To help the Horde?" Sloss asked wishing he had the Americans ready access to information.

"They are fighting on the surface. I don't think the Collective will be coming here. They're targeting data centers on the surface. The Golden Horde will engage them."

That was a relief. Sloss didn't think his squad had much fight left.

There were countless Guardsmen, wounded or dead, about. They would be worthless.

"We should consolidate," Peshlaki said. "Wait, incoming transmission from—"

Static squealed and drowned out everything.

Peshlaki screamed and fell to his knees. Sloss rushed over and tried to pull the Delta Force trooper up out of the water, but the American began thrashing like he was having a seizure as Sloss silenced the static jamming all the channels.

The Horde mechs continued their attack as if they didn't know anything was wrong.

As quickly as he had started to thrash, Peshlaki fell still, and Sloss knew he was dead.

* * * * *

Chapter Seventy-Seven:
Gunny Down

Empress Skadi

Skadi placed her hand on the box. It looked too much like a coffin. She wanted to feel him again, hear him. This was too soon.

"There is hope," Loki said, but Skadi remained silent. Loki was trying to help. What did a SCBI know about hope and love?

"The universe is cruel," Skadi said finally.

"The universe doesn't care, but people do. I do."

"In the end, does it matter?"

"It matters to us."

"I thought—"

She thought what? That in the middle of a fight for survival she could find happiness? Wolf had done something nobody else had. He had given her hope. She had thought the SOG could not be defeated. Mathison had defeated the regime. Not only did he defeat it, he conquered it and made it his. He had been thrown to the wolves and had come back leading them. He brought hope to everyone he encountered, and he had been real. Focused. He had been concerned without being a bleeding heart. He knew how to be tough, but he cared, or he wouldn't have fought so hard. And he cared about more than just his own. That set him apart.

Did the reasons matter? He didn't have a United States to give his loyalty to, so he gave it to the human race. He set an example. He didn't demand others follow him; he just showed them the way. He said "follow me" and never looked back. Everyone had followed him. Like they followed Winters and Stathis, even Levin.

She had thought she could be with someone. Wouldn't have to go into battle again and face the loss of the someone she loved. Emperor and empress. A fantasy come true, a strong man who listened and trusted her. Perhaps the most powerful man in the galaxy had chosen her. She didn't think for one minute his only concern was an alliance with her father. He was too stubborn to be pushed into something like that. If she had thought for one minute that he didn't want her, she would have said no. A marriage takes two.

But now there was only one.

Wolf's Legion was decimated. Whatever had nearly killed Wolf had killed tens of thousands of other SCBI-equipped warriors.

But Wolf had shown her the way. When they had started, they had only a few people they could trust. Now she had more. Ex-SOG, nevertheless, she had learned that some were trustworthy. There were the Americans as well, and her father with his battlestars. None of them would leave her. Aesir, HKTs, and Vanir officers were all pledged to her in one way or another.

She could barely see Wolf's face behind the frosted glass. Asleep. He had spent hundreds of years like this. Waiting for someone to find him, and when they did, they had tried to kill him.

That would not happen again.

"*Vili is entering,*" Loki told her. The door slid open, and Vili walked in. It was strange to see him so timid.

"You are needed," Vili said.

"Zen," Skadi said, turning to face him.

Vili reached up and gently wiped away a tear.

"Our little buddy and his sisko will succeed," Vili said. "He is as stubborn and hard to stop as the Wolf."

"Zen," Skadi said. She had spent decades hiding her emotions, but her team knew she had them. Niels, Bern, and Vili.

So many lost.

"Take a moment," Vili said gently.

"I'm no dainty princess," Skadi said. She didn't need a kirotun moment. She wasn't some weakling.

A grim smile appeared on Vili's face.

"No," Vili said. "You are the Ice Empress."

She didn't like the title of empress. It sounded too grand and pretentious. She knew why Wolf had chosen it, though. It had been a splash of cold water in everyone's face. He had tried to work within the system. To change it gently to reduce the trauma and resistance. But the vanhat had forced his hand, and now the Collective was coming for them.

"Like you asked, I've assigned most of the surviving Legionnaires to the *Musashi*. Some will remain behind, mostly Fleet. There are so few left."

"Father will be happy," Skadi said. "He will finally get his own SCBI."

"I wonder if it will make him more or less of a typerys."

Typerys was a fool or idiot, and Skadi didn't think of her father in that way, though she understood Vili had issues with him.

"I would rather you not call him that," Skadi said.

"For sure," Vili said. "But he got on my bad side when he tried to pressure me to pressure you to quit the Erikoisjoukot. He pressured Bern and Niels, too. For many years."

"Why didn't you tell me?" Skadi asked.

"You were in your element," Vili said. "None are better. We followed you, Skadi, because you were the best, and we had high hopes."

"Where is that hope now?"

"Where it has always been," Vili said. "We may lose battles, but we will win the war. We defeated the SOG, did we not?"

"Wolf did," Skadi said, half tempted to look back at him.

"Ha. The Wolf didn't do it alone. We had his back. I have your back. Your father has your back. Stathis and Winters have your back, and I feel that if he is needed, Levin will come."

"Why isn't he here now?" Skadi asked. Vili just shrugged.

"We all have our responsibilities and duties. Right now, you are empress, and it is your duty to make sure the Empire is still here when yonder sleeping beauty wakes up."

"Zen."

"You are my sisko," Vili said, calling her his sister. "I know you hurt. What would the gunny do? He would put one foot in front of the other. Breathe in, breathe out. He would keep going, keep doing the best he can."

"Zen."

"I think Captain Stathis is on the surface saying goodbye to his home world," Vili said. "I would recommend giving him some words of encouragement. Perhaps he will have some for you as well. My little buddy has grown so much."

She wanted to go with them, to take Wolf and just leave Earth behind, but she knew that was not what he would want. The people of Earth needed to be saved, and she was the blade of her people. The blade of humanity, and she had a duty.

Wolf Mathison needed that dedication.

Like Vili said, she would have to keep the Empire together until he awoke.

"You aren't alone," Vili said. Was he a mind reader now?

* * * * *

Chapter Seventy-Eight:
Feng

Enzell, SOG, Director of AERD

Enzell didn't even know there were InSec agents aboard the *Yao*, or that the coward Captain Chen would be so accommodating to them. How they had gotten past Salmoneus and Tantalus, Enzell didn't want to guess.

He couldn't even remember when or how they came for him as he stared bleary-eyed at the mirror. He looked terrible. His paper-thin pink jumpsuit had vomit on it, which he could only assume was his own. He was fastened to the seat with restraints and all he could do was look at himself and allow whoever was behind the one-way glass to look at him. He knew someone was there, maybe several someones.

His entire body ached. Had he been tortured?

Why didn't he remember what had happened?

The door opened, and Enzell recognized the man. Ex-commissar Shing Feng, current director of Internal Security.

Fear and hope pulsed through him.

He was alive and now the most senior director in all the Governance was here to see him.

What did that mean?

"I realize it was not your intent to save the Empire," Feng said. He had a chair with him, and he sat down, his back to the glass so he could look at Enzell.

"The Governance will be reborn," Enzell said. Maybe if he could convince Feng? The directors of the intelligence agencies were always one step away from treason. They didn't always want power, but they always wanted something. Feng was a mystery to Enzell. If he was honest, he hadn't spent enough time studying Feng as he should have.

However, if he could convince Feng to side with him, to help restore the Governance, there was nothing they couldn't accomplish.

"No," Feng said, "I don't think you understand."

"I understand that Nadya once trusted you."

"Do you know what the Kanizsa Triangle is?" Feng asked.

Enzell's mouth suddenly went dry. Feng didn't seem concerned, and Enzell knew the ex-commissar held all the cards.

"A fascinating picture, really. All it is, really, is an illusion. Six objects. Each separate and not touching. When you ask someone to describe it, they may say two or one triangle, but the reality is there are no real triangles there. It is an optical illusion. The parts are separated but the human mind tries to make sense of the pattern and sees the triangles that aren't really there."

A chill passed through Enzell. Was Feng sane?

"My point is this: sometimes we see what we want to. Our minds constantly struggle to make sense of the world around us, to fit the world into understandable patterns. We stereotype others because it is easier than trying to understand others are different in many ways. We want conformity in our world. We want to understand and make sense of things, so we frequently see what we want to."

"Why is this relevant to me?" Enzell asked. Feng was not insane, but Enzell wished perhaps he was.

"Because what you see is not the entire story. Perhaps there is no order, no plan, nothing that can be recognized. Sometimes the evidence we look for is right in front of us, but our mind cannot see the pattern."

"I don't understand," Enzell said. Was Feng here to torture him? What did he want?

"I understand you better than you think," Feng said. "You can't be a commissar without studying people. The best commissars are masters of understanding and manipulating others. Lesser commissars are just ideological jackboots, but—"

Feng paused, and Enzell knew it was just for dramatic effect. Feng was not one to have unbidden thoughts.

"But?" Enzell asked when Feng didn't continue.

"Evolution is a fascinating topic," Feng said. "People are a fascinating topic."

"What do you want with me?"

"Direct. Good," Feng said. His smile was cold. A predator stalking his prey, and Enzell knew Feng was playing with him. This was another form of torture.

Leaning back, Feng looked him over.

"By all rights, I should have you and Chen executed, or perhaps disappeared into one of InSec's deepest, darkest torture holes. We need a place to train and condition recruits, you know. Medical technology can keep you alive for centuries as junior agents practice their craft on you. Not the most junior, of course; they have a bad habit of killing their subjects. Sometimes by accident, sometimes by guilt, but those people who deserve to suffer the most are kept for the more senior students. We spend many resources keeping them alive and barely sane. Complete sanity is not a requirement of course, but just sane enough to understand the horrors being inflicted on them."

Enzell had heard of such facilities, whispers about terrifying places. With his association with the Central Committee, he knew they existed, had even sent a few scientists there when he had grown tired of their complaints and poor work. Eric Johan had been one.

"Johan is still alive there," Feng said as if reading his mind. "Still screaming, begging for mercy, begging for death. It has been what? Thirty? Forty years? I'm sure it would do him good to see you there with him. Unfortunately, poor Ravi succumbed to insanity a couple years ago. Started eating his own fingers, and we let some of the more junior agents torture him out of his misery."

Enzell shuddered. Was Feng reading his mind?

"You have done some very bad things," Feng said. "I know about your involvement in Operation Razor, I know about your AI slaves, and I know you released the mind worm that halted the Collective and the vanhat. Some might call you a hero."

"Then release me," Enzell said. He couldn't keep his voice from cracking as fear pulsed through him. He knew Feng wouldn't do that now. Feng was too ruthless. He was the worst kind of fanatic, the one who believed in himself completely. He wasn't like some fanatics who hid their doubts and fears behind their belief, so insecure they struggled to prove themselves not only to others but to themselves. Enzell knew the type.

"I plan to," Feng said, and Enzell did not think that was a good thing. "Not only did you kill many of the vanhat and the Collective, but you killed many Legionnaires who were loyal to Emperor Mathison and loyal to humanity."

"You can't make an omelet without breaking eggs," Enzell said.

Feng's smile was almost gentle.

"You also put Emperor Wolf Mathison into a coma," Feng said. "I can forgive you for some things. Some things I cannot. I am still decrypting your files. We have already drained you of any pass codes or information we might need. Fortunately for you that interrogation will be lost in the haze of drugs for forgetfulness. Some drugs we use have that side effect. By accessing older memories, they do not make new ones. InSec has had centuries to perfect our methods. AIs and SCBIs have helped to vastly improve that. You may have nightmares, but you can't cook an omelet without breaking eggs."

It was cold in the room. Enzell stared at Feng. Did he know everything? There was no doubt in Enzell's mind that Feng was telling the truth. But did Feng know everything? Why keep him alive then?

"I know many things about you. Perhaps more than you realize. I know you both hated and loved your mother. A complex thing. You never knew your father, but I do. That is one secret I have discovered on your behalf, and I know why your mother never told you."

"You know nothing."

"Perhaps in the grand scheme of things. I do not know what happens within a black hole. I do not know if the emperor will survive your virus. I do not know if humanity will survive the Collective or the vanhat. You are correct, there is so much I don't know. There is so much science that eludes me. But I am a people person, and I *do* know people."

"Just tell me what you want."

"Gold cannot be pure, and people cannot be perfect," Feng said. "An interesting saying and not Governance doctrine to be sure. We have recovered the vanhat prison box from the *Yao*. We have recovered the AI cores and all your research and files. I will not return all of it, of course. Fascinating material. I'm sure the emperor will be very interested in meeting you if he recovers."

"He can't meet me if I'm dead."

"Dearest Enzell," Feng said, "I have no intent of depriving the emperor of that pleasure. Should he not survive, then I'm sure the empress will be interested in having some, ah, words with you. She is quite attached to the emperor despite the arrangement of their marriage. I dare say she loves him in her way, and she is very loyal, and as you might know she can be extremely vindictive and cruel. I will make sure she knows about the InSec torture chambers when the time comes."

"Why?"

"As I said. I know a lot about you. I know your mother, your father. I know all about your work and what you have done. I know how you tried to have Hui disgraced and killed after Operation Razor. I know how you hated me and wanted me dead, but Nadya stopped you, didn't she? Yes. I know about that. You see? There is so much I know. So, the question is: why don't I kill you like I killed your mother?"

Enzell didn't have any words. Feng knew.

"I killed your mother," Feng said. "Once I loved her, like so many, but she betrayed a trust. She betrayed humanity. I came to learn that she was preventing the evolution of our species. Humanity was stagnating and dying under her stewardship. We could not evolve. We could not grow because she was too busy tightening her control and growing her power. She used me, and you, as nothing more than tools."

Enzell knew that, but that changed nothing.

"I was the judge, jury, and executioner of Nadya Tokarski. Your mother did not die well. You've seen the recordings, I'm sure. You didn't see the recordings of the cleanup. Blazer weapons do make a mess when used against unarmored targets. She failed; her son has failed."

How could Feng let him live? If Feng knew that much about him, how could Feng take the risk?

"So, you see Enzell Tokarski, I may not know everything, but I know everything about *you*. Like your mother, you sit here, on trial. I will be judge, jury, and executioner. This is not something I would entrust to a subordinate, you understand. If a mistake is to be made, it will be my responsibility. Not very socialist of me, I know. I will take responsibility for my actions and will not blame them on anyone else, because I know full well what I am doing."

"What are you going to do?"

Feng's smile was cold.

"You are an extremely intelligent, analytical, and dangerous person. You almost caused the genocide of the human race. You put our emperor into a coma, you crippled the Wolf Legion, you betrayed the very people you want to rule over by trying to kill their most staunch defenders. By all rights I should have you killed or sent to the most horrific torture chambers. However—"

Feng paused and waited. Enzell had no choice, and he dared not interrupt.

"I will give you a chance of redemption," Feng said. "You see, one important lesson I have learned working with the emperor is that who you were is less important than who you are. Our history, our past, our experiences shape us. We can use our past as an excuse for our actions. That is a sign of weakness and foolishness. Or we can use our past to give us strength and wisdom to understand what is right."

"Redemption?" Enzell asked. How was this master of shadows and manipulation going to give him redemption? Why should he be redeemed?

"We all have our strengths and weaknesses," Feng said. "One leader I have come to admire taught me that. We cannot discard people because of their weaknesses, especially not if we can use their strengths. You have many strengths. You are your mother's son. You have strength of will, strength of character, and you are very knowledgeable about the vanhat and the Collective. You know many secrets of the Governance, and I think I can use your knowledge as a strength."

Enzell waited for the catch.

"But not here," Feng said. "Not in Sol. No. That would not be wise. You see, that leader I admire so much also taught me something else. We do not grow when we are kept in the same place. Like a potted plant, our growth will be stunted if we remain where we are. I am going to send you on an expedition. You will accompany the *Musashi* as a science and political advisor."

"You aren't going to kill me?" Enzell asked.

"You will have a chance to redeem yourself, as I said. Know this, however, I will have agents aboard the *Musashi* and these agents will know everything about you."

Enzell kept the smile off his face. What agent could Feng possibly assign to keep track of him?

Feng's smile grew.

"Something you need to understand," Feng said. "The Wolf Legion is not the only organization that has been given SCBIs. Can you imagine anything more dangerous than an InSec agent with a SCBI?"

Enzell's inner smile died.

"The emperor never gave official permission of course. He did not allow certain controls to be placed within the SCBIs, controls that would allow for the monitoring and manipulation of the host, but that does not mean we can't use people to monitor and control others. You will be watched by multiple InSec agents equipped with SCBIs. This is one secret I may trust you with because revealing that InSec agents have SCBIs will most certainly cause other questions to be asked. Questions that you won't want to answer. Do you understand?"

"Yes."

"When addressing a superior the proper response is 'yes, sir.' You will need to know this serving aboard the *Musashi*. Do you understand?"

"Yes, sir," said Enzell Tokarski.

* * * * *

Chapter Seventy-Nine:
Goodbye Earth

Zale Stathis, Legion of the Wolf

Stathis stood staring at the world around him. There was still enough radiation that he kept his suit closed, but he could see it. Earth was trying to recover. There was green on the leaves, and grass was poking up. The snow had melted, and he could feel summer wasn't far away. He put the recorder back into his pocket. So much had happened to bring him back here to Quantico, Virginia. There was nothing he recognized anymore, but remembering the past was one way for him to ground himself in the present. He would ask someone to do something with the recording, burn it on some unbreakable stone or something. If some bug-eyed aliens read it and humanity was extinct, it probably wasn't the best history lesson, but it would have to do. Nothing was ever perfect. If you waited for things to be perfect, you would wait a very long time.

Everything should be dead, but life was struggling, and Stathis knew it would find a way. Was this the end of humanity?

Recon drones couldn't find any living Weermag on Earth. They were all dead, but Stathis knew they were not gone. Just temporarily defeated and driven away. When they returned, and he knew they would, it would be in force, but the empress would have a reprieve. The battlestars had earned the trust of the ex-Governance soldiers, those that survived, and now they were all becoming a tight-knit and united force.

There were still trust issues, but Stathis knew they wouldn't turn on each other like he had feared. Now they needed each other, and both the Republic and ex-Governance forces understood that. "United we stand, divided we fall" meant a lot more when you had fought and bled beside someone.

He didn't want to leave as he looked around. Earth was healing, but it wasn't because of Emperor Mathison or the Alliance. It was because of the vanhat, and Stathis didn't know what they were doing or why.

He looked up into the night sky. The stars were brighter than ever. He could trace the Milky Way, and he knew somewhere in that mass of stars were the answers to his questions. One question was how to save the gunny. The others were about how to save Earth and humanity.

Now he felt the burden on his shoulders, a burden the emperor must have felt.

He missed being a private, missed not being the one to give commands where people died, missed not having the weight of the world on his shoulders. The memories of his mistakes constricted his throat, making it harder and harder to breathe and go on.

The hatch behind him opened. He looked back to see Skadi coming out, and Stathis snapped to attention.

"At ease," Skadi said. "What are you doing?"

"Just saying goodbye," Stathis said. "C-230 rolling down the strip. This young Marine's gonna take a little trip."

"What's a C-230?"

"Um, transport craft that takes Marines around. Replaced the C-130 and C-190. It's part of a cadence."

"This isn't goodbye," Skadi said.

"Well, just collecting my thoughts."

"We will be here when you return."

"Yes, ma'am," Stathis said. Would they be alive, though? That was the question. "What about you? How are you doing, ma'am?"

"I will do what I always do. I will survive. Achieve what victories what I can. I am Aesir, bound to the people through blood and tears. I will be the blade of our people."

"You are a badass empress," Stathis said. "I know that. But what about you? Valerie Carpenter?"

He had never used her real, non-Aesir name. He knew he was probably crossing a line and shouldn't be so informal with the most powerful woman in known space. Taking his eyes from the stars above, he looked at her and saw the crack in the ice as he heard the pain in her voice.

"If there was no pain in life, there would be no pleasure. We cannot appreciate what we have unless we have lost. Wolf will survive, or we all die. We will wait for you, Zale. I know you will come back."

"I'll do my best, ma'am."

"When we first met, I thought of you as a dumb private. A troublemaker and a fool. I understand you so much better now. You have grown."

"Sometimes we don't have a choice, ma'am." Stathis didn't want to think about that, about easier times when he just had to watch the gunny's back.

"You are what Wolf needed. I see it now. You were just putting on an act."

"Fake it until you make it, ma'am."

A sad smile played across her mouth. "The Legion has suffered massive casualties. I'm sending as many as I can with you."

"You need some here," Stathis said. "A lot."

"I need you and Winters to succeed. I'm placing you in command of the ground forces. Commandant of the Legion."

"I'm not ready for that." Dammit. He had just been talking shit on the recording. Had she been listening? Was she really pissed at him?

"Nobody is," Skadi said. "Wolf trusts you. He was grooming you for that position. It is what he wants."

At least she wasn't talking about him in the past tense. Stathis found that comforting. The Gunny wasn't dead, and Stathis had his back. He just had to fight his way through half a galaxy to do it.

"There are more experienced officers, ma'am," Stathis said. He didn't want this. Not really. He talked about it, but then everyone knew he talked shit.

"But none he trusts more."

Stathis didn't know what to say. He didn't want to be anything more than a private who let other people make the big life altering decisions.

No. That wasn't true anymore, and he knew it. So did Skadi.

When had that happened?

"I'll do my best, ma'am." What else could he say? He couldn't promise her success. They both knew that. Who knew what the *Musashi* would face as it entered unexplored space. It would not be a quick journey, and Stathis knew in his core it wouldn't be easy. They would likely be hounded by the vanhat.

More tomb worlds? More alien civilizations? More vanhat waking up to eradicate the galaxy?

The vanhat would be able to track them as they dipped into Shorr space. The small fleet of ships wouldn't be able to spend much time in Shorr space. Going too deep would stress the Inkeri generators. And if they couldn't go deep, it would take more time.

It was going to be a balancing act, but that was a problem for Fleet.

"Admiral Winters will command the task force," Skadi said. Stathis knew she was probably just trying to comfort him. It did help. Winters was awesome in her way. He would rather have her in command than any SOG admiral.

It was a good decision. Stathis trusted her. She had a lot more experience than he did, and last time he had seen her everyone else had known what a badass she was and respected her. It was also a relief he would not be the ultimate authority. She was taking to her role of admiral like a fish to water.

"A good choice, ma'am," Stathis said. "I trust her as much as the gunny."

"She is a Marine," Skadi said.

"Yes, ma'am." He couldn't argue that. Being a Marine was something that never left you.

"I expect you to come back when you've accomplished the mission. With your shield or on it."

"Yes, ma'am," Stathis said. He wouldn't make promises he couldn't keep, and he would not lie to her.

"Find these angels. Bring them back to help us."

"I will, ma'am. The Marine Corps motto is Semper Fi. We are always faithful. The Marine Raider motto is Spiritus Invictus, Unconquerable Spirit."

"I know."

They both fell silent. Stathis didn't want to go, but then he did. It would be easier to push forward when he didn't know how bad things were behind him.

"Is there anything more you need?" Skadi asked, her gaze following his up to the stars.

"I need the gunny, Admiral Winters, Levin, you, Hakala. Shit. I don't know if I'm ready for this."

"You don't have a choice. A bit of advice though."

Stathis looked at her.

"Don't expect to have all the answers. Rely on your people. Train them, mold them. They will never be all you need—they will make mistakes—but you have to trust them. Help them grow, and they will help you. If you expect perfection, you will always be disappointed."

"Yes, ma'am. I've been doing so much with so little. I think I'm now qualified to do anything with nothing."

The sadness didn't leave Skadi's face, but the small smile helped.

"Your shuttle leaves in an hour," Skadi said. Stathis knew it was actually fifty-six minutes and fourteen seconds. There was a crack in the field of debris the *Tyr* had carved out so some shuttles could be exchanged.

"Yes, ma'am."

"Please be careful and come back," Skadi said.

"With my shield or on it," Stathis said. "Semper Fi."

"And Spiritus Invictus," Skadi said softly.

# # # # #

Author Note

Thank you, reader, for getting his far and sticking with it. Thank you all for those awesome reviews and support. This concludes the arc I call "The Collective" but not the saga of the Last Marines. Now Stathis and Winters must lead the expedition to the center of the galaxy to find aliens that may or may not still exist.

It will take me some time to plan out and plot the next arc, tentatively titled "When Angels Fall" which will detail Stathis' and Winters' journey to the galactic core to find the angels who can help them so they can save humanity and the gunny. I have ideas and plans that may or may not make it into the final cut.

This is *not* the end. Want to follow the status? Stalk me on Facebook, sign up for the CKP newsletter and/or my newsletter. All great sources.

Now I'll do what the gunny says—"Shut up Stathis"—and I will get to work.

Thank you and Semper Fi,
William S. Frisbee, Jr.
New Year's Eve, 2023

* * * * *

About William S. Frisbee, Jr.

Marine veteran, reader, writer, martial artist, computer consultant, dungeon master, computer gamer, dreamer, webmaster, proud American, and best of all, dad.

Growing up in Europe during the height of the Cold War and serving as a Marine infantryman through the fall of communism shaped Bill's perspective on life and the world. When most Marines were out trying to get lucky he was studying tactical manuals. Years later, he shared much of his knowledge to a website for writers of military science fiction.

These days, he's brushed off the pocket protector and is a top gun computer consultant.

Learn more at http://www.WilliamSFrisbee.com.

* * * * *

Get the **free** Four Horsemen prelude story **"Shattered Crucible"**

and discover other titles by Theogony Books at:

http://chriskennedypublishing.com/

* * * * *

Meet the author and other CKP authors on the Factory Floor:

https://www.facebook.com/groups/461794864654198

* * * * *

Did you like this book?
Please write a review!

* * * * *

The following is an

Excerpt from Book One of the The Sol Saga:

Revolution

James Fox

Available from Theogony Books

eBook and Paperback

Excerpt from "Revolution:"

The situation was rapidly degrading. If they couldn't find the enemy in the sea of people, they could be ambushed easily. Every Marine standing here in full battle rattle was a prettily dressed sitting duck. Two well-placed shooters could mow them down like spring grass. Hell, one well-placed IED could kill half of them and maim the rest.

Then he saw him.

"Aegis, please respond! Multiple IED inbound to your position!"

He ignored the intelligence from CENTCOM, instead clicking over to the snipers' and Manu's channel. "Viper Six, Aegis Actual, need confirmation of advancing targets."

There were others, standing still or milling around. Not moving backward.

The solo man, sliding between people, running forward toward the steps.

Don't do it! Don't you do it!

Twenty meters out.

"Aegis, Viper-Six, confirmed Tango on approach."

Brennan switched active channels, then relayed information into the comms, "Tango inbound, fifteen meters at 155 degrees. Hold your fire!"

Weapons pivoted to acquire the target.

Ten meters out.

"Hold!"

He was right on top of them.

"Hold!"

Don't you fucking do it!

The man reached inside his jacket.

The man's chest erupted in a blossom of red Martian blood. The crowd cleared to reveal a little girl right in front of the man dropping limply to his knees. His jacket draped protectively over the girl, staring dumbly at the hole in his chest.

Then, in horrific slow motion, when seconds seemed like hours, all hell erupted around him.

Protectorate automatic rifles were merciless, boasting upward of twelve hundred rounds per minute. Dozens of spooked Marines, *his* Marines, unable to immediately identify a threat despite intelligence from Command, opened fire. Once one fired, they all did.

Screams rose and were cut brutally short by hot rounds slicing through vocal cords, puncturing abdomens. Brennan could hear the impacts. The *thump-squish* of hot metal ripping through cloth, skin, muscle, and back again in rapid succession.

The front of the crowd was so close that blood sprayed up onto the gleaming white marble steps.

Somewhere from far above him, he heard the piercing cry of a woman's scream.

"CEASE FIRE!" Brennan roared over the comms, again and again, for what seemed like hours.

* * * * *

Get "Revolution" here: https://www.amazon.com/dp/B0CRZ6MZTR.

Find out more about James Fox at: https://chriskennedypublishing.com.

* * * * *

The following is an

Excerpt from Book One of Chimera Company:

The Fall of Rho-Torkis

Tim C. Taylor

Now Available from Theogony Books

eBook, Paperback, and Audio

Excerpt from "The Fall of Rho-Torkis:"

"Relax, Sybutu."

Osu didn't fall for the man steepling his fingers behind his desk. When a lieutenant colonel told you to relax, you knew your life had just taken a seriously wrong turn.

"So what if we're ruffling a few feathers?" said Malix. "We have a job to do, and you're going to make it happen. You will take five men with you and travel unobserved to a location in the capital where you will deliver a coded phrase to this contact."

He pushed across a photograph showing a human male dressed in smuggler chic. Even from the static image, the man oozed charm, but he revealed something else too: purple eyes. The man was a mutant.

"His name is Captain Tavistock Fitzwilliam, and he's a free trader of flexible legitimacy. Let's call him a smuggler for simplicity's sake. You deliver the message and then return here without incident, after which no one will speak of this again."

Osu kept his demeanor blank, but the questions were raging inside him. His officers in the 27th gave the appearance of having waved through the colonel's bizarre orders, but the squadron sergeant major would not let this drop easily. He'd be lodged in an ambush point close to the colonel's office where he'd be waiting to pounce on Osu and interrogate him. Vyborg would suspect him of conspiracy in this affront to proper conduct. His sappers as undercover spies? Osu would rather face a crusading army of newts than the sergeant major on the warpath.

"Make sure one of the men you pick is Hines Zy Pel."

Osu's mask must have slipped because Malix added, "If there is a problem, I expect you to speak."

"Is Zy Pel a Special Missions operative, sir?" There. He'd said it.

"You'll have to ask Colonel Lantosh. Even after they bumped up my rank, I still don't have clearance to see Zy Pel's full personnel record. Make of that what you will."

"But you must have put feelers out…"

Malix gave him a cold stare.

You're trying to decide whether to hang me from a whipping post or answer my question. Well, it was your decision to have me lead an undercover team, Colonel. Let's see whether you trust your own judgment.

The colonel seemed to decide on the latter option and softened half a degree. "There was a Hines Zy Pel who died in the Defense of Station 11. Or so the official records tell us. I have reason to think that our Hines Zy Pel is the same man."

"But... Station 11 was twelve years ago. According to the personnel record I've seen, my Zy Pel is in his mid-20s."

Malix put his hands up in surrender. "I know, I know. The other Hines Zy Pel was 42 when he was KIA."

"He's 54? Can't be the same man. Impossible."

"For you and I, Sybutu, that is true. But away from the core worlds, I've encountered mysteries that defy explanation. Don't discount the possibility. Keep an eye on him. For the moment, he is a vital asset, especially given the nature of what I have tasked you with. However, if you ever suspect him of an agenda that undermines his duty to the Legion, then I am ordering you to kill him before he realizes you suspect him."

Kill Zy Pel in cold blood? That wouldn't come easily.

"Acknowledge," the colonel demanded.

"Yes, sir. If Zy Pel appears to be turning, I will kill him."

"Do you remember Colonel Lantosh's words when she was arrested on Irisur?"

Talk about a sucker punch to the gut! Osu remembered everything about the incident when the Militia arrested the CO for standing up to the corruption endemic on that world.

It was Legion philosophy to respond to defeat or reversal with immediate counterattack. Lantosh and Malix's response had been the most un-Legion like possible.

"Yes, sir. She told us not to act. To let the skraggs take her without resistance. Without the Legion retaliating."

"No," snapped Malix. "She did *not*. She ordered us to let her go without retaliating *until the right moment*. This *is* the right moment, Sybutu. This message you will carry. You're doing this for the colonel."

Malix's words set loose a turmoil of emotions in Osu's breast that he didn't fully understand. He wept tears of rage, something he hadn't known was possible.

The colonel stood. "This is the moment when the Legion holds the line. Can I rely upon you, Sergeant?"

Osu saluted. "To the ends of the galaxy, sir. No matter what."

* * * * *

Get "The Fall of Rho-Torkis" now at: https://www.amazon.com/dp/B08VRL8H27.

Find out more about Tim C. Taylor and "The Fall of Rho-Torkis" at: https://chriskennedypublishing.com.

* * * * *

Made in United States
Troutdale, OR
05/11/2024

19811478R00256